MW01697793

The Lost Voices

Paul Rushworth-Brown

HISTORIUM PRESS

Printed in Australia

Historium Press USA/UK

Paperback ISBN: 978-1-964700-90-8

Ebook ISBN: 978-1-964700-91-5

https://www.paulrushworthbrownskulduggerywinterofred.com/

https://www.facebook.com/authorpaulrushworthbrown/?ref=pages_you_manage

https://www.instagram.com/paulbrown630/

https://twitter.com/Brown9Paul?lang=en

This book is for my children

Rachael, Christopher, Hayley,

my friend Pammie Brown,

and my wife Clare Brown

whose support and patience made it possible.

The Lost Voices

Paul Rushworth-Brown

Step into a world where history comes alive and adventure awaits on every page. In 'The Lost Voices,' the captivating best-selling novel by Paul Rushworth-Brown, you'll be transported through time to experience the vivid tapestry of 17th century Yorkshire. Born in the United Kingdom in 1962, Paul's journey from Charles Stuart University in Australia to becoming a passionate writer in 2015 led to the creation of this remarkable tale.

Immerse yourself in a story that transcends the confines of a mere history lesson. As you turn the pages of 'The Lost Voices,' you'll embark on a thrilling odyssey, seeing the world through the eyes of your ancestors. This is no ordinary historical account – it's a gripping narrative that will leave you breathless with anticipation.

Travel alongside John and Robert Rushworth, two sons of the moors, as they set out to make their fortune in the bustling city of Leeds. With a blend of adventure, intrigue, and forbidden romance, their journey unfolds against the backdrop of a society filled with colourful characters, each with their own secrets and desires.

Meet John Wilding, a man of brutish demeanor and lowly origins, determined to capture Robert Rushworth for a reward that could change his fate forever. Encounter Milton Killsin, a Puritan with a hidden yearning, and Captain Girlington, torn between the call of the sea and an unexpected love. In a world teeming with beggars, thieves and prostitutes, every step is fraught with danger, and every decision could lead to a life-altering consequence.

As the tension mounts, 'The Lost Voices' weaves a tapestry of murder, mystery, and mayhem that will keep even the sharpest minds guessing until the final revelation. Will Robert pay the ultimate price for his misdeeds? Can the Rushworths rise above the challenges that threaten to engulf them? The answers lie within these pages, waiting for only the most astute readers to uncover.

Paul Rushworth-Brown's masterful storytelling will transport you to a bygone era, where dreams of courage ignite against a backdrop of hardship and perseverance. If you crave heart-pounding adventure, intricate intrigue and a taste of history brought to life, then 'The Lost Voices' is your next must-read. So, open the book, turn back time, and let the Rushworths' legacy of determination and bravery inspire you. Your journey begins now.

OTHER NOVELS BY PAUL RUSHWORTH-BROWN

SKULDUGGERY

Step back in time to the tumultuous year of 1590, where the pages of history come alive in a gripping tale of shenanigans, skulduggery, and a love that defies all odds. As the sun sets on the glorious reign of Good Queen Bess, a new era dawns with King James taking the throne of England and Scotland.

Amidst the backdrop of political upheaval and societal unrest, we are introduced to Thomas, a young man thrust into the responsibilities of manhood as the elder brother. But his fate is intricately woven with that of Agnes, a woman intended for an arranged marriage, setting the stage for an unforgettable love story that blooms amidst the chaos.

Join these two captivating souls as they navigate treacherous waters, where loyalty is tested, secrets unravel, and danger lurks at every corner. 'Skulduggery' takes readers on a rollercoaster ride through the cobbled streets of a bygone era, vividly capturing the hardships and landscapes that both characters and readers alike must traverse.

With masterful prose that evokes the sights, sounds, and emotions of the past, the writer skilfully crafts a narrative that keeps you on the edge of your seat. As the tension rises and the stakes grow higher, you'll find yourself entangled in a web of suspense, wondering if good will ultimately triumph over evil.

Prepare to be transported to a world where honour clashes with deceit, love blooms against all odds, and the fate of our protagonists hangs in the balance. 'Skulduggery' is a must-read for history buffs, romance aficionados, and anyone seeking an immersive escape to a time long past.

Don't miss out on this mesmerizing journey through a richly detailed and captivating historical landscape. Order your copy of 'Skulduggery' today and embark on an adventure you won't soon forget!

RED WINTER JOURNEY

In a literary landscape where few dare to venture into the past, Rushworth-Brown emerges as a master storyteller, deftly transporting readers through the annals of history with unparalleled skill. Critics and readers alike are enraptured by the artistry, atmosphere, and depth of emotion woven into this extraordinary novel, hailed as a triumph by the prestigious US National Times.

Step into the shoes of 17-year-old Tommy Rushworth, a young soul thrust into the relentless maelstrom of history. Kidnapped into the heart of the Parliamentary Army, Tommy's indomitable spirit becomes a beacon of hope amid the chaos of war. As he navigates the unforgiving landscape of battlefields and brotherhood, his struggle for survival becomes an inspiring testament to the human capacity for resilience.

But this isn't just Tommy's tale; it's a sweeping saga that intertwines the lives of generations. Follow the footsteps of his father, Thomas Rushworth, a man driven by the fierce determination to rescue his son from the clutches of war. Alongside him, the irrepressible John Hargreaves, a larrikin grandfather whose humour and heart provide a poignant counterpoint to the grim realities of conflict.

Amidst the turmoil, a fragile love story blossoms, threading its way through the narrative like a delicate wisp of hope. Will Lucy and William's love endure the trials of a world torn apart by strife? As their hearts are tested and tempered, their journey becomes a testament to the enduring power of human connection.

Prepare to be swept away by a narrative that knows no bounds—where every twist and turn, every unexpected revelation, is expertly crafted to keep you guessing until the very last page. 'Red Winter Journey' is not just a novel; it's a symphony of emotions, a masterpiece of historical authenticity, and a breathtaking exploration of the human spirit's unyielding strength.

Join the chorus of praise from critics and readers alike! Embark on an unforgettable adventure where the past comes alive in all its splendour and sorrow. Order your copy of 'Echoes of Resilience' today and experience the transformative power of a truly remarkable literary journey.

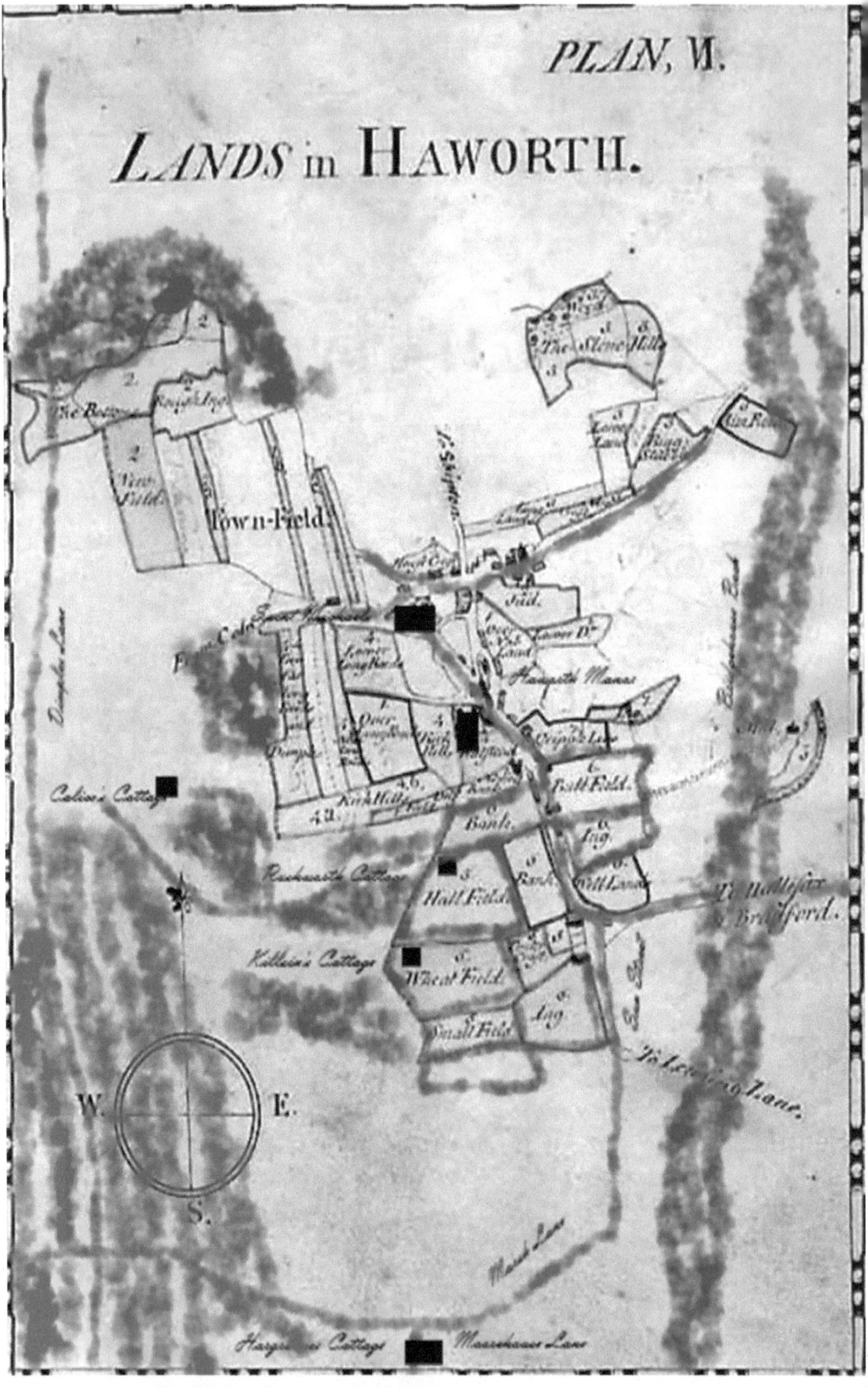

PLAN, VI.
LANDS in HAWORTH.
Town-Field
Hall Field
Wheat Field
Small Field
Bank
Ing
To Hallifax
& Bradford.
W.
E.
S.

Contents

The history of these people is rarely thought of and even less often written about because there are few records as most were illiterate. There is much written about the nobles of the time, but what about the common people? At this time, eighty-five percent of people were peasants, our ancestors, and yet their story is mostly untold.

Now let their story begin…

Paul Rushworth-Brown 2019

PROLOGUE

The echoes of battle still reverberated through the blood-soaked fields of England. A kingdom once united under the rule of monarchs now lay shattered, torn asunder by the tempestuous winds of revolution and the thirst for power. King Charles, a man consumed by his own desires, had sown the seeds of his own downfall, attempting to wield authority without bounds. His ambition had become the catalyst for a cataclysmic upheaval that would forever change the fate of the land.

As the sun dipped beneath the horizon, casting an ominous hue across the skyline, the guillotine's blade fell with a resounding finality. King Charles, the embodiment of absolute authority, met his end on the executioner's block, his dreams of dominion and dominance extinguished by the swift stroke of justice. England's trampled liberties and forgotten rights found a voice in the grim chorus of the condemned, and a new era was born.

From the ashes of monarchy emerged a republic, with Oliver Cromwell at its helm. His iron fist gripped the reins of power, his vision of a new order taking root. The halls of Parliament echoed with the voices of the people, their newfound authority shaping a nation no longer shackled by the whims of a single ruler. Yet, even as the republic unfurled its banner, the specter of the past loomed large.

Across the sea, in the grand courts of France, an exiled heir watched as his father's fate unfolded. Charles II, the rightful successor to the English throne, treaded a perilous path. Fear etched lines upon his brow, for he knew that returning to his homeland could lead to the same gruesome destiny that had befallen his sire. The allure of power was overshadowed by the dread of retribution.

In the heart of England, amidst the whispers of change and the clamour of conflicting loyalties, a fragile equilibrium danced upon a knife's edge. The Parliamentarians held dominion over a realm still haunted by divided allegiances. Royalist sympathisers, their fervour hidden beneath veils of caution, yearned for the resurgence of the crown. Their secrets, like precious gems, were hidden in the recesses of their souls, lest the pendulum of power swing once more.

The battlefields may have fallen silent, yet the war's harrowing aftermath painted a gruesome tableau. A nation scarred and fractured, its political, social and economic foundations razed to the ground. The rivers of England flowed not only with water but also with the tears of those who had witnessed the horrors of war. Mercenaries and soldiers, driven by greed and desperation, had marauded and pillaged, leaving behind a trail of destruction and despair.

In the idyllic village of Haworth, where once lush meadows had thrived, now lay devastation. Cattle and sheep had been stolen or slaughtered, and homes reduced to smouldering ruins. The Rushworth family, however, clung to their ancestral soil, unwavering in the face of adversity. Little did they know that their resilience would intertwine their destiny with the winds of change, setting them on a course destined for glory or tragedy.

As the embers of conflict dimmed, a new breed of power rose from the ashes. Middle-class landowners, beneficiaries of Cromwell's largesse, ascended the rungs of influence, altering the landscape of privilege and prestige. Among them, Lord Birkhead, once the master of Haworth Manor, had vanished into the shadows. Whispers of his fate drifted through the air like leaves carried on the wind, some claiming he had sought refuge in the embrace of distant lands.

In a land scarred by war and propelled by the winds of change, the tale of a kingdom's fall and the birth of a republic was far from over. In the heart of the chaos, a story of love, loyalty, and unbreakable bonds was about to unfold, weaving together the threads of fate for generations to come.

CHAPTER 1

All Is Not What It Seems

The gentle rustling of cornstalks and the soft caress of a sunlit breeze greeted Tommy as he strolled through the expansive fields of Hall Green. His calloused hands trailed along the emerald beards of corn, a bounty that promised prosperity. The distant echoes of rising prices in York and London had cast a golden glow over their lives, ushering in a glimmer of hope. It was a bountiful year, the promise of a bumper crop that would carry them through the harsh embrace of winter and bring coins for the necessities they couldn't cultivate themselves.

As a yeoman, Tommy had ascended from the ranks of labour, owning his own land, and casting off the chains of rack rents and fines. The weight of his newfound status hung upon him like a finely tailored garment. A VanDyke collar adorned his neck, a mark of a man who belonged to the higher echelons. His tall capotain hat, dark and dignified, crowned him with an air of distinction. His attire, a testament to his toil and determination, spoke volumes to those who might pass judgment.

He stopped for a minute and gazed up at the bright blue sky allowing the sun to warm his face. Now a yeoman, Tommy owned his own land and didn't pay rack rents or fines for the lease to his grace.

The cruck house where he grew up was gone and replaced with a stone farmhouse. There were windows and a stair led up into the bedrooms. The animals moved to a newly constructed barn outside.

The moors of the Pennine, the pink and purple radiance coloured by a Godly painter. The mounds of blooming heather danced in the breeze and whispered their ancient secrets. Sloping pastures bordered by vivid green, unsymmetrical squares separated the countryside. White sheep, their thick snouts dotted the hills and dales. The bleating and ba-a-a-ing of their lambs echoed through the valley.

As the sun reached its zenith, a silvery beck wound its way through the landscape, a glistening serpentine ribbon that whispered of secrets known only to nature herself. The moors sang their ancient song, a chorus of wrens and warblers striving to court the favour of unseen mates. Tommy halted in his tracks, allowing the woody, mossy fragrance of heather to envelope him in its embrace. He closed his eyes, savouring the scent that spoke of untamed beauty and whispered promises.

He heard Isabel's voice in the distance. Her calls became louder, slowly separating him from his thoughts… no… his dream.

Tommy's eyes fluttered open and he found himself ensconced within the confines of their modest cottage. The warmth of a candle's glow cast a dim light, illuminating Isabel's figure as she sat upon the edge of their bed. Her voice, a gentle reminder of duty and responsibility, tugged him from the embrace of slumber.

'It's late and I must start me day or else the kersey won't be finished in time.'

Tommy opened his eyes, rubbed them, but then closed them to the candle she lit.

He failed to hold onto the last remnants of his dream. 'I was havin' a dream, a nice dream, the corn… the sun… erggh! Now lost.'

Isabel stood but had to stoop because of the low roof in the loft. 'Husband, dreams start with the first nod and melt with the rooster's call and you know the only corn 'round here is on the Killsin's land.'

'Errgh.' Frustratingly, Tommy pulled the blanket over his head to delay the inevitable.

'Come now… up ya get, I'll wake Will and get him off to the beck for water.' Isabel put on her wimple and kirtle.

Their cottage, slightly larger than before accommodated the loom and a window that let in a sliver of daylight, became a hub of activity. The loom stood as a silent testament to their toil, and the small window allowed the promise of a new day to trickle in. A flickering fire beckoned in the hearth, casting dancing shadows that waltzed to a silent rhythm.

Isabel, Tommy, Will and their daughters Morwen and Mirth, spent their days weaving, carding and combing wool. The monotony of their task was tempered by the knowledge that this labour was the thread that stitched together the fabric of their existence. The long-staple fibres yielded to their touch, slowly transforming into a tapestry of sustenance and survival.

Some called the wool industry 'The Staple', the fibres and strands of hope. It wasn't because the quality of wool was not what it was.

Cunning broggers, shifty middlemen, kept the best. They bought in bulk and monopolised the industry. They acquired a bad reputation in the west for villainy and crookedness. Often unscrupulous in their dealings with farmers, they demanded far less than what the wool was worth. They borrowed money then bought all the best wool, hiding it away which raised prices. This made it difficult for home spinners and weavers.

The Rushworths struggled. Even so, the family did their best to provide a good kersey for sale with wool they could get, but they knew it wasn't enough to support themselves.

Lack of good wool for the household weaver forced Tommy to buy dirty wool at higher prices. The difference between what they paid and the coin they could get for the kersey at market was pitiful.

Gone was the open green expanse, the rolling fields that once stretched as far as the eye could see, a canvas of arable promise. In their place lay a fragmented tableau, a landscape divided, imprisoned, suffocating under the weight of overgrazing and neglect.

The remnants of a once-thriving community were scattered like fragments of a forgotten dream. The few tenants who clung to their ancestral soil were burdened with the responsibility of managing ten-acre plots, their efforts a testament to both their resilience and the unrelenting demands of survival.

And then there was Hall Green, a seemingly forgotten corner, its worth dismissed as inconsequential. Tommy, in his humility, had assumed that nobody would cast their gaze upon its humble terrain. However, the currents of fate are unpredictable, and he was about to be proven wrong.

The Rushworths, their determination unwavering, laboured tirelessly upon the land they had left. Barley, a grain less noble than its wheat and corn counterparts, became their reluctant companion. Their life-hold, a stronghold of heritage and tradition, remained steadfast, yet the landscape had shifted. The common crop fields that once nourished their hopes and sustenance had been lost to the ever-changing tides of fate.

Small cottages, once witnesses to the laughter of children and the warmth of hearth, stood desolate and abandoned, their timeworn facades a reflection of the community's decline. The air hung heavy with a sense of nostalgia, a mournful dirge for a bygone era, a melancholic song of a once-vibrant past now overshadowed by sorrow.

Due to enclosure, the days of fine wool in the north were gone. All the family could hope for was the sale of long course wool for draperies. At least it got them through, unlike other poor, desolate souls.

The popularity for English wool in Europe had declined and some broggers fell afoul of rich tradesmen because they couldn't pay their debts. Some broggers were out of favour, some found beaten and others locked up. Most had to disappear and earn an income in other dubious ways.

Jacob Wilding, one such brogger, danced dangerously close to the precipice of ruin. His debts, a weight he could no longer bear, forced him into the shadows of the Briggate, a man marked by his own avarice. Unbeknownst to him, his fate would intertwine with that of the Rushworths, a web of destiny woven by the hand of circumstance.

The tradesmen of The Company lent Wilding money to buy wool, but now he couldn't pay it back. He went into hiding in Leeds.

The Company were a group of rich trading families who held power in Parliament. It was they who rose to the forefront and now controlled trade in and out of England. Publicly, The Company personified respectability and class; however, there was a more sinister side. They made their fortune exporting wool, cloth and… opium grown in India and sold to China for considerable profit. These landed families originally made broad cloth. Their empires grew they turned to exporting cloth out of Selby and Hull. They began to outdo the merchants of London and Hull and became the most powerful in England.

Mr Wilding took a large loan from 'The Company' to buy wool from shepherds outside Leeds. He made a good living until brogging became outlawed. Following an act of parliament, licences were restricted to approved, honest merchants. Jacob Wilding was not one of them.

For broggers, a fine twice the value of their wool was a deterrent. Wilding was in strife. He didn't own a licence so couldn't sell it. He also couldn't pay off his loan, which carried an interest rate of two hundred percent. Wilding was now incognito and hiding in the Briggate.

The Rushworth's ten acres of land was harsh and rocky but had good, lush green feed for their small herd of sheep. The four acres of barley allowed them to make bread when harvested. The vegetable garden allowed fresh potatoes and onions in spring and summer if they didn't rot from the damp.

Groggily, Tommy dressed and climbed down the old, crooked, rickety ladder which led from the loft. He could hear Isabel trying to raise Will as the rooster welcomed the start of a new day. He opened the shutters. It was dark except for the candlelight coming from the Killsin's two-story house, which sat on a rise a quarter of a mile away.

He peered at the unripened wheat swaying in the moonlight and couldn't help but feel jealous of his crop. *It doesn't seem right, all that land fer one man.*

Tommy yawned and examined the sky which was ablaze with a billion stars and stretched as far as the eye could see. He coughed the night-time phlegm from his throat and spat it through the opening. Taking a deep cold breath in and out he watched it curl, circle then vanish into the darkness.

Tommy's off white, long neck shirt was open to midway down his chest. His indigo, buttoned tunic revealed curled chest hairs and worn leathery skin. His breeches were baggy and his woollen stockings loose around his lower leg. His cut-out latchet shoes had strips of leather wrapped around the foot poking through holes in the upper part of the shoe. A man of medium height, his face weathered by the northern elements. He had thick dark brown eyebrows, deep-set eyes, a chiselled chin and a previously broken nose from the 'ball' he played as a young man. His cheeks were reddened by the constant wind blowing across the moors. His hands strong, rough and scarred from the dry wall he was building for his grace.

Isabel climbed down the ladder trying not to step on her kirtle. Will, their eldest followed. When he got to the bottom he turned and tried to shake away the grogginess.

Isabel put her hands on her hips and shook her head in frustration. 'Tommy, the children will get a chill with the shutter open. Goodness me, close it before their humours get out a' sorts.'

Isabel hurried toward the fire. She bent down and stoked it, placing a small piece of dried peat on the embers and blew to raise the flame.

'Wife, ya worry too much.' He closed the shutter to the early morning and shuffled toward the hearth. There he squatted warming his hands on the growing flame.

Isabel's heart swelled with maternal pride as she cast a fond glance at her son, his towering stature for his age a testament to their family's heritage. 'He's tall for his age, is our Will,' she proclaimed, her voice a soft murmur of pride.

Will's groans and yawns echoed through the cottage as he struggled to shake off the remnants of sleep. His doublet, now too snug for his growing frame, clung to his shoulders, the fabric bearing witness to his recent growth spurt. Only the two ties at the bottom managed to unite the garment in front, a testament to the rapid passage of time.

Isabel ambled back over to the stairs, peeked up and called out, 'Morwen, Mirth, up ya get now my loves, there's work to be done.'

'I feel heartbroken, Tommy. Will and the girls must grow up in this world, what of their future?' Isabel whispered.

Tommy heated the combs in the fire on a stone slab. 'He'll make do just like I did, and me da, and his da before 'im.'

'Oh Tommy, I worry about them so much!' Isabel shook her head.

'The moors are in his blood and no matter what happens nobody'll ever take it away from him. He'll be right, he's a Rushworth and he'll do what we've always done, survive!'

Tommy inserted the combs into the fire to heat so they slid through the oily wool much easier. Having the fire on all day, especially in summer, made the one-room cottage unbearably hot and humid. The ceiling rained and the walls ran with the humidity but it was better than the alternative.

Will grumbled, he had a petulant expression; he wasn't a morning person. He walked over to the water bucket sitting on the floor and poured some into the ceramic bowl. He splashed his face, he wiped the night's gritty sleep from his eyes.

Will had a rugged and weather-beaten appearance. His sun-kissed, wind-bitten skin bore the marks of countless hours spent toiling under the open sky. His blonde hair had a sun-bleached wheat colour. His locks were unruly and unkempt, and fell in shaggy waves.

His attire was simple, he wore a coarse tunic and breeches made from wool and a heavy, weather-resistant cloak.

His lean and muscular frame spoke of a life of hard labour, where he tended to sheep and worked the land with his father and uncle.

Despite the physical challenges and simplicity of his existence, his eyes held a spark of resilience and youthful hope. The moors were his home, and he possessed an intimate knowledge of the land, its ever-changing seasons, and the nuances of its flora and fauna.

Dreams and aspirations danced in his heart, even amidst the daily grind. He longed for a better future, and harboured a desire for adventure beyond the moors, fuelled by the timeless spirit of youth. Picking up the other water bucket, he grabbed his hat hanging on a nail near the door. The door creaked as he opened it. Stepping out into the morning's light sky, his steamy breath billowed before him.

Will traipsed around the side of the cottage and let their twelve sheep out of the keep. The sheep had been shorn and the wool already woven and sold. The lambs had been shorn with stud combs for protection from the cold autumn nights. The sheep relished the freedom from the keep and darted off in the same direction. The lambs followed in haste with a bounce and kick of their hind legs.

Will headed east toward the beck. Glimpsing at the first rays of sun peeking over the horizon, he listened to the dawn chorus; the blackbirds, robins and wrens sung their morning song. The dark silhouette of the kingfisher flashed past on its way to the beck.

W*hat is my future?* he thought as he strolled along, thinking about his mother and father's whispers. *Me parents aren't getting any younger. I need to do more. I'll visit the manor, see if I can get work at their new mill.*

He crossed Sun Street then walked down the slope. Reaching his favourite water collection point at the beck, he turned and paused to see his trail of steps in the dew. He peered north to the manor.

As the day unfurled its possibilities, the manor beckoned, its secrets and promises intertwined with the threads of his destiny. He glanced towards it, a beacon of wealth and intrigue that loomed on the horizon, its allure tinged with a hint of apprehension.

Will had heard the stories, mostly bad, and knew his mother wouldn't like him working there. The grand building was lit up on both floors, the chimney chugging grey smoke from preparations for the first meal of the day. The thought of it brought pangs of hunger, so he quickly collected water and headed home.

Isabel poured water from the jug into the cauldron. She stirred the unripe barley and silverweed roots, 'Tommy, we 'ave little grain left. I need to go to the village and sell something to tide us over.'

Tommy grumbled, 'Aye, but it's so expensive! The engrossers took theirs and the rains took the rest. Bad weather, higher taxes, summer rain, drought and frost.'

How are we to get on? Isabel asked herself desperately.

Tommy stared at her and mumbled, 'Things were better under the king.'

Isabel's eyes grew wide with fear. 'Tommy, please!'

Isabel wasn't used to seeing Tommy in this type of mood, but she knew what he'd been through in the war. The memory of almost losing him was like a shadow on her heart.

''Usband, you'll end up hanging from the Tree and the rest of us will end up beggin' in the street.'

'Well, what do ya expect, every time I go up ta village, they've put their grain prices up.'

Isabel sighed. 'Aye, I hear ya. Seems poor folk are the only ones livin' the dearth.' She ladled pottage into wooden bowls and placed them onto the table.

The familial bond between Isabel and Tommy stood firm, a bastion of support in a world fraught with uncertainty. 'We must forge ahead, Isabel. For our children, for our family, we must weather this storm and find a way to thrive.'

Tommy slurped some of the watery stew, 'Even with the little coin we 'ave, victuals are scarce.'

'Beggars grow in their number and those who don't give do too. Even poor relief is failing in the Parish,' claimed Isabel.

'Milton Killsin's got the job of handing out poor relief among the Parish,' Tommy explained.

'Can't blame 'im, Tommy, there's only so much coin ta go 'round.'

'Aye, and I know where it's goin' ta… buyin' more bloody sheep! His herd has grown threefold since he got 'ere.'

Isabel gazed at Tommy sternly, 'Husband you 'ave no proof!'

Tommy stood and pointed toward the Killsin's farmhouse, his eyes squinted with rage, 'Two storeys, four windows, come now, how can they afford it in these times?'

Isabel raised her hand to calm him. 'Husband, he comes from money in Halifax, Mrs Killsin told me. Has the backin' of Jasper Calamy who he fought with in the war.'

Tommy's face grew red with frustration and anger, 'Aye, well I fought in the war and what did it get me? Nothin' but a head full a' bad dreams.'

Isabel stepped closer and put her arms around his neck affectionately, ''Usband, you were very brave and I thank God you returned to us.'

Tommy put his arms around her. 'Wife tis not right! How are we ta get on?'

Isabel always tried to look on the brighter side. *I don't know how or when but things will get better. They 'ave to. Dear God they 'ave to.* Every night she prayed.

The Puritan Milton Killsin leased land from Jasper Calamy at a low price in return for his services in the war. It was enclosed to keep Tommy's sheep from it and what was once common land was now gone.

Milton Killsin was out of favour with the people in the parish because he bought sheep at a pittance from families who were turned off for not paying rack rents. He also took their lands and had amassed forty acres.

The Rushworths didn't know it at the time, but now he wanted theirs and would do anything to get it. He didn't want this lowly sort living next to him.

After the war, parliamentary backed Puritanism caused huge political and religious divides encouraging suspicion and tension in villages and towns throughout Yorkshire. The 'witch panic' was the result and accusation and fear grew widespread.

Isabel was fearful the same tension and suspicions would reach Haworth. Her fears would soon be realised.

Isabel stood closer and whispered so the girls couldn't hear, 'All this darkness, Mrs Killsin says it's the wrath of God. Only after fasting and repentance will the famine and pestilence end. She says its devilry!'

Tommy listened then smiled. 'All this talk of devils, demons and witches, it's Cromwell scarin' people to go to church. I don't believe any of it.'

Isabel stared into space nervously. 'Some say, the Devil is on Earth collecting souls ready for the end of the world. Many speak of witches and their wicked ways turnin' poor souls and leavin' their mark.'

Tommy sighed. 'Load of nonsense if you ask me.'

Isabel frowned. 'Tommy!'

'Well, what do ya expect? It's Killsin, he starts all the rumours about witches and demons and his wife is no better.'

'Tommy! Don't you dare speak about Mrs Killsin, she's a kind soul.'

'Mrs Killsin says they are hangin' 'em down south. Witchfinders, they go from village to village finding women who've made a covenant with the Devil. Nineteen convicted in Chelmsford, hanged 'em all, they did.'

'So, that's where ya been hearin' all these fanciful stories, Mrs Killsin? I wouldn't be believing everything you hear from her.' Tommy shook his head.

Isabel glared at him. 'Quiet now, she's a blessin', gives me vegetables from her garden and flour, well when her husband isn't about.'

She frowned. 'He blames her fer them not 'aving children. She's lived with guilt for twenty years. He treats her so poorly.'

The girls were giggling upstairs, Isabel lowered her voice. 'Mrs Killsin said the witchfinders inspect a person fer the Devil's mark.'

'Witches, witchfinders? Are you seriously worried?'

'Tommy, Mrs Killsin is a kind soul and if she believes it, then I do too.'

'A load a' bloody rot if you ask me.'

'She told me, they bring in a witch pricker who watches fer blood and if there isn't any, they're branded a witch.'

'Witch pricker?' Tommy smiled.

Isabel frowned. 'Don't laugh Tommy, poor women get dunked in water to see if they float. If they come up, God's turned his back on 'em, they're branded a witch and put to the hangin'… or worse!' *What a horrible way to go.*

Tommy wasn't a believer. He stood confidently and gently put his arm around Isabel's shoulders. 'Don't worry, luv, there are more things between heaven and earth that could do more harm to common folk than witches, devils and demons. The less said about it the better.'

Morwen and Mirth started to climb down the ladder.

'Shooosh, 'usband, all this talk about devils and witches will scare the girls.'

Tommy lowered his voice, 'The dearth will kill more than your witchfinders you mark me words.'

'Shuuush!'

'John Pigshells told me those turned off their land by Calamy, are travellin' to Leeds fer work. Poor bastards will be ripe pickin's fer highwaymen and footpads.'

'I've heard they're mostly former Royalist soldiers turned from their lands by Cromwell's generals. They don't rob the poor and homeless, just the new rich,' stated Isabel confidently.

Tommy smiled at her forthrightness and replied cheekily, 'And wife, what would a woman know of such things?'

Isabel rolled her eyes. 'I hear and know as much as you, 'usband!'

'Mornin', Ma, mornin', Da.' The girls gave their parents a peck on the cheek, celebrating the birth of another day.

Tommy smiled and winked at Isabel. 'Girls, the day is gone, you may as well go back up and climb back under yer blanket the sun is settin'.'

Morwen and Mirth laughed. 'Tis not, Da, it's risin' silly!' They both giggled.

Thomas opened the door wider. 'And how do ya know girls?'

Morwen strode over. 'Cause the sun rises in the east and sets in the west, hahaha! Yer tryin' ta trick us.'

Isabel shuffled over and handed them both a small basket, 'Aye, well yer da's right, if you'd slept any longer, you would 'ave missed the day.'

Mirth whined, 'Oh, Ma, but it's sooo early! I should still be under me blanket.'

'Stop whining, now go on you two, off with ya. Go collect the eggs.'

Tommy sat down at the loom; his smile changed to a frown. 'Some 'ave gone to the city. Others 'ave returned tellin' tales of people starvin' on the side of the road. Whole families with neither bread nor seed or coin to buy either.'

Isabel sighed. 'I hope John and Robert are okay, it's been so long.'

'Time will tell, they're good lads probably workin' in a mill somewhere. Just wish they'd send word,' replied Tommy.

John and Robert, William's sons, went to the city. They'd been gone two years and nobody heard from them. Some thought the worst.

Isabel sensed Tommy's frustration, 'Mrs Killsin told me Milton bought sheep from down the road. Another family turned off.'

Tommy threw the weft threads across the warp threads.

'Rap! Trap! Rap!' 'Rap! Trap! Rap!'

He paused and rested his forearms on the breast beam. 'Yea, well if they keep turning crop to pasture, there'll be no grain fer anybody!'

Jasper Calamy was awarded the common land by Parliament. Most of his tenants were gone. The only ones he couldn't get rid of were the plots owned by freeholders. He also couldn't evict life-holders like the Rushworths unless there was reason.

Gone was the open green expanse of arable open fields. The land was divided, imprisoned, suffocating from over grazing.

The few tenants who remained were responsible for ten-acre lots. As for Hall Green, it wasn't arable like on the other side of the beck. Tommy assumed nobody would be interested in it. He was wrong.

The Rushworths made do with what they tried to grow mostly barley which was cheaper than wheat and corn. They held their life-hold; yet, lost access to common crop fields.

Small cottages once graced the countryside but were now abandoned and desolate. It was a sad old, sad old place.

'Rap! Trap! Rap!' 'Rap! Trap! Rap!'

'Ya know, wife, they be weavin' in Keighley, lots of men and women weavin' and cardin' wool under the same roof. I hear Calamy's doin' the same over at the manor.'

Isabel sat down at the spinning wheel. 'Suppose ya gonna want ta rush right off and join 'em, husband.'

'Rap! Trap! Rap!'

'Me, noooo!'

'Tommy 'ave you 'eard how they're treated in those places, no sunlight, workin' from before dawn till dark? Ya get a whippin' if ya so much as raise your eyes from the wheel of the loom. I'd rather be at home, thank ya muchly.'

'Rap! Trap! Rap!' 'Rap! Trap! Rap!'

Tommy's hands moved with a steady determination, his voice a reflection of his steadfast commitment. 'Aye, the coin we earn at market may not be much, but at least we're together.'

'Rap! Trap! Rap!' 'Rap! Trap! Rap!'

'THE ONLY ONES LIVIN' WELL ARE THE BROGGERS AND ENGROSSERS.' Isabel yelled.

'Rap! Trap! Rap!' 'Rap! Trap! Rap!'

‘John Pigshells told me broggers are havin’ problems paying back loans. Somethin’ about the state of the pound and the quality of the cloth.

‘Rap! Trap! Rap!’

‘Europeans aren’t buyin’ as much wool. Broggers get stuck with it. If they can’t sell it they can’t pay back their loans. They deserve everything they get, thievin’ bastards!

‘Maybe William will do better at the market,’ replied Isabel as she slowly spun the wheel.

In Halifax, a new middle class arose, merchants and craftsmen were supporters of Cromwell’s government. Their commercial power was boosted and ownership of property was taken from previous noble landowners by order of Cromwell and his eleven generals.

Lord Birkhead was forced out of Haworth Manor by order of Colonel Robert Lilburne. Jasper Calamy was anointed with administrative power over Keighley, a mantle he embraced with fervour.

Calamy was a Puritan scholar and Justice of the Peace. He was commanded to uphold the orders of Cromwell, in Keighley and for the people’s acceptance of strict Puritan ways.

Things changed since the departure of the king. The Kings Arms lost its usual merriment and the usual past times and sports were gone.

Oliver Cromwell was the protector of England. A Puritan, a highly religious man who believed the future of England rested in his hands. He thought he alone was responsible for ensuring the Godliness of its citizens. This was a doctrine which was upheld and any who didn’t follow the ways were punished.

There was no longer rat baiting or dog fighting and frivolous pastimes were banned. Dancing and play on a Sunday was frowned upon and festivals like Christmas were cancelled. Anybody found not conforming to the strict religious ways were publicly whipped or placed in the pillory.

The Maypole was removed from the village square and villagers were presented at court leet, by Milton Killsin, for non-payment of the taxes and tithe even when they were destitute. Times were tough.

In the village, the old vicar was charged for not reading set Puritan prayers and for non-Puritan irregularities. The churchwardens were cited for nonconformity and a lack of respect to Puritan ways. They were all presented at the court leet and fled soon afterwards.

As the village grappled with the shadows of change, the figure of Milton Killsin emerged as both enforcer and arbiter of the new order. A man of cunning and ambition, he rode the currents of power, driven by a relentless desire to secure his own fortune. With a two-story farmhouse and plots of land, he wielded his authority, his gaze fixated upon the Rushworths' domain.

The new churchwarden, Milton Killsin, approached Jasper Calamy and requested a new Puritan clergy for Saint Michael's.

Milton Killsin and his wife moved to the village from Halifax to build their fortune. Killsin came from a family of rich cloth merchants who lost their fortune during the war. Anything of value was inherited by his older brother Oliver, much to Milton's annoyance.

Milton Killsin was responsible for ensuring all who lived in the village and surrounds abided by Puritan ways. He was responsible for collecting the hearth tax and distributing relief to the poor.

Milton rode his horse carriage around on a Sunday watching for those who broke the laws of the Sabbath. Any found to be contravening the will of the church were presented at the court leet.

In return, Jasper Calamy provided him with a two-story farmhouse and a thirty-acre plot at Hall Green. He also promised him more land as it became available.

Milton Killsin was a rather short, pompous, plump little man with beady eyes and several chins. His wispy, fine hair curled to his shoulders. His clothes were always pressed and his wife was under strict instructions to ensure his Vandyke collar and cuffs were bright white.

Milton tended to walk with his chin up trying to make himself seem taller.

When he wasn't tending to his wheat or sheep, then he was at church. When he wasn't at church he was watching, all the time watching. Much of the time standing outside his house motionless, just scrutinising the Rushworth's cottage, and planning what to do with their land.

Milton was friendless and his only family was his wife and his brother's family. He rarely visited them and rarely spoke to locals unless he presented at court leet. It was here where he felt superior and acted like he was still a clerk in the Parliamentary army.

Milton Killsin wasn't liked in the village and some speculated it was only a matter of time before he got his just deserts.

If he heard Milton's name, John Pigshells would squint his eyes and clench his fist, 'FUCKIN' CUMBERWOLD! I know what he deserves, and I'll be the one to give it to 'im one day, mark me words!'

John was never backwards in coming forwards and spoke his mind whenever and wherever he chose. Most often this was the reason why he ended up in the pillory, but more often for fighting, cheating at cards or being with women of questionable character. He knew his three bastard children around Keighley.

Isabel tried her best to get on Milton's good side and would often wave if she saw either him or his wife outside.

Mrs Killsin often smiled and waved back. Milton would order her to put her hand down.

If he noticed Isabel waving, he'd ignore her and turn away.

My lambs and ewes won't make it through winter and Calamy's no help. I'll 'ave to take care of this myself. Milton spent a good part of the day thinking about this conundrum.

Often Isabel would see him peering at her from behind a lace curtain upstairs. He gave her the creeps.

Isabel liked Mrs Killsin. She and her daughters would often call out and go up to the dry bap wall which divided their land. She knew the latest news from Halifax, offered vegetables from her garden and sweets to share. Isabel knew she was a kind-hearted soul and thought no ill of her.

Mrs Killsin's hair was tied in a bun underneath her wimple. Her kind face appeared older than her years. She was quite portly but was always smiling and this was the reason people in the village liked her.

Both her and Milton's family were traders and they knew each other for years in Halifax. They played together as children and it was only fitting she and Milton married when they become of age.

On Sunday after Church, Milton did not socialise with other members of the congregation. He would order Mrs Killsin to get into their small carriage and leave without as much as a God bless or farewell. He knew they despised him for his many presentments to court leet.

In the shadow of hardship, the Rushworths clung to their unity, their resilience a testament to the enduring power of love and family. As the sun journeyed across the sky, casting its golden glow upon the landscape, the Rushworths continued their unyielding march, propelled by a shared conviction that no matter the trials they faced, their spirit would endure.

CHAPTER 2

The Heather Was Seeded by Blood From His Hands

English wool used to be the finest in Europe and was called the 'staple' as it was so important to the economy and Cromwell's standing army. The enclosure of fields, in the north, put an end to this because sheep were fed too well. This increased the weight of fleece reducing its quality. The product grown in Keighley became longer, courser and less popular. Their wool industry was dying and so were the livelihoods of its residents.

Tommy and his Uncle William bought wool from broggers. They were lower sorts who clawed their way out of serfdom by buying up fleece for the Company on loan. Some were ex-soldiers, vicious and unruly types who wavered on the line between morality and impropriety. Jacob Wilding was one of these types.

William took the finished kersey to the cloth market in Halifax each week. The family always ensured it was the correct width and length so he didn't get on the wrong side of the aulnager. Others weren't so lucky and were taken before the magistrate.

Prices were much lower now in Halifax, especially for the long course wool they wove. Now, the finest wool came from Wiltshire in the southwest where open fields still existed. This was the wool, turned to cloth, to make quality clothes for the rich.

The ten-hour round trip in the rain with the thirty-pound bundled kersey strapped to his back was long and tedious. It was all they could do to supplement the food they grew lest they join the multitude of wondering beggars and vagrants. William knew they were better off than most presently, but was fearful of the future.

The roads were full of former wives and children of soldiers killed in the war. Poor wretches, once copyholders and yeomen. Now they scoured the countryside looking for any means to put food in their bellies. Most often than not, they were turned away from parishes by the nightwatchmen. Eventually, they would find their way to the alms-houses or workhouses in the city. Others turned to more unfavourable pursuits like prostitution and thievery. William prayed his family wouldn't succumb to such shame. How wrong he was.

The shutters were still open, it was well into the night and the sun dropped below the horizon waving to the full moon shining in the sky. Small clouds played with it and clung to its beam like moths to a naked flame. Tommy could see the small grey circles which adorned it. He and other farmers believed the rings caused the rains that damaged crops.

They continued their spinning and weaving. It was hard work and the floating wool fibres made them itch and cough. Will sat by the fire combing the wool, he removed the short fibres, tangles and clumps making it suitable for his mother to spin.

Isabel was tired and yawned loudly then called out, 'MORWEN, MIRTH COME IN NOW.'

They didn't hear her.

The girls fulled the cloth at the back of the cottage.

Isabel got up from the spinning wheel, opened the door and stuck her head out. 'Come in now, girls, tis getting late!'

It was eleven-year-old Morwen and twelve-year-old Mirth's job to do the fulling. They stood in a half barrel of collected urine for hours at a time stomping on the cloth to rid it of its oils and impurities. It was also their job to go from cottage to cottage with a hand-pulled cart. It held a barrel to collect the urine from those in the parish. This was getting harder and harder since many families moved away.

Morwen and Mirth sauntered over to the door, the bottoms of their matching blue kirtles tucked in the string belt at the front.

Isabel opened the door wider for them. 'Come now, girls, go over and wash the putrid smell from yer feet and legs.'

Mirth was the more outspoken and cheekier of the two. 'But Ma, tis a lovely smell, I might take it as my par-fume.'

Isabel frowned. 'Parfume, where on Earth did you hear that?'

Mirth giggled. 'Heard this lady talkin' about it in the square. Well-dressed she was.'

Morwen was more like her father, a strong quieter personality rarely speaking. She frowned. 'You just keep ya parfume to yerself or else you won't be sharin' me bed if ya do!'

They giggled.

'Well, it would smell a lot better than some of the smells comin' from yer side of the bed durin' the night,' declared Morwen.

'And what do ya think, you smell like, a rose?' Mirth smiled cheekily.

Isabel interrupted, 'Right you two, wash and up and sit at the table!' She knew the smell of urine and manure would never depart no matter how much they washed.

Will removed the combs from the fire. He was a good loving son to both Tommy and Isabel. He doted on his mother and respected his father, not through fear but through admiration for the man he was. Will heard the whispers about his father's exploits in the war from his Uncle William, but until now, dared not ask.

Tommy stood from the loom and took a break stretching his back. He washed up and sat down in front of the fire.

Will sat down opposite. 'Da, what was the war like?'

Tommy pretended like he couldn't hear him, somewhat put off by his question. He stalled answering by taking out his pipe and filling it with tobacco. He frowned and looked at Will wondering where the blond hair came from. His and Isabel's was the darkness of soil. Will's hair was like a silvery, white gift from the heavens.

He was a hard worker like Tommy, spending his days with his father combing and ridding the barley of Armyworm and Mealybugs.

It would be two months before harvest if the rains stayed away and the cool weather didn't slow the crop and bring on mites and aphids.

Isabel looked up from the spinning wheel slyly to see how her husband would respond to Will's question.

Tommy turned and glanced at her. He raised his eyebrows as if waiting for the day when his son would ask.

Memories of the war were difficult and Tommy always tried push them to the back of his mind. When the bad memories came back, he found it difficult to wash them away and was constantly plagued by nightmares and cruel dreams.

Tommy glanced at his son; he didn't have the maturity to realise the difficulty of the question. 'One day I'll tell ya, lad, but now's not the time, the pain's too fresh.'

Tommy turned pale. 'All I'll say, is a lot of good men, including yer mother's father, were lost for a reason which escapes me. Me da always said it was never our war.'

Isabel could feel how difficult it was for Tommy to speak about it. She could feel the tension in the room. 'Come on you two, I 'ave ta finish this skein or else you won't have enough yarn to work the loom tomorrow.'

Isabel picked up the fleece and started to tease it. She stepped on the treadle and the wheel began to turn and whir. She expertly twisted it into a consistent strand.

While he sat by the fire, Tommy remembered the time he and his father Thomas spoke of war. A long time ago now and how naive he was.

'You've never seen what a matchlock musket ball can do to a man. Imagine a hot ball of solid lead three-quarters of an inch in diameter. At thirty yards it pierces yer skin, breaks your bones and splatters part of yer guts. It leaves a hole you could fit yer thumb in. If you were lucky enough to survive, a musket ball it would have taken a bit of material from yer tunic in with it. Left there, it would fester and rot. You'd get the sweats and a fever would take over. No matter how much they tried ta help ya, the wound would start to pong like a dead lamb left in the sun on a hot summer's day.'

Tommy thought of the reeve's brother and how lucky he was not to meet the same fate. Once again, he tried to dismiss it from his mind. He couldn't and took another gulp of ale to dull the memories.

Tommy stood, ambled over, and placed his hands on the top of Isabel's shoulders lovingly.

Tommy didn't like talking about the war because the news of the atrocities committed were fresh. The killing and maiming of female Royalist sympathisers repulsed him. *How could they do such a thing?*

It was some years since he fought for the Roundheads but remembered too well the horrors he'd braved. It also brought back memories of his friend James Fewtrall who saved him from certain death and the corporal. He often wondered if they both made it back.

He scrutinised Will and could see the resemblance of his father and he sadly thought of the day he passed. Passing away from consumption shortly after Will was born. He and Isabel often climbed up the hill to Saint Michael's to lay heather flowers on his grave.

His father would often say the heather was seeded by the blood from his hands. To be buried there amongst the pink and lavender was fitting.

'Will, best ya be getting yourself off ta bed. There's work to do in the morning and ya know we can't do it on the Sabbath lest both of us end up in the pillory.'

'Da, I'd rather wait fer Uncle William ta get home.'

'Won't be home fer ages, Will, now off ta bed with ya.'

'Tommy, please don't be sa harsh on the lad.'

'Tis alright, Ma. I should get some sleep.'

'There is some truth to the pillory. Milton Killsin caught Henry Tussler grinding grain t'other Sabbath, told the bailiff. Now poor old bastard has ta face the court leet.'

'Milton Killsin is a snivellin' creepy little man,' exclaimed Isabel. 'I can feel him watching me when I'm working in the vegetable patch or collectin' eggs from the coup. Whenever I spot him, he turns away.'

In the quiet corners of their idyllic village, Isabel's heart ached with empathy and concern. She couldn't help but exhale a heavy sigh as she whispered, 'His poor wife,' the words carrying the weight of a painful truth. 'Dare not peek over here, not even a smile when he's home, lest she bear the brunt of his temper.'

The secret anguish hidden behind closed doors had become an unbearable burden. 'I've heard him,' she continued, her voice filled with both sorrow and indignation, 'calling her a whore, even kicking her out in the middle of the night.' But it was the memory that haunted her most – a chilling testament to his cruelty: 'One day, I heard him beating her because of the meal she put on the table.' It was clear to Isabel that this man was a dark presence.

Will tilted his head, 'Seems ya can't do anything anymore cause of Killsin, can't play ball on a Sunday, fasting on a Friday.'

Tommy grumbled. 'Yer, well, times 'ave changed, we have ta change with 'em, nowt we can do, Will.'

Now growing weary, Will strode over to his mother who was still sitting at the wheel and gave her a peck on the cheek, 'Night, Ma.'

'Night, night, my luv, sleep tight, don't let the bed bugs bite.'

Will smiled. 'Not much I can do ta stop that, Ma.' He climbed the ladder to the loft.

Tommy watched him go and smiled proudly. 'He's grown, not a boy anymore. A man in his own right.'

Realising Isabel had been spinning all day, Tommy sauntered over and placed his hands on her shoulders, 'Come, wife, rest.' He leant over and smelled her hair; it had an earthy, natural, herbal scent. He gave her a kiss on the top of the head.

'Tommy, this skein won't spin itself!'

'Aye true wife, but ya can't do anymore t'night. You need to rest.'

Isabel inspected the yarn. 'I suppose I can finish it in the morning.'

Isabel never complained and besides spending hours on the wheel, tended to family's needs as best she could. She often went without food so both Tommy, Will and the girls could eat. After filling their bowls of the watery pottage or barley oats, she would often wipe the cauldron with her fingers and lick it.

This didn't go unnoticed by Tommy, who would often fain fullness and give the rest of his bowl to her.

Tommy loved his wife. She was younger, a country rose. Her freckled face and bright persona improved the mood of all who met her. The high cheek bones and fresh, pale skin was flushed with a rosiness from the heat of the fire. When she untied the ties of her wimple she would shake her dark hair loose allowing it to drop down past her shoulders. Her blue eyes glinted with glee.

She wore a stained, dark brown linen kirtle, pulled tightly with drawstrings held the top together and accentuated her bosom. Her waist was thin and her legs long.

Happily married, she still attracted the attention of the men in the village. She would smile but never look at them as she wandered past the stalls of the market. They often stared at her in a lecherous manner, whispered and laughed.

The quieter of the two sisters, Isabel was more laid back than her sister Lucy who was the more spirited. She still missed her deeply. Lucy died during childbirth some years ago now.

Tommy's Uncle William never got over it and when he wasn't journeying to Halifax, spent his time solemnly combing wool alongside Will. The sparkle in his eyes was gone.

Tommy sat in his favourite chair near the hearth of the fire and took his muddied shoes off. He embraced the warmth in the candle lit room. The radiant heat flushed his cheeks and warmed his heart.

He took his white, long-stemmed, clay pipe from the pipe holder, which his great grandfather made. It took pride of place on the large oak mantel piece above.

His peace was disturbed by his daughters laughing so he called out to them, 'Ooy… you two… quieten down now before I come up there.'

'Okay, Da.'

He grumbled, 'I had a chat with John Pigshells the other day, they been pinchin' corn from carts on the way to market in Halifax, people are starvin'.'

Isabel held her hands to the fire. 'We havn't had a good harvest for four years, summer rains, drought then frost! Low wages, high food prices.'

'Aye, with people like us, things can't be worse off.'

Will called down from the loft, 'I'm gonna go to the manor tomorrow, ask about work at the new mill.'

Isabel feared Jasper Calamy and his men and the consequences for her son if he got mixed up with him. 'Will, there's plenty a' work to be done round here. No need to get mixed up with that lot.'

Tommy sensed Isabel's concerns. 'I'll go with him, wife, doesn't hurt ta try, must be something he needs doing, probably more stone walls I'd say. Will's getting older now, wouldn't hurt him to start payin' his way. I'd rather him do that, than take off for the city like Will's boys.'

Annoyed, Isabel glanced up. 'At what price, Tommy? Besides if he sees ya, he'll probably ask fer the lease fines.'

'Well, wife, he can't get what we don't have,' stated Tommy stubbornly.

Isabel's breathing quickened. 'I just don't want ta lose the life-hold, don't want us ta be turned off like the others.'

Tommy straightened his posture and took a puff of his pipe. 'It won't happen, wife, we've been on this land fer too long. Don't you worry yerself.

Isabel, when William gets back we'll pay some of the lease fines God willin'. He must have good cause to see us off and he doesn't.

'Rest now, my love.' Tommy's voice was a tender murmur, an invitation to find solace in the embrace of sleep. 'Tomorrow is a new day, and we shall face it together.'

Isabel, her weariness evident, acquiesced, her spinning wheel finally stilled. The fire's gentle crackle provided a soothing backdrop to their shared reprieve, a moment of respite in a world that seemed ever poised on the precipice of upheaval.

As the night deepened, the Rushworth cottage fell into a slumber, the echoes of the day's labour carried away by the soft whispers of dreams. In the quietude, the embers of determination burned bright, a testament to the unyielding spirit that defined their lives in a world fraught with uncertainty.

☆

The next morning Tommy woke to the sound of thunder. The skies opened. The rain started dripping through the thatch which he hadn't the time or inclination to fix.

Isabel placed a wooden bucket beneath to catch it. She narrowed her eyes glaring at Tommy.

Isabel stood beside the bucket, her face a mask of annoyance. 'At it again, Tommy. Rain's seeping through, drippin' on the floor. Should've fixed that thatch ages ago.'

'Wife, put yer dagger look away. I told you, I'll fix it soon,' Tommy's voice a mix of resignation and mild irritation. He donned his cloak, woollen hat, and motioned for Will to follow as he set off toward the manor. Tommy pulled his cloak around him tighter. 'This rain's good for the feed and barley and better now than at harvest time.'

Will walked ahead, his steps matching his father's determined pace. He stopped and turned to face Tommy, raindrops decorating his young face like glistening jewels. 'Da, ya don't have to come with me.'

'Aye, I do! Don't trust Griswold or Calamy as far as I could throw 'em,' Tommy responded, his voice heavy with caution.

The drizzle continued, painting the world in varying shades of gray. In the midst of the storm, a ribbon of bright orange emerged on the horizon, a valiant attempt by the sun to break free from the shroud of clouds. The sky above was a canvas of shifting grays, with the promise of a new day hidden beneath the layers.

Tommy stopped and looked up, a sense of wonder flickering in his blue eyes. 'Sun is tryin' to get through, Will. Only a shower, and it's movin' Southwest. Won't last long.'

The rain began to subside, as if taking its cue from the sun's tentative appearance. Birds overhead sensed the impending respite and burst into song, their melodies a celebration of the storm's passing. Some ventured down to the fields, their beaks digging into the damp earth in search of breakfast.

The moors were touched by the first rays of morning light, the heather and grasses awakening with the promise of a new day. As the clouds slowly parted, the landscape transformed, revealing hues of pink and purple in the heather, and vibrant greens in the fields.

Tommy and Will strode up the driveway of the manor, gone was the hubbub of times gone by. There were no manicured gardens or newly trimmed hedges. The once magnificent display of pruned roses was an unruly mess of thick thorns and yellow and black spotted leaves. The air of decay hung heavy, a reflection of the changing times.

Tommy rapped his knuckles against the big oak door at the back of the manor, its solid surface echoing the uncertainty that lay within.

There was a commotion inside. A woman grumbled, 'YES? 'OLD ON. Who is it at this bloomin' hour?' After a moment, the door creaked open, revealing a stout woman in an apron, her scowl revealing her annoyance at the early morning interruption.

Mrs Stuart, the housekeeper, looked Tommy and Will up and down with disdain, 'And what, pray, do you want at this time of day?'

Tommy and Will took off their tricorn hats. 'We're here to see his grace.'

'Are ya now? Mrs Stuart grunted, 'Master Calamy is barely awake.'

'Missus, he asked fer us,' Tommy lied.

'Oh, all right, wait 'ere. I'll get Mr Griswold.'

She closed the door abruptly and left them out in the drizzle. Their cloaks were soaked through, and shoes caked with mud.

Will looked up and scanned the grey sky then closed his eyes, allowing the cold rain to drip on his face. He opened his mouth and stuck his tongue out.

Before long, the door swung open, revealing a man dressed in the attire of a Puritan, his presence commanding attention. This was Mr Griswold, the man who often stood by Calamy's side, his scarred face telling a story of battles fought and loyalty earned.

Tommy dipped his head. 'Mr Griswold, we are here to speak with his grace.'

The man's deep voice echoed. 'Come, his grace will see you.'

Tommy and his son glanced at each other raising their eyebrows curiously.

As they followed Griswold through the corridors of the manor, Tommy couldn't help but take in the faded grandeur that surrounded them. The once bustling halls now echoed with the ghosts of better times, and Tommy's mind drifted to memories of a time when the Rushworths and the manor were more intertwined.

Finally, they entered a grand hall, the table set for breakfast, and at its head sat Jasper Calamy, the master of the manor.

His grace Jasper Calamy sat in a high backed, carved and embroidered chair. He watched them make their way toward him. They marched with their heads held high and with a confident and proud stagger above their standing.

Calamy heard of Tommy Rushworth's service for Parliament in the war. For this reason, he decided not to turn him off the land like the others. Well, for the time being until he could find reason.

As they got closer to the fire, Will could feel his woollen cloak start to steam. They stood in front of his grace then bowed in unison.

When Will straightened, he glanced at Griswold who took up his position at the side of his grace.

Calamy said nothing for a moment scrutinising his visitors.

Tommy's faded indigo, tunic was missing buttons and frayed. His breeches were baggy and his woollen stockings loose.

Finally, Griswold leant down and whispered to his master.

Calamy nodded. 'Ahh Rushworth, I've been meaning to call for you. It appears your neighbour would like to lease the land you hold. He's prepared to pay more coin for it. He's purchased more sheep and requires more feed for them. I'm sure you understand.'

Will frowned then glanced at his father, waiting for his response.

Tommy bore the weathered countenance of a life shaped by the unforgiving landscapes and the toils of rural existence. His face, etched with the lines of time and labour, told a story of resilience and endurance.

Weathered and tanned by the harsh northern elements, his skin was deeply creased, like the rugged contours of the moorland itself. The wind and sun had left their mark, bestowing a leathery texture to his complexion. Sunspots and freckles scattered across his cheeks and nose, testament to years spent working under the open sky.

His eyes, framed by a network of crow's feet, were the colour of stormy skies, a muted blue-gray that seemed to mirror the ever-changing moods of the moors. They held a quiet wisdom, a deep well of experience that came from a lifetime spent in close communion with the land. Though they spoke of hardships endured, they also sparkled with a spark of determination that refused to be extinguished.

A thick beard covered his lower face, a testament to his rustic existence. Strands of silver were intermingled with the dark brown, giving his beard an almost salt-and-pepper appearance. It was coarse and wiry, much like the heather that blanketed the moors.

His nose, slightly crooked from an old injury, jutted out with an air of rugged character. The lines around his mouth were etched deep, a map of laughter and solemnity, smiles and sorrow. A faint scar traced a path along his jawline, a reminder of some long-forgotten mishap.

Despite the years of hard work and exposure to the elements, there was a quiet strength in his gaze and a sense of dignity in his features. He was a man of the moors, shaped by the land and the life he had known, a living testament to the resilience of those who made their home in Yorkshire's rugged and unforgiving terrain.

'I beg yer pardon, yer grace, but me family has been working this land since before I was born. My grandfather worked it and his father before 'im.'

'Means nothing Rushworth, times are changing,' said Griswold.

'With all respect, we've got life lease hold. Me da told me we have it for the lives of me, and my son Will, or fer ninety-nine years. Got the parchment to prove it.'

'Ninety-nine years? A long time.' Master Calamy and Griswold smiled.

Tommy put his hand on his chest. 'I know we been a bit slow with the fines fer the lease, but we'll pay the rest soon as the barley's harvested.'

Jasper Calamy turned and stared into the fire. *'As justice of the peace I would come afoul of the magistrate, if I tried to turn them off without good reason.'*

Griswold became angry at Tommy's impertinence. 'Rushworth Hall Green is not an alms-house for the poor. How dare you speak to his grace in such a manner!'

Calamy continued, 'Tommy come now, surely you do not believe in all those ancient land laws. The value of my land is almost double what you pay.'

Tommy looked submissive but stayed defiant. 'With all respect yer grace, we 'ave life lease hold and have had for many years.'

'You are merely tenants-at-will and it is only by his grace's kindness you're not evicted,' added Griswold.

Jasper Calamy glimpsed up at his man then spoke quietly and confidently, 'No, Griswold, he is quite right.'

'You are behind on your lease fines as Griswold informs me. You have yet to pay the fine which was renewable on the passing of your father.

You have already passed the twelve-month term by three months. It seems time is of the essence if you wish to remain.'

Tommy put his hand on his heart. 'Your grace, part of the fines fer the lease will be paid when my uncle returns.'

Calamy didn't say anything but paused and glanced sideways at his benefactor. 'What say you Griswold?'

Griswold leant down to whisper to Calamy, 'Tis true what he says, unless something happens to them or they leave, they cannot be turned off. They have paid some of the fines and it would be seen to be improper if we turned them off now. If they complained to the magistrate...'

Will frowned and leant forward straining to hear what was being said.

Calamy sat forward. 'I tell you what I'll do, Rushworth, if you agree to pay the same lease your neighbour has agreed to pay, I will say no more about it.'

'But yer grace, I 'ave a parchment.'

'If you cannot pay it, then I will ask you to leave, is this understood? The magistrate would have no other option other than to support my claim.'

Tommy's eyes grew wide with concern. 'But your grace, with the increase in grain prices, tithe and tax, we are destitute.'

Calamy became annoyed. 'What of the poor relief Milton Killsin distributes and the alms house in Haworth and Halifax. Are you not aware I and other landowners pay handsomely into it each year?'

Tommy knew Killsin spread the poor relief but was sure he kept a tidy sum for himself. 'Aye, I am your grace, but with the recent bad harvests and lack of grain available, times are difficult.'

'That is not my concern, I'm afraid it is my final offer, one month! Will you continue with the lease or not?' Calamy asked with confidence knowing they wouldn't be able to afford it. *If they reneged on their life hold he would have his land back and Killsin would stop complaining.*

Tommy lamented knowing he didn't have a choice, he dropped his chin and mumbled, 'Yes, your grace, I'll find coin for the lease fines somehow.'

With all their labour, Tommy could barely pay their lease fines as it was. Now they needed to pay it within the month or else be turned off like the others. *Where would we go, what would we do?* Tommy was distraught.

Calamy sat back in his chair, pleased with the outcome. 'Very good, Griswold will keep you to your agreement. Now, is there anything else?'

Will straightened. 'Your grace, I humbly ask if you ha-ave any work hereabouts I could do.'

'What say you, Griswold, is there anything the lad can do?'

Griswold bent down and whispered, 'We wouldn't be fined if we're seen to be taking on another pauper apprentice. He seems like a strong lad; we could put him to work.'

Griswold peered at Will.

'Well, the stables need muckin', your grace. Terrible job in this rain and as you know, Bobby the hand is otherwise disposed.'

Calamy, understood what he meant. 'Are yes, best to leave Bobby.'

'Very well then, it's settled. Griswold, take him to the stables.' He felt good about himself after re-negotiating the lease.

Tommy and Will bowed, turned and followed Griswold across the stone floor toward the door.

Calamy stood in silence, his eyes tracking their departure, fixated on their mud-splattered hose. The weight of their sodden, woollen cloaks seemed to drag them down, a poignant symbol of their struggles. He couldn't help but shake his head with a sigh, murmuring, 'Poor wretches, they won't be able to pay their lease. It's only a matter of time.' A faint, rueful smile played at the corners of his lips as he contemplated the upcoming reckoning. 'Killsin better appreciate this,' he mused, his thoughts a mix of compassion and frustration.

Being the justice of the peace in the parish, it was required to be seen to be fair and impartial as he didn't want trouble like they had in the Midlands. He heard about the enclosure riots, shepherds knocking down walls and fences and illegally claiming back common land from landowners.

Calamy thought for a moment. *Using the law to force them out is certainly in my power. If they don't pay their lease, any magistrate in the land would surely support my claim. It's best this be done right and I stay on the right side of the magistrate. Besides, how much longer can they last?*

Calamy relished the power given to him by Robert Lilburne, a supporter of Oliver Cromwell. After hearing of the importance of the Yorkshire wool industry to Cromwell's standing army, Calamy dedicated himself to its prosperity, and his.

Calamy surrounded himself with the loyal officers who served with him in the war. Archibald Griswold and Milton Killsin. They stood by his side at the battle of Tadcaster. They and their families were loyal Puritans, and he was tasked with ensuring their wealth and prosperity.

Griswold strode to the door and opened it, stepping through into the kitchen. Tommy and Will followed. They smelt and heard the bacon sizzling. They noticed the bag of corn sitting on the bench, its yellow goodness spilling onto the tabletop. They were in awe.

Tommy placed his hat back on, lifted the latch and proceeded out into the drizzle. He peered back through the raindrops dripping from his eyelashes.

Griswold stared at him then shut the back door abruptly.

Making his way down the drive to the gate, Tommy stopped to wave, 'I'll see ya back at home when yer done. If ya do a good job they might ask you to stay on.'

'Okay, Da,' he said, his voice filled with both concern and tenderness, 'get home quick and get out of the rain.'

He lingered, watching his father with a deep sense of longing as he disappeared through the gate. It was a fleeting moment, but it held the weight of their worlds. That gate, a simple structure of iron and wood, stood as a stark border – a dividing line between those who possessed plenty and those who had little. In that moment, it symbolised the profound disparities of their existence.

Tommy didn't look back again but walked ahead quickly. He was confused by what happened at the manor. *Milton Killsin the fucker! His land is double the size of ours and much more arable. I Suppose much wants more. I'll pay the lease fines, but how?*

The Killsins were devout Puritans having little to do with the Rushworths, or any of the lower sort, who they considered to be clodhoppers barbarous, uncivil and vulgar.

In church, The Puritan minister preached against immoralities and read the statutes prohibiting blasphemy, swearing, cursing, perjury, drunkenness and profanations of the Lord's Day.

It was believed by some cursing, and blaspheming was the greatest threat to England's relationship' with the Almighty. This was this culture the Puritans hoped to eradicate. Ridding the village of people like the Rushworths was the first step. The land they acquired was a gift from God.

☆

Like other men in the village, Tommy refused to acknowledge Milton Killsin in any way.

Milton was despised by all, especially John Pigshells who often whispered 'what he'd like to do to with the ledger' the church warden always carried.

Will looked up to see the curtains move and somebody peering through a window on the second floor. He quickly strode toward the stables to get out of the rain.

As he entered the stable, he heard the neighing, stomping and clopping of hooves. He could tell the horses were disturbed by the weather and displayed their annoyance. They stomped and kicked their hind legs back in anger at the stall walls.

He took off his brown tricorn hat and cloak which were saturated, limp and heavy. He sighed heavily and was soaked through to his undershirt. Will shivered, rubbing the tops of his arms to get circulation back.

The straw, coarse and golden, was the canvas on which this olfactory masterpiece was painted, its union with horse manure birthing a distinctive, earthy aroma that spoke of hard work and humble living. The horses themselves, noble creatures, contributed their own unique bouquet – a blend of sweat, urine and breath that added a robust, animalistic essence to the air.

He loved the smell of the freshly cut hay and lifted his nose and closed his eyes to savour it. He smiled, pleased with himself.

Stepping into the first box stall he confidently rubbed the white mare's muzzle. She nervously pulled away, stomped her hooves, and moved away to the other side.

Will grabbed the halter from the wall and gently placed it over her muzzle and neck.

She reared up a little, but he patted her on the neck, and she settled.

'There, there girl, I'm n-not gonna hurt ya. Gonna be cleaning up, that's all.' Will led her out of the box stall and tied the halter to the outside gate.

He grabbed the pitchfork leaning against the wall, stopped and peered out the door.

The rain was starting to slow; the wind picked up over the moors. The barn door slammed on its hinges which spooked the horses and caused the white mare to rear up again.

Will took hold of the halter and patted the mare on the neck to settle her again. A cold swoosh of wind rushed into the barn causing a cold shiver to run down his back. He grabbed the wooden wheelbarrow pushed it back toward the stall.

Will heard something and at first dismissed it. Hearing it again, he stopped and listened; there was something happening next door. He heard a grunt, so he put the wheelbarrow down and strode up to the wooden planked wall. He heard it again and put his left ear against to it to listen. There it was again. Will peeked through the crack in the timber and by candlelight, could see somebody stacking full hessian bags up against the far wall.

He turned around nervously, paused then peeked back to have a second look through the crack. *Engrossers! Calamy, he keeps it all for himself.*

He felt it, a sharpness in his back. He froze and raised his hands.

'Turn around slowly.' He recognised Griswold's voice. 'You should learn ta keep yer nose out of other people's business, lad.'

As Will cautiously turned, he glanced down to see the sharp end of a rapier sword pointed at his mid-region.

He stared up at Griswold nervously, 'I h…heard a noise yer grace.'

Griswold lowered his sword. 'And what sort of noise did you hear? More importantly, what did you see through the crack in the wall, lad?'

Will peered toward the wall. 'Not a lot, yer grace, it was too dark.'

'Too dark?' Griswold grumbled and peeked through the crack.

Bobby blew out the candle. There was nothing but darkness and silence.

'Well, you make sure it stays this way and keep ta shovelling shite 'cause the way I see, it's all your good for.' Griswold put his sword back in its scabbard and proceeded toward the door.

'Aye, yer grace, of course.' Will sighed with relief.

Picking up the wheelbarrow again he pushed it over to the stall. He lifted a dollop of horse manure and gave it a shake with the pitchfork dropping the straw back to the ground. He scraped the top layer of sawdust noticing the dark patches of urine then exposed the larger wet patch beneath. Inhaling the strong smell of ammonia, he coughed as he lifted the wet patch. He pushed the dry shavings and straw to cover it.

The rain stopped so he took the wheelbarrow out back to empty its contents onto the muck mound.

Will turned around to see if anyone was about, then strode over to the far side of the barn. Peering in, he was surprised to see straw bales stacked from floor to ceiling but no hessian bags. He climbed up the wall of straw bales. Reaching the top, he sat trying to figure out what... *Where are the sacks?*

Griswold secretly spied on him. He appeared once more and peered in the stable and grumbled, 'Yer a nosy little bastard, aren't ya? Stop what yer doing, his grace wants to see ya, follow me!'

Will rolled his eyes. *Oh no, now I've done it, probably get a whippin' and told to go 'ome. He's right, I am a stupid bastard!*

Will led the mare back into the stall and once again rubbed her on the neck. He ran to catch up to Griswold ensuring a respectful distance behind. They continued into the kitchen where Mrs Stuart gave him the filthiest of looks.

They walked through the great hall. Will stopped and inspected the roof trusses twenty feet above his head.

The great hall was forty-five feet in length and over half in breadth. At the end, was a tall, narrow window capped by a sharply pointed arch and another clerestory window at the side. There was wood panelling and an entrance to a small chapel with a table and a crucifix. Opposite the clerestory window, there was a fireplace and a high chimney. Opposite the fire, was a large table where his grace sat.

The table was set for breakfast. Master Calamy didn't pay him a thought but continued to gorge himself on his meal. The cornbread, trout stew and boiled eggs made Will's mouth water. He'd never seen so much food on one table.

Griswold strolled around the table and whispered in Calamy's ear.

The master ignored Will. He tapped a boiled egg on the table and picked the shell from it. After he placed the full egg in his mouth, chewed and swallowed. He eventually glanced up. 'Young Rushworth, my man Griswold tells me while you were mucking out the stalls you saw more than you needed to.'

Will dropped his eyes and pondered his situation. *Christ, what am I gonna tell Da?*

Calamy drank from a goblet. 'Young man, such interest in other's affairs could make things difficult for you and your family. What say you?'

'There was a noise your grace, I saw nowt!' Will declared brazenly.

'And the sacks you claimed to have not seen, what of these? Show him!'

Griswold marched into the kitchen and returned a few moments later with an opened sack. He tipped it, releasing a steady stream of corn onto the table.

Will's eyes grew wide with wonder.

'Is this what you saw?' Calamy asked, squinting ready to decipher Will's response.

'I've ne-never seen sa much corn!' Will's excitement grew, more from hunger than surprise.

Calamy handed Griswold a piece of cornbread who in turn offered it to Will.

He glanced up nervously at Calamy.

'Go on, take it, lad! Griswold tells me you've worked hard today.'

Will raised his hand slowly and took the cornbread devouring it quickly then taking another from Griswold stuffing it in his tunic.

Calamy smiled. 'You know we may have other uses for you 'round the manor, but these duties need... a level of secrecy. I'm sure your family could use some extra coin and corn, if you keep your mouth shut.'

Will's voice quivered with unease, his words halting as he confronted the enigmatic figure before him. 'And wha-what du-duties might they be, your grace?'

His inquiry was laced with a blend of curiosity and apprehension, mirroring the same unyielding determination Calamy had observed in his father.

In that fraught exchange, a thread of familial resilience seemed to pass through generations, connecting him to his father in ways they could not comprehend.

Jasper Calamy wasn't a dishonest man but thought he deserved more than he got from Lilburne. *Now stuck away in this God forsaken place?*

He wanted to make the most of his position while he could, increase his fortune then return to Leeds. The demand for long-staple for draperies was increasing, but he required more of it to be hidden away for it to be profitable. Shepherds were reducing their stock herds, so he acquired more sheep to fill his pastures. The price of grain was going up and he would soon start to release some of his to market in Halifax and Bradford for almost double the price.

Griswold marched back across the stone floor. He stopped and waited for Will to catch up. They went back to the stable then continued round the other side. Griswold climbed up the steps of straw bales then disappeared over the top.

Confused, Will followed, he peered over the top and noticed a small gap between the straw and the wooden wall. There was a small set of iron bolts sticking out of a vertical wooden beam, which Griswold clambered down.

'COME ON, BOY, I HAVN'T GOT ALL DAY!'

Will carefully followed.

At the bottom, Griswold pushed on a wooden plank in the wall and it opened. He lit a candle in a lantern and stepped inside. Two rats chirped and scattered all except the one caught in the trap. This one squealed and bit the metal cage; its gums bled around its long yellow teeth.

Will followed and there it was, a secret store full of corn and wool bales from floor to ceiling. He stood there in amazement, the store was hidden by a false wall.

'I've ne-never seen sa much corn and the sacks of wool, there must be a king's fortune in 'ere.'

'Aye and you won't again, if ya sa much as whisper to anybody about our little secret,' whispered Griswold.

Griswold turned and made his way back to the opening in the wall, 'Remember what his grace said, now all you need do is keep quiet and do his bidding.'

'But what is his grace's biddin'?'

'You'll find out, for now come each day to the mill down the back. The master will give you the odd job for you. Play yer cards right and you and your family might eat better. And remember, keep your bloody mouth shut!'

Griswold threw a sixpence to Will then turned to leave with the candle.

Will was left in the dimming light. He didn't catch the coin so dropped to the ground and rummaged around in the dark. Finally feeling it through the straw and spilt grain. He picked it up being sure to grab a couple of handfuls of loose grain as he stood. He lifted the flap to the leather pouch which hung from his belt and quickly placed it inside.

Will closed the opening to the false wall behind him and followed Griswold up to the top. He watched him go through the door of the barn.

Engrossers, Da won't want me getting involved with all this lot. Will heard his father speak of engrossers, those who bought grain in bulk from farmers before it went to market. They would control the supply and demand and sell it at a higher price later. Those who could afford it, ate well, those like his family went hungry.

Will knew his mother would be wondering where he was. He meandered out into Sun Street and turned right down the hill. A rainbow formed, a spectrum of arched colours over the east horizon towering above the woods ahead. The bleak grey sky broke giving birth to patches of blue.

Will passed the odd cottage and tenant farmer trying to scare away the birds from their crop. He gazed up Weavers Hill and heard a loom working. The thicket started on the left-hand side of the road. It led down to the beck and then the cleared pasture of Hall Green. He gazed south noticing the neighbour Milton Killsin and his wife working the hoe.

Mrs Killsin looked up, smiled and waved. 'Husband, the Lord says love thy neighbour, why do you treat them so?'

Milton stared at her. 'I do not like their ways. I will not associate with them and nor will you! Do you understand? The sooner they are off the land the better!'

Mrs Killsin was saddened by this but dared not argue. She feared his temper and couldn't stand another beating like the last one.

Secretly, Milton was infatuated with Isabel Rushworth. He would often secretly watch her working in the vegetable garden. She was much younger and prettier than his wife and he sometimes dreamed of her in ways not appropriate for a Christian man.

He didn't believe, like other Puritans, that the sexual act was only for procreation. He and his wife couldn't have children, it was years since they tried. Isabel Rushworth brought out all what was unholy in him and his guilt was all consuming.

Milton stopped work and glanced over. He noticed Will but didn't acknowledge him, then continued hoeing the weeds.

A dog barked in the distance. The Pennine's ghost-like mist haunted the hills and valleys. A few sheep watched on disinterested, they grazed on green grass, their lambs hidden from view.

Will stumbled across the fallow field and made his way up the side of their strip of land. He approached the cottage and couldn't hear the loom. He could hear his father rummaging out the back, so he went around.

'Ayeup Will, how'd ya go son?'

'Alright da, they want me back.' He reached into his pouch and opened his hand to reveal the six pence.

Tommy smiled. 'Well done son, yer ma will be pleased.'

The air inside the Rushworth cottage was thick with the scent of the meager meal being prepared. Isabel was huddled over the fireplace, tending to a pot that contained the sparrow chicks her husband had brought in.

'Ma,' Will began hesitantly, 'I got something for ya.' He held out his hand, revealing the small handful of corn.

Isabel turned from the pot and looked at the offering in her son's hand. Her tired eyes brightened for a moment as she took the corn, her fingers brushing against his. 'Thank you, Will,' she said softly, her voice a mix of gratitude and weariness.

Tommy walked in from the back, his boots heavy with mud, and caught sight of the corn. He grinned at his wife and son, a rare expression of happiness spreading across his weathered face. 'Well, ain't that a fine surprise.'

Isabel's smile was faint, but it reached her eyes as she added the corn to the cauldron.

Will's chest swelled with a mix of pride and relief. His efforts had earned his family a small comfort, and he was determined to keep doing whatever was necessary to provide for them.

'Sit down, Will,' Tommy said, gesturing to the worn wooden table. 'Tell us 'bout your day.'

As they settled around the table, Will recounted the events at the manor, carefully omitting the secret store of corn and wool he had stumbled upon. He spoke of the tasks he had been given.

The family sat in a quiet moment of unity, appreciating the small warmth the cottage provided against the chill of the outside world. The crackling fire created a soothing rhythm.

Will's gaze met his father's and he nodded solemnly. The weight of his family's well-being rested heavily on his young shoulders. He knew that he would have to navigate a world of hidden truths and unspoken agreements, all while preserving the fragile existence they had.

As the evening wore on, the Rushworths shared their meager meal, their conversation drifting to the village and its people. They spoke of Milton Killsin, the cold-hearted landowner, and his wife who seemed to be a prisoner in her own home. The Killsins were respected in the community for their devoutness, yet they were shunned by many for their callousness.

'Killsin's a strange one,' Tommy muttered, taking a sip from a mug of weak ale. 'He preaches of righteousness on Sundays, but his actions speak of greed.'

Isabel sighed, her gaze distant as she stirred the pot. 'It's a cruel world, Tommy. We must do what we can to survive, even if it means dealin' with folks like him.'

'True enough,' Tommy conceded. 'But we must never forget who we are and what we stand for.'

Will listened to his parents, the flickering fire casting shadows on their faces. He thought of the hidden store of corn and wool, the mysterious tasks he was being asked to do, and the delicate balance between survival and integrity.

As the night deepened, they retired to their simple beds, the fire's embers providing a dim glow that illuminated their modest home. Will lay in his straw mattress, his mind racing with thoughts of the future, of the secrets he had discovered, and the path he would need to tread carefully.

In the midst of uncertainty, a sense of purpose began to take root within him. He had glimpsed a world beyond the confines of their village, a world of hidden truths and complex alliances. Will knew he held a role to play in this intricate dance, and he was determined to navigate it with the same unwavering determination that had carried his family through generations of toil and hardship.

And so, under the watchful gaze of the moon and stars, young Will Rushworth drifted into an uneasy sleep, his dreams filled with visions of cornfields, hidden stores and a future waiting to be shaped.

CHAPTER 3

To Hull, Hell or Halifax

The land was not fertile nor arable. It was located on the south-eastern corner of the Pennines. The town of Halifax was built on the prosperity of the wool trade. The area around it became the third most prosperous manufacturing district in England. The land on the outskirts was now home to rich yeomen, and traders. It was only they who could afford grandiose 'Halifax Houses'.

These houses were built of dressed stone, gritstone and mullioned windows. They sat amongst the overcrowded streets filled with filth, poverty, hunger and vagrancy.

Halifax was also home to the 'gibbet'. Decapitation was a common method of execution in England but Halifax was unusual as it employed a guillotine-like machine.

William peered up at St James Church which was the biggest building in town. He arrived tired and thirsty. The rope dug into his shoulders. The back of his shirt was sweaty, sticking to him underneath the folds of cloth clinging to his back like a needy infant.

William's grey hair was long, pushed back off his face and tied in a ponytail. His aged and weathered appearance was a testimony to the life he . Crow's feet spread from the corners of his eyes; wrinkles on his forehead were like deep furrows in a field. The glint in his eye was gone and they lacked the spirit they once had. A light grey moustache and beard adorned his face and met with his bushy, grey sideburns. His dour expression was a shadow from the life he lived.

He wore a thigh-length, brown leather patched tunic with cut off sleeves. His coat was done up at the top and opened as it neared his thigh. His brown leather wrist bands accentuated his muscular upper arms. Dirty, mud-stained breeches reached to above his knees homemade garters held up his hose. He wore muddied brown leather ankle height boots on his feet which were caked in mud and caused blisters.

William travelled to the markets in Halifax each week to sell the kersey. It took three hours to walk each week in rain, hail or shine. He wasn't to know at the time, but this journey was going to be different than all the others.

He often passed the empty horse packs heading out of town. Beggars and vagabonds heading into town. He would see them turned back to their home parish by constables and night watchmen. They would wait on the outskirts of town begging for coin from clothiers leading packs of horses on their put-out runs.

Most were fatherless families. Children begging and crying from hunger or their mother's pinches. *Not all casualties occurred in the war, nope, not in the war,* he thought to himself.

William arrived in Halifax with the cloth early so he could get a bed and a good position at the market the next day. The one kersey they managed to weave each week was a yard wide by twenty-four yards long. It was hard-wearing, weatherproof and heavy.

The alehouse was the most important building in town, as they were places to socialise, eat a meal, discuss various matters of the day, and for most to get drunk.

William always stayed at the Crosse Inn, he knew the publican, James Mitchell. He knew he could get a pot of ale and a noggin of pottage for two pence.

The cockfighting held in Whewall's Courtyard outback was a bonus if he could pick the right bird.

James Mitchell was a bit of a swill-belly but he also knew he had any news worth hearing. Prices, exports, imports, quality of wool and cloth, he knew it all. James knew all the broggers, clothiers, inspectors and overseers in the district.

William entered the courtyard through the stone archway and walked past the coach. He lifted the latch of the large oak door and went in.

The inn was crowded with all manner of down and out former soldiers, tinkers and tradesmen. Puritans, with their black felt hats and ruffled collars drank and spoke of trade. Gone were the card games and frivolous chit chat of old. The talk was mostly of Cromwell's government, the gibbet and the expected price of cloth at the market.

William undid the rope and took his kersey from his back and placed it down on the floor beside him. He sat down at the end of a trestle and noticed James.

The inn was noisy; the floor covered in a mixture of horse manure, mud and soggy straw. There was an opening next to the bar leading to the kitchen. Behind the bar were shelves of pewter dishes, earthenware mugs and pitchers.

In the corner beside the fire, a clothier and a buyer whispered the price of a kersey. They laughed and tried to settle on a price before the market which they knew was forbidden.

'Ayeup William, good evenin' ta ya, how was your trip?' James called out over the hubbub and laughter of the patrons. He poured two ales from the barrel into pewter, wooden tankards and placed them on the trestle near William.

'What's the word, James?'

James whispered, 'Same as usual, you know, nobody's sayin' nowt till the mornin, 'cept those two cunnin' bastards over there. The gibbet's on tomorra,' James replied while sitting down opposite.

William rubbed his shoulders where the rope left its mark. 'Another poor bastard having his head lopped off fer nothing more than trying to feed his family.'

'Aye, constable and Hunincri caught two of them hiding in Scarr Woods between Copely and Skircoat. They made off with kerseys drying out the back of Daniel Grains cottage, tried to dye them a different colour.'

'Constables said it was worth three pounds.'

'So?'

‘Haven’t you heard? A new law passed by Parliament, anybody caught stealing cloth or fleece worth more than thirteen and a half shillings goes to the gibbet!’

William shook his head.

James continued, ‘I went the last time, there were hundreds watchin’ and cheerin’ like it was a celebration. It was a bloody mess! Executioner didn’t sharpen the blade so the poor bastard didn’t die with the first drop. He groaned for a while until they lifted the axe head and dropped it again.’

‘Poor bastard.’ William turned to look at a Puritan family sitting at a long table.

The table was dressed halfway down with an embroidered tablecloth. The husband with his tall black capotains hat tried to convince his wife to stay for the gibbet.

The inn hound gazed up at the table waiting for a morsel of food to be tossed his way. The Puritan man pushed him away with his shiny black, buckled shoe. The dog growled with dissatisfaction, licked its lips then moved to the next table.

Seeing the family, made William think of Lucy and their child who would be a young boy by now. A wave of melancholy overcame him as he thought of that fateful night.

☆

The evening hung heavy with a sense of impending loss as William stood outside their humble cottage, the crisp air biting at his cheeks. His gaze was fixed on the door, his heart pounding with a mixture of anxiety and hope. Isabel, his beloved wife, had been labouring for hours and every minute that passed felt like an eternity.

Then, finally, the call came. Her voice, like a soothing balm, cut through the darkness and beckoned him inside. He stepped over the threshold, his heart in his throat, only to be met with a quiet, solemn atmosphere that clung to the room like a heavy fog.

With cautious steps, he approached the bed where Isabel lay, her body weary and her eyes heavy with the weight of the world. But as he moved to offer his comfort, her trembling hand came to rest on his chest, a barrier between them.

The tear that glistened in her eye spoke volumes before she even uttered a word. 'I tried everything I could.' Her voice trembled like a fragile leaf in the wind. 'Bairn's feet came first, no breath, bleedin' wouldn't stop.' The words hung in the air like a haunting melody. 'She told me to tell you she loved you and the boys. Prayed for God's salvation and passed. I'm so sorry, William, so sorry.'

His world shattered in that moment. He knelt by the bed, his heartache tangible, and gently brushed the cold, wet strands of hair off Isabel's forehead. Tears welled up in his eyes, a dam threatening to burst as he peeled back the woollen cover to reveal their newborn's face. His anguish poured out in a torrent, his face buried in the blanket that held the scent of both life and death.

Time seemed to blur as Isabel and two women from the village came to perform the sombre task of preparing their departed loved one for her final rest. The bundled form of the infant was placed in William's trembling arms, a fragile bundle of what-ifs and dreams cut short.

The realisation struck him like a bolt of lightning – since the child had not been baptised, the sanctity of the church could not welcome their little one. A heaviness settled upon him, a burden of profound sorrow and a sense of helplessness. With a heavy heart and a determined resolve, he took up a shovel and trudged to the outside back wall.

As the earth gave way to his efforts, the hole grew deeper, a grave for the unmarked soul who never had the chance to draw breath. Gently, he placed the wrapped infant inside, a gesture of tenderness and love, and began the slow process of covering the tiny form with the earth that would be its eternal blanket. Each shovelful of dirt felt like a piece of his heart, falling into the abyss of loss.

A small, flat stone was chosen, a makeshift marker for a life that had barely begun. A prayer escaped his lips, a whispered plea for mercy and a promise to remember. Tears flowed freely, a river of grief that could never wash away the ache in his soul. With one last glance at the makeshift grave, he turned away, his footsteps heavy but resolute.

The moonlight painted a silver path as William made his way back to the cottage, his steps haunted by the echoes of a life forever changed. 'How am I to go on without her?' His voice broke the silence, a lament to the heavens. 'And the boys without a mother.'

The walls of their home seemed to hold the weight of his anguish, the absence of her laughter and her touch an ache that could never truly heal. As he looked upon his sons, the heaviness of his responsibility pressed upon him, a mantle of fatherhood worn with both pride and sorrow.

In the midst of darkness, the love that had once filled every corner of their existence now felt like a fragile thread, threatening to unravel at any moment. Yet, within the depths of his pain, William found a glimmer of strength, a flicker of resilience that whispered of a future built upon the foundation of love and loss.

And so, under the silent gaze of the moon, William stood as a testament to the human spirit's capacity to endure, to find hope in the face of despair, and to carry the legacy of those who had gone before. The journey ahead would be fraught with challenges, but within the shadows, he would discover a light – a light that would guide him through the darkness, a light that would forever be fuelled by the love that once bloomed under the silent moon.

☆

William stared off into space, trying to put the sadness to the back of his mind. 'Got a bed fer me ta rest me aching back, James?'

'Aye, old mate, 'course, but because of the coach you'll 'ave ta share one.'

'No matter, I'm sa tired, I could sleep on the back of an 'orse.'

James re-filled his tankard and smiled. 'If I 'ave ta pay any more tithe and tax, I might be joinin' ya. 'Ere, 'ave ya heard about the engrossers?'

William looked up, his eyes widened.

‘Aye, ya missed all the ruckus, engrossers! Been all sorts of trouble at market, fightin’ and lootin’.’

‘Money hungry bastards.’ William skulled his ale.

James continued, ‘They’re all bein’ put before the magistrate and losing their goods. Walk down the road and there’s three of them in the pillory and stocks.’

‘When they get out they’re banned from coming into Halifax again. It won’t make a blind bit of difference. Magistrates can’t compel ‘em to sell it proper. The hard times was God’s sendin’ but tis they who cause the dearth.’

The bar maid placed a noggin of pottage in front of William. ‘There ya go, luv, get it into ya.’

‘Thanks muchly I’m sa hungry I could eat a bear.’ William picked up the wooden spoon and stirred the contents, hunting for signs of meat. There were a couple of morsels, but mostly pieces of overcooked grain, onions, carrots and potatoes.

James leant forward and lifted his gaze toward the Puritan minister sitting at the long table. He whispered, ‘He’s a minister, on his way up your way. Bein’ sent up there to rid the area of evil doin’s by Robert Lilburne himself.’

William felt a mixture of curiosity and wariness as he watched the minister move through the room. The Puritans had gained influence in recent years, and their strict beliefs and practices had caused a divide among the townsfolk. Some saw them as a beacon of hope, while others viewed them as oppressive and judgmental.

William took another gulp of ale. ‘The Puritans are in a good position since the war.’

‘Aye, they believe their fasting and solemn humiliation will reverse the dearth.’

William glanced at him curiously. ‘And what of the cock fights out the back, are they on tonight?’

James looked down, disappointed. ‘Can’t ‘ave ‘em anymore. Cromwell’s put an end to ‘em, said they were the work of the Devil.’

'I was hopin' to get a bit of extra coin.'

'It's too dangerous, and if ya go against 'em you spend weekends in the stocks, whipped, or worse.'

'Poor Sara Warren was put to the gibbet last week, convicted by the magistrate fer bearing a bastard and not going to church. Poor woman was just trying ta survive. She used to come in 'ere often with her rumpers.'

William took another spoonful of pottage, blew on it and swallowed. He wiped the drip on his chin with the back of his sleeve.

James paused. 'And what news from home, William?'

The old man spoke with a heavy heart, his eyes filled with a weariness that only time could etch. 'Nothin' really.' He sighed. 'Aven't 'eard from me sons, still in Leeds, I'd say,' he continued, his voice tinged with longing.

In this once-thriving community, bleakness had settled like an uninvited guest. Many had been forced to leave, seeking solace elsewhere. The culprit behind their misfortune was none other than Calamy, a figure whose name was whispered with disdain. With a ruthless fervour, he continued to confiscate lands, relentlessly raising rack rents and turning a blind eye to the plight of the locals.

'Aye, they be hard times, anyway I best get off, good luck tomorra with the kersey. God willin' you'll get a good price. You know where the bed is, I'll leave ya to it.' James stood and went about his business.

William could hear the calls of the night watchman outside; he knew this was his cue to head to bed. He wanted to get the best position for the night in front of the fire.

Picking up his kersey, he strolled through the inn and made his way out the back to the bedrooms. He opened the door; there were two rows of simple box beds. The walls were adorned with the history of the Bible including a crude painting of Daniel in the lion's den.

William chose a bed near the fire just in case one of the other men decided to pay extra for it to be started.

He undressed down to his undershirt, put his kersey underneath the bed then climbed onto the pea-shuck mattress which rustled with his weight.

The sheets weren't washed and he was always assured of a nasty rash in the morning.

It wasn't long before other men, women and children came in. They all chose their beds and started to undress.

A baby started crying so its ragged, tired mother took out her flat, floppy breast and fed it.

William laid there on his back, one eye open, hoping there were enough beds so he didn't have to share.

He heard the door open and heard the footsteps and the cling clang of a tinker rambling toward the bed. He wore an old mottled, unshapen black hat and a faded brown tunic. He struggled with his wooden bellows and toolbox. His apron, tied to a button on his tunic, was dirty and frayed. A small hammer dangled from his belt. He dropped his belongings on the floor with a clang.

He peered at William who closed both eyes, feigning sleep. 'Christ, I 'ope the bairn aint gonna cry all night! 'Hope ya don't mind sharin'. Been a long day, it has.'

William sensing the tinker knew he was awake, reluctantly opened his eyes.

The tinker whispered, 'Gonna be a longer one tomorrow with the market and all who've come to the gibbet. Never seen one meself, bit of a spectacle they say.'

William sat up. 'Not really interested ta be true. Just 'ere to sell me kersey then get on 'ome.'

The tinker glanced down at William. 'They like to 'ave a good turnout ta remind common folk of their sinfulness. They 'ave pamphlets printed, 'ere look at this.'

William sat up and took the small, creased pamphlet from the tinker. 'No good, I can't read.'

He stared at the rudimentary woodcut image on the front. There was a wooden structure with two wooden uprights, capped by a horizontal wooden beam. Underneath, there was an axe head attached to the bottom of a wooden block.

On the back were written words that meant nothing to him. 'I wonder what it says?'

'Don't rightly know, can't read nowt meself,' replied the tinker.

He leaned down close to whisper. William was, immediately stunned by the blackness of his teeth and the rankness of his breath and turned away.

'What I do know, is I was there in London when the king met his end. There was a huge crowd, ya could hear a pin drop. They brought him out onto the scaffold, I'll never forget it.'

The tinker continued, 'I found out the next day he said he was innocent of the crimes and a martyr to the English people.'

William was curious. 'Go on.'

'Well, I couldn't see much 'cause there were Roundhead guards all around blocking the scaffold, so I moved and stood on steps a' Banquet Hall. I watched him. He calmly laid his head down on the block and after a moment, stretched his hands forward and the executioner dropped his axe. There was a large groan from the crowd as the executioner lifted his head to show them. I'll never forget it!'

The old tinker slid under his blanket beside William. 'Night, old son sleep tight, don't let the bed bugs bite,' he grumbled.

Eventually, weariness overtook William once again. He settled into the lumpy mattress, the events of the day swirling in his mind. Despite the hardships and uncertainties, he felt a glimmer of hope deep within him.

He closed his eyes, allowing himself to drift into a more peaceful sleep, if only for a few hours.

Little did he know that the events unfolding in Halifax were just a small part of the larger tapestry of history, and that the winds of change were blowing in unexpected directions. The town, like the rest of the world, was on the cusp of transformation, and William would soon find himself caught up in a series of events that would test his resilience, challenge his beliefs, and shape the course of his life in ways he could never have imagined.

William woke early the next morning and sat on the side of the bed tired and sore from his previous day's march. He put his head in his hands and wiped his face trying to revive himself. He turned to see the tinker still mumbling and snoring.

William leant down and picked up the ceramic chamber pot. Releasing a steady stream into it he smiled, farted and groaned with satisfaction. He dressed quickly, picked up his boots, picked up the kersey and left quietly through the door.

James was already up and noticed William walk through the door, 'So are ya coming to the gibbet, William?'

'Nah, I better be off home.'

'Come on William, come wi' me, got the cart outside. I'll take ya ta the outskirts a' town after. Besides, we might get a runner.'

William frowned as he wasn't really used to the ways of the city. 'Runner?'

James placed two tankards of ale on the table and William sat down.

James whispered across the table, 'If the culprit escapes before the blade drops, and gets across the river before the executioner catches him, then they let him go free.'

Come on bring yer ale, it's a celebration; some of the wealthy even 'ave their own platforms built so they get a better view.' James stood and waited for William to follow.

James plodded out the back to the cart and climbed aboard with William following slowly behind still considering whether he should go.

'Geeup,' James shook the reins and trotted forward through the arch. They rode down Crown Street to Pellon Lane then left on Bedford Street.

James pulled on the reins and stopped the cart just in front of the gibbet. They sat higher than the crowd to get an uninterrupted view.

The gibbet sat on a stone platform. A wooden structure standing about five yards high with an axe blade hanging from a heavy wooden block at the top. A rope was attached to the axe affixed to a wooden peg attached at the front of the platform. This wooden peg was fastened to a rope which led to a horse being calmed by its owner. At the time of execution, the horse went forward releasing the pin, causing the axe to drop between its two upright timber posts.

The excited crowd who came to see the spectacle were cordoned off by wooden rails surrounding the stone platform. Soldiers armed with a halberd were positioned every few metres on the inside of the wooden rail.

The executioner was dressed in a long black robe, his face half-covered with a leather mask. He stood silently beside the gibbet. Twelve men, the jurors, dressed in black Puritan robe stood on the other side.

A few moments later the crowd started to stir. William saw the bailiff; a minister and two soldiers escort the bound prisoner. The thief could barely walk and dragged his bare feet. Two soldiers supported him as he had spent the last two days in the stocks.

He was bent over, his clothes muddy and ripped. He wore no shoes or hose, stolen by the poor lest they go to waste. Dried congealed blood could be seen on his forehead where citizens, passing the stocks, inflicted their punishment. His long, matted, dark hair dangled in his face.

As the soldiers helped him up the stone steps the crowd surged forward trying to get a better view. Some called out, but most remained quiet and whispered to the person standing beside them.

Standing on top of the platform the soldiers turned the prisoner, so he was facing the crowd.

The bailiff stood beside him and unrolled a parchment. Clearing his throat, he took a breath, then peered at the parchment. He called out, 'ROBERT RUSHWORTH, YOU'VE BEEN CONVICTED OF THE CRIME OF THIEVERY OF THE *STAPLE*. A CRIME WHICH IS

PUNISHABLE BY DEATH!'

Robert Rushworth? William, hearing the name, glanced at James, 'WHAT? Tis me son!'

James looked at William in disbelief. 'Nah couldn't be, there could be many with the same name.'

William jumped down from the cart and ran over but the crowd were to many. He pushed through much to the annoyance of those in front.

'William!' James called out after him then jumped down from the cart and followed quickly.

Eventually, William made his way up to the railing and stood before the platform calling out, 'ROBERT! ROBERT!'

A soldier stepped forward, lowering his halberd. 'STOP THERE!'

Worriedly, William ignored the soldier, 'ROBERT, ROBERT, tis me, your father. ROBERT!'

The crowd gave William space and allowed him to get closer to the railing. 'ROBERRRRT, let me through!'

Robert, almost comatose from his time in the stocks, could not hear him above the murmurs of the crowd.

William screamed, 'ROBERRRRT!'

James appeared at William's side. 'Come on man, it couldn't be, you said he was in Leeds!'

'Yes, tis me son Robert, I 'ave ta do something.' William bent down to climb under the railing.

Two soldiers heard and saw the commotion. They hurried over and pointed their halberds at him. 'STOP!'

James grabbed William by the arm and pulled him back under the railing, 'Come, William, follow me!' James tugged at William.

They wrestled their way through the crowd to get closer.

‘Make way, make way, it’s his son, let us through and let the man say his goodbyes. MAKE WAY!’ James screamed and led William through the crowd.

‘ROBERT RUSHWORTH, DO YOU HAVE ANYTHING TO SAY BEFORE GOD AND BEFORE THE BLADE IS BROUGHT DOWN UPON THY NECK?’

The crowd shushed waiting for the prisoner’s last words.

Robert lifted his head. ‘I admit I am guilty; I repent and accept my punishment before God.’

The bailiff repeated so the crowd could hear his words. ‘ HE ADMITS HE IS GUILTY. HE REPENTS AND ACCEPTS HIS PUNISHMENT BEFORE GOD!’

The crowd clapped and cheered.

He paused and swallowed. ‘I pray I die well and may God forgive me.’

The bailiff repeated, ‘HE PRAYS HE WILL DIE WELL AND GOD FORGIVES HIM!’

The crowd cheered again.

The Puritan minister stepped forward, cleared his throat and opened his book of prayer.

‘O God of my Exodus,

great was the joy of Israel’s sons,

when Egypt died upon the shore,

far greater the joy when the Redeemer’s

foe lay crushed in the dust.

Jesus strides forth as the victor,

conqueror of death, hell, and

all opposing might.

He bursts the bands of death,

tramples the powers of darkness

down, and lives forever.

Thy death is my life, thy resurrection

my peace, thy ascension my hope,

thy prayers my comfort.

Resurrection, a prayer from the

Puritan Valley of Vision

I hope your risen Saviour

is an encouragement to you today

wherever life has taken you.'

The bailiff turned toward the executioner.

He nodded his head then gestured to the two soldiers who struggled to carry him. They placed him on his stomach face down under the blade.

The executioner ripped his shirt then gently guided his head onto the block ensuring his neck was exposed.

William and James made their way through the crowd and stood five yards in front of the stone platform.

Robert's eyes were closed.

William called out, 'ROBERT, son, can ya hear me? ROBEERT!'

Robert heard a familiar voice and momentarily opened one of his eyes, the other swollen and shut. He groaned then whispered, 'Fath… er.' He closed his eye. He mumbled, 'For…give me.'

The atmosphere was heavy with the weight of the moment, the gravity of life and death palpable in the air. Robert's eyes met William's from across the platform, a brief but powerful connection between father and son. Despite the circumstances, a glimmer of love and understanding passed between them.

'Yes, son, it's me.' William's eyes started to well up with tears; he wiped them away.

'God have mercy, ROBERT! I forgive you, I FORGIVE YOU, SON!'

Robert opened his eyes, he whispered, 'I'm sorr—'

The executioner stepped forward, his dark robe billowing in the breeze. He adjusted the leather mask over his face, his identity hidden from the eyes of the world. The axe blade gleamed in the sunlight, a chilling reminder of the imminent finality.

The crowd held its collective breath as the executioner moved to the horse that was to release the axe. The tension was almost unbearable, a sense of morbid fascination gripping the onlookers. Even those who had initially come for the spectacle now found themselves caught up in a moment of reflection.

Robert's lifeless body slumped forward, held only by the ropes that bound him. His journey in this world had come to an end, his fate sealed by the judgment of the law.

William tried to jump over the railing.

James held him back. 'NOOOO!'

The blade didn't cut all the way through the neck.

William screamed again, 'NOOO!'

His son's eyes opened and his lips worked in rhythmic contractions for five or six seconds. His pupils were fixated on his father. A lone tear pooled and dropped from the corner of his eye. It found its way across his face and dripped to the stone.

William screamed again, 'ROBERRRRT!'

At this point, without any spasm, his eyelids lifted. Undeniably living eyes fixed themselves. He wasn't dead!

William screamed, 'ROBERRRRT!'

The executioner used the rope to pull the axe back up to the top of the vertical frame then dropped it again.

There was no further movement – and the eyes took on the glazed appearance which they have in the dead.

As the reality of what they had just witnessed sank in, the crowd began to disperse, each person lost in their own thoughts. James placed a comforting hand on William's shoulder, offering silent support in the face of an unimaginable loss.

'NOOOOO, NOOOOOOOOO!'

The tinker shoved him. 'Oy… Oy, wake up, old son, yer havin' a bad dream. You scared the bejesus out of me,' he growled.

William opened his eyes, shook his head and sat up. 'Errggh, sorry I woke ya.'

'Tis alright, old son,' the tinker pulled the blanket up, turned over and went back to sleep. It wasn't long before he started snoring.

The baby started to cry again.

William placed his feet on the floor and groggily sat up on the side of the bed. He sighed with relief.

In the darkness, he picked the sleep from the corners of his eyes. He sat there for a moment dismissing the remnants of the dream.

It would serve as a reminder of the fragility of life, the power of justice and the enduring bonds of family. And as the sun dipped below the horizon, casting the town in a warm, golden glow, a new resolve began to take root in William's heart – a resolve to navigate the challenges that lay ahead, to find strength in the face of adversity.

He laid there in the darkness, his eyes open, wondering if he would see his sons again.

Sleep, fitful and fleeting, eventually overcame William. Dreams of a better future mingled with the haunting specters of loss and uncertainty, and as the night pressed on, the tavern's walls seemed to bear witness to the collective hopes and fears of those who sought refuge within its embrace.

CHAPTER 4

The Halifax Market

As the baby's cries persisted, William's gaze shifted inward, his thoughts turning to his sons and of course Tommy and Isabel. They were his anchors, his reasons for facing the daunting hardships of life in Haworth. Their innocent faces flashed before him, filling him with a renewed sense of responsibility. He had known struggle and adversity intimately, and he was determined to shield them from the harshest blows of fate.

Lucy, his beloved wife, was a constant presence in his memories. Her strength and unwavering love had sustained him through the darkest hours. Even in her absence, her spirit guided him, a guiding star lighting his path through the storm.

'Are ya coming to the gibbet, William?'

'No, my friend, I better be off after market. Besides, watchin' some poor bastard havin' his head lopped off? I can think of other ways ta spend me mornin'.'

It was Thursday, market day and William wanted to sell the kersey quickly and get home.

As he stepped out into the early light of day, William carried with him the weight of his past and the promise of his future. The town of Halifax was awakening, its streets once again bustling with activity.

The sun was coming up. The marketplace, stretched on either side of Southgate and Northgate. The streets were deep in mud and sludge runoff from the rain overnight. The bridge was occupied by farmers, yeoman, clothiers and their wives.

Preparations were in full swing. There were scenes of chaos and disorder. Pick pockets picked and lifters lifted. Men yelled and women argued for the best position to sell their wares.

There was a multitude of lads and lasses crowding the square vying for each other's company; the young folk came to enjoy themselves and each other. Their mothers watched on nervously.

Carriers, cartmen and gigs teemed into the narrow nearby lanes. Dogs barked, pigs snorted and chickens clucked disapproval from their wooden cages.

An old woman emptied her chamber pot from the upper window of her two-story trader's house. It missed the ginger, stripped tabby cat which hissed then darted out of the way.

On the south side of High Street, there were butchers, ale-sellers and hawkers of timber and faggots. 'FAGGOTS, DRY FAGGOTS 'ERE. GET 'EM 'ERE! DRY FAGGOTS.'

In the middle of the road sellers of coarse bread, earthenware, and coals were vying for coin on offer. Between All Saints and the east gate, straw-sellers bellowed, 'CLEAN STRAW, CLEAN STRAW! GET IT 'ERE. CLEAN STRAW.'

On the west side of Northgate, sellers of rushes and brooms loudly spruiked their goods.

On the east side of the square there were tanners, poulterers and between the Cross inn and the North Gate, sellers of dry corn.

In the middle of the street were sellers of hay, overpriced cheese, eggs and this morning's warm milk. Over on the west side of St. Aldates Street were sellers of pewter dishes and scullery ware.

The lanes between the stalls were full of the posh and poor, the honest and the deceitful.

The local beggar sat at the main entrance to the square, his head down, hands up in a gesture of humility. The nightwatchman moved him on much to his annoyance.

The bread seller's limited stock was sold at a premium and she was bartering a price with a woman who objected.

She let her know it. 'Tis highway robbery, ya old COW! Ya should be disgusted with yerself!' She stormed off.

The fishmonger yelled while trying to keep the flies away, 'FRESH FISH, LOVELY FRESH PIKE. GET IT 'ERE. FRESH FISH! COME AND GET IT! ONLY SIXPENCE EACH. FRESH FISH!'

The blacksmith's hammer beat to a rhythm. The street dogs sniffed while others humped. Ragged children chased one another around the stalls. One mother pleaded for them to stop or else receive a 'beltin'.

William strolled purposefully toward his designated spot in the bustling square of Halifax. The vibrant energy of the market pulsed through the air, a symphony of voices, colours and textures that brought the town to life every week. Long trestles, weathered by time, were strategically positioned along the bridge, creating a tapestry of commerce where the town's artisans and traders showcased their wares.

The market square was a well-orchestrated dance, a choreography of commerce that played out with each toll of the chapel bell. Each week, as the sun climbed its arc in the sky, the townsmen meticulously set up their stalls, arranging wide boards for woollen and linen drapers, glovers, and leather tanners. The rhythm was familiar to all, a ritual observed by those who understood the importance of being ready when the bell tolled, signalling the commencement of trade.

Weavers and put out men arrived, their arms laden with bundles of cloth. The colourful fabrics unfurled along the wooden boards, a vibrant display that transformed the market into a canvas of textures and hues. Among them, William carefully laid out his own kersey, its rich, sturdy weave a testament to his skill and dedication. He stood before it, a quiet pride emanating from him, a craftsman confident in his creation.

Everybody knew their place as most came every week and knew the importance of being set up and ready for the bell.

The weavers and put out men arrived with their cloth and unravelled them lengthways along the boards. William did the same and stood in front of his kersey proudly.

Its solemn toll reverberated through the air, marking the moment the clothiers had been eagerly anticipating. They understood that the intricate dance of bargaining could commence only when the bell fell silent once more and so they stood poised, ready to engage in this age-old ritual.

In that suspended moment, as the bell's mournful chime echoed, an eerie silence gripped the crowd. Time seemed to stand still, the world holding its breath in anticipation. William counted each toll with a precision born of years of tradition. Three… four… five… six… The tension in the air grew taut and then, with a sudden, explosive energy, all hell broke loose.

The chapel bell's chime, once a symbol of tranquillity, now marked the onset of chaos. It reverberated through the hearts of the gathered clothiers, signalling the commencement of a frenzied exchange that would determine their fates and fortunes.

Clothiers and traders, their eyes sharp and discerning, moved along the trestles. Fingers traced patterns, assessing weaves and textures with a practiced eye. The cloth was turned and examined, threads scrutinised for any irregularities – a testament to the meticulous scrutiny that defined the market.

The aulnager, a figure of authority in this realm of fabrics, paced back and forth. His keen eyes took in the marks of the weavers, a signature stitched into the fabric, a silent testament to the creator's craftsmanship. Measuring the length, he held the cloth against his chin and extended his arm, counting threads and calculating value. Sometimes, a shilling could smooth over minor imperfections, a wink and a nod to the practicalities of trade.

Among the array of fabrics, William's kersey stood out, woven in a distinctive twill pattern. He knew that his choice of weave made it easier for finishers to raise the nap, a detail that added value to his creation. As the buyers made their rounds, one finally reached his spot. Leaning in, he inquired about the price, and William responded in a hushed tone, 'Four shillin' a yard.'

The buyer's brow furrowed as he considered the offer. 'Three,' he countered, his voice a quiet negotiation between aspiration and practicality.

Undeterred, William leaned in, his confidence unwavering. 'Even better, tis good cloth, ya may colour it ta ya choice. It's not stretched like some of the other cloth 'ere.'

In the intricate dance of market bargaining, William knew the value of his creation. The twill weave he had chosen had transformed his kersey into a canvas of both practicality and artistry. It was not just cloth; it was a story spun in threads, a testament to the toil and creativity of its maker.

'Four shillin',' William persisted, his voice a steadfast declaration of his worth.

As the market continued to hum around him, William held his ground. The square was alive with movement, a tapestry of people and possibilities woven together by the common thread of commerce. Each transaction was a thread in the grand fabric of Halifax Market, a story waiting to be told – one that would intertwine the destinies of all who participated in this age-old ritual of trade.

The buyer shook his head and went to leave.

William relented, 'Orl right, orl right, three shillin,' he whispered frustratedly.

The buyer smiled and dropped just over three pounds into William's outstretched hand. 'Pleasure doing business with ya.'

William folded up the kersey, tied it back up with the string and passed it to the buyer who gave it to his partner waiting with the pack horses.

He moved off swiftly to another trestle to purchase more. Within an hour all the buyers were gone, and the townsmen started packing up the trestles. Any remaining cloth was taken back to the inn.

The traders, and burdened pack horses, made their way out of town east toward Leeds. There they would sell the cloth which would end up on a ship in Hull bound for the Baltic.

William was disappointed with the coin for the kersey. However, it would provide enough to pay part of the fine for the lease, purchase more dirty wool and buy victuals to sustain the family. He went back to the inn.

James placed a tankard of ale in front of William. He always treated him to a penny ale aftermarket to reflect and cheer his sale before the long trek home.

'How'd ya go, William, did ya get a good price?' James asked.

William peered in his pouch. 'Coin fer sale a' the kersey is gettin' lower and lower, three pounds and change.'

'I thought as much,' replied James. 'They're not buyin' in Flanders anymore, buyin' fine wool from Spain.'

James sat down, 'Fine English wool's finished mate. Only thing sellin' in the Baltic is worsted and course wool, but they're not paying as much. The only traders doing well now are those in Lincolnshire 'cause a' the fine wool they can grow down there.'

'I didn't have a good night.' He sculled his ale, bid farewell and proceeded toward the door. 'See ya next week, James.'

'Aye, safe journey.'

William lifted the latch and stepped through the large oak door. The sun was rising but was blanketed by whispery cloud. There was a crisp, morning chill so he pulled his cloak together.

Marching through the archway, he went down Crown Street and turned northwest on Pellon Lane. It was uphill, and he could feel the perspiration running down his back.

The houses sprung up when the demand for English wool was at the forefront in Europe. The clothier's houses were solid and grand. Timber framed, constructed with chimneys, mullioned windows, and he assumed private chambers. He was in awe of the circular rose windows above the doorway.

Inside, he could see men milling about in the lower rooms of the house moving cloth to storage. The men who owned these houses could afford to live well. He wished for such things for himself but was reminded of his reality.

The sun cast a golden glow over the town of Halifax, William Rushworth stood at the crossroads of past and future. With every step he took, he carried with him the legacy, two sons and the love of a wife who remained his guiding light, and the unyielding determination to shape his own destiny. And as he gazed into the horizon, he knew that his story was far from over – a story of resilience, courage and the unbreakable spirit of a man who had weathered the storms of life and emerged stronger on the other side.

William continued up Mount Tabor Road to the Crossroads Inn. He usually stopped there before the last push toward Ovenden Moor. It was a lonely, desolate place even in spring. From then on, it was downhill toward Oxenhope then thankfully, home. He could see for miles as the lay of the land sloped eastward.

As the sun started its descent, he heard the muffled clomp, clomp of hooves in the mud and the clatter of rein and bit. He stepped off the road to let the carriage pass.

The red and black coach splattered mud up the side of its doors from the large oak wheels. It was mostly enclosed except for the gap above the door. The luggage was strapped to the roof tray with the lad who sat up there holding on to it. Four brown well fed horses pulled the coach. They frothed at the mouth. The driver whipped them onward and upward, up the muddy hill.

As they passed, William noticed the Puritan minister from the Crosse Inn who gazed down at him with contempt. William turned away to protect himself from the flicked mud. The passengers were on their way to Oxenhope where the horses would be rested, watered and fed.

It was an uncomfortable ride for those inside because the roads were always difficult and often impassable after rain. At the top of the hill, the carriage would need to stop and unload its passengers. With less weight, the driver could urge the horses up the hill with some assistance from the male passengers.

He continued climbing and as he got to the top, saw the stagecoach stationary. He squinted, his eyesight not being what it was. *Has the carriage lost a wheel?*

The driver held his hands above his head. A masked rider pointed his pistol.

William backed off down the hill out of view. He crept down the grassy slope then parallel to the road. He crawled up the slope and listened.

'DELIVER YOUR PURSE!' The highwayman's voice carried authority and a touch of menace. This was a highway robbery, a scene straight out of a tale of old.

Some Royalist soldiers turned to a life of crime as highwaymen. After the war, many of them were turned off their family estates by Cromwell so they were forced into this life until the king's son returned.

The Puritan minister took his wife's outstretched hand and helped her down. The other four passengers stepped down on to the muddy road. They all stood with their hands up in the air all except the minister's wife.

She complained about the inconvenience of it all. 'I fear this journey will never end.' She gaped at the masked stranger. 'This is an outrage! Do you have any idea who my husband is?'

'QUIET, WOMAN!' The highwayman growled.

Flabbergasted, she put her hand to her chest. 'Arthur, will you allow this wretch, this criminal to speak to me so?'

Appearing intimidated by the situation, Arthur took a deep breath. His face flushed as he braved himself. He stepped forward. 'What say you, wretch! You shouldn't speak to the gentile sort in such a way.'

The highwayman ignored his attempt at bravado. He raised his pistol and pointed at the minister's head. He threw a small cloth bag at him. 'Put the coin and jewellery in the bag, do as I say and nobody will be hurt.'

William kept out of sight behind the mounds of heather. He was in earshot of the coach and could hear the highwayman's demands.

'BE QUICK ABOUT IT!' Impatience seeped into the highwayman's tone, making it clear that he wouldn't tolerate any delay.

Hidden behind the heather, William observed the scene unfold. His heart raced with a mixture of fear and fascination. The highwayman's appearance was intriguing – an enigmatic figure cloaked in a beige knee-length coat, a black waistcoat and breeches. A ruffled shirt peeked out from beneath the waistcoat. A black cloth covered the top half of his face, tied tightly at the back. A brown, curly wig crowned his head and atop it sat a beige felt Cavalier's hat adorned with a plume that billowed in the wind.

As the highwayman continued to issue commands, the Puritan minister's wife handed over her possessions with an indignant air. The other passengers followed suit, their movements cautious and measured.

'BE QUICK ABOUT IT!' The highwayman was starting to lose his patience.

Hidden though he was, William couldn't shake the feeling that he was bearing witness to a pivotal moment – an encounter that would be etched into his memory forever. The highwayman's audacity, the passengers' compliance and the stark contrast between social classes all played out before him like scenes from a drama.

Once the highwayman had collected the passengers' belongings, he instructed them to face the coach, their backs turned to him. A final command rang out: they were to recite the Lord's Prayer in unison, their voices merging into a chorus of supplication. The scene held an eerie reverence, a blend of vulnerability and defiance as the passengers obeyed their masked captor's directive.

The Puritan minister reached inside his coat and pulled out a drawstring purse which he placed in the bag.

'You there, yer pouch and the brooch.' He pointed his pistol at the other three passengers. And the ring! Now, you, driver, come down and keep your hands where I can see them. You there, pick up the driver's pistol and throw it.'

The driver climbed down and raised his hands. 'You'll ney get away with this.'

'Seems, I already have, now, all of you face the coach and don't turn around until you've said the Lord's Prayer. If any of you do before it's done, you'll wish you hadn't, I assure you.' A change of accent seemed to creep into his voice.

The highwayman rode his horse around the other side of the coach. 'GOD SAVE THE KING!' He took one last glance back and rode off into the moor.

They all started to recite the prayer some in sync, others not,

'Our Father, which art in heaven,

'allowed be thy name. Thy kingdom come,

thy will be done, in Earth as it is in

heaven. Give us this day our daily bread.

And fergive us our trespasses, as we

fergive them who trespass against us.

And lead us not into temptation;

But deliver us from evil. Fer thine is

the kingdom, the Power and the Glory,

fer ever and ever. Amen.'

The driver was the first to peek around then turned and ran toward the lower slope. 'He's well long gone by now!'

William fearing reprisal, ducked down below the heather not twenty yards away.

The driver started to search for his pistol in the clumps of heather but it was getting late and the light wasn't so good. He wondered back and forth peering down, moving the pink flowers and long stems with his foot.

Discouraged, the driver gave up and started making his way back to the road. 'I'll never find me pistol. Come on, best we be off. You lot walk to the top of the hill.'

The minister's wife glared at the driver. 'We must report this to the authorities! Come, Arthur, we'll request an audience with his grace when we reach Haworth.'

The driver whipped the reins and encouraged the horses up the slippery slope. At the top, the Puritan family and the other passengers climbed aboard.

It was getting dark and William's journey was long. He was curious about where the highwayman fled. He crossed the road and climbed up the slope to see if he could see his tracks. There was no sign of him. Climbing down he noticed something in the heather, he reached down and picked up the pistol. He inspected it, turning it back and forth in his hand; it wasn't loaded. William tucked the pistol into his breeches then continued northwest along Cold Edge Road.

A few minutes later he could hear galloping hooves. He ran off the road and laid down, once again fearing the highwayman's return. He watched as the rider got closer. There were two horses, one horse followed another with two large sacks of wool.

After he passed, William stood and watched the silhouette ride northwest.

The road stretched ahead of him, beckoning him toward his journey's end. But in that moment, in the fading light of day, he was acutely aware that his own path was forever intertwined with the events he had just witnessed. And as he turned his gaze toward the horizon, he carried with him the memory of that highwayman – a mysterious figure whose presence had ignited a spark of intrigue and adventure in his heart.

After some time of walking, William's weary steps carried him closer to the welcoming lights of Haworth. The village lay ahead, a haven after the day's exertions. With a sigh of both relief and exhaustion, he stumbled down Marsh Lane, his worn boots finding their familiar path onto Sun Street. The hill leading up to the cottage awaited him, a final ascent before he could rest. A dog's bark greeted him, a familiar companion signalling his return.

Inside the humble cottage, Isabel had heard his approach. She swung the door open, concern and warmth etched onto her face.

'William, come in. Let me get you some food. How did the kersey trade go?'

William offered a tired smile, his fatigue evident as he removed his hat and undid his cloak, draping it on the nail by the door. 'Three pounds and change,' he replied wearily.

'Is that all?' Tommy chimed in, his curiosity piqued.

William's weariness seemed to deepen as he explained, 'The demand is not what it was. The kersey fetches only a fraction of the price it used to in Halifax. Times have changed.'

Tommy, ever the voice of reason, added his insights. 'James Mitchell was saying they've shifted their wool trade from Flanders to Spain. Fine wool from Spain, coarser wool for draperies from the Baltic. The Lincolnshire clothiers are exporting fine wool from Hull. The market has shifted, and we're caught in its wake.'

The weight of the evening's events still hung heavily on William's mind. 'Wool trade has truly gone to shite,' he mused, his thoughts swirling with a mix of weariness and concern.

Tommy's gaze held a hint of sadness as he looked at his uncle. 'More importantly, we're facing trouble at the manor. Calamy threatened us, said he'd raise the fines for the lease. We've got one month to settle it.'

Slumping into a chair at the table, William sighed and reached for the bowl of pottage that Isabel had set before him. 'He can't simply turn us off,' he muttered, trying to find some semblance of reassurance.

Tommy's voice was tinged with worry. 'He's the Justice of the Peace, though. He's claiming the old land laws aren't holding up anymore. He won't be reasoned with. He even offered Will some work.'

William blew on the steaming pottage before taking a tentative spoonful. 'We'll pay him what we can, to keep him off our backs. Can't turn us out if we've paid something,' he mumbled between bites, his mind already strategizing.

Tommy's concern persisted. 'And the rest?'

A glint of determination sparkled in William's tired eyes. 'We'll find a way, nephew. We always do. Don't worry yourself.'

Shifting gears, Tommy changed the subject, attempting to divert their attention from the weighty matters at hand. 'So, how was the journey?'

William's features darkened slightly as he recalled the unusual encounter. 'I saw a highwayman holding up a coach on the way home.'

Tommy's eyebrows shot up in surprise, 'Did he see you?'

Shaking his head, William replied, 'No, I hid in the heather until he rode off. But I found this.' He reached behind his breeches and pulled out a pistol, its metallic gleam reflecting the flickering firelight.

Tommy's eyes widened as he reached out to inspect the pistol, his fingers running along its cold surface. He peered down the barrel and examined its mechanisms, a ghost of his wartime experiences surfacing. He handed it back to William with a sober expression.

Isabel's voice rang out, a mix of concern and caution, 'Be careful, Tommy.'

Tommy's fingers deftly tested the pistol's mechanisms. 'It's not loaded, and there's no powder. It won't fire,' he reassured her. Demonstrating, he pulled back the hammer and squeezed the trigger, the distinct click echoing in the room.

The sound seemed to transport Tommy back to another time, another battlefield. With a shake of his head, he handed the pistol back to William. It found its place on the mantelpiece, a curious relic that held tales of its own.

'It must be worth something to someone,' William mused, his gaze fixed on the firearm, an object that had journeyed from one life to another.

As the fire crackled and the room settled into a momentary quiet, the pistol's presence on the mantel served as a reminder of the ever-shifting tides of life. Challenges arose, burdens were carried, but in the midst of it all, the resilience of the Haworth villagers endured, finding strength in their bonds, their resourcefulness, and the flickering flames that danced in their hearths.

CHAPTER 5

The Devil's Work

In the heart of a land where tradition held its sway, where the echoes of history reverberated through cobbled streets and stone-walled villages, a movement emerged – a group of fervent souls who sought to reshape the very fabric of their faith. They were the Puritans, a community bound by an unyielding devotion to their beliefs, and their journey would become a defining chapter in the annals of England's history.

During the reign of Queen Elizabeth, a time when the power of the crown intertwined with the spiritual compass of the realm, the Puritans stood out like stars against the night sky. Their fervour, their unwavering commitment to a singular cause, set them apart from the traditional norms of their age. They were not content with the state of the Church of England, for they saw it as burdened with rituals and practices that bore no scriptural foundation. To the Puritans, the Bible was more than a book – it was their guiding light, their unerring compass, their sole authority.

-PUBLIC NOTICE-

Working on the Sabbath, not

fasting on a Friday and engaging

in frivolous pastimes and other

Satanical practices are

FORBIDDEN

with the offender liable to a fine of two shillings or punishment

by whip or stocks

In the midst of the ancient village of Haworth, where time seemed to have slowed to a measured pace, a new figure had arrived – one who bore the weight of a mission, a calling that he believed to be ordained by the Almighty. The newly appointed Puritan minister, Arthur Baxter, strode into the hallowed walls of the village church, his presence commanding attention even before he uttered a single word. He was a figure of solemnity, dressed in the sombre attire of his creed – a black skull cap crowning his head, a long Geneva robe flowing down his frame. His countenance was a mixture of smug satisfaction and nervous anticipation, a potent blend that mirrored the tumultuous currents coursing through his heart.

As Arthur ascended the pulpit, a hushed reverence fell upon the congregation that had gathered to witness his inaugural sermon. Two pristine preaching bands adorned his neck, stark symbols of the spiritual authority he now held. It was his first service, his virgin voyage into the hearts and minds of the faithful, and he was determined to leave an indelible mark.

'Let us quieten our hearts.' His voice resounded, breaking the stillness like a bell tolling in the distance.

The newly appointed minister entered carrying his Bible. Wearing a black skull cap and a long black Geneva robe, he had a smug look on his face. Two bright white preaching bands drooped from his neck like metaphoric chains.

Once the room went quiet, he bellowed, 'THE DEVIL IS PRESENT IN THIS VILLAGE!' The declaration, like thunderclaps, echoed off the stone walls, reverberating through the hearts of those who had gathered. It was a statement that sent shivers down spines, a rallying cry that demanded attention.

The women in the congregation gasped, the men hushed, Tommy and William frowned.

'YESTERDAY MY FAMILY AND I WERE SET UPON BY THE FORCES OF EVIL on the road to Oxenhope,' he continued, his voice carrying an air of gravitas. 'A dark spirit, a harbinger of malevolence, dared to cross our path. It threatened my wife, and its malevolent eyes locked onto mine. But by the grace of my deliverance from sin and the Lord's divine protection, I stand before you today. Be warned, my brethren and sisters, for these are perilous times, and even darker days may lie ahead! We must repent!'

The parishioners muttered their uneasiness.

Milton Killsin noticed Tommy's expression then called out, 'IT'S THE DEVIL, his soldiers have come to bewitch us all.'

The murmuration got louder.

A parishioner at the back, stood and yelled angrily, 'The dearth, we haven't seen a GOOD harvest in three years, tis the Devil's work. WE MUST REPENT! REPENT! REPENT!'

An elderly Puritan lady fainted. Those beside her fanned their hands in front of her face to revive her.

Shocked, Tommy glanced at his wife, winked at Will then turned to smile at William who sat in the pew behind.

In the midst of this swirling maelstrom of emotions, one man stood apart. Tommy, his features etched with scepticism, exchanged a knowing glance with William, a shared understanding passing between them like a whispered secret. It seemed they shared a common sentiment, one that stood at odds with the fervour that had taken root.

As the sermon continued, the congregation navigated the tempestuous waters of fear and doubt, their minds tossed between the call for repentance and the familiarity of tradition. The village of Haworth, a canvas of human emotion and spiritual turmoil, bore witness to a clash of ideologies – a battle for the soul of a community, a test of faith in the face of uncertainty.

'QUIET!' Milton Killsin yelled trying to assert his authority.

He was ignored.

The vicar raised his hands. 'MY BROTHERS AND SISTERS, please, please, PLEASE!'

The parishioners quietened.

Tommy and William looked at each other, folded their arms defiantly and looked on uninterested.

The vicar continued, 'Only our belief in God can keep us out of harm's way and rid us of the dearth imprisoning us. The wrath of God will befall all of those who do not see unto his light. So, we must cast aside the spirits of the night and give ourselves unto the Lord in Jesus Christ's name. Amen!'

'Amen!' The congregation whispered; they were apprehensive about the vicar's words.

'BEWARE, the weakest at upholding Puritan values and morals are women and children. They will be chosen to carry out the Devil's work. It is these pour souls which we must protect.'

Isabel looked worried and peered at Tommy for comfort.

The vicar continued, 'There are demons and witches amongst us who cause misfortune with harmful magic. Ye must repent, come to church and be one with the Lord. Amen!'

'Amen!' The congregation repeated not quite knowing how to react to the vicar's claims.

Arthur's wife Mrs Baxter sat in the front pew with a proud look on her face. She mouthed some of the words of Arthur's sermon.

The minister continued, 'To rid the village of this EVIL, there is to be no cursing, swearing and no unlawful games. Under no circumstances is one to eat flesh on Friday. There shall be no profaning of the Sabbath by absence from St Michael's Church and no working hereabouts. Only then will the Lord's peace and protection be returned.'

'If you see unholy things, failure of crops, sickness, illness or the death of livestock, report it immediately. This must be investigated!'

'The village will be rid of frivolous pastimes. No longer will Christmastide customs or the carnival of Martinmas be celebrated. There will be no joyous and exuberant occasions, no merriment, dances, or amusements. Absolutely no merrymaking by proclamation of our Lord and our Protector OLIVER CROMWELL!'

And as Arthur's words hung in the air, his stern visage projected an air of authority, his voice a vessel for the convictions that burned within him. It was a sermon that marked not only his entrance into the role of a minister but also a turning point for the village: a crossroads where the past met the future, where tradition met revolution and where the bonds of community were tested against the backdrop of a changing world.

The murmuration got louder.

'No Christmastide and no Martinmas celebrations?' Isabel whispered as she glanced sideways at Tommy.

Will peered at his father for a response.

None came.

Tommy sensed Will's fixed stare then winked and smiled.

Tommy turned and stared at the preacher impassively.

Isabel saw this and was not amused. 'Tommy tis no time fer foolery!'

'Yes it is, nobody's gonna tell me what to do in me own home. Pigshells said they been protestin' in the streets in London and Leeds, had to bring the guard out. No Christmas, we'll see about that.'

'Well, let's hope they don't do the same thing 'ere,' whispered Isabel.

'What bring the guard out? Closest thing we got to a guard is old Griswold! What's he gonna do, the ol' fart.' Tommy grumbled stubbornly.

The vicar spoke again, 'THE NEW CHURCH WARDEN, Milton Killsin, will be the overseer of the ways of our church. It will be his position to flush out the evil among us.'

Milton Killsin's gaze, cold and calculating, swept over the assembled villagers. His eyes bore into the souls of those before him, a chilling reminder that his newfound authority was not to be taken lightly. His words held a veiled threat, a promise of retribution to those who dared to question his intentions.

He glared at Isabel then at Tommy and William. *You'll get yours one day and that day is fast approaching. By God you'll be off that land soon.*

The minister read his last prayer while the new churchwarden meandered up one side of the aisle with the collection bag hanging from a long pole. Each parishioner placed what coin they could in the bag. Tommy dropped a penny in.

While extending the collection bag, Milton peeked slyly down Isabel's partlet.

Isabel's discomfort was evident as she felt Milton's gaze upon her. She shuddered, her instincts warning her of his unsettling intentions. Her husband's hand on hers brought a modicum of comfort, a gesture that spoke of unity in the face of looming challenges.

She glanced up at him as he turned his gaze. She shuddered and whispered, 'He gives me the creeps.'

Tommy put his hand on the top of hers and whispered, 'Probably jealous, checkin' out what he can't 'ave and I can.' He looked ahead and grinned.

Isabel removed her hand from underneath his. 'Tommy Rushworth, you will do no such thing. I can't believe you would say such a thing in church!'

'Tis only natural, God says ta procreate.'

'Tommy Rushworth, you behave yourself now, yes he says procreate and have children. Not what you're thinkin'!'

'Hahaha, no difference, same beginnin' same endin'.'

Isabel raised her eyebrows, blushing. 'Tommy, please stop!'

One by one, they made their way toward the grand wooden doors, where the minister, a pillar of unwavering faith, stood shaking their hand as they left.

In the heart of the village, the lingering echoes of the Puritan minister's sermon still hung in the air, like a spectral reminder of the tumultuous words that had been spoken. The congregation had dispersed, each member carrying with them the weight of the minister's fervent warnings and the unsettling prophecies that had woven their way into their hearts.

As the villagers spilled out of the church, the atmosphere buzzed with a mixture of uncertainty and hushed murmurs. The public notice, posted on the door, had left an indelible mark on their minds, a proclamation that spoke of change, authority and a shifting of power. And now, the new churchwarden, Milton Killsin, stood before them, a sentinel tasked with the solemn duty of guarding the sanctity of their faith.

Authur felt pleased with himself. He nodded slightly and smiled falsely uttering to all who passed him. 'God bless you.'

'God bless.'

'God bless you.' The words flowed from the minister's lips like a benediction as the parishioners filed out of the hallowed sanctuary of St Michael's. He stood at the imposing doors, extending his hand with a charismatic grace that masked the depths of his ambition. With each handshake, he felt the palpable surge of influence coursing through him, a power that tightened its grip on the hearts and minds of those who sought solace and guidance within the church's embrace. In that fleeting contact, the minister realised that his hold over the congregation was not merely spiritual but also deeply personal, a testament to his ability to shape their beliefs and, perhaps, their destinies.

It was a beautiful day and the lush green pastures in the distance capped the view, their beauty a contrast to the choking stone grey cottages nearby.

Tommy and the family walked down the shale path, past the granite horizontal headstones to Main Street.

As William passed, he smiled and nodded but felt a quiet contempt for the ranting sermon he heard. *Times are tough enough without scaring the be-Jesus out a' people.*

Tommy, Isabel and Will followed William outside and greeted the other townsfolk.

Outside the church, the lush green pastures offered a stark contrast to the solemnity within. The beauty of the landscape seemed at odds with the inner turmoil that had taken root within the villagers' hearts. Tommy, his mind racing, caught sight of Will and his companions engaged in conversation with a young girl from the manor. The image sparked a moment of warmth amid the chill of uncertainty.

Milton Killsin stayed behind counting the coin and discussing the sermon with the minister. 'Well done, it'll get 'em comin' to church more often. Those bloody Rushworths, they'll get theirs.'

Outside, Mr Griswold approached Tommy. 'Ahh Rushworth, I would like to talk to you about taking on young Will as an apprentice for the mill.'

Apprenticeships were supposed to prepare boys for becoming independent craftsmen in adult life. However, what they were to be taught was not always specified. Some masters spent very little time with their young apprentices and only gave them menial tasks to complete, proverbial slaves. Was this to be Will's future?

Tommy didn't want this for his son; he heard how some apprentices were abused and mistreated. He remembered a case in Leeds. *Apprentice was beaten until he couldn't piss upright and spat blood for a fortnight afterwards.*

Rushworth, 'As there will be no statute hiring at the carnival of Martinmas. I would like to take him into my employ.'

'Well, I'm not sure yer grace. We need him for work around home.' Tommy looked around to see where his son was.

Will, Morwen and Mirth were chatting with a young girl from the manor.

'How long ya been workin' there?' Morwen asked curiously.

'About three months now,' replied Margaret.

Will was curious. 'Me grandma used to work there years ago, what's it like?'

'Tis orlright, Mrs Stuart is a bit of a fusspot, but the other girls are nice. Rarely see his grace 'cause I'm always stuck in the kitchen. Old

Griswold sticks his head in occasionally, usually to complain about somethin' or other.'

Margaret didn't speak to other boys so she shyly enquired, 'What about you?'

Will noticed his father peering over. 'Just help me da' on the lease. We got ten acres ' barley growin' and twenty breedin' ewes and lambs.'

Will was shy with the girls in the village, so cut his chat short. 'Anyway, we better get on home, come on girls. Bye, Margaret.'

'Okay then. Bye.' Margaret took an instant liking to Will. 'Nice talking to you.'

She watched them head down the road. *I would love a family like that, brothers, sisters and of course a ma and da. They're so lucky.*

Will looked back at his father as he went. He was in deep discussion with Mr Griswold. 'Ere, wonder what they're talkin' about?'

'Who cares?' Both Morwen and Mirth giggled and ran ahead, leaving Will to stroll down the hill by himself.

'In return for his services, I will provide arles, God's Penny of eight shillings for you to use however you wish. You may like to put it toward your lease fines. He will be fed and well looked after at the manor.'

'Take it.' Griswold placed eight shillings in Tommy's hand. 'If by sunset you do not return it, then I will assume there is an agreement between us.'

Griswold frowned and stared into Tommy's eyes. 'Think well on it, Rushworth, for there are difficult times ahead and it will be easier with one less mouth to feed.'

Tommy dropped his chin, a poor attempt at a bow, turned, and left. He stopped outside the Kings Arms and went around the back. He knocked on the door three times, with a pause after the second. This allowed him entry. Tommy walked over to his uncle William sitting on a form. William was swigging ale from a pewter tankard contemplating the vicar's sermon. The barkeeper poured a tankard for Tommy and placed it on the trestle.

Tommy and William found solace in the dimly lit tavern, a place where secrets could be shared away from prying eyes and ears. The tankards of ale before them provided a momentary escape from the uncertainties that loomed on the horizon.

The atmosphere was quiet. Patrons spoke in whispers about the events in church. The shutters were closed to prying eyes. Smoke from the white long-stemmed clay pipes collected among the trusses. A handful of men stood at the bar berating each other over the price of grain. Yeomen, by the fire, complained about the hearth tax.

One of the local sisters lifted herself up and down slowly on the lap of Robert Ferguson. Her partlet was untied and hung at her waist to expose her breasts. Robert held her waist his eyes closed and his head tilted back. The young woman rolled her eyes with boredom and continued her rhythm.

Tommy didn't speak; he could tell his uncle was deep in thought.

After a while, he whispered, 'William, tell me about your run-in with the highwayman, I hear Calamy has put a reward of ten pounds for information leading to his capture.'

'Not much to say really, he didn't see me, I hid in the heather. I watched him rob the minister and the other passengers as the coach got stuck in the mud near Oxenhope. Then he took off on horseback into the moors. After he bolted, I waited until the coach left then I found the pistol.'

'What on Earth are you going to do with it.'

'Don't rightly know yet, must be worth something ta somebody.'

'William, I need ta talk to you about somethin'.'

'Aye?'

'Griswold wants Will working at the manor, gave me eight shillings fer arles.'

'Tight BASTARD, Will's worth ten, if not fourteen, give it back!' William paused and thought about it. 'Hold on, Tommy, times is tough, let the lad earn his keep, might even learn somethin'.'

Tommy leaned in toward his uncle. 'Will told me about the secret stash of corn, he said there's sacks of it hidden out the back of the barn. Griswold warned him if he told anybody we would be turned off.'

There was a knock on the front door and the back door but with no pause. 'OPEN UP 'TIS THE CONSTABLE!'

Robert stood quickly dropping the young woman on the floor. He pulled up his breeches and tucked in his shirt.

She stood up and protested demanding the coin before running up the stairs.
The publican whispered for the men to put away their cards and coin then walked slowly to the door. He opened the door slightly. The door was forced open and he stood back.

The constable walked in with several Puritan men including Milton Killsin.

All in the room peered at them, then turned back around and continued drinking and whispering insults.

Tommy smiled and glanced up. 'Oh ayeup John?

'Constable to you, Rushworth,' said Milton Killsin.

'William, tis constable Pigshells. What can we do fer ya constable Pigshells?' he asked sarcastically.

John Pigshells and his father John Snr were friends of the Rushworths for years.

The constable glared at William and Tommy. 'Come on you two, don't make this more fuckin' difficult than it is.'

The part time constables were usually land-owning shepherds and only did it to escape the fine. The constable of the village checked pubs, restrained loose animals and collected parish rates.

Pigshells narrowed his eyes and his face went red. 'Ya know I don't 'ave a fuckin' choice in the matter. Fuckin' well turned it down twice then they fined me. Missis wasn't very happy, I can tell ya.'

Pigshells had no coin to pay somebody else to do it. Now he was responsible for the pillory, where he spent many a night himself.

Pigshells had a long record with the court leet. Now he was responsible for others who committed the same crimes. It was his job to punish poachers, drunks, prostitutes, church-avoiders and fathers of bastards.

Milton Killsin pushed in front of John. 'BY ORDER OF THE NEW MINISTER, THIS ESTABLISHMENT WILL BE CLOSED ON A SUNDAY. ANY FOUND PARTAKING IN GAMES, DICE OR WOMEN OF DISREPUTE WILL BE PUNISHED BY FINE, WHIP OR STOCKS.'

Most of the patrons ignored him and continued whispering insults.

Milton continued, 'Parliamentary legislation has been enacted to ensure every Sunday is stringently observed as a holy day – the Lord's Day. After sermon, all must be home fer prayer. CLEAR THE PREMISES!' Milton stepped outside.

Pigshells rolled his eyes. 'Come on you lot, get home fer Christ's sake!'

William watched Milton writing the names of the men leaving the tavern in his ledger. He knew they would be presented at the next court leet.

Pigshells' name was a regular entry in the ledger, usually on a Saturday. His time in the pillory was usually uneventful as most passers-by feared him.

When Milton was distracted, the barkeep handed Pigshells a tankard of ale. He skulled it then wiped his mouth with his sleeve.

Pigshells, like his father before him, was a tough, rough man who liked the cards, liked to fight and liked to be with women of disrepute. Now, hecould take into custody any man who didn't comply. Although, John was more likely to take a bribe. That was unless it was somebody he didn't like, then he would provide a thumpin' until they gave him a bribe.

Anybody breaking God's laws would be placed in the pillory without the need for sentencing although Pigshells turned a blind eye usually, unless Killsin was watching.

William and Tommy, along with the other patrons who came to wet their whistle, skulled their ale and left. The publican stood at the door with a quizzical expression on his face.

Milton watched them go and added William and Tommy Rushworth's name to his ledger.

They trudged home, made harder by the strong wind coming from the east. Two dogs fought for territory barking and growling in the distance. Passing the manor house they made their way down Sun Street, muddied and slippery underfoot, their woollen cloaks doing little to protect them from the elements. The looms were quiet and the shutters were closed. Residents hid from view. The wind blew in the rain as it picked up force across the moors.

'This wind is gonna blow the thatch right off the roof!' Tommy declared.

They went across the fallow field and made their way to the cottage. Some of the sheep laid low in the grass trying to hide their lambs from the blustery gusts. William and Tommy shepherded them into the keep then walked around to the front of the cottage and opened the door. They ducked their head and went inside.

As the winds outside grew stronger, carrying with them the promise of change and upheaval, the Rushworth family remained steadfast, bound by blood, and resolved to face whatever trials the future may hold.

CHAPTER 6

Just Up a Nick in Briggate

Among the bustling streets and hidden corners, a new world unfurls before the Rushworth brothers, revealing the stark contrasts of a city both alluring and foreboding.

The twittering calls of linnets and twite serenaded the air as Robert Rushworth approached his home, the last vestiges of daylight casting long shadows across the landscape. Knotgrass and mayweed whispered tales of the avian wanderers who sought refuge in the local orchard, their respite from a day of feasting echoing the fleeting moments of peace the brothers yearned for.

The weight of newfound success bore heavily on Robert's mind as he traced his steps homeward. A trader in fine wool from Lincolnshire, an exporter through Hull – his words rehearsed for the discussion with his father, a moment that had now become an emblem of his aspirations. Yet, despite his accomplishments, memories of Ursula lingered like ghostly silhouettes, their dance a testament to endings both strange and unfulfilled.

The thought of Ursula's beauty and their passionate connection stirred Robert's senses, dispelling any notion that their time to together had been mere fantasy. As his heart quickened, he focused his mind on the journey he and John had embarked upon since their departure from Haworth, a moment etched with a bittersweet argument between brothers – bound by blood, separated by necessity.

☆

John and Robert were standing out in the middle of the barley field weeding and looking for pests.

'THEY DON'T WANT US TO GO,' yelled John.

‘SHUUUSH, they’ll hear ya! Of course, they don’t!’

‘Look Robert, this is our home, I don’t want ta leave.’

‘‘Ave ya noticed Isabel hasn’t been eating. There’s not enough food fer all of us, John.’

John’s protests still echoed in Robert’s ears, a plea to remain in the familiar embrace of their home. The spectre of Isabel’s waning health, a poignant reminder of their family’s plight, had compelled them to brave the unknown. A tense farewell under the watchful eyes of loved ones, their father’s blessings a testament to a shared hope for better days and then, they embarked on the road to Leeds.

It was a sad time for the family when Robert and his brother left. Food was in short supply and they knew they were old enough to start making it in the world on their own. They said their farewells and like many others from the area, started on their way to Leeds to find work.

Isabel filled a knapsack and market wallet with as much food as they could afford to give. She provided them with a woollen blanket and their father scraped together a couple of shillings.

On the morning of their departure the family waited outside. Tommy and Isabel were sad about their departure but knew it was for the best.

William stood away looking out into the green hills, but not really seeing them. He thought of his wife Lucy. He was saddened by the occasion because she wasn’t there to see her boys as grown men.

John and Robert appeared, they hugged Isabel, Mirth and Morwen then slowly approached William. ‘Da, we ‘ave ta go.’

William turned, coming to terms with his son’s imminent departure.

He was a proud father. ‘Robert… John, I hope your years at home are remembered with fondness, kindness and happiness. Your mother, God rest her soul, and I, truly did our best. If we failed at times, it wasn’t our intent. My son’s… go with my blessing.’ He pulled them both close and held onto them briefly.

John and Robert embraced him. They swallowed the lump in their throat. They'd never seen their father this way. They turned and headed down the hill waving as they went, 'Bye Da, bye Isabel, ta-ra Tommy.'

☆

The outskirts of Leeds greeted them wearily after a long journey, the city's expanse unfurling before them like a tapestry woven with threads of life's complexities. John's awe mirrored Robert's confidence as they navigated through a metropolis fuelled by stories of its woollen past. The whispers of John Pigshells painted a city built on deceit and promise, a place where dreams could either flourish or fray.

They made their way across the bridge over the river and past the burgage plots. People out front, sold chickens, vegetables and piglets bred on their plots out back.

They passed the tofts, the small wooden houses which sat at the front. They were very compact and close together. The timbers deeply scarred with rat holes teaming with life. The houses opposite each other were so close in the narrow alleys occupants could reach out and touch hands.

Some houses were made of stone and the odd rich tradesman owned a slanted tiled roof. A network of dark laneways and alleys ran diagonally off the main street. There were hidden shanties and hovels; sick, coughing, roughly clad children hung about outside.

Above Kirkgate end stood Moot Hall. Robert was impressed with the building. *How beautiful.*

Hidden alleys and bustling markets painted a tableau of contrasts – opulence and squalor woven into the fabric of everyday life. Vibrant shanties and hovels stood alongside the affluent homes of tradesmen, the very air carrying the symphony of life's diverse symphony – ballad singers, beggars and rogues composing an ensemble that mirrored the soul of the city.

Noxious fumes came from tanning sheds and the stench from dung-pots left in the streets by rakers made them cough. Pigeons flew out from under the eaves of the old houses and their droppings left white streaks on the daub and wattle walls below.

Beggars, ballad singers, street vendors, disabled soldiers, rogues, vagabonds and prostitutes went about their business. Some in plain view others not.

In Leeds, the availability of money and valuables grew, and the size of the vagabond population provided ample prospects to make a dishonest living.

Overhanging houses kept light out and the smell of dung, rubbish and excrement in. A wily tammy cat sat on a step waiting for his feed to dart out from the pile of rubbish and faeces in the middle of the lane.

Robert strolled up to a potato badger selling outside the front of his toft. 'Ooy, where's the best place ta stay around 'ere?'

He glanced up. 'Just up a nick in Briggate. The Whitelocks, The Ship Inn and The Swan closed courtesy of our Lord Cromwell. Just down ta road a way the Nags Head at the corner of Commercial Street and Albion Place. Good brew in there.' He drawled.

'Right ya are, come on, John, good day ta you. The Nag's Head it is!'

They traipsed down the narrow lane then saw the wooden sign for the tavern. The Nag's Head, their haven for the night – a refuge and a vantage point from which to observe the intricate dance of humanity. The swaying sign creaked as if welcoming them into the fold, a reminder that within the city's depths, destinies and encounters awaited, some kind and others sinister.

A drunk old man staggered toward them. He was not in a good way as he staggered on approach. As he got closer, he lost his balance and bumped into Robert who tried to stop him from falling.

'You orl… right there old man?' Robert kindly supported him.

The man mumbled something incoherently then steadied himself holding onto Robert to steady himself. Robert turned his head away from his rank brewer's breath.

The drunkard staggered down the laneway, under the arch then disappeared into the hustle and bustle of the crowd.

In this city of contrasts, the brothers stood on the precipice of opportunity and adversity. Through its labyrinthine streets, their fate intertwined with beggars and thieves, traders and cutpurses, each thread weaving a tapestry of choices that would shape their futures. Within the layers of Leeds' complex existence, they would uncover not only the treasures of the city but also the hidden gems within themselves.

They made their way into the tavern. The first thing that embraced their senses was the stale tobacco, a testament to the countless pipes that had been drawn upon. The hearth crackled with burning wood, casting a warm, flickering glow upon the weathered faces of patrons. Aye, the scent of burning wood and coal danced with abandon.

The tavern's lifeblood, ale, flowed freely, its yeasty and malty aroma intertwined with the whispers of patrons and the echoes of countless tales. Beneath the wooden floorboards, fermenting beer barrels exhaled their own unique bouquet.

Amidst the clatter of wooden tankards and the hearty laughter of men and women, the tavern's kitchen offered pottage, roasted meats, bread and cheese. The rich, savory aroma of these simple but hearty dishes mingled with the tantalising spices and herbs that seasoned them.

Yet, as one lingered, the earthy, less enchanting notes of body odour made themselves known. Crowded and bustling, the tavern was a melting pot of humanity, each soul contributing their own essence to the air.

Occasionally, a four-legged companion was welcomed within, introducing the rustic scent of straw and hay to the tapestry of odours. Stale ale and spilled drinks left their mark as well, a slightly sour undertone to the tavern's symphony of smells.

Candles and tallow lamps cast their warm, wavering light, their distinct fragrances adding to the sensory mosaic. Conversations flowed like the very beer from the taps, and the mirthful cacophony of human activity swirled around, intertwining with the myriad scents.

The Nags Head, constructed out of stone, had a large fire and many wooden tables. There was a large oak bar topped with an ale barrel rack and pewter and wooden mugs. Large wooden beams crossed the ceiling and a set of thick oak stairs led up to the rooms. A large wrought iron candle chandelier hung from the ceiling. Wax dribbled down the length of the candle fashioning a wax sculpture stopped by time.

Two men sat at a table near the window, one asleep with his chin leaning against his chest. A wooden tankard knocked over in front of him drips of ale dripping to the floor. His companion leaned his elbow on the table his head in his hand commiserating over his loss.

Women sold their services with a smile and a whisper for two shillings and sixpence. The sisters were marred by venereal disease, alcoholism and physical abuse. They were often mistreated by landlords who took rent and a percentage of their takings. Often landlords would squeeze as many of them as he could into damp, miserable cold rooms.

The owner of the Nags Head was different. He was respected by the sisters and all who frequented his tavern, both rich and poor. Beggars and vagabonds knew they could get out of the weather, warm themselves by the fire, and be treated to slops.

The stairs were much travelled by the clientele, and the sisters who disappeared up them. When they reappeared, men were smiling. The sisters flicked their hair and plumped up their bosom to entice the next customer. Some with no modesty performed their services downstairs in full view.

Three large ale barrels stood at the end of the entrance to a storage alcove. There were boxes of grain ready to brew the Leeds manufacture.

Robert and John never saw so much grain in one place and it reminded them of how hungry they were.

They both strolled up to the bar and placed their bags on a stool.

'Tavern keeper, two ales.' Robert turned his back to the bar and rested on his elbows. He looked around.

There was a small amount of coin in the middle of the table. Two men were playing cards deep in thought about their hand. Their pupils darted back and forth trying to decide on a bet or bluff.

John turned to the tavern keeper. 'Won't those men fall foul of the constable if they're caught playin' the cards?'

'Not here, charlies turn a blind eye, besides they're too busy with the lifters.'

A pretty, young barmaid darted back and forth filling up tankards and bringing used ones back to the bar. She carried three tankards in each hand and smiled at John as she approached.

Rosie, the barmaid, flicked her auburn hair; her large, deep blue eyes were very attractive. Her smile was delightful. She wore a long green kirtle made of sturdy twill. The upper part was close-fitting and cut with a centre front placket with wooden buttons. A sewn-on skirt piece gathered at the waist highlighting her slim waist.

She rushed up to the bar and smiled. 'Aye up y'orl right?' Not waiting for an answer from the boys. She took hold of two clean pewter tankards and a ceramic ale jug and went back to refilling.

John was infatuated and watched her go.

'Don't bother with her lad, she's as fresh as they come,' said the tavern keeper.

'What's her name?' John asked with interest.

'Rosie, moved up here from London some time ago, works 'ere part-time and lives upstairs. Let's just say she has a specific set of talents not required by the men in 'ere.'

Robert frowned, turned back around as the barkeep placed the tankards down in front of them.

He reached down to take two pence out of the pouch inside his tunic, but it wasn't there. He gazed down curiously patting his waist. 'Me pouch tis gone!'

In a panic, John glared at him. 'What da ya mean it's gone!'

'Somebody's pinched me pouch!'

They both ran to the door.

The tavern keeper called after them, 'You won't catch 'im now – yer coin is as good as spent!'

They stopped and traipsed slowly back to the bar. Robert dragged his feet. 'It was our only coin, now what?'

The tavern keeper glanced at them while he polished a tankard. 'You wouldn't be the first to 'ave yer coin pinched 'round 'ere, mate.'

'Erghh!'

'Look, lads, don't worry yerself. It's on the house. Drink up, I'll get ya some grub.'

In the Briggate, there was a criminal underground where fences would provide shelter and coin for stolen goods. The fence provided advice, tips, targets and crime techniques, but most importantly, alibis and false bills of sale. This tavern keeper was one of them.

Dejected and forlorn, Robert and John took their tankards in hand and drank from them greedily.

'What are we gonna do now?' John asked. 'I suppose we'll 'ave ta go 'ome. Can't stay here with no coin and no work.'

'We can report it to the constable,' replied Robert.

Rosie the barmaid heard him and stared at them sympathetically. 'Not much point, lads.'

'No?'

'No! Waste a' time.'

'Why?'

'There's a workhouse on North Street, but it won't 'ave room.' She glanced at the tavern keeper across the bar and winked. 'Smythe, don't we 'ave ale to be brewed?'

The tavern keeper paused. 'Seems like yer a couple of likeable lads. Look, I'll let ya stay 'ere the night, ya can brew some ale, work fer ya grub.'

'Very generous of ya. We'll pay ya back.'

‘Bloody too right you will!’ The tavern keeper smiled mischievously.

The door opened, and a man trudged in; he made his way over to the furthest table and sat down.

He was a solidly built man; a bent grey felt hat with a rusty roped band sat atop his head. The peak was lowered. His dark brown hair was long and oily and drooped to his shoulders. A bushy, brown beard and moustache covered his face. He frowned in a distrusting manner. The bags under his eyes did not conceal the sleepless nights.

The stranger wore an armless leather brown tunic atop a wool-lined short coat and dirty breeches. A grey stained angular collar sat around his neck.

As soon as the tavern-keeper saw him he became distracted. ‘Here, just give us a minute, will ya? Rosie, watch the bar.’

John watched her step past the tavern keeper and go behind the bar. ‘Tavern-keeper says yer from London.’

‘Where you two from?’ Rosie asked.

‘Place called Haworth, Northwest of ‘ere.’

‘Never ‘eard of it.’

John smiled, ‘Not many people ‘ave, it’s a small village near Halifax.’

‘Never ‘eard of it.’

One of the patrons yelled out, ‘ROSIE, FER CHRIST SAKE, ‘OW LONG DOES A MAN ‘AVE TA WAIT FER A TOP UP.’

‘COMIN’!’ She walked away with a jug of ale.

The old tavern keeper ambled over to the table and sat down opposite the stranger. Everybody in the tavern knew not to sit at this table for it was here where the tavern keeper conducted business.

John was intrigued and noticed the stranger take out a small linen bag from inside his tunic and give it to Smythe. He opened it, smiled then examined the contents. He closed the bag quickly and put it in his tunic.

The two men began an in-depth discussion, the tavern keeper shaking his head in disagreement. A few moments later he reached into his money pouch and handed coin to the stranger.

The stranger stood and left the tavern in a hurry.

The tavern keeper ambled back over to the other side of the bar, discreetly putting his cloth bag underneath.

Rosie and John were in deep conversation. They were both resting their elbows on the bar flirting.

'Come on, Rosie, those tankards aren't gonna fill 'emselves,' exclaimed Smythe.

The tavern keeper filled John and Robert's tankards from the barrel and put them on the bar in front of them. He leant forward and whispered, 'You will meet my acquaintance, Mr Wilding, this evening.'

John glanced at Robert, wondering about Mr Wilding. *Wilding doesn't seem like the sort of person I wanna meet.*

He wasn't to know his and Wilding's fate would be inextricably entwined.

'Come on, you two, follow me, come downstairs and stow yer gear,' ordered Smythe.

They went outside and then down some stone steps to a small wooden door. It was a one cellar room with a small opening just above ground level. The stone floor was covered in wet straw where the rain came in through the broken window.

Three box beds with grubby looking straw mattresses and holey, frayed blankets laid next to each other. The one in the middle hosting a cat laying curled up comfortably.

Smythe shooed away the cat. 'Tis not much but it beats sleeping under the bridge. You'll 'ave ta share a bed as I 'ave three ladies rentin'.'

Smythe turned to leave. 'Oh, and best not be here during the evening 'cause they use it fer "business" if ya know what I mean.'

John and Robert were put to work mixing the ingredients for the brew. John started the fire in the alcove. Robert poured malt, oats, water, yeast and oak chips into the cauldron at the quantities the tavern keeper instructed.

'Right now, pour three quarts of boiling water over the grain. Don't stir. Put the cover on the tun and let it stand for ten minutes. Then add one more quart of boiling water. Put the lid back on and wait twenty more minutes. Take the lid off and stir it all up and add three more quarts of boiling water and stir. Wait a while then add four more quarts of boiling water. While ya waitin' ya can crush more malt, then mix it well, with the dry oats. Got it?' Smythe stared at the boys.

John, the quieter of the two, answered, 'Three quarts, don't stir, one more quart, wait twenty minutes, three more quarts, wait a while, four more quarts!'

'Right you are then, I'll leave ya to it.' Smythe walked away to tend the bar.

They spent most of the day brewing, but John was distracted by the coming and going of Rosie and she knew it.

John was still distracted. 'Leave off, she's pretty!'

'Brother, you've only been 'ere fer a couple of hours.'

Rosie flicked her hair and smiled each time she sauntered past the alcove. John watched her and smiled every time she past the alcove.

The brewing was hot and thirsty work so Rosie brought them ale whenever she could.

In the evening, Mr Wilding returned; he was as mysterious as the last time they saw him. He sat down at the same table and moved the candle away. The tavern keeper took two tankards of ale and sat opposite.

'Who are those two?' Mr Wilding asked in a gruff deep tone. He leant over and placed another linen bag on the table. 'Yer, well one of them looks nosey, couldn't take his eyes off me before.'

‘They’re harmless, two lads from the north-west Robert and John Rushworth, thought we could put them to work if ya know what I mean.’

Smythe opened the bag and grinned. ‘It has been a productive day.’ He put it in his tunic.

Mr Wilding glanced up. ‘What do ya know about ‘em?’

‘Country boys, tryin’ to find work; their coin was pinched yesterday. Brewster I’d say, he left as they came in. I gave ‘em some grub and said they could stay ‘ere the night.’

Mr Wilding growled. ‘Bloody Brewster, can’t trust anybody these days. Fuckin’ lifters and cut purses own the streets!’

The tavern keeper didn’t know how to take his comment but laughed then coughed. Wilding showed no emotion, he never showed emotion.

Rosie sashayed over and refilled the two tankards. ‘Good day ta ya, Mr Wilding.’

Wilding ignored her and took a swig of his ale.

Smythe glanced up. ‘Rosie, tell the two lads to come over ‘ere.’

She made her way over to the alcove and gestured for John and Robert to go to the table. ‘Smythe wants ta see ya.’

John and Robert strolled over.

John bit his lip nervously.

Robert held eye contact with Wilding.

‘What ya lookin’ at, BOY?’ Wilding grumbled.

‘Now, now, John, Robert, I want you to meet my acquaintance, Mr Wilding. He’s been some assistance to me over the years. We may have some work for ya.’

An excited look spread over Robert’s face as if the worry of the world was lifted from his shoulders. ‘WORK? Aye, nything’.’

Mr Wilding glared at Robert, trying to decide if he could trust him.

Robert's grin was wiped from his face as the stranger kept staring. 'Me and me brother, we'll do nything'. Anythin I tell ya!'

The tavern keeper glanced at Mr Wilding then back at Robert. 'You look like a bright 'en so this evening we'll teach ya how ta make a livin' in the Shambles. Now, gew on earn ya keep, back ta boilin' and mixin'!'

John continued stirring the malt, wheat, oats and spices in the tun. Robert put another log on the fire.

John continued to stir. 'What the hell was all that about?'

Robert stoked the fire. 'Let's just wait and see. A job, I'm not sure but it might be a bit dodgy, but to be honest we don't 'ave much of a choice.'

John shook his head. 'Da wouldn't like it if he knew we were up to no good!'

Robert straightened. 'Da isn't 'ere, let's just see what 'e has ta say, doesn't hurt. Might not be as bad as I think.'

Later in the evening the tavern keeper shoved an old man who was passed out at one of the tables. His head rested on his arm, one hand still holding onto a dripping tankard.

'Come on, Harold.' Smythe glanced at Robert who was stirring the brew. 'Give us a hand, lad.'

Robert helped the tavern keeper lift him from the table. They both put one arm around their shoulders and escorted him to the door.

He grumbled and started to come out of his stupor. Harold shook the drowsiness from his head. 'What ya doin' Smythe, can't be time ta go, let's 'ave another.' Harold stopped and took his arms from around them and turned to go back inside.

'No, nooo Harold tis late, gew on now, you get 'ome.' They pointed him in the right direction watching him stagger down the road into the darkness.

When they went back into the tavern, Robert peered over near the bar and rolled his eyes.

Rosie was smiling and flirting with John who stood there trying to impress her. She flicked her auburn hair and smiled touching his arm in a gesture of building intimacy.

Robert could never understand why John always attracted the prettiest girls in the village.

Growing up, he always thought John was the favourite twin even when their mother was alive. Of course, she always made out she loved them both the same.

Robert always felt jealous of John and his closeness to their mother. For this reason, he strived for ways to impress his father with manly pursuits. Robert was always better at ball than John, was stronger, faster and could shear more sheep.

The twins both had dark hair like their father when he was younger. Robert looked more like their father and John like their mother. Robert was taller and more extroverted, and John was the quieter of the two. The ladies seemed to like it. This always annoyed Robert.

Little did Robert know his life was to be forever changed by a beautiful, mysterious woman.

It was late when the tavern keeper shut and barred the doors of the tavern. 'Right, you two come upstairs so ya can get more acquainted with Mr Wilding.'

Robert and John followed the tavern keeper up the stairs. He knocked on the wooden door three times and waited for it to open.

'Alright, Mr Wilding?' They entered.

Mr Wilding did not answer but closed the door. He sauntered over to a straw dummy of a body, shirt, tunic and breeches full of straw. It hung from the rafters from a piece of rope. Small bells hung on various parts of the figure.

The flickering candlelight painted eerie shadows on the walls, casting an otherworldly glow upon the straw-stuffed figure that danced like a marionette from the rafters.

As Mr Wilding's enigmatic gaze bore into them, the twins stood in the dimly lit room, their hearts pounding like the distant drums of fate.

The straw figure, now stilled, seemed to hold the secrets of the night, an embodiment of the clandestine world they were about to enter.

Robert and John gazed at it curiously.

Mr Wilding stood beside the figure and pushed it, so it swung in front of him. He blew on his fingers, reached into the dummy's tunic and in one swift motion took out an embroidered handkerchief, a gold trinket and a pouch.

He returned the items and swung the figure once more, nodding at John to try it.

John glanced at Robert then stepped forward. He tried to put his hand inside the tunic but pulled back as the figure swung past. He moved closer, thrust his hand inside the tunic. He grabbed the handkerchief, but the bells jingled. John blushed.

Robert laughed at his embarrassment.

'Gew on then, you 'ave a go,' demanded John.

Robert took a step forward for his turn and blew on his fingers like Mr Wilding.

Wilding pushed on the figure.

While Robert waited for the straw figure to slow its swing. He let it go by once more then shifted his weight onto the other foot and stepped in the direction of the swing. In one swift movement he reached into the tunic with his right hand and slowly removed the handkerchief. The bells were silent.

'Do ya know what we do 'ere, lads?' Smythe whispered.

Robert glanced at John then back at Smythe, not really knowing what to say. 'I've got a pretty good idea.'

The tavern keeper opened the door. 'Let's go downstairs fer an ale.'

Robert and John went through the door followed by Smythe then Mr Wilding.

Smythe called out as he stepped down the stairs, 'Rosie, four ales and get one fer yourself, luv.'

Smythe led the brothers to a table and pulled out two chairs for them.

Rosie plonked five tankards of ale on the table and sat down with an exhaustive thud. She flicked her hair. She was pretty and she knew it.

The tavern keeper lit the candle in the middle of the table and sat, as did Mr Wilding.

Mr Wilding's silence was a challenge, a test of their mettle and resolve. In the span of a heartbeat, the twins found themselves standing at the crossroads, their future balanced upon a delicate precipice. With each breath, they inched closer to a destiny unknown, their choices echoing like ripples in the night.

Smythe never liked Wilding much and knew how dangerous he could be if provoked. He heard stories of his exploits in the Parliamentary army. Sneaking through Royalist camps in the dead of night, he would slit the throats of senior ranked officers then disappear into the darkness.

'Drink up,' demanded Smythe.

Rosie lifted the tankard and chugged the tankard empty. She wiped the froth from her mouth with the back of her hand.

John and Robert fixed their gaze on her, smiling in awe.

'Whaaat?' Rosie didn't know what they were smiling at.

Smyth whispered to Mr Wilding, he nodded.

Smythe's grin held a spark of mischief, a spark that ignited the twins' curiosity. 'Ladies and gentlemen, ye've got nimble fingers, lads, and the heart of adventurers. We want ye to join us, to learn the dance of shadows and secrets, to become a part of something greater than yer own selves.'

The room seemed to hold its breath, the air heavy with the weight of decisions yet to be made. In the span of that fleeting moment, the twins glimpsed the threshold of a new world – a world where their destinies were no longer bound to the windswept moors of their past.

To change the subject, Rosie smiled and propped up her bosom. 'Ohhh, I've been called many things but never a lady!'

John glimpsed at her shyly, dropped his eyes down at the table. 'I think yer a lady, Rosie.' John blushed, smitten by her charms.

Robert frowned at John and punched him on the arm.

Blushing, Rosie grinned at John. 'You and me are gonna get along just fine, young man.'

'As I said, what we 'ave 'ere, is what I like ta call sanctuary. Free from city authority and protected by the beaut-ee-ful church 'cross the way. If someone's on the run, they head to the church, charlies won't go in there.

'I provide lodgin' and services and all you 'ave ta do is provide lace, plates, jewels an' coin. We split the spoils at the end of the day.'

Smythe continued, 'Of course, I take a tiny bit fer let's say… agent's fees.

'Now, if ya do 'appen to get caught, a little coin to the bailiff or constable, my alibi and the magistrate, lets you out.'

Robert noticed when Smythe was around Wilding, his accent changed and he exaggerated his speech patterns to that of a Tyke.

'Now tomorra, ya can go out with Rosie and watch 'er at work from a distance. If ya like what ya see and you want ta join our little business venture…'

Mr Wilding lunged forward, planting the tip of a huge blade into the middle of the table with a THUD!

Rosie screamed and brought her hands to her face; she stepped back from the table fearfully.

Robert and John, stunned by his aggression, stood instinctively, knocking over their chairs.

The knife stood there like a pillar, Robert and John mesmerised by the blade's glint.

Mr Wilding said nothing, his hand clung tightly to the handle of the eight-inch blade. The blood drained from the top of his clenched fist. He glared at John and Robert with menace and growled under his breath.

Smythe sat up straight in his chair. 'Ahhhh then there's that!'

'If by now you 'aven't noticed, Mr Wilding is a man of few words. He considers himself a man of doin' and that was his little… er… warnin'.'

'If ya should stray from the course and let the authorities know of our… er… little arrangement… then… well he'll cut you up into little pieces.'

Mr Wilding bared his teeth, took a deep breath then ripped his knife back out of the table.

John and Robert relaxed then looked at him tentatively.

He glared at them. A coldness and evil in his eyes. In one swift motion, he threw the knife at a downright beam ten feet away, the blade stuck in then vibrated back and forth. He stepped toward the beam and wrenched his blade from the wood putting it in the sheath in the back of his breeches. He said nothing then disappeared up the stairs without looking back.

Smythe, not a newcomer to Wilding's ways, continued, 'Now, Rosie 'ere is the best decoy, prig and cheat you'll ever find. Came up 'ere all the way from merry old London, she did. She'll show you how ta play the foist, the nip, the stall and the stand. Listen to what she says and remember, we're all watchin'.'

The tavern keeper stood. 'You can call me Smythe. I will let you know, what I know about who, what, when and where. Any personal projects you happen to engage in, you bring me the goods and I coin it up fer ya.'

Smythe stood and walked toward the alcove to check on the brew bubbling away.

'Oh, before I forget.' Smythe turned around, reached into his tunic and threw something at Robert.

He caught it with one hand. Robert glanced down and opened his hand to discover his pouch stolen earlier in the day. His face had a quizzical expression. 'How on Earth did…?'

Smythe continued toward the alcove and did not look back. Feeling sorry for them, he retrieved the coin from Brewster. *There was some honour among thieves after all.*

Robert realised it was best not to ask questions, so he lifted his eyes curiously and put the pouch back on the inside of his tunic.

'Right, you two, let's call it a night, big day tomorra!' Rosie blew out the candle, stood and continued up the stairs to her room.

John stood there in the dark and watched her go.

Robert pushed him in the back. 'Come on, you got no chance tonight, she's a "lady" remember.'

John picked up the candle, they bid their goodnights then made their way down to their room in the basement. When they got there, the room was empty all except for the cat who once again took up its position on the bed.

The brothers took off their boots and laid down.

John whispered, 'Sleep here the night and we'll head home tomorra.'

Robert sat up. 'Don't be in such a rush brother, we only just got 'ere.'

John sat up. 'Da wouldn't want us involved with this lot! We'll both end up in the shite.'

Robert frowned looking at John with contempt.

'Orlright, orlright we'll stay, I'm not leavin' you 'ere by yerself. You do what ya must but I'm lookin' fer honest work.' He blew out the candle.

Robert elbowed his brother. 'Look, the rich get richer and the poor get poorer, I'm sick of scrimpin', sick of being hungry and sick of seein' me family battlin'. If you wanna go home then go! I'm gonna stay and make Da proud.' For Robert, this was to be a decision he might one day regret.

As the candle flickered and the shadows waltzed, the twins stood at the precipice of choice, their paths entwined with the allure of the unknown. In that dimly lit room, their lives were forever altered, the die cast and the secrets of the night calling them to dance within the embrace of the shadows.

☆

The next morning John and Robert followed Rosie south of the Briggate,

'Come with me, lads.' She strode ahead.

They meandered down the dirty lanes and small, crooked streets arriving at the river. There was a mass of barges pulled along by horses. They plodded up the side of the river, their drivers clicking and urging them on. The water was putrid and stunk of rot, rubbish and excrement.

Fulling mills lined the banks, their large wheels turning with the speed of the current. A great noise emanated from the mills and there was a hive of men coming and going carrying bales of cloth.

Rosie pointed. 'If you're after honest work, it's where yer gonna find it. All the cloth in Yorkshire ends up 'ere at these fullin' mills but they're not as busy as they used to be. Doesn't pay much but you won't end up branded or dangling from a rope.'

John thanked Rosie and bid farewell as he crossed the bridge and went to the first mill on the river. He asked for the headman, found him, then enquired about a job. Luckily for him, the headman informed him he lost one of his men and was looking for another. The headman took him around and showed him the process.

John watched men take the cloth from the horses and throw it into a wooden trough filled with stale urine. This released the cloth of its grease and impurities. They would then use fuller's earth to complete the process.

The cloth was pounded with wooden mechanical beaters. Depending on the type of cloth, this could take up to six hours. The cloth would be rinsed in soapy water and then rinsed in clean water. It was then taken out the back to the tentering frames to stretch and bleach in the sunlight. Other men raised the nap with a thistle-like plant and then sheared it to make the cloth smooth.

A couple of days later the carriers would collect it and load it onto horses and start the two-day trip to The Haven. Here it would be loaded onto ships bound for the Baltic.

The headman stopped his tour. 'The job pays eight pence a day. If you're late ya lose a day's pay, second time two days' pay. If ya show up drunk, I'll turn you away. Oh, and any fighting or thieving and the others will beat the shit out a' ya. You can start now, help the others take the washed cloth out the back to the frames.'

CHAPTER 7

Shadows and Desires

Amidst the turmoil of their new lives, the bonds of brotherhood are tested as Robert grapples with his own desires and the growing tension between him and John.

In the dimly lit basement room of the tavern, the air hung heavy with unspoken tension. The flickering candlelight cast dancing shadows on the walls, mirroring the turmoil that brewed between the two brothers.

Leeds and Hull became the headquarters for trade to Europe and the Baltic. Tradesmen, clothiers and skilled professionals increased their wealth, carried valuables and increased amounts of readily available cash.

The economy of the middle class grew. Leeds and Hull became places of grandiose buildings, gardens, theatres and gambling resorts built amongst the filth and squalor.

The population increased as the number of poor were forced to sell their labour in the city. Others survived by crime. All of this justified by a growing social unrest and a supposedly honest world of increasing material wealth.

Robert followed Rosie back up to the Briggate. He could hear wooden wheels of coaches grinding over the cobbles and the hammering of blacksmiths and candlestick makers. Rakers drove their dung-carts around. Men gathered around a cockfight shouted and cheered their choice of bird. Vendors pushed their carts bellowing their prices. Neighbours leaned out their windows chatting and watching the hub bub below.

Rosie whispered, 'What you'll find is there are three types of people coming to the Briggate, those who need and those who don't.

Then of course, there's us. What we do, is take from those who don't need, to give to those who do. It all works out in the end.'

Robert was curious.

Rosie smiled. 'Professional beggars, cutpurses, felons, debtors, lifters, prostitutes, sneak thieves, you'll find 'em all 'ere.'

She never wore a wimple and Robert liked her free-flowing hair. *Shame she has eyes for John,* he thought to himself.

As gentlemen passed her in the street they would dip their hat and smile appreciating her attractiveness.

Rosie sensed Robert's attraction and mentioned his brother to distract him. 'Tis a shame yer brother changed his mind about our little venture. You two are so similar and yet so different.'

'Aye, always been even as young boys, John was always the good looking, sensible one.'

'Ayeup! Ya see the oak over there, watch this…' Rosie wandered over to a rather well-dressed, portly gentleman.

He was speaking to one of the sisters at the entrance to one of the lanes leading off the Briggate.

Rosie went to squeeze past him, feigned a trip and bumped into him. She reached to steady herself then feigning a sprained ankle, dropped to the ground.

The gentleman politely dropped to assist her. Mary strolled away. He helped her up and she appeared grateful flirting with him and leaning on him for support.

He was a rather large man and he used his walking stick to support his weight. He assisted her to a nearby broken wall where she sat down. He fussed over her ensuring she was okay.

Robert observed from afar being sure not to act too suspicious. He watched as Rosie slapped the gentleman's face. Embarrassed, the man rushed off quickly before he attracted any attention. When he was out of sight, Rosie stood, smiled and sauntered over to Robert.

'What was all that about?'

Rosie fluffed her hair. 'He thought I was a lady of suspect morals, so I set 'im straight.' She smiled, reached into her bosom and pulled out a pouch. She jingled it and Robert could hear coin rattling.

Mary sashayed over from her usual location and held out her palm. Rosie opened the pouch and placed some coin in her palm. Mary glanced at the coin, closed her hand and went back to the entrance to the lane.

Robert gazed at Rosie. 'Aren't you worried he'll go get the constable?'

'He's respectable, a gentleman, married probably has children. Won't wanna bring any attention to his little… hobby.'

'So how often do ya do it?'

'Whenever the chance presents itself really, but this is just pocket change. By the time I give Smythe his cut, not much left. The big money is in the housebreaking. Silver, flaxen sheets, head-cloths, handkerchiefs, jewels.'

'Don't ya worry about getting caught?' Robert asked nervously.

'Yea I do, I fear a whippin' or a brand or a hangin', but I been savin' and I won't be doin' this fer much longer. Another three months and I'll be finished then I'll find a good man, settle down and 'ave some sprogs.'

Robert smiled. 'And what about Mr Wilding, what's his story?'

'Mmmm, be careful with him, he's as nasty and crooked as they come.

'He, me darlin', started off as a brogger. He got caught and they confiscated his wool and fined him. Been in and out of the Courts of Assizes caught stealin' wool from ships on the Humber among other things.

'Now he's a thief-taker, makes out he's an honest man and gets hired to find stolen goods by the rich. In most cases, he's the one organising their theft.

‘Gets paid by the owner of the stolen goods to find ‘em, then fences most of it. Usually returns bits and pieces so they believe he’s done what he was hired to do.’

As there was no longer any money in the wool trade, Wilding took to becoming a thief-taker, a private enforcer whose duties sat on the fringe between legality and lawlessness.

They turned around and started walking to Moot Hall. They walked up Lands Lane and reached Upper Headrow.

Standing there was a huge red brick building. There were three large gables and whitewashed mullioned windows. It possessed three chimneys, a slate roof and a panelled oak door. Large cornices overhung the windows and huge quoins cornered the walls.

A lady servant hung out the side window, shaking dust from a tapestry into the side lane.

‘I aint never seen a house like it before,’ said Robert.

‘Red Hall, they call it. Rich wool merchant turned alderman owns it, imagine the treasures in there.’ Rosie turned and gestured for Robert to follow her back towards the Briggate.

On their way back they heard a commotion outside Moot Hall. A large crowd gathered to watch a man being put into the pillory. He’d been caught stealing chickens and chicken feathers were pricked into his undergarments scratching his skin as further punishment. Of course, the more he struggled, the more they scratched.

‘Whenever there’s a large crowd’s the best time, people are too busy watchin’. Hangins’ are the best,’ Rosie whispered then went about her business.

Purses, pocket handkerchiefs, pins and brooches dresses, were all on offer.

It was a few days before Robert gained the courage to embark on his newfound career, but he did manage to get exceptionally good at it over the coming weeks. He shared his spoils with Smythe, and he and John even managed to be able to afford a room upstairs in the tavern.

Robert watched as Rosie and John become close. It made him jealous; he wanted the same.

They would flirt and John with his sense of humour would make Rosie laugh as she flitted about the tavern serving ale. At times they would disappear upstairs. Rosie would reappear a few minutes later with flushed red cheeks. John blushed, everybody in the tavern knew what they were up to.

In their room in the basement, away from the eyes of others, the two brothers often quarrelled.

Robert paced the small chamber, his frustration gnawing at him like a persistent ache. The spoils of their illicit endeavours lay scattered on the worn wooden table – glittering trinkets, jingling coin and the remnants of their daring escapades. But amidst the stolen treasures, an invisible divide had taken root, threatening to cleave the once unbreakable bond between the twins.

John leaned against the wall, his gaze fixed on the flickering flame of the candle. A palpable unease emanated from him, as if the very air crackled with unspoken words. He could feel the rift widening between them, a chasm that seemed insurmountable.

John tried to convince his brother to stop his thieving ways. 'Robert, you've gotta stop this, it's not right! Your gonna end up swinging from a rope!'

'You know, John, I thought we were in this together.' Robert's voice was tinged with bitterness, his frustration finally bubbling to the surface.

'We are, Robert,' John replied softly, his eyes never leaving the candle's dance. 'But I never wanted this life. I never wanted to be a thief.'

Robert's jaw clenched, the muscles in his neck taut with restraint. 'And what did ye want, John? To toil away in some wretched mill, breaking yer back for a pittance?'

'I wanted an honest living, Robert. I wanted to make Da proud.' John's voice wavered, the weight of his own desires evident in his words.

‘Look, brother, I came ‘ere to make me fortune, I’m not gonna wile me days away in a mill fer eight pence a day.’

John shook his head. ‘And what da ya think Da would say if he knew what you were up to?’

‘Da’s not here, fer Christ’s sake, John, listen ta reason. I’m gonna get as much money as I can and give da the life he deserves. In case you haven’t noticed, he’s not gettin’ any younger.’

‘I’ll not be a part of it!’

‘I didn’t sign up for this to tear us apart.’ John’s voice was a whispered plea, his vulnerability laid bare.

Robert’s anger began to wane, replaced by a pang of guilt. He hadn’t meant for their newfound endeavours to drive a wedge between them. Yet, the allure of the shadows, the thrill of the stolen moments, had clouded his judgment, blinding him to the cost it exacted.

Sighing heavily, Robert crossed the room and placed a hand on John’s shoulder. ‘I know, John. I know. But we’re in this together now and I won’t let it tear us apart.’

John nodded, his shoulders sagging as if releasing a heavy burden. ‘I just… I can’t keep doing this. It’s not who I am.’

Robert’s grip tightened, a silent promise passing between them. ‘We’ll find a way out, John. We’ll find a way to escape these shadows.’

As the candle burned low, casting elongated shadows on the walls, the brothers stood there, their bond reaffirmed amidst the darkness that had threatened to consume them. In the quiet of that basement chamber, they forged a silent pact – to navigate the treacherous waters they had set adrift upon, to overcome the allure of the shadows, and to emerge unscathed on the other side.

Their journey was far from over, and the path ahead remained uncertain. But the brothers knew one thing for certain – they would face it together, hand in hand, their bond stronger than the secrets that whispered in the night.

‘Robert, I’ve got somethin to tell ya. Rosie and me… we’re getting married. She’s giving up her ways. We’re gonna move into a house. Robert, she’s with child.’

Robert’s anger melted from his face, he turned. ‘WITH CHILD? Yer gonna be a father?’

Robert grabbed his brother and squeezed him tight, lifting him off the floor. ‘Come ‘ere, ya big lug.’

John groaned. ‘Errgh, leave off, yer crushin’ me.’

‘John I’m so pleased fer ya! I’M GONNA BE AN UNCLE! COME ON, we ‘ave ta celebrate.’

☆

Three weeks later the Banns were said and Robert, Smythe, Brewster and two men from the mill attended the hand fasting at the church across the road.

John and Rosie moved to a small house on the south side of the River Aire. The cottages on the river were made of rough timber, low built and close together, but it was home.

John continued the long hours at the mill. Every morning he would be up before the break of dawn and trudge down to the river before the carrier’s horses with new cloth arrived.

Rosie left the tavern because she started to show. She had managed to accumulate some wealth so they purchased basic furniture and household items. The rent was minimal and they planned one day to acquire their own house.

Their humble cottage stood sentinel on the riverbank, a sanctuary amidst the bustle of life. John’s days began before dawn, a relentless rhythm as he toiled at the mill, the ebb and flow of the river a constant companion to his labours.

Rosie, her rounded belly a testament to their blossoming family, embraced the quiet life of a homemaker. She left behind the tavern, her laughter and allure, in favour of nurturing the new life that stirred within her. The future held promise, a dream of owning their own home, a haven for their growing family.

Robert remained at the Inn and continued with his thieving ways. He tried to steer clear of Mr Wilding who continued as the local thief-taker. It wasn't easy.

Overtime, Robert and Smythe became good friends. Robert amassed a small fortune. Smythe tried to convince him to give the thieving a rest but he wouldn't. Smythe asked Wilding to let him be. Wilding's plans differed.

One fateful evening, their whispered conversation at the back table cast a pall over the room. The air crackled with tension as Smythe's voice lowered to a conspiratorial murmur, the gravity of his words etching lines of concern on Robert's face.

'I've a job for you,' Smythe began, his gaze unwavering. 'But it's unlike anything you've done before. Dangerous, it is, and it'll require the utmost precision.'

Robert leaned in, his curiosity piqued. 'What sort of job?'

Smythe's eyes flickered, a mixture of apprehension and determination. 'A heist, my friend. A grand endeavor that could secure our futures if executed flawlessly.'

Robert's heart quickened. The allure of the challenge, the promise of untold riches, set his mind ablaze. 'Go on,' he urged.

Smythe outlined the details – a well-guarded estate, a valuable cache of treasures, and the need for a masterful thief to slip through the cracks. The plan was intricate, a delicate dance of deception and daring. As Smythe's words wove a tapestry of intrigue, Robert felt the shadows deepen around him, beckoning him toward a fate he couldn't quite fathom.

Robert's mind raced, grappling with the audacity of the proposition. It was a far cry from his usual exploits, a perilous dance on the precipice of danger. Yet, the prospect of a life beyond the shadows, of wealth beyond measure, stirred a tempest within him.

'Can it be done?' Robert's voice was a whisper, a testament to the gravity of the decision before him.

Smythe's gaze held his, a mixture of hope and caution. 'With your skills and my guidance, aye, it can. But know this, Robert – once this is done, there's no turning back. The shadows will become your realm, and the line between truth and deception will blur.'

As the weight of Smythe's words settled upon him, Robert felt a mixture of trepidation and excitement. The path he had chosen had always been one shrouded in darkness, a journey where the line between right and wrong had blurred long ago.

In the quiet of the inn, amidst the murmur of patrons and the clinking of tankards, Robert made his decision. The die was cast, and the shadows that had long been his companions would lead him toward a destiny unknown.

With a determined nod, Robert met Smythe's gaze. 'Tell me everything, my friend. I'm ready to step into the shadows once more.'

And so, the die was cast, and Robert Rushworth's fate became inexorably entwined with the shadows that beckoned from the depths of the unknown. The winds of destiny whispered through the room, and the stage was set for a daring gamble that would challenge his skills, his loyalties, and the very essence of his being.

☆

Robert didn't see much of his brother and when they did meet, they argued constantly.

John swore he wouldn't stop annoying him until he gave the thieving away. 'Robert, you've got to stop! Rosie and I don't wanna be visiting you in the lock up or be present at ya hangin'.'

'John just a little while longer, one more job, I swear. Then I'll return to Haworth. Imagine what difference it will make?'

Robert promised. 'Think about Da, he wouldn't have ta worry anymore.'

Robert was hooked; he liked the coin and was sick of missing out on the material wealth others seem to accumulate. *Besides,* he thought, *the justice system is as crooked as me.*

Well, it was the way he justified it.

The justice system was full of corrupt magistrates, prison keepers, legal officials and arrangers who bribed officials and swearers to perjure in the court of law.

With his newfound wealth, Robert bought new clothes and a fancy hat. He became well known around the Briggate.

Mr Wilding didn't like it and thought of ways he could dispense with this young upstart who was working his turf.

☆

One evening, Robert wandered down the Briggate past Moot Hall and past the butcher's shops in the Shambles towards Headrow. He made his way along Guildford Street and stood outside Red Hall. *One more job,* he thought to himself. *One more job.*

He admired its magnificence. There was a wrought iron fence at the front and a row of Poplar trees standing like sentries guarding it. Servants eagerly paraded backwards and forwards past the windows. The house's boot room was attached to the south side. Late at night he watched the servants leave through it one by one. *My way in.*

The next night was a dark night, a night of a misty quarter moon. Robert waited behind one of the Poplar trees until the candle in the master bedroom went out. He waited some time then crept around the side to the boot room. He made sure he wasn't seen by the street walkers.

He broke the small square window being sure to hit the corners to reduce the noise. Pulling the pieces of glass out one by one he reached through and lifted the latch. Quietly and stealthily, he opened the door, crept inside and took off his boots. He scurried through the boot room, opened the door to the kitchen, then went through the dining room into the hallway. He went up the stairs one step at a time until he was at the landing.

There were four doors, and the master bedroom was the closest. He quietly opened the door and stepped in being sure to pause after each step. The master of the house was snoring loudly, the lady of the house absent.

He tiptoed over to the chest of drawers and quietly slid the drawer open. There it was. He lifted out the box. Going back downstairs, he picked up his boots and left the way he came in, the box tucked under his arm.

Robert made his way through the back lanes and dismissed the attentions of the street walkers. He recognised one of them. It was Mary from their first day in Leeds; the one who took coin from Rosie. This worried him as she stared and recognised his face. He pulled his hat down further over his eyes.

Mary smiled. 'Want some company, luv?'

He ignored her and scurried past.

She watched him go down the lane and smiled. *Worry not, Robert Rushworth, fer all is well.*

When he got back to the tavern, he went straight up to his room. He jimmied open the box with his knife and opened the lid. There it was. It was so beautiful he didn't even notice the other gold ring and brooch in the box. A magnificent piece, swirling jewels, a painted opaque enamel bow and a dark blue Sapphire.

The next morning, Robert gave Smythe the ring and the brooch, but the tavern keeper refused to take the sapphire. 'No, and you know why.' Two men were eavesdropping. 'It's too recognisable. I'll never get rid of it around here, me old son.'

☆

A couple of days later, Smythe sat down opposite Robert and whispered, 'Ooy, you gotta get out of 'ere quick, those two the other night they heard us. Wildings on the hunt for the alderman's necklace. There's a reward a ten pounds fer your capture.'

Is this to be my end, to be caught by Wilding on my last job? Robert felt uneasy, his breathing quickened and his face turned pale.

He didn't know what to do or where to go. *That bastard will 'ave me strung up.*

Alderman Thomas Metcalf made his fortune as a cloth merchant. He amassed great wealth and power. He also managed to sway the local authorities and most importantly often dined with the magistrate.

After discussions with the magistrate, Metcalf decided to take Wilding under his employ. He also provided him with a warrant for the arrest of the individual who swiped the necklace.

Smythe continued, 'Robert, people been complainin' to the magistrate about the amount of thieving going on, so because the charlies can't do anything, he's passed a law allowing thief-takers to do the job.'

Thief-takers were often recruited from the criminal underground and provided with powers of a general warrant which allowed them to arrest and detain on grounds of suspected crime. Having come from the criminal structures existing, most could easily move among the criminal world undetected. They employed spies to find out who committed crimes and what goods they acquired. They were also employed by prison keepers to arrest criminals and reap the benefits of blackmail and extortion. Often thief-takers would inform thieves of targets then arrest them returning the stolen goods to their owners for a fee. 'Wilding has been asking around about who swiped it. Only a matter of time before he comes hunting fer you.'

Robert remained quiet, thinking about what he should do; he peered at Smythe for advice.

Smythe frowned at Robert and whispered, 'If he catches ya, I won't be able to help you!'

'What should I do?'

'I've organised a horse fer ya, I suggest you get out of 'ere today, take the necklace to Ye Olde Black Boy in The Haven. Ask fer Captain Girlington and no other, use my name. And Robert… be careful lad and God Speed.'

'What about John? I must tell him!'

'You can't tell anybody, especially yer brother or else Wilding will find out and ya don't wanna be putting him and Rosie in danger. Now get before he finds out I've helped ya!'

Ignoring Smythe's advice, Robert rode through the Briggate and crossed the bridge. He rode up to the mill where Robert worked and tied up the horse outside. He stood for a while watching John hauling large piles of wet cloth from the fuller to the tentering frames out the back.

Robert walked up behind him. 'John?'

John recognised his brother's voice and dropped the cloth. He turned. 'What are you doing 'ere?'

'John, I must go.' Robert was concerned.

'Go where?' John knew something was wrong.

'It's Wilding, he's after me. Remember "last job"? Well, there were some complications. I 'ave to leave town.'

John shook his head. 'Dammit, Robert, I knew this would come to no good. I begged ya, you fool!'

'I have ta go, look after Rosie, I luv ya brother.' Robert turned away and strode back to his horse.

John watched him go. *Robert, what 'ave ya done?*

The headman noticed the stranger leaving and John standing there idle. 'ERE, WHAT YOU DOIN', GET BACK TA BLOODY WORK!'

John paused, worried about his brother. *What can I do? I can't leave Rosie and the baby.*

After work when he arrived home he kissed Rosie on the cheek. 'Robert's gone.'

Rosie looked up at him flustered. She was elbow deep washing clothes in a bucket. 'Where?'

John sighed. 'He wouldn't tell me, Wilding's after 'im. The last job I told you about, well, seems it didn't go to plan.'

'Oh, good heavens, John, what can we do?'

☆

As the sun began its descent over the rooftops of Leeds, casting long shadows across the cobbled streets, Robert spurred his horse onward, its hooves clattering against the uneven stones. The weight of the alderman's necklace pressed against his chest beneath his tattered coat, a constant reminder of the perilous journey he had undertaken.

Robert's heart was heavy with a mixture of determination and regret. He thought of John, his younger brother, left behind to face the wrath of Wilding and the law. He wished he could have shared his plan with John, but the stakes were too high, and Rosie and their unborn child's safety came first.

The journey to The Haven was treacherous, the road winding through dense forests and rolling hills. Each rustling leaf and snapping twig sent shivers down Robert's spine, his senses heightened by the constant fear of pursuit. His mind raced with thoughts of Wilding, tracking him down like a bloodhound, his eyes fixed on the ten-pound reward that hung over his head.

The sun had fully set when Robert finally arrived at the outskirts of The Haven, a small coastal village known for its clandestine activities and discreet harbor. The salty sea air filled his lungs as he dismounted and led his horse through the dimly lit streets. The flickering lanterns cast eerie shadows on the weathered buildings, giving the village an otherworldly aura.

At last, Robert stood before Ye Olde Black Boy, its ancient timbers creaking in the wind. He tied his horse to a nearby post and entered the dimly lit tavern. The air was thick with the scent of tobacco and ale, and the low hum of hushed conversations filled the room.

Spotting a weathered figure nursing a tankard at the bar, Robert approached cautiously. 'Captain Girlington?' he whispered, his voice barely audible over the raucous chatter.

The man turned, his weather-beaten face framed by a mop of unruly gray hair. His eyes bore into Robert's, assessing him with a mix of curiosity and suspicion. 'Who's askin'?' he grumbled, his voice gravelly.

'Smythe sent me,' Robert replied, his heart racing.

'Don't know nowt about any Captain Girlington. Go and speak to the barkeep.'

CHAPTER 8

Pursuit to the Haven

Mr Wilding entered the tavern at his usual time and sat at his usual table.

Smythe ambled over and sat opposite. 'Ave a good day, did we?'

He took the cloth bag and examined the contents. 'Oh yes, yes these will do fine.'

Smythe put the cloth bag in his tunic and went to stand up.

'Sit down!' Wilding growled, 'The sapphire necklace, where is it?'

'What necklace are you talking about?'

Wilding stared into Smythe's eyes menacingly. 'Where is it?' he uttered in a seriously threatening tone. 'I know you know its whereabouts!'

'Mr Wilding, I know nowt, ya know I don't deal in things valuable, no, bit a lace and silver does me.'

Mr Wilding continued to stare. 'Ya might not deal in it but ya know who has it.'

'I told you I know nowt!'

Suddenly, in one quick move, he reached for his knife and planted it in the back of Smythe's hand which was resting on the table. The blade went straight through his hand and into the wood beneath.

'Argggghhh!' Smythe grabbed the top of Wilding's hand, holding the blade. He panted heavily. 'Errrgh… let it go!'

A pool of blood started to spread over his hand and on to the table. The men sitting around turned to see what the commotion was but knew not to get involved.

Wilding leaned closer and stared into his eyes, he whispered, 'Next… it will be a finger… then a thumb!'

'Errrgh… FUCK! Alright… alright LET GO!'

Mr Wilding pulled the knife from his hand and the table in one motion and wiped the blood from the blade on Smythe's arm.

'Errrrgh.' Smythe pulled his hand away and held it to his chest, squeezing trying to stem the flow of blood. 'You know who has it, I don't 'ave ta tell ya.'

'Where is he?' Wilding asked.

Still holding his hand, Smythe stood. 'He left, went to Hull, The Haven… YOU BASTARD!'

Wilding stood and glared at him. 'And the necklace?'

'Took it with 'im, Errrgh.'

'When did he leave?'

'This afternoon! He left this afternoon.'

Wilding growled. 'HOW?'

Smythe didn't want to tell him about the horse. 'I DON'T KNOW, just left in a bloody hurry.'

Wilding's eyes grew narrow and he stared at Smythe trying to tell if he was telling the truth.

'The Alderman of Leeds, Thomas Metcalf has hired me to find the necklace and the criminal who stole it. He's also given me a warrant for his arrest.'

The Alderman told him of the significance of the necklace. The painted opaque enamel bow and sapphire was imported from France for his wife's birthday.

'There wasn't another like it in England,' Metcalf said. 'It would be difficult to fence without raising suspicion.'

As she went over to bandage Smythe's hand, the new barmaid moved back as Wilding rushed past her.

He climbed the stairs then crept down the hallway to Robert's room. Kicking open the door, he lit the candle and sat down on the bed. He slowly peered around the room then peeked under the bed and found the valuables box. He opened it. It was empty.

He strolled down to his room and went inside planning to keep the box as proof of his findings. Now all he needed was the lad, he couldn't be hard to find.

Wilding considered his next move. *I'll hunt Rushworth down, flog the necklace and reap the ten-pound reward. Give the empty box to the alderman as proof. Rushworth will hang, I'll be rich, and Metcalf will be none the wiser.*

Wilding didn't sleep well and rose early to get to the coach house before six o'clock. It was on the east side of the Briggate opposite the junction with Boar Lane. He knew the coach set out to Hull every Monday and Wednesday and it would take eight hours to get there. Rushworth was at least a day ahead of him.

The alderman gave him some money for expenses.

The stagecoach was already waiting outside when he arrived, so he quickly paid the £1 for the ticket.

Luggage was being thrown up to the lad standing on the roof of the carriage. The four horses were stomping in anticipation of the journey and the four outside passengers, including Mr Wilding, were waiting to climb aboard.

It was a good hour before it set off. The rain overnight made the roads out of Leeds muddy and travel was slow and uncomfortable.

The inside passengers complained. They sat three abreast in padded leather seats facing each other. Each of them held baggage on their laps and the occasional jarring lifted them from their seats.

On occasion, the men would all alight from the coach and assist the driver to push the coach wheels out of a large, muddy rut in the road or up a slippery hill the four horses struggled with.

Wilding noticed the perspiring, over enthusiastic, overweight, Puritan lady who was going to Hull to visit with her sister. She introduced herself to the other passengers as Mrs Bertha Simpson. She held onto a large, expensive, heavily embroidered silver and gold bag with ivory handles. Wilding could tell by the way she was holding it that it was here where she kept her money and valuables.

The passengers endured the discomfort with varying degrees of patience. Mrs. Simpson maintained an air of superiority, though her incessant complaints revealed her true displeasure. The other travellers exchanged weary glances, their weariness turning to camaraderie as they collectively bemoaned the conditions.

They trotted north to York Street then east along York Road and galloped toward Selby Road heading south. They passed through Thorpe Wood and then Selby Common finally arriving at Selby where the horses were changed.

The driver urged the horses down Gowthorpe and turned left on Finkle Street. He drove the horses through the carriage entrance of the Londesborough Arms Hotel into the yard.

For Wilding, the town of Selby brought back memories of the war as it was here the Parliamentary infantry surrounded and captured the Royalist army. It was here Royalists were beaten and they later took York under the leadership of Lord Fairfax.

Wilding served as a sergeant under Captain Archibald Griswold and Colonel Jasper Calamy. It was they who gave him those dangerous jobs nobody else would do.

The noise of the horse hooves in the cobbled yard brought him out of his trance.

'EVERYBODY OUT, YOU 'AVE THIRTY MINUTES TA 'AVE SOME GRUB AND TAKE CARE OF CONSTITUTIONALS!' the driver bellowed.

Wilding climbed down from the carriage and stretched his back, raised his arms and relished the solid ground. He gazed up at the balconies and windows of the three-story building from the yard then went inside. He sat at the host's table, ordered toast and ale.

Mrs Simpson step down from the carriage with assistance from her girl servant. She ordered a private chamber, waddled over to the table and ordered sack, mutton stakes, pigeons and a goblet of imported wine. She dismissed her servant to the communal table.

Lizzie sat down opposite Wilding and ordered toast and ale. 'G'day ta ya, are ya goin' far?'

'As far as tuppence a mile will take me,' growled Wilding.

'Well, if yer goin' to 'ull we're 'alfway there, just sayin'.'

'You've done this trip before then?' asked Wilding as he took a mouthful.

'And you and yer mistress, business in Hull?'

Lizzie relished the company, 'Nooo, never been there before, don't get away much, usually stuck in the 'ouse dustin', polishin' and sweepin'. Mistress needed me this time 'cause the upper housemaid was too busy with the day ta day dealins' of the 'ouse.'

'And yer mistress?'

'Married to a gentleman trader, exports cloth and imports wine, salt, iron from France, well so I 'ear from the other maids. 'Avn't been there long.'

A few moments later the driver stuck his head in the door. 'ALL ABOARD FER 'ULL, NEXT STOP!'

Wilding gulped the last of his ale and stood, he threw his tuppence on the table and plodded across the stone floor towards the door.

Fresh horses were being bridled and a hostler led the other horses away for water and feeding.

Wilding climbed up on the back of the carriage and watched as the servant girl assisted her mistress.

The driver placed a wooden step to help Mrs Simpson up into the carriage.

Lizzie grabbed the driver's hand and took her seat beside him. It was only the rich who could afford a seat inside. The four outside passengers climbed aboard.

With a whip of the reins and a, 'HEYAHHH,' the horses were guided out through the archway and down Finkle Street turning left on Gowthorpe Road.

It wasn't long before they were back in the countryside, it was late and the sun was going down. They continued their journey toward Newport where the horses started uphill toward the small village of North Cave and the hamlet of Everthorpe. Just outside town, the horses started to struggle with the rise and couldn't manage more than a slow canter on the soft road.

The woods came right up to the side of the road. It would take a firm hand with the whip to get the horses up and over the hill at South Cave.

The carriage continued along Swinescall Road and the horses slowed at Comberdale. He drove the horses on; white froth dripped where they strained against the bit. There were thick woods on both sides of the road and as he turned the bend he saw it, a large tree trunk across the road.

The driver pulled up hard on the reins. 'WHOA!'

The passengers inside, shocked by the sudden slow, were flung forward. The Puritan lady's purse dropped to the floor but the gentleman sitting opposite picked it up and gave it back.

'Thank you, you are so kind,' said Bertha.

Jumping down, he inspected the trunk of the tree to see if there were any axe marks. There wasn't so he calmed himself. 'OKAY, EVERYBODY OFF!' The driver assisted the servant girl to get down from the seat.

Lizzie scurried around the side of the carriage. 'Are ya okay, Mistress Simpson?'

'Yes, yes I'm well and fine, assist me Lizzie.' She opened the door and was about to step onto the wooden step.

Wilding appeared from around the back of the carriage he heard the servant girl called by name. 'Could I be of some assistance, Lizzie?'

He shuffled past her then held up his hand with a mischievous smile. 'Please take me hand mistress.'

'Why thank you kind sir, I am indebted to you.' Bertha took his hand and gingerly climbed down from the carriage. She would one day regret this kind gesture.

Wilding helped her down carefully, all the while keeping an eye on her embroidered purse, 'There ya go, mistress, if I can be of any further service don't hesitate to call on me.'

'Why thank you, Mr…?'

Wilding smiled falsely. 'Wilding, Jacob Wilding at yer service.'

He took off his hat and bowed to reveal a bald head all except for a few whispers of hair snaking across it. Long oily strands hung down the side of his face.

'Now, I must make haste and assist the driver to remove the tree from the road, please excuse me.'

The driver, the young lad, Mr Wilding and the three other outside passengers stepped up to the tree.

'Right, three on one side and three on t'other,' commanded the driver.

Just as they bent to try and move it, a masked horseman bolted through the woods. 'STAND AND DELIVER!'

CHAPTER 9

Trouble on the Road to Hull

The air hung heavy with tension as the highwayman's demands echoed through the forest clearing. Mr. Wilding's heart raced, his mind assessing the situation. The highwayman's pistols, glinting ominously in the dappled sunlight, left no room for defiance. One wrong move, and the consequences could be dire. The highwayman sat straight atop a beautiful brown horse holding out two pistols.

Mr Wilding reached behind him and grabbed the handle of his knife, contemplating whether to use it…

The highwayman noticed this and pointed the pistol directly at him and cocked the trigger. 'AHT… AHT, throw it down!'

The highwayman urged his horse forward. 'Slowleey.'

Mr Wilding gaped at the pistol aimed straight at his chest and thinking better of it brought his blade out and dropped it on the ground.

The driver peered at the highwayman and tried to memorise what he was like for the authorities. He wore a black knee length coat, a soldier's waistcoat and breeches with beige stockings and a ruffled shirt. The top of his face was covered with a black cloth tied at the back with two holes cut out to see through. Brown curly hair rested on his shoulders below a beige felt Cavaliers' hat decorated with a billowing plume. His brown floppy boots were a testimony to his previous time in the military.

'Right, the six of you put yer hands behind your back and sit down in front of the tree. Be bound or else die! Makes no difference to me.'

The highwayman jumped down from his horse then one by one bound Wilding and the others.

He jumped back up on his horse and rode to the carriage all the while keeping one pistol aimed. He peered into the carriage at the three terrified women sitting inside.

As the highwayman turned his attention to the carriage, Mrs Simpson's trembling voice filled the air. She clutched her purse tightly, her face a portrait of fear and desperation. The highwayman's words were a stark reminder that even the privileged were not exempt from the threats of the road.

'Hand it over and nobody will be hurt! You there, the purse!'

Mistress Simpson shook with fear. 'My word, this is all I own in the world. Surely you won't be so barbaric to take it from me.'

'My dear lady, I'm sure this is but a drop in the sea to you and yours, now spare a thought for others, please! Consider it a donation toward the king's return.'

'COME HERE, GIRL!' The highway man threw a linen bag to Lizzie. 'Hold out the bag for them!'

'Put it in the bag, the rest of you, money pouches, rings, brooches, lace, all in the bag!'

Lizzie, the youngest of the passengers, tentatively reached for the linen bag, her hands shaking as if she held her fate itself. Her wide-eyed gaze met the highwayman's for a moment and in that fleeting connection, a flicker of understanding passed between them. She knew that compliance was their only option.

With a mixture of trepidation and resignation, the passengers began to relinquish their valuables, placing them into the outstretched bag. Rings, necklaces, coins and trinkets all tumbled together, a jumbled testament to their vulnerability in the face of the highwayman's power.

☆

All in the carriage proceeded to untie their money pouches and take off their rings and necklaces placing them in the bag.

'Close your eyes and repeat the Lord's Prayer out loud,' the highwayman commanded, his voice carrying an air of authority that brooked no disobedience. If any of you move before the finish, you'll be sorry, for your next word will be with the Almighty.'

The highwayman took a quick glance back at the six men sitting in front of the log. He called out, 'God save the King!' He rode off into the woods from where he appeared.

Except for Mr Wilding, they started to recite the prayer, their voices mingling in a chorus of desperation and hope. Each word uttered was a plea for salvation, a fervent wish for the ordeal to end without violence.

'Our Father, which art in heaven,

'allowed be thy name. Thy kingdom

come, thy will be done, in Earth as it is

in heaven. Give us this day our daily

bread. And fergive us our trespasses,

as we fergive them who trespass

against us. And lead us not into temptation.

But deliver us from evil. Fer thine is

the kingdom, the Power and the Glory,

fer ever and ever. Amen.'

As suddenly as he had appeared, the highwayman's figure vanished among the trees, leaving behind a sense of unease and uncertainty. The passengers slowly opened their eyes, their gazes darting around the clearing as if expecting him to return at any moment.

'Is it over?' Mistress Simpson's voice quivered, her fingers clutching her purse as if it held her last vestige of security.

Mr Wilding rubbed his bindings against the tree trunk after he was bound but to no avail. 'LIZZIE, UNTIE ME!'

Lizzie picked up the blade he threw to the ground and cut the bindings of all the men.

The forest seemed to hold its breath, the leaves rustling softly as if whispering secrets to the wind. The passengers gathered their belongings, their faces pale but resolute. As they untied their bindings and helped each other to their feet, a collective determination settled over them.

Mr Wilding snatched his blade from Lizzie and ran into the woods in the direction the highwayman fled. He followed the tracks of the horse south through the trees. It was a dense woodland, but he could see where the horse meandered through the trees. He peered back to ensure he kept an idea of the direction, so he didn't lose his way. Suddenly he heard the click of a pistol and stood motionless raising his hands slowly.

'You are either very brave or very, very foolish!' The highwayman stood ten feet behind him pointing the pistol at the middle of his back.

'Are the few coins I took from you worth yer life?'

Mr Wilding did not move. 'Hahaha, I'm not scared of dying, I want information.'

'What information?' The highwayman asked in a deep low tone.

'A lone man, on horseback… yesterday heading to Hull, did you see him?'

'I didn't, now I suggest you turn around and follow your tracks back to the road and be on your way lest this meeting become… complicated.'

'MR WILDING, MR WILDING, they need yer help!' It was Lizzie in the distance sent to find him.

The highwayman took out his other pistol and nervously ran into the trees.

Lizzie appeared. 'Oh, Mr Wilding, they need your help, they said to come at once to help move the tree.'

Mr Wilding lowered his hands and turned to see if he could see the highwayman or his horse, but the scrub was too thick, and it was starting to get dark.

The highwayman circled back around and crept through the trees his pistols still drawn. He could see the girl and watched as Wilding followed her back to the road. The highwayman made his way back to the horse and took off his hat, wig then his black mask. It was only by coincidence Robert noticed him from the balcony above the yard at the Londesborough Arms Hotel.

Robert purchased the knee length coat, soldier's waistcoat, breeches, brown wig and felt Cavaliers' hat from the hostler back at the inn. A Royalist soldier left them after the war wanting to rid himself of the garb. It was a fitting disguise for a highwayman and by the time they moved the tree, he would be well gone.

He stayed off the main thoroughfares and rode southeast through Howden then followed the line of the Humber River to Hull which rested on the banks of the Hull River. Hull was a busy seaport and the import and export made it one of the wealthiest and most important towns in England.

He rode past the old earthworks from the war, went across the draw bridge and entered through Hessle gate at the end of Humber Street. An interval tower rose sixteen feet above the street and was at least three feet thick. The hornwork and outer defences had taken a battering during the war, so workers were busily repairing it.

Smythe told him trade was conducted via The Haven, a series of wharves on the west bank of the river Hull. He was told to find a tavern called Ye Olde Black Boy among the merchant's houses which backed on to the wharves along High Street. It was here, he was told, he would find Captain Girlington.

The streets and alley ways were full of people coming and going. They carried market produce on their carts, or merchandise on the smooth-running sledges used at the riverside.

He turned right on High Street and continued north until he came to Ye Olde Black Boy. He tied his horse up outside and entered the tavern through the front door.

A handful of seamen stood at the bar playing shove ha'penny on a rectangular wooden board. The shelves behind, housed leather jacks, wooden bowls and tankards. Most of the light came from the sporadically placed candles which provided enough light for the card games and dice. The tavern smelt of fish, the smell emanated from the straw on the floor.

One seaman's attention was directed to a young woman with her top half undone. She sat on his lap giggling, whispering her intentions and her price. Another woman, her kirtle lifted around her waist, and his breeches around his ankles. She was bent over before him. He grunted with each thrust and she answered with a similar reply.

As Robert strolled across the stone floor the room became quiet as the locals stopped what they were doing and eyed him suspiciously. They were not used to strangers in Ye Old Black Boy and were very suspicious of outsiders.

Tide waiters, who were tasked with boarding ships to check for smuggled goods, refused to go in there. One did… and was never seen again.

Robert wasn't dressed like the other men in the tavern and attracted some discerning, curious stares. Most of the men wore the garb of merchant sea men: red dirty caps, stockings, blue or white shirts, cotton waistcoats, cotton knee breeches or slops. Some wore leather, flat heeled shoes but most were bare feet giving them better traction aloft in the rigging.

'He's got a lot a' nerve comin' in 'ere,' one sailor whispered to another.

'Fuckin' toff, he'll be lucky if he leaves in one-piece.'

Robert stepped up to the bar confidently and slapped a penny on the rough wooden counter. 'Tavern keeper, ale!'

The tavern keeper stared at him, leaning against the barrel wiping the wooden and pewter tankard. He was a bald, heavy-set man with large silver earrings dangling from both ears. He donned a long, thick, red moustache which was plaited and dangled down to his chest. The sleeves of his tunic and shirt were cut off emphasizing his muscular upper arms born of years spent in the rigging.

Robert gazed around, noticing the room was deathly quiet. 'One ale.'

The tavern keeper stayed where he was, wiping the wooden and pewter tankard. 'We don't serve the likes of you round 'ere. Why don't you be a good lad and go find an ale somewhere else, there's plenty of other taverns in town.'

'I just rode from Selby, I'm only gonna be in town a short time, I'm tired, I'm thirsty and I need ale to quench it.'

The tavern keeper peered over Robert's shoulder and nodded. He turned to fill up the tankard from the barrel. Once full, he turned back around and plonked it down on the bar in front of him, spilling the froth everywhere. 'Drink up and get out!'

The clientele went back to spinning sea yarns and sailor's tales of shipwrecks, tyrannical captains, and a lovely German lass.

Robert picked up the tankard staring at the tavern keeper the whole time, he didn't blink. He chugged down the ale and wiped the froth from his mouth. He then reached in his tunic and pulled out a shilling and slapped it down on the bar. 'ANOTHER!'

The tavern keeper glanced over Robert's shoulder once again then refilled his tankard. He then took the shilling and placed the change on the bar in front of him. 'Yer pushin' yer luck!'

Robert leaned across the bar and whispered, 'No, you keep it, and there's more, I'm trying to find somebody… a man, a captain by the name of Girlington.'

He stared at the tavern keeper who was once again peering beyond him. He went to turn to see who he was looking at. He felt a massive wallop on the side of his head… and darkness.

As consciousness slowly seeped back into Robert's senses, he found himself in an unfamiliar and disorienting situation. The rhythmic sway of the ship beneath him and the faint smell of saltwater in the air were stark reminders that he was no longer within the confines of the tavern. His head throbbed from the blow he had received and he was keenly aware of the rough surface beneath him.

Robert slowly opened his eyes it was dark, and he felt claustrophobic and could hear water slapping at his side.

The top of his head stung. Remaining still and feigning unconsciousness, Robert strained his ears to catch fragments of conversation that floated through the air like echoes in the darkness. The hushed tones of the men in the room hinted at a clandestine discussion, their words punctuated by the occasional sound of a creaking ship and distant waves.

Edwin was sitting on a bale of wool whispering, 'Nobody knows, just showed up, an 'orse was outside; just strolled in an' started askin' questions.'

Edwin's voice, tinged with concern and intrigue, reached Robert's ears. He grasped at the tidbits of information being shared, piecing together a puzzle that seemed to revolve around his unexpected presence in Ye Olde Black Boy.

Horace was surprised. 'Won't need a horse where he's goin' hehehe.'

'Captain Girlington wants ta chat with 'im before we send 'im ta the deep,' replied Edwin.

Robert smelt a complex blend of scents saltwater and stagnant water created a foul, lingering stench. The mingling scents of human and animal waste filled the air. Mold and mildew contributed a musty layer to the symphony of odours.

With a slow and deliberate movement, Robert shifted his body, feigning a groggy awakening. The cloth covering his face allowed him a limited view of his surroundings, and he could see the faint glow of a candle. As his eyes adjusted to the dim light, he assessed his surroundings – the cramped confines of a ship's hold, the stacks of cargo around him, and the shadowy figures of his captors.

Horace saw Robert move. ''ere, I think he's awake, fucker's listenin' to us!'

Robert winced at the pain on the top of his head and tried to lift his hands to feel, but they were bound. 'UNTIE ME!'

Edwin stood, stepped up to Robert, clenched his fist and punched him in the side of the face.

‘Hmumph.’ Robert was slightly dazed, shook his head and tried to get his senses back.

‘Shut yer face, er else I’ll shut it fer ya,’ grumbled Edwin.

With a sudden burst of movement, Robert lunged upward, tearing the cloth covering from his face and startling his captors.

The candle’s flickering light cast eerie shadows across the faces of the men who had imprisoned him. Their expressions ranged from surprise to alarm as they realized that their captive had regained his senses far sooner than anticipated.

Without hesitation, Robert’s instincts took over. He sprang to his feet, his movements swift and calculated. One of the men lunged forward, attempting to restrain him, but Robert’s years of experience as a thief had honed his reflexes and agility. He dodged the man’s grasp, his movements fluid and deliberate.

‘Don’t worry, Horace, once Girlington is ‘ere we’ll put ‘im on ‘is way,’ he scoffed.

Robert peered through the weave of the linen bag over his head; they were in the hold of a ship. It was dark except for one candle. The ceiling beams were low and the hold was filled with ballast stones, bales of cloth, barrels, rope and sacks of wool.

In the confined space of the ship’s hold, chaos erupted as Robert fought to free himself from his captors. Fists flew, bodies collided and the dim light of the candle flickered amidst the tumultuous struggle. With each blow he landed, Robert’s determination grew stronger, his resolve unwavering in the face of danger.

Amidst the chaos, a voice rang out – a command that cut through the melee and brought a sudden halt to the violence. ‘ENOUGH!’

‘Captain Girlington?’ Edwin nodded with acknowledgment and they both stood tall. Robert leaned back on the mast and slid down onto the hull, his wrists still bound.

The tense silence that followed was broken only by the heavy panting of the men, their faces flushed and bruised from the altercation. Captain Girlington's gaze bore into Robert's, a mixture of curiosity and scrutiny.

'I hear you've been looking for me. Do you know what happened to the last tide waiter who ask too many questions?' the captain asked threateningly.

It was a woman's voice, he squinted and glanced up just making out the gentile cheekbones and slender, pale skin of a woman in the candlelight. Black eyeliner was painted around each eyelid and a tattoo on the fleshy part of her hand between her thumb and finger. She wore a felt, black tricorn hat and her long, dark, curly hair landed on her shoulders. She wore a dirty, white shirt, with a dirty ruffled collar.

Robert looked her up and down and noticed the brown, knee-length boots and dark green woollen doublet. A brown, leather belt with pistol, sword and knife gave her an intimidating appearance. A large black belt with a huge buckle hung diagonally and met up with the hilt of her sword.

She stood there resting her hand on the grip of the pistol in her belt, the other on the hilt of her sword. Every finger on her hand held a silver, jewelled ring, some fingers two. She possessed an air of superiority and Robert could the sense fear in the room.

She lifted her foot and placed the sole of her boot on Robert's throat and applied pressure. 'I said, I hear you've been trying to find me!'

Robert took a deep breath. 'Aye, man by the name of Smythe in Leeds told me to come and find Captain Girlington!'

She applied more pressure. 'How do I know your tellin' the truth? I don't know any Smythe!'

'Hmumph.' Robert tried to take a breath but it was difficult with the pressure of her boot. 'Please… I can't… breathe!'

Edwin and Horace smiled their gummy, toothless, cavernous smiles and cackled like a couple of ravens fighting over a morsel of food. They glanced at each other in anticipation of what was going to happen.

Girlington released some of the pressure from her boot, but just enough to allow him to speak with some difficulty.

'The… the… Nags Head…. Leeds…. Smythe… told me to… come to… Ye… Olde… Black Boy and… find… Girlington and no other.'

The captain increased the pressure on his throat with her boot. 'Well, you've found me, now what do you want?'

'I can't… breathe. He… said…you… might… help!'

The captain turned to the two sailors who were enjoying the entertainment. 'Slit his throat, put him in a sack and we'll throw him overboard when we're out in the river.'

She took her boot off his throat and marched away in the direction of the wooden steps.

The two sailors stepped forward. Horace took his knife from its sheath and knelt before Robert. He grabbed a handful of his hair and tilted his head back to further expose his throat.

Robert screamed. 'WAIT, WAIT, I 'AVE JEWELS!'

She stopped and turned back around. 'WAIT!' She sauntered back. 'What jewels?'

'Untie me and I'll show ya,' Robert pleaded.

She glanced at Horace then back down at Robert. She pulled the knife from her belt.

Robert was panic stricken and feared the worst. 'NO, PLEASE, A SAPPHIRE…YOU CAN 'AVE IT! I SWEAR! It's why I'm 'ere, Smythe said you'd help me.'

Horace let go of Robert's hair and stood.

Edwin got excited. 'Gew on Captain, finish 'im! We don't need the trouble.'

She bent down slowly with her knife in front of Robert, holding the tip to his throat. She lowered the knife, grabbed the ropes binding him and cut them. 'If you are lying, I will cut your throat and throw you overboard.'

'I… I'm not lying, I swear, tis the reason I'm here, reason Smythe sent me.

The two sailors immediately drew their knives.

'What do we do with him now? We're setting sail on the tide,' Horace complained.

She stood and stared at Horace.

Edwin moved away from him sheepishly.

Girlington placed her hand on the pistol in her belt and stared up into his eyes.

Her presence and authority made Horace nervous and he wished he'd kept his mouth shut.

Horace turned his gaze away fearfully. 'A… a… pologies, Captain Girlington, don't know what I was thinkin'.'

'Hmf.' The captain frowned then dismissed his apology.

Robert used the mast to help him stand and rubbed his wrists where the rope dug into his skin. He pulled his arm out of his tunic and reached in which put them all on edge.

Girlington drew her pistol and pointed it straight at his chest nervously.

Robert raised one hand. 'Wait, wait, I need to get it out, give me your knife!'

The two sailors gawked at him suspiciously as did Girlington who cocked her pistol.

She pulled the blade out of her sheath in one slick motion without taking her eyes off him or moving her pistol. She turned it around and handed the blade handle to him.

Robert took off his coat, turning it inside out spreading it out on the floor. He preceded to cut some stitches one by one on the bottom edge of the inside of the coat. He reached in with his thumb and finger, lifting the sapphire for all to see. It glinted in the candlelight.

The two sailors and Girlington watched, fascinated by the jewel. She used the blade of the sword to take the necklace letting it slide along the blade toward her.

Edwin picked up the candle and trudged toward her excitedly so he could view the gem. He was mesmerised by its beauty and whispered, 'Ahhh, tis beautiful.'

'Worth a fortune, I'd say,' said Horace with a smile, knowing he would get his share of the spoils.

She took off her hat, placed the necklace inside then put it back on her head. 'Come with me,' she demanded. 'You two, go deck side and start readying for sail.'

The two crewmen stood tall and waited for her to march past them and climb up the stairs.

After she was gone, Edwin turned to Horace. 'What ya say that fer? Yer lucky yer not hanging from the yardarm. You will be if Beaman finds out about yer cheek, ya stupid bastard.'

'I was only askin',' Horace replied worriedly.

Edwin shook his head. 'Yeeer, well, in future, don't bloody ask!'

Robert followed Girlington up the stairs to the tween deck then up another set to the top deck. She made her way to the port side and along a small plank onto the wharf.

He followed her in silence as she marched down the road back into Ye Olde Black Boy.

Inside, the patrons stopped talking as the door opened then on seeing her went back to what they were doing.

She took off her hat and strolled over to a table at the back of the room. 'SIT!' She demanded. She placed her tricorn hat on the table so she could inspect the necklace more closely.

Robert obeyed the captain's command and took a seat at the table. He watched as Captain Girlington delicately handled the sapphire necklace, her fingers tracing over the intricate details of the pendant. The dim candlelight danced across the gem's surface, casting mesmerizing reflections.

The captain's intense scrutiny shifted from the necklace to Robert's face, her piercing gaze locked onto him. 'Explain yourself, lad,' she demanded, her voice firm but tinged with curiosity.

Taking a deep breath, Robert recounted the events that had led him to The Haven – the encounter with Smythe, the whispered instructions and his perilous journey to find Captain Girlington. He spoke of the alderman's necklace, its significance, and the growing threat posed by Mr Wilding and the looming specter of capture.

Girlington listened intently, her features betraying no emotion as she absorbed his tale. She continued to turn the sapphire pendant in her fingers, studying it as if evaluating its worth beyond the monetary value.

When Robert had finished speaking, a thoughtful silence settled between them. The weight of his words hung in the air, and he could sense that his fate rested in the captain's hands. The room seemed to shrink around them, the ambient noise of the tavern becoming distant background chatter.

Finally, Captain Girlington leaned back in her chair, her gaze never leaving Robert's. 'You've found me, lad, and you've brought me something of value,' she mused, her tone contemplative. 'But what's to stop me from taking this necklace and sending you to the deep?'

Robert's heart raced and he realised that his destiny hinged on this pivotal moment. He leaned forward, meeting her gaze with unwavering determination. 'Because I have information,' he said, his voice steady. 'Information that could prove invaluable to you and your endeavours.'

The captain's eyebrows raised slightly and a flicker of interest passed across her face. 'Go on,' she prompted, her curiosity piqued.

'I know the inner workings of Mr Wilding's operation,' Robert explained. 'I can help you navigate the underworld of thieves, smugglers, and those who seek to profit from chaos. I can be an asset to you, a partner in thwarting Wilding's schemes.'

Girlington regarded him with a mix of scepticism and intrigue. 'And why should I trust you? You could be spinning tales to save your own skin.'

'Because my life is on the line as much as yours,' Robert asserted. 'If Wilding finds me, I'm as good as dead. But together, we have a chance to outwit him.'

The bar maid sauntered over and placed two penny ales on the table.

The captain's fingers drummed softly on the table as she considered his proposition. The tavern around them buzzed with activity. Girlington looked up at the barmaid. 'Please ask Beaman to come over here.'

Robert chugged down his ale and then putting the tankard on the table was about to say something…

'Aht! I'll do the talking, where did you get it?'

'Let's just say I acquired it in Leeds and had some difficulty dispensing with it. Smythe told me to come here and see you and only you.'

'It's a wonderful piece and so unique, no wonder Smythe didn't want anything to do with it.'

'So ya do know 'im?' Robert stared at her, perplexed.

Girlington smiled. 'Yes, I do, we've done business in the past.'

He could tell she was holding something back, but what? He started to wonder if he made the right decision in coming here. *Surely, I can trust Smythe.*

Robert leaned his head back and rolled his eyes. 'So what was all that about then? Ya scared the be-Jesus out of me.'

'Had to be sure, there's been a lot of searchers and tidewaiters hanging about checking seals and manifestos. They're making imports and exports very difficult. They tried to get me and my crew once before. If you hadn't mentioned Smythe, you'd be in the same place he is right now.'

Robert hadn't the nerve to ask where, but it was surely not a place he wanted to go.

The tavern keeper ambled over; Girlington kept her eyes on Robert and lifted her hat up to the bartender.

Beaman picked up the candle from the table and peered into the hat closely. 'Mmm, swirling jewels, a painted opaque enamel bow and the dark blue Sapphire. French I'd say, no chance to get rid of it 'round 'ere cause a' the enamel.'

Beaman put the hat back down on the table and stepped away.

Girlington picked up her tankard. 'Sixty-forty! I 'ave to find somebody who wants it. We sail for the Baltic on the high tide the day after tomorrow.'

Robert gawked at her. 'Fifty-fifty! And how am I to know you'll return with the coin?'

'You don't!' She smiled cheekily.

Robert glimpsed at her then focused on the top of the table sadly. 'It seems you 'ave me at a disadvantage.'

'I tell you what, since you are a friend of Smythe's, I'll give you some fine wool for collateral and you can have your horse back.'

Robert nodded his approval. 'Sounds reasonable, my family are spinners and weavers, and it's time I returned home. When will you be back?'

'Two months give or take, we sail to Antwerp, Stade then to Riga and Danzig.' *After we spend a few days building up our manifesto with further goods from the ships on the Humber,* she thought to herself, not giving too much away about their plans.

Robert leaned in toward her and whispered, 'There's something else!' He paused. 'There's a very dangerous man hunting me and the necklace, a thief-taker. His name is Wilding, I know him from Leeds, and he will do anything to get me and retrieve the necklace.'

'Well, we sail the day after tomorrow. Why don't you come with us? My crew will take care of your thief-taker if he shows up.'

Girlington gazed at him and appreciated the honesty of her prisoner. She also liked his quiet strength and the way he held himself. She peered into his, green deep-set eyes; they seemed to look beyond her rough, hardened appearance. He had a proud, intelligent way about him but there was a secrecy she couldn't make out.

She loved his shortish, curly, brown hair and the short growth moustache and beard gave him a handsome ruggedness. His white shirt was opened to reveal his broad chest covered with dark chest hairs. His arms were muscular and his hands large and strong. He was taller than her but not by much and he held himself with confidence.

I haven't had the company of a man for such a long time, she thought. She tried to imagine feeling his taught firm body against hers.

Robert felt guilty. 'I thank you for your offer, but I cannot, it's been almost two years since I've seen me family and I know nothing of their wellbein'. When I left, they were struggling to make ends meet and me father is not a young man anymore. I should go home.'

The captain appreciated his loyalty to his family. 'Okay then, let's get the wool and put you on your way.'

They walked along back toward *The Pearl*. A mist rolled in off the bay. The anchored tall bobbing grey, white sails of ships had a ghost like appearance. Their rusty hinges squeaked, canvas flapped and halyards slapped against their masts.

As they got closer to *The Pearl*, the creaking was interjected with flatulence, belching and profanity from inside.

Captain Girlington stopped before boarding. 'By the way, it's fine wool from Lincolnshire and we should get a pretty penny for it. Put it out, bring it back and we'll get a good price for the cloth. Full it, but don't dye it because we sell it in Danzig and they have their own craftsmen.'

'I know exactly what to do with it and once again, thank you.'

She smiled, fluffed her hair and gestured for him to follow her. 'Where are you from?'

Robert spoke as they left the tavern. 'Small village, Haworth near Halifax to the west. Tell me, you 'ave a different accent where are you from?'

'Portishead, my father and I moved away after mother died. He was a seaman. He sent me away to boarding school in Kent. I don't see him much these days. So how on Earth do ya know the tavern keeper?'

Robert considered her question. 'If it wasn't for him me brother and I would 'ave been lost when we first arrived in Leeds. He put us up and taught us how to brew, among other things.' Robert smiled. 'Ah yes, he has many notable talents, and curses, my father and I have known him for many years, and he has been a valued and trusted friend.'

As the weight of the situation settled over them, Robert found himself faced with a pivotal moment – one that could determine the course of his quest and the fate that awaited him in the unforgiving world of The Haven.

CHAPTER 10

Veil of Shadows

The stagecoach trudged wearily through the darkness, the weight of an obstinate tree trunk forcing a reluctant pause. As the silver light of the moon bathed the scene, the weary travellers found themselves on the cobbled streets of Hull. A sense of frustration hung heavily in the air, as the horses were unhitched with laborious precision to clear the path ahead.

Minutes stretched into an eternity as the passengers, lost in their vexation, bemoaned the loss of their treasured possessions. Bertha Simpson's voice cut through the night like a shrill wind, her dissatisfaction echoing off the walls of the nearby buildings. The gentlemen, in their tailored suits and impeccable manners, fumed over the lateness of the hour, their tightly wound tempers threatening to snap.

Hull, under the moon's ethereal glow, revealed its dual nature – the enchanting bow-windowed shops gleamed, beckoning with their allure, while the damp, winding streets exhaled a symphony of repugnant odours and discarded waste. As if participating in a clandestine ballet, the old doors shut firmly, secrets held within their wooden confines. Shop signs danced erratically, casting eerie shadows that whispered of mysteries concealed beneath the surface.

And there, under the watchful eye of the moon, stood the George Hotel, a bastion of respite for the weary and the curious. Wilding, a man with a shadowed past and a determination etched into his features, knew that time was not on his side. The reputation of the Haven, Hull's labyrinthine underbelly, hung over the city like a fog, but it was precisely within those murky depths that Robert Rushworth, a master of illicit trade, would inevitably surface.

He strolled through the archway located on the left side of the inn, a young lad came out to open the gate and allow him entry. Wilding followed the young lad inside. The other passengers, some complaining about not having money to pay for a room, followed.

Lizzie and her mistress paid the six shillings for supper, bed and breakfast up front. Seeing this, Wilding assumed the woman possessed more money hidden. He ambled up to Lizzie and Mistress Simpson once again.

Mistress Simpson, her flushed countenance betraying her fatigue, addressed him with gratitude, a hint of vulnerability in her voice. 'Mr. Wilding, your assistance this afternoon was a godsend.'

Hat in hand, Wilding executed a courteous nod. 'It was my pleasure, dear mistress. Should the need arise, consider me at your service. Thankfully, not all your treasures fell prey to the thief's grasp, a stroke of luck, I dare say.'

She smiled and whispered. 'No, fortunately Lizzie hid most of my valuables; nobody would suspect a servant girl, hehe. One must be very careful these days.'

Wilding peered at Lizzie who was standing away from the counter, he frowned and forced a smile. 'You are very shrewd, Mistress Simpson.'

'Mr Wilding, I hate to impose on you further, but would you be so kind as to have my luggage brought up to my room, it is very late and after the excitement of the day. I feel absolutely exhausted.'

'It would be my pleasure; I will speak to the driver immediately.'

'Thank you so much, Mr Wilding. Come upstairs and I'll give you something for your trouble.'

She turned away. 'Come, Lizzie, let us make haste before the sun rises again.'

Wilding watched as Lizzie followed her mistress up the stairs to their rooms. Then she stopped halfway up and descended the stairs. 'Mr Wilding, Mistress wants me ta show ya which trunk is 'ers.'

The two of them went out to the carriage.

Lizzie pointed to a large wooden trunk with brass handles and corner protectors which was just offloaded.

Mr Wilding walked over, picked up the trunk and slung it up onto his broad shoulder with a grunt and followed Lizzie upstairs. He heard the rest of the passengers complaining to the inn keeper about what happened on the road and fretting about how they would pay for their rooms.

Lizzie stood at the top of the stairs waiting for Mr Wilding. 'You alright?' she asked.

Mr Wilding didn't answer but struggling, placed the trunk on the landing with a thud.

'I could use a hand,' he stated.

She turned and grabbed the brass handle on her end of the trunk and lifted. 'Tis so heavy, I need to put it down for a minute, Mr Wilding.' Lizzie was puffed; she dropped the trunk.

A surge of adrenaline coursed through Wilding's veins, quickening his movements as he advanced. Yet, the fabric of destiny had been woven with unexpected threads, and in a heartbeat, the scene transformed. His once steady hand, now a vise, closed around Lizzie's throat. Terror painted her features, her eyes wide with disbelief and fear. A deep gargle came from the back of her throat as she tried to pry his fingers away.

Keeping one hand on her mouth and one on her neck, he squeezed harder and harder until her eyes grew wide, white and terrified. She started to wriggle frantically and tried to push him away.

He was too heavy and when she tried to kick him, he stood closer, trapping her against the wall with his hip. He put all his might into squeezing her neck and he could feel her strength wane under his grasp.

Lizzie thrashed her head from side to side; her face was bright pink. She couldn't remove his hand from her throat.

Fury and anguish mingled in her gaze, her struggle palpable yet futile against his unyielding strength. The dance of life and death commenced, a private performance cast in shadows and silence, a prelude to a revelation yet unknown.

Wilding grinned.

Her terrified stare started to weaken as her strength slipped from her body. She pushed against his chest weakly. She tried to beg for her life but it was muffled.

A moment or two later, she stopped struggling and went limp.

As Wilding held her lifeless form, a disturbing calm settled upon him. He glanced around the room, his gaze landing on the bedroom door beside him. With a swift movement, he lifted the latch and dragged her body across the threshold. The door creaked shut, sealing away the scene of his malevolent act.

Laying her on the floor, he felt over her kirtle. He felt around her waist then her breasts and finally felt the pouch hidden there. He ripped her partlet open and ripped her undershirt down the middle, exposing the pouch attached to the inside of her undershirt. He ripped it off and put it in his tunic before lifting and pushing her lifeless body under the box bed.

Wilding opened the door slightly to see if there was anybody in the hallway, then stepped out.

The passengers from the carriage were still downstairs arguing about how they would pay for their rooms.

Wilding took out a skeleton key and opened the trunk quickly rummaging through it. There was nothing but clothes and a small box which contained a man's silver ring which he immediately put in his pouch. He threw the box back in the chest.

Wilding shuffled down the hallway, down the stairs, through the archway and quickly out into the street. He fumbled around inside his tunic and felt the ring.

Sometime later, one of the gentlemen from the carriage opened the door to his room. He recognised the trunk. He read the name on it then called for the boy.

The boy dragged it to Bertha Simpson's room. He knocked on the door.

Bertha opened the door slightly. 'Your trunk, mistress. The other boy took it to the wrong room.' He pulled it in for her, doffed his hat and left.

Bertha followed him to the door, looking down the hall for Lizzie. *Where has she gone?*

Alone in her room, Bertha approached the trunk with a sense of anticipation. The key, kept close to her bosom, glinted as it found its place in the lock. With a turn, the trunk yielded its secrets. Her gasp was audible, a shocked exhalation of disbelief. The once-ordered contents had been transformed into a chaotic jumble, a testament to a ruthless violation of her privacy. Bertha's heart pounded in her chest, her voice rising in an anguished cry.

'HELP… HELP… I'VE BEEN ROBBED!' She stepped to the door and called out again. 'HEEELP! HEEELP!'

The sound of her distress echoed through the corridors, a chorus of alarm spreading like wildfire. A tapestry of deception had been woven, each thread carefully spun by Wilding's callous hands. As the inn's patrons converged, Bertha's cries pierced the air, a chilling reminder that darkness often lurked beneath the surface of even the most innocuous surroundings.

☆

Wilding turned right on Manor Street then left into Silver Street. He noticed the pub signage for Ye Olde White Harte and headed toward it.

Strolling through the archway, he went inside and up to one of the brown panelled bars which were split by a staircase.

The publican was wiping the last of the pewter plates and stacking them on the shelf behind him.

'Ale and a room!'

The publican poured the ale from the barrel and plonked it on the table in front of where Mr Wilding was seated. 'Two shillin'.'

Mr Wilding reached into his tunic and pulled out the pouch; opening it, he saw it contained about three pound and some change. He reached in and pulled out two shillings, tossing them on the table.

The publican pointed. 'Through the door, up to first floor, first on the left.'

Mr Wilding took a gulp of his ale. 'The Haven?'

The publican stared at him curiously. 'Down Silver Street, cross Market Place and follow Scale Lane until you reach High Street. I wouldn't be wanderin' around there at this time a night, if ya know what I mean.'

'I'm trying to find somebody.' He paused. 'What other inns are about?'

'Well, there's the William Hawkes, The Lion and the Key and Ye Olde Black Boy, but I wouldn't venture in there, full a' seaman and they don't take kindly to strangers. Last stranger who ventured in there never left, never seen again so they say. Yer better off stayin' away.'

Mr Wilding finished his ale, stood and climbed the staircase to his room. He took out his knife and placed it under the pillow, took his boots off and laid down.

He didn't sleep much. He got up as soon as there was a glimpse of light in the sky, put on his boots and went downstairs and sat at the table. The publican put a bowl of oats in front of him which he gobbled down greedily. He left quietly through the door and meandered down the cobble stones of Scale Lane toward the River.

Morning mist clung to the River as Mr. Wilding made his way toward The Haven. The air was tinged with the scent of saltwater and the distant cries of gulls echoed in the distance.

The bustling maritime activity along Scale Lane was a stark contrast to the quiet of the previous night and the olfactory experience of such a location was a complex mixture of scents. There was a pungent, briny aroma of the sea carrying hints of seaweed and the sharp tang of brackish water.

There was also whiffs of tar and pitch commonly used to seal the seams of ships, repair sails and maintain the overall integrity of vessels.

Merchants were unloading and storing a wide array of goods, and each item had its own distinctive scent. Spices like cinnamon, cloves and nutmeg would infuse the air with their exotic, aromatic notes, while sacks of grains contributed a hearty, grainy aroma. Barrels of salted fish and cured meats emitted a potent, savoury scent that could be both inviting and overpowering.

The wharf was also a place where fishermen brought in their daily catch. The unmistakable odour of fish, both fresh and salted, was prevalent, sometimes mingling with the faint undertones of fishnets, ropes and the brine-soaked gear.

The sailors, dockworkers and vendors brought their own personal fragrances, combining to create an amalgamation of sweat, leather, tobacco and even a hint of rum from nearby taverns.

The ships in The Haven, all except one *The Pearl*, were triple banked. Preparations were in full swing with carts, horses and bales of cloth, wool and sacks of grain being loaded onto them.

Merchant seaman spent the last few minutes with their lady and others staggered out of the taverns still coming to terms with the rum the night before. Tradesmen counted sacks being loaded onto ships and land-waiters and excise men went about their business checking manifestos and arguing with captains if they found extra goods.

Dogs barked and cats sniffed around the crates of fish unloaded from fishing vessels arriving back from Norway and Russia.

General labourers off loaded timber from Norwegian ships and beggars and vagrants begged for pennies from recently paid sailors on shore leave.

The loud hammering of hammer against metal and wood could be heard coming from the shipyards where whalers and warships were being built.

Carts loaded with hemp and bags of lead crisscrossed the cobbled wharves taking their goods to ships ready to sail on the next high tide.

Captains yelled orders and seaman climbed masts to check rigging while others swabbed the decks and readied sails.

Wilding watched patiently. He knew to fence such a necklace; Rushworth would have to do it here on the docks.

Mr. Wilding's thoughts were interrupted by the sound of hooves on cobblestone. A horse-drawn cart laden with goods rattled past him, its driver shouting orders to a pair of porters who scurried alongside, loading the cargo with practiced efficiency. He watched as the bales of cloth and sacks of grain were secured on board, the ship's crew members bustling about, their faces etched with a mixture of weariness and purpose.

Turning his attention away from the loading process, Mr. Wilding followed the path along the water's edge. The River was a tapestry of sights and sounds, a living canvas that told stories of trade, adventure and secrets hidden beneath the surface. Fishermen cast their nets into the depths, their weathered faces reflecting years of toil and perseverance. Seagulls circled overhead, their cries a haunting melody that resonated with the ebb and flow of the tide.

He walked along the quay, past weathered warehouses and busy docks, absorbing the energy of the place. The scent of brine was almost intoxicating, a reminder of the vastness of the sea and the boundless possibilities it held. Yet, beneath the surface, he sensed a tension, an undercurrent of uncertainty that seemed to ripple through the very air.

He headed back up Scale Lane passed the William Hawkes and stood on the corner of high street peering at those coming and going from the Lion and the Key. He leaned against the wall, pulled his hat down and smoked his pipe patiently waiting, all the time watching.

A while later he thought about what the publican said about Ye Olde Black Boy; he scurried down High Street and stood at the walled entrance to Dunwell's Forge.

Moments passed like eternity, his thoughts swirling in the cool morning air. Just as he was about to abandon his vigil and retreat, the creaking of a door hinges reached his ears. The entrance to Ye Olde Black Boy swung open, and a trio of seamen staggered out into the street. One a captain with a tricorn hat, dark green woollen doublet and black leather jerkin and two others, regular seamen with striped shirts, jackets and baggy slops.

Robert Rushworth followed the captain and two seamen down Scale Lane toward the docks. He followed from a distance stepping into doorways if it seemed like one of them was going to turn around. Arriving on the docks he stopped and watched them stagger along the gang plank and board a sloop.

Mr Wilding withdrew further into the shadows, his curiosity outweighing the urgency to confront them directly. He strained to hear their words as they conversed on the dock.

Robert followed Girlington and the two seamen onto the deck. 'Never been on a boat before.'

Girlington stopped; she waited for Robert to catch up. 'Boat? It's a Sloop!'

Robert gazed at her curiously. 'What?'

Girlington stopped, turned and gazed at him impatiently. 'It's not a boat, it's a ship, a sloop, built in the Caribbean and sailed all the way here by my father! She's a fine vessel, *The Pearl*.'

'From the Caribbean?' Robert lifted his eyebrow with curiosity.

Girlington smiled. 'Oh yes, there is much you don't know about my family, and much more you will never know, now come with me.'

They marched along the top deck, past seamen singing sea shanties and headed to the stern. She opened the door to the captain's cabin and stepped inside.

The captain's cabin on *The Pearl* was a world of its own, a sanctuary within the confines of the ship. Girlington led Robert Rushworth inside, her demeanour shifting from the enigmatic figure on the docks to a more welcoming presence. The space was surprisingly spacious, illuminated by the soft glow of candlelight and the dim sunlight filtering through the glass windows at the rear.

There was a bed, dressing table, ledged shelves, cabinets and a ledged oak desk. On the desk there was an hourglass, a map, a quill, ink, parchment and a thick black glass bottle and pewter goblet. All things required by a ship's captain.

She lit the candle in the lantern above the desk.

Robert noticed the quill and parchment. 'You can write?'

Girlington smiled. 'And "read" if you must know. Can you not? I suppose that's how you got the sapphire?'

Robert's admission was candid, his voice tinged with a touch of vulnerability. 'Me… no, I'm from humble beginnings, poor folk, tenant farmers and shepherds. The only thing I know is wool, cloth and a set of skills I learnt recently.' He winked.

Robert's smile was fleeting, a mask to hide the complexity of his emotions. 'The moors, most beautiful country you've ever seen in Spring, when the heather blooms,' Robert reminisced. 'I miss it.'

Girlington stepped to the desk, poured some wine out of the thick blue glass bottle into the goblet and handed it to Robert. 'Imported wine, from a place called Bordeaux in France.'

Robert took the goblet, inspected it cautiously and smelt it then turned up his nose. 'Tis red, like blood!'

Girlington smiled. 'It's an acquired taste, take a sip and keep it on the tongue before swallowing.'

Hesitantly, Robert took a sip and shuddered. 'Tastes like dirt, mud and mushrooms.'

He smiled and chugged it all down then held out the goblet for more. 'Where did ya get it?'

Girlington took another pewter goblet from a cabinet filled up hers and Robert's again. 'Let us just say we acquired several bottles some time ago. Now come, sit, tell me of Smythe, is he well?'

Robert skulled the next goblet and held it out to be refilled. 'Yes, very well, doing what he does, he brews a good ale and the tavern's always full.'

Not used to the imported wine, which was far stronger than ale, Robert started to feel tipsy. He started to slur his words. 'Tastes much better now.' He held out his goblet again.

As the evening wore on, the conversation meandered from tales of the moors to the origins of the imported wine. Robert's initial hesitance gave way to a more carefree demeanour, his tongue loosened by the intoxicating liquid. Girlington listened with a knowing smile as he shared stories of his past and his connection to Smythe's tavern.

Girlington went to fill it but as she turned it upside down only a couple of drops came out of the bottle. She stood and went back to a large oak storage chest with many brass handles which sat underneath the ship's windows spanning the width of the room. She lifted a panel. 'It's alright, plenty more.'

Girlington reached in and grabbed another bottle, then used her knife to cut the wax from the top and pried out the cork. She filled up Robert's goblet and her own.

'I c… c… could get used to this.' Robert grumbled.

Girlington's eyes lit up. 'Yes, well, don't get too used to it, it's worth about a guinea a bottle.'

Robert coughed then looked down into his goblet. 'G… Guinea a bottle?'

Girlington could tell he'd drunk enough and although cute, his sloppy drunkenness was annoying. 'Robert, come with me!'

She stood up from the chair and stepped toward the door, opening it to allow Robert to go through albeit unsteadily. 'You can sleep in here.' She opened the door to the cabin next door.

Robert peered in, it was a tiny cabin with a small, enclosed bed, a stool and a ledged shelf with a candle on it.

'So, what was yer father doin' in the Ca… a…ribbean and how did he come by The Pea… r… l?'

Girlington put her hand on the door handle. 'That is a long story for another night, sleep well.' She closed the door.

Robert heard her enter her own cabin and close the door.

The ship's bell rang to mark the start of the gangway watch. Robert took his boots off and climbed under the blanket. The slow gentle rocking of the ship and the imported wine put him straight to sleep.

Girlington locked her door then went to her strongbox and opened it to reveal the necklace. She took it out and placed it on the desk and inspected it. *So intricate, so beautiful,* she thought to herself. Would fetch a tidy penny in Antwerp. And as Girlington gazed at the sapphire, she knew that the threads of destiny were unravelling, leading them all toward a future yet to be written.

All the wine and all the talk about the Caribbean brought back memories. Her past was woven with threads of mystery, adventure and sacrifice. Her memories of her father were a tapestry of fleeting moments, of embraces shared under the cover of night, and tears shed in the shadows. The absence of his presence was a constant ache, a reminder of the cost of his chosen life upon the seas. Yet, in the midst of that absence, there were moments of profound connection that shaped her destiny.

She didn't see much of her father when she was younger and even less when she was sent to boarding school. He was away at sea for months at a time. When he was home, he remained incognito often arriving and leaving in the middle of the night. One day he would be there, then the next gone. Mother told her he always kissed her gently on the cheek before he left.

She still remembered the night. She told him about mother. As a young girl she tried to console him as he dropped to the ground and wept.

She left with him two days later and joined him on *The Pearl*. It was an adventure she would not soon forget.

It took some time before the crew accepted her. They said it was unlucky to have a woman on board until Beaman gave one of them a hiding. As time went by she became one of them. They taught her how to replace yards and sew up sails, climb the shroud lines and stand on foot ropes thirty feet above deck.

Occasionally, a sailor standing on the foot ropes would call out, 'SHIP AHOY!' Her father would order her to his cabin. She would sit there, sometimes for hours, hearing the shouting and clambering and movement of men on the deck and the occasional loud boom of a cannon.

Sometime after, her father sat her down in his cabin and he told her about boarding school. She pleaded with him to let her remain, but he was against it.

Her father explained how when they arrived back in Ports a gentleman would be waiting to take her to a boarding school in Kent. 'A ship is no place fer a lady.'

She begged him through teary eyes. 'Father, please, don't send me away.'

It was a sad day when they docked in Portishead and the first mate, Beaman and all the crew came dockside to see her off. The Boatswain whittled her a dolphin out of some scrap wood and her father gave her a pouch with her share.

'Now then, if ya ever need me, tell the headmaster and he'll get a letter off to the ports where I'll be landin'. Never tell anybody else.'

She threw her duffle into the carriage and climbed aboard all the time waving to the crew sadly as she and the headmaster departed.

It would be a month and a year before she saw him and the crew again, but her father would write to her. His letters were always typical and very rarely mentioned where he was or what he was doing.

One day, she received a letter from her father asking her to come to him. He said he was getting old and tired and was ready for a quieter life. He was tired of looking over his shoulder all the time and being chased on the open seas.

When she arrived in Hull, she was so pleased to see his cheerful smile and doting affection.

In a quiet moment, he explained how he was tired of being at sea and explained *The Pearl* was in The Haven. The crew were away on leave for a fortnight until he could sell it.

She was devastated.

He explained how Cromwell's new navigation act allowed only English vessels to transport English cargo; it wouldn't take long to sell.

It took the full month to convince him to let her take over the ship, but there was one condition.

It was over five years ago now, but she still remembered when her father introduced the 'new captain' to the crew and their cheers.

She was voted in by the crew because they respected her and knew she was capable of commanding and navigating the ship. Her skills with the sword and pistol were renowned she was taught well by both her father and Beaman. Of course, it took a few years for her to build up her knowledge but Beaman was the best first mate around.

The bonds between Girlington and her crew were more than just professional; they were bonds of family, woven through shared triumphs and trials. Her leadership style was one of fairness and compassion, ensuring that her crew received their due share and were treated as equals. Loyalty flowed both ways, a mutual understanding that extended beyond the confines of the ship. For this reason, they were loyal to her and besides, they knew what would happen if it got back to Beaman or her father she had been wronged.

CHAPTER 11

Shadows of Doubt

The sun hung high in the sky, casting a brilliant radiance over the bustling ship deck. The salty air mixed with the pungent aroma of tar and sweat as the crew worked diligently, their rhythmic shanties filling the air like an ancient chorus. Robert squinted against the harsh sunlight, his head throbbing as if a thousand hammers pounded within his skull. Girlington's laughter seemed to dance upon the wind, taunting his discomfort.

Erghh, me head feels like it's gonna explode.

Robert blinked his eyes, because they were dry, then closed them again. He could hear the ship's bell ring and seaman on deck yelling, bumping and banging. His ears were ringing.

Struggling to regain his composure, Robert steadied himself against a weathered railing, his bleary eyes fixed on the formidable figure before him. Captain Girlington, a woman of unparalleled strength and charisma, stood with an air of command, surveying her domain with an unmistakable aura of authority. Her tousled ebony hair framed a face etched with tales of adventure and her eyes, sharp as the glistening sea, held a depth of knowledge that spoke of countless maritime escapades.

Girlington was standing on the upper deck proudly and she turned around to greet him. 'Morning, Master Robert, or should I say good afternoon.'

She could sense his distress, she checked him out; his eyes were red, hair dishevelled and he still looked as if he was still three sheets to the wind.

Girlington laughed. 'Good to see you up and about! Are you sure you wouldn't like to join us on our voyage? Your liking of the mud, dirt and mushroom tasting blood is certainly a pre-requisite.'

He squinted and felt somewhat inadequate after his late rise and massive headache.

Robert tried to put on a bravado to this woman who scared him but also, who he felt attracted to despite her bossy ways.

Robert put his hand on his forehead. 'Why'd ya let me drink fancy stuff? Me tongue feels like it's wearin' a fur coat.'

Captain Girlington smiled. 'Let's just call it an initiation.'

As the crew continued their boisterous work, Robert's attention was drawn to the intricate ballet of maritime preparation. The ship, an imposing vessel with timbers weathered by countless storms, was a world of its own, alive with the synergy of man and nature. The sails unfurled like giant wings, ready to carry the ship across uncharted waters. The masts, like ancient sentinels, reached toward the heavens, their rigging a labyrinthine web that connected every corner of the vessel.

Girlington's voice cut through the cacophony, bringing Robert back to the present. 'You look like you've weathered a storm, Master Robert,' she remarked, her lips curving into a mischievous smile. 'But fear not, for the sea has a way of tempering even the most stubborn of souls.'

The crew were in the process of preparing the ship for sail. The masts were being refurbished, sails being sewn and others were scraping, re-caulking and tarring the joints of the boards on the deck. All the while they sang very loudly and deeply with their rugged baritone voices.

The crew's shanties reached a crescendo, their voices harmonising with the very essence of the ship itself. Robert's gaze shifted from Girlington to the sailors, each one a cog in this intricate mechanism, bound by a shared purpose and an unbreakable camaraderie. He felt a pull, a yearning to be a part of something greater than himself, to embrace the unknown with open arms.

Farewell an' adieu to you fair Spanish ladies,
Farewell an' adieu to you ladies of Spain,
For we've received orders for to sail for old England,
An' hope very shortly to see you again.

We'll rant an' we'll roar, like true British sailors,
We'll rant an' we'll rave across the salt seas,
'Till we strike soundings in the Channel of Old England,
From Ushant to Scilly is thirty-four leagues.

We hove our ship to, with the wind at sou'west, boys,
We hove our ship to for to take soundings clear.
In fifty-five fathoms with a fine sandy bottom,
We filled our maintops'l, up Channel did steer.

The first land we made was a point called the Deadman,
Next Ramshead off Plymouth, Start, Portland, and Wight.
We sailed then by Beachie, by Fairlee and Dungeyness,
Then bore straight away for the South Foreland Light.

Now the signal was made for the Grand Fleet to anchor,
We clewed up our tops'ls, stuck out tacks and sheets.
We stood by our stoppers, we brailed in our spankers,
And anchored ahead of the noblest of fleets.

Let every man here drink up his full bumper,
Let every man here drink up his full bowl,
And let us be jolly and drown melancholy,
Drink a health to each jovial an' true-hearted soul.

As the crew's resounding chorus enveloped them, Robert stepped forward, his heart alight with anticipation. The sun glinted off the sea's expanse, its shimmering waves a promise of adventure and discovery.

Robert tried to shake off his bottle ache and tried to look as sober as he could. He staggered up, standing and swaying beside her, trying to hide his discomfort. 'Looks like yer ready ta set sail.'

The captain frowned. 'No, not yet. It's Friday, we won't set sail on a Friday, bad luck. Besides, it will take us another day to get provisions on board. High tide on Saturday then we'll up anchor.'

Robert was struggling. 'Erggh I've got a banging headache and me mouth is as dry as ash.'

'Come on, let's help you get rid of the bottle ache.' Girlington made her way back to her cabin.

Robert followed cautiously.

She strolled back up to the desk, pulled the cork out and poured some wine, turning to Robert and holding out the goblet to him. 'Hair of the dog, it works!'

Robert stared at the goblet as if it held the secrets of the universe. He shook his head weakly, his tousled hair falling into his eyes. 'Erggh, I couldn't.'

Girlington waved off his protest with a grin. 'Go on!' she urged, her hand gesturing for him to take the offered drink. 'It's either this or Goddard's drops.'

Robert's brow furrowed in confusion. 'Goddard's Drops?'

The captain's smile widened. 'Powdered human skull, dried snake, and spirit of hartshorn,' she explained matter-of-factly.

He took the goblet from her, his nose wrinkling at the pungent scent emanating from the mixture. 'Errrgh, can't believe I'm doing this,' he muttered under his breath, 'but beats the drops!'

'It'll help, the crew swears by it, don't smell it just drink it all down!'

Robert chugged it down then shuddered.

Girlington smiled at him and his boyish ways.

The goblet of wine seemed to appease and wake him. It also gave him a tipsy feeling again. He caught sight of his saddle bag.

Girlington saw him looking. 'Yes you can take your saddle bag. Your horse is out the back of Ye Olde Black Boy fed and watered, tods of wool ready to be packed. I will lend you another horse to carry the wool.'

Robert was appreciative. 'I'll wait until you set sail, if it's alright, get me head clear. It'll take a good three days to get back to Haworth with the horse laden with wool.'

A sense of relief washed over him, mingling with a renewed surge of energy. 'Thank you,' he murmured, his voice filled with genuine gratitude.

The captain's smile softened, revealing a hint of tenderness beneath her confident exterior. 'I will lend you another horse to carry the wool,' she offered, her words a reassuring promise.

Girlington walked toward the door then stopped and turned back around, 'Well, if ya gonna stay, why don't we dine together this evening? Say at seven bells, you can tell me more of Smythe and Leeds, it must have grown. Now I must go.'

Robert staggered over and picked up his saddle bag. 'Until this evenin' then?'

Girlington marched off a spring in her step. She did not look back.

Robert watched her go and couldn't help but imagine her thin waist and long legs hidden by her loose-fitting garb.

As Robert's fingers brushed against the cool leather of his saddle bag, he couldn't help but marvel at the unexpected twists and turns that life had brought him. And as he stood, his head still slightly fuzzy from the strange concoction, he couldn't shake the feeling that he was on the brink of a new adventure.

He followed her out and strode along the deck being careful not to get in the way of seaman coming and going. He stepped carefully along the gang plank onto shore and headed for Ye Olde Black Boy.

The High Street bustled with the activity of the day, yet Wilding remained concealed, a shadow lurking in wait. His eyes narrowed as he spotted Robert emerging from the ship. He had been tracking Robert's every move, biding his time for the perfect moment.

As Robert walked along the cobblestones, his steps echoing through the air, Wilding seized his opportunity. He bolted across the street, closing the distance between them with swift and purposeful strides. With a quick and calculated move, he pressed his hand onto Robert's shoulder and the cold point of his knife against his back.

'Make a noise, you fucker, and I'll run ya through,' Wilding hissed, his voice a venomous whisper. He guided Robert down an empty alley, his grip unyielding, the knife a constant reminder of the danger that loomed.

They reached the shadowed entrance of Dunwell's Forge, the rhythmic clang of the blacksmith's hammer reverberating in the background. Wilding pushed Robert's face against the rough stone wall, his grip unrelenting. The blade of the knife dug into Robert's neck, drawing a thin line of blood.

'Where is it?' Wilding growled, his eyes aflame with a deadly intensity.

'I don't have it anymore!' Robert retorted, his voice trembling with a mixture of fear and defiance.

Wilding's grip tightened, his patience wearing thin.

They could both hear the clang, clang, clang of the hammer hitting the blacksmith's anvil.

Wilding pushed Robert's face against the wall roughly and held it there, putting his knife to his neck. 'Where is it?' he growled.

'I don't have it anymore!' Robert replied.

'You didn't fence it yet, too fine a piece, now where is it?' Wilding pushed Roberts face harder against the wall and pushed the knife deeper into his neck drawing a line of blood.

'WAIT! WAIT! It's on the ship, the captain has it! Takin' it to Europe to flog! They set sail tomorra on the high tide!'

'It seems as if yer little wench has taken a likein' to ya. NOW, yer gonna get the necklace back, da ya hear? And if ya don't, I'm gonna slit yer slut's little throat!'

'She's nothin' ta me, I'll get the necklace fer ya, bring it to ya tonight, where ya stayin?' Robert lied.

Wilding grumbled, 'Oh no ya don't, can't 'ave you trottin off again. LISTEN 'ERE. You'll bring it 'ere at nightfall, I'll be waitin' and watchin' and if ya should even look the wrong way, she gets it!'

Wilding pushed his face into the wall one last time then scurried away up High Street and disappeared down a lane.

Worriedly, Robert staggered into Ye Olde Black Boy and ordered an ale and a noggin of pottage. The patrons stared suspiciously at first until they saw Beaman's wife put them on the table in front of him.

'Captain Girlington said to lend you another 'orse until she gets back. When ya headin' off?' Beaman asked as he sat down opposite.

Robert was distracted then he realised Beaman asked him a question. 'Er… tomorra after the ship sails.'

'Mmmm, seems Captain Girlington 'as taken a bit of a likin' to ya. You know who her father is, don't ya?' Beaman asked.

'Sea Captain?' Robert was curious as Girlington was so sheepish about her father.

'Sea Captain?' Beaman put his hands on his waist and laughed a deep chesty laugh.

Other sailors joined in, 'HAHAHAH,' when hearing Robert's reply.

Robert was confused and peered around at the patrons who continued to laugh at his expense.

Beaman stopped laughing and the room went quiet. His smiling face turned to a serious glare.

He put his huge hands on the table and whispered, 'Now, you look 'ere, mate, if anythin' should happen to our Captain Girlington, if she should break a nail or shed a tear? There are twenty blokes in 'ere who will come huntin' fer ya! And more when the word gets out.'

Robert nervously peered around and all eyes were on him, then he glanced back at Beaman who hadn't taken his eyes off him.

'They will follow you to the four corners, mark me words,' Beaman whispered menacingly.

Suddenly, a knife landed in the wooden post behind Robert with a thud. He turned, his eyes widened, he took a deep breath and swallowed hard.

With a nervous gulp, Robert understood the depth of the loyalty these sailors held for their captain. As he glanced around the room, he realised that he was entangled in a web of danger, betrayal and fierce camaraderie, all set against the backdrop of a world brimming with secrets and uncertainty.

Beaman smiled a big gaping smile then stood. 'Just as long as we understand each other.' He turned and strode back to the barrels.

Robert's mind spun like a ship caught in a tempest. He sat in the courtyard, absentmindedly tending to his horse, his thoughts consumed by the tangled web of deceit and danger that had ensnared him. Beaman's warning echoed in his ears, a constant reminder of the dire consequences that awaited him should he fail to retrieve the stolen necklace.

I'll tell her, he thought. *She won't think kindly of me asking for the necklace back, but what else can I do? I don't want to involve her in this mess.*

Walking out into the courtyard, Robert tended his horse, checking her legs and lifting each hoof to check the shoes. He brushed her slowly, but all the time thinking about what transpired earlier in the day. He could feel the weight of the necklace back in the seam of his tunic.

He inspected the wool and took some from the sack. He felt it and realised how soft it was, beautiful short staple, then thought about getting it home to Haworth.

What will I say, no one would believe me? He thought about it for a while. *I'll tell Da I'm a trader and I got the coin to pay for it.*

He went up to the other horse and patted her on the neck then checked her shoes, gave her a brush and strapped the oat bag to her neck.

Robert went back inside and upstairs to one of the rooms and tried to sleep his bottle ache away.

When he awoke, the dim light filtering through the small window indicated that evening had fallen. Robert washed his face and hands, attempting to rid himself of the remnants of the day's ordeal. He wet his hair and tried to tame its unruly strands, then carefully shaved using his knife blade, wincing as he nicked his chin.

It was late, and Robert knew he had to act swiftly. He descended the stairs and slipped out of the inn. His heart pounded as he scanned the surroundings, spotting Mr. Wilding lurking behind a wall, a sinister figure concealed in the shadows.

Robert walked quickly to the docks. He nodded to the gangway watch who were told of his impending arrival. He made his way up the gang plank and onto the deck, then climbed the stairs to the captain's cabin. He gently knocked on the door.

'Come in,' Girlington's voice called from within.

As he pushed open the door, a flicker of surprise crossed his face. The cabin was bathed in warm candlelight, the transformation striking. Gone were the charts and nautical instruments, replaced by elegant silver candlesticks and fine china.

Girlington was nowhere to be seen, then he noticed the oak fivefold screen in the corner of the cabin.

An alluring voice came from behind it. 'Do you like it? It's from Flanders, the screen I mean.'

Suddenly, Girlington stepped out from behind the screen, gone was the dirty, white shirt, dirty ruffled collar, large dirty and stained, white cuffs and brown, knee-length boots.

She wore a magnificent green velvet dress, the skirt and bodice joined at the waist with shiny light green ribbon and decorated with white glass beads. The collar and sleeves were decorated with bright white lace and her hair was pushed back off her face all except two ringlets. Red lip colour was applied to her lips and cheeks and there it was, the sapphire, resplendent around her neck.

Robert just stood there in awe for a moment not thinking about the difficulties of the day or the sapphire. 'You look wonderful and this room, the silver and china and… Captain Girlington… you…'

She cut him off. 'In here you can call me Ursula,' she said charismatically.

'Alright, Ursula.' He smiled. 'Where did the name "Girlington" come from?'

'My mother and father didn't want me named anything which could tie me to him, so they gave me my mother's maiden name Arlington. He felt my real name wasn't going to work so, a girl captain... Girlington.'

The knock at the door signalled the arrival of the cook, his presence heralding the start of an unexpected feast. The cook stepped in with a tray filled with silver plate covers. He placed them individually on the table then left quickly closing the door behind him.

'Please sit, we don't dine well at sea, so I make an effort before we set sail.' She removed the silver plate covers to reveal one plate of lamb and one of fried chicken covered in nutmeg, cloves and cinnamon. There was a plate full of sweets, cakes, comfits and fruits.

The lamb was marinated to perfection, its juices mingling with a harmonious blend of spices that included nutmeg, cloves and cinnamon. Each inhalation revealed a symphony of aromatic notes, with the warm, woody spices dancing delicately around the rich, savoury essence of the meat.

The crispy, golden-brown exterior of the chicken crackled with a symphony of satisfying sounds and the scent that rose from it was nothing short of enchanting. The chicken, bathed in a fragrant blend of nutmeg, cloves and cinnamon, seemed to capture the very essence of comfort and indulgence. The spices had fused with the golden crust to create a tantalising crust that held within it the promise of tender, juicy meat.

Beside these savory delights lay a plate overflowing with a rainbow of confections. Sweets of every kind were arranged with care, forming an edible masterpiece that teased the senses. Cakes, their sugary exteriors adorned with delicate frosting flowers, exuded a heavenly scent of vanilla and buttercream. Comfits, small candies coated in vibrant sugar coatings, added a burst of fruity and floral fragrances to the air. 'Ursula, can I?' Robert reached for the wine bottle and filled both their silver goblets with imported wine.

A genuine smile touched Ursula's lips. 'Of course, Robert. Enjoy.'

‘I’ve never seen so much food; this would feed me family for a week.’ Robert ripped off a chicken leg and started to chew and swallow it hungrily.

She picked up her goblet and took a sip, watching him devour his chicken then reach for the lamb. He pushed a cake into his mouth while chewing the lamb with his mouth open.

The clinking of silverware and the soft murmur of their surroundings filled the cabin as they dined. Robert, feeling the effects of the wine, emptied his goblet in a single gulp before continuing to feast.

‘Robert, we don’t set sail until tomorrow, there’s ample time,’ Ursula remarked, her tone gentle as she watched him slow his eating.

Realising, he lifted his eyes, with his mouth full of food. ‘Sorry, I’m not used to bein’ in the company of fine folk.’ He was apologetic and slowed his eating and chewing.

He swallowed his mouthful, burped then filled the goblet with more wine wash it down.

‘I’ve something important to tell you,’ he began, his voice more serious now. ‘The man I mentioned earlier, the one who’s been pursuing me for the necklace... he’s here. I encountered him in High Street this afternoon. He wants the necklace back.’

Ursula’s brows furrowed as she considered this new development. She rose from her seat and paced, her thoughts churning. ‘This could indeed complicate matters. Where is he staying?’

Robert’s eyes were troubled as he answered. ‘I don’t know. He wouldn’t reveal anything, just demanded I meet him outside Ye Olde Black Boy tonight, or he’d harm you.’

A determined glint sparkled in Ursula’s eyes as she made a decision. ‘Describe him to me.’

Robert’s description painted a vivid picture of the man – his attire, his facial hair, his appearance. Ursula’s mind raced as she considered her next move.

'Wait here,' she instructed before calling a seaman and issuing a quiet command.

Moments later, she returned, a reassuring smile on her lips. 'I've sent word to Beaman. He'll handle the situation. You're not alone in this, Robert.'

Her words brought a sense of relief to Robert's heart. He couldn't help but feel a growing admiration for this enigmatic captain who had shown him unexpected kindness and support.

'Maybe I should go, Ursula. I don't want to put you in any danger.' Robert hesitated, his concern for her evident.

Ursula reached out and touched his hand, her touch gentle yet firm. 'Don't worry, Robert. Beaman is a loyal and capable friend. He will ensure our safety. For now, let us enjoy the night. Eat, drink and forget your worries.'

As the wine continued to flow and stories were exchanged, Robert found himself opening up to Ursula in ways he hadn't anticipated. The walls he had built around himself began to crumble, replaced by a sense of camaraderie and connection that defied the circumstances that had brought them together. And as the candlelight flickered and danced, casting shadows across the cabin, a bond was forged, one that would carry them through the stormy seas that lay ahead.

The cabin was bathed in the soft glow of candlelight, and the night was now in full bloom as Robert and Ursula exchanged stories that wove the fabric of their lives. They shared their pasts, the experiences and memories that had shaped them into the individuals they were today.

They spoke of Smythe and Leeds and Robert told her of his twin brother John and his wife Rosie. He told her of the early days in Leeds and told her of Leeds.

As Robert spoke of his twin brother John and his wife Rosie, Ursula found herself captivated by the vivid picture he painted of his family and their life on the moors. She listened intently as he described the struggles and triumphs of his family, the legacy of their land, and the challenges brought on by the enclosures in the north-west.

She listened intently with her chin in her hand and marvelled at how their lives were so different.

Ursula told him of the boarding school in Kent and how she was taught to be a lady all the while dreaming of being on the open sea. She spoke of the good times with her mother and father and how they revelled in each other's company when he was home.

They laughed, they shared, and they flirted, their conversation flowing as freely as the wine in their goblets. Time seemed to suspend, cocooning them in a momentary reprieve from the worries that had plagued their thoughts earlier.

As the night deepened, Robert's mood shifted, the weight of his predicament settling back upon him. He mentioned the looming threat of Wilding and the stolen necklace, a sombre note that dimmed the joy of their evening.

It started to get late and thoughts of Wilding and the necklace dampened Robert's mood. 'I should go.'

'Or… you could spend the night here with me. It's probably a safer option because there'll be a security watch stationed outside my door all night.'

Robert's gaze met hers, torn between his desire to protect her and his own longing for safety and companionship. He whispered his concerns, his worry etched across his features. 'I appreciate your offer, but I don't want to put you in any danger.'

Ursula reached across the table, her fingers brushing against his. 'Robert, I've navigated dangerous waters and faced many storms. I can handle myself. Besides, I've made my choice and I choose to help you. You're not alone in this.'

A mixture of gratitude and warmth flooded Robert's heart as he met Ursula's gaze. Her unwavering support gave him a sense of comfort he hadn't expected to find. He considered her offer, his mind racing as he weighed the possibilities.

In one swift motion and before Robert could react, Ursula lifted the knife she was eating with and pointed it at his throat.

Robert didn't move but swallowed gazing at her curiously.

She smiled and lifted the knife under his chin. He stood slowly as she applied more pressure.

She also stood, then cut one button after another until all buttons of his tunic were sitting on the floor of the cabin.

He reached for her wrist and grabbed it forcing the knife out of her hand, it dropped to the floor.

As the candlelight flickered and cast dancing shadows across the cabin, Robert and Ursula stood in companionable silence, a newfound connection bridging the gap between their worlds. The night held a promise of safety and the magic of possibility, the weight of their troubles temporarily set aside beneath the starry sky.

In that dimly lit chamber, time seemed to slow to a tender crawl. Their lips met in a dance of longing, a kiss that spoke of all the unspoken words, all the emotions swirling between them. Soft, yet powerful, it was a connection that sent shivers down their spines and ignited a fire deep within their souls.

She gasped for air as his lips traced a path along her neck, sending electrifying sensations coursing through her. Her heartbeat echoed in her ears, a rhythmic symphony of desire. As his fingers deftly worked at the ribbon of her bodice, a sudden surge of uncertainty gripped her. Her hand halted his, their fingers entwined in a silent plea.

They embraced and kissed a long soft kiss. She breathed heavily as he kissed her neck. He pulled the ribbon from her boddice, but she grabbed his hand.

'Blow the candles out,' she whispered. She sauntered over and disappeared behind the screen.

Robert blew the candles out excitedly and started to undress, first his tunic then his boots and then his breaches. He crept over to the bed and lifted the elaborately decorated blanket and climbed in. It was only a single bed but much softer and more comfortable than what he was used to.

The moonlight revealed her in all her naked splendour, a masterpiece of curves and contours. Her breasts, softly illuminated, beckoned his gaze, a delicate invitation that stirred his senses. He averted his eyes, yet found himself drawn back by an irresistible force, his desire intermingled with a reverence that left him breathless.

She sashayed over to him and he raised a hand to her. Lifting the blanket, he shuffled over toward the wall so she could slide in.

In that hushed moment, time held no sway. The world outside ceased to exist, leaving only their entwined destinies and the unspoken promise that hung between them. Love, longing, and vulnerability converged, a symphony of emotions too powerful to be contained within the confines of that moonlit chamber.

They kissed gently and she could feel his manhood against her leg. She gently caressed it until it hardened.

Robert moved to lay on top of her, but she stopped him and pushed him back down on the bed. She lifted herself up and swung her leg over so she straddled him. She could feel his manhood on her lower back and reached around and caressed it once again. Lifting herself from his lower abdomen, she angled his manhood inside her. She slowly moved her buttocks then allowed her weight to drop, she paused, then lowered herself once again.

His member was fully engulfed.

She gasped then lifted herself slowly up and down.

He moved her hair so he could see her breasts and gently rubbed them, touching the nipples delicately. She rolled her hips and murmured with delight.

He closed his eyes then opened them and was fascinated by her love making as she threw her head back and groaned.

She continued to roll her hips; her breaths started to quicken so she rose and lowered herself as far as she could murmuring.

Robert put his hands on her buttocks and supported her; he could hear and feel the wetness.

She quickened her pace up and down then put her hands on his chest for extra support. Quicker, quicker she could feel it rising in her, quicker, quicker, she started to perspire. The pressure in her loins increased she let out a slight moan as did Robert. She started to grind her pubis against his, quicker, faster.

She let out a small whimper and collapsed on him totally spent, breathing heavy. She shuddered then shuddered again and took a deep breath.

Robert let her lay there on his chest to catch her breath; he could feel his manhood becoming flaccid.

She lifted her buttocks and slid herself off, kissing him gently on the cheek.

He put his arm under her neck.

She stroked his chest hairs and they laid there quietly in the darkness.

Her breathing eventually returned to normal she closed her eyes and laid there quietly listening to the beat of his heart. He moved the sweaty hair from her face and gaped at her in the moonlight. He smiled as he thought about Oliver Cromwell's decree, *Intercourse should not be enjoyed.* He grinned and kissed her gently on the forehead.

After some time, she whispered, 'I suppose you're wondering… well… I'll tell you… many years ago… my father took me to the Caribbean, a small island full of sugar plantations and of course slaves. We stayed in this huge house, you could sit on the balcony and watch the slaves working the sugar cane.'

She continued, 'The slave's village was on the west coast of the island, nobody else could go there. One night, when the slaves headed home, I snuck out and followed them. They went through the jungle up hills and then down to the most beautiful cove you could imagine.'

'The water was so clear and the sun was going down; there were parrots in the trees and monkeys. There were small huts made of wattle and thatched palm rooves. Children were swimming and playing on the beach until their mothers called them in as it started to get dark.

'I watched a young couple frolicking along the beach smiling, laughing and holding hands. They scurried to one of the bohios' and went inside.

'I slid quietly down the hill and crept up to the side of their hut and peeked inside between the wattle. There was a small fire in the middle of the hut and the smoke arose and dissipated through a small hole in the roof.

'They sat down together on a small mattress on the sandy floor and kissed. Then he undid her pareo and it slipped down.'

'She was so beautiful, so dark I'd never seen anything like it. He stood and untied his pareo, allowing it to drop, although it did catch.' Ursula giggled. 'I watched silently. They kissed and then she pushed him down on the mattress and… well I watched; it was almost heathen. Their black bodies shiny with perspiration thrusting and gyrating to the sounds of the jungle. I never forgot; it was one of the most memorable moments of my life.'

Robert laid there in the darkness, his fingers tracing delicate patterns along her arm, the soft contours of her skin a comfort against the turmoil in his mind. The events of the day replayed like a relentless loop, each scene etched into his consciousness, a haunting reminder of the choices that had brought him to this point. The room was enveloped in silence, broken only by the gentle rhythm of their breathing.

She nestled closer, seeking refuge in his embrace, her warmth seeping into the very core of his being. The rise and fall of her chest, so steady and peaceful, served as a stark contrast to the storm brewing within him. As sleep claimed her, he envied the tranquillity that had eluded him, his eyes remaining open, fixated on the inky abyss that surrounded them.

Wilding's face danced before his eyes, a kaleidoscope of emotions reflected in those hauntingly familiar eyes. Doubt gnawed at the edges of his resolve, tugging at the threads of his carefully constructed plan. He couldn't shake the nagging feeling that there was more to the story, hidden layers of truth that had yet to be unveiled. But he had come too far to turn back now. The stakes were higher than he could have ever imagined.

'I must stick to the plan, no matter what,' he whispered into the darkness, the words a solemn vow that echoed in the stillness. He had made a promise, not just to himself, but to those who depended on him, to a cause that transcended his own desires. The weight of responsibility settled heavily on his shoulders, a burden he carried willingly, even as uncertainty gnawed at his resolve.

Time seemed to stretch on, each passing moment laden with the weight of his contemplation. The room remained cloaked in shadows, a sanctuary where secrets were both kept and unearthed. His mind was a labyrinth, his thoughts twisting and turning, tracing the intricate paths that led him to this juncture. He couldn't afford to falter now, not when the pieces were finally falling into place.

He glanced down at her, her face a portrait of serenity in slumber, a reminder of the fragility of the moments they shared. He brushed a strand of hair from her forehead, a tender gesture that masked the turmoil that churned within him. He would protect her, he vowed, just as he would see this through to the end. The echoes of Wilding's voice, a whispered plea for justice, resonated in his mind, a driving force that propelled him forward.

With a final, lingering touch, he allowed himself to close his eyes, a silent prayer whispered into the void. The darkness welcomed him, enfolding him in its embrace, as he embarked on a journey that would test the limits of his courage and the depths of his convictions. The path ahead was shrouded in uncertainty, but he was resolute. He would face whatever challenges awaited him, armed with nothing but his unwavering determination and the memory of a promise made in the dead of night.

As the hours stretched on, dreams and shadows intertwined, a tapestry woven from the threads of hope and doubt. And through it all, Robert remained, a solitary figure in the quietude, poised on the precipice of destiny.

CHAPTER 12

The Tides of Fate

The knock echoed through the cabin, pulling Robert from his restless slumber. She was already dressed, the urgency in the air palpable as she yanked her boots on. The ship's wooden planks creaked beneath her steps as she rose from the bed, her heart racing with a mix of anticipation and trepidation. Roberts eyes met hers as if sensing the gravity of the moment.

'Quickly, dress and meet me on deck!' Ursula's voice was edged with a determined urgency, her gaze locking onto his before she swung open the door and disappeared into the corridor, the door closing with a soft thud behind her.

She climbed down the steps and the ship's first mate was waiting for her. 'Captain,' he whispered in her ear.

Ursula waited, she watched as Robert stepped through the doorway, 'Follow me, Robert!'

They climbed down the steps to the tween deck then down the ladder to the hull.

It was dark but by the light of the one candle, Robert could see a bloodied man tied to the main mast. His chest was bloodied and his long hair was wet, his bald head bled. He slumped unconsciously.

The captain nodded at Beaman.

He picked up a bucket of water and threw it on the unconscious man.

The stranger groaned.

Ursula's gaze settled on Beaman, the ship's burly crew member whose face was etched with a mixture of grim determination and weariness. Ursula watched intently, her eyes unwavering, as Beaman took hold of the man's hair and directed his gaze toward her.

'Blacksmith next door to the tavern seen him wandering around fer the last couple days. Hidin' in the entrance ta Dunwell's Forge watchin' who was coming and going from the tavern. He crept up behind him and knocked him on the head with a poker, then called us. We thought we best bring 'im straight 'ere. Oh, we found this on 'im.' Beaman handed Girlington a parchment, which she unrolled and read to herself.

A chill ran down Ursula's spine as the puzzle pieces began to click into place. The man before her was no ordinary stowaway; he was a spy, an infiltrator in their midst. Her fingers reached out, accepting a parchment from Beaman, its surface worn and crinkled from its clandestine journey.

With a sense of purpose, Ursula unrolled the parchment and perused its contents, her eyes narrowing as the words came into focus. The words painted a picture of intrigue and deception, weaving a tapestry of conspiracy that threatened to unravel the fragile balance of their world.

'Is that him?' Girlington glanced at Robert who was still adjusting his eyes to the poor light.

He took a step closer and stared at the man's face while Edwin held the candle closer. 'Yeah, that's 'im alright.'

Girlington turned to Beaman. 'You know what to do… and Beaman, make it last.'

She climbed up the ladder and Robert followed her. 'Ursula… now what?'

As she read, a steely resolve settled over Ursula, her gaze lifting from the parchment to meet Robert's. In that moment, they shared an unspoken understanding, a silent promise to unearth the truth hidden within the shadows. The sea whispered its secrets, the ship's timbers groaning in agreement, as Ursula folded the parchment and looked once more at the man before her.

When Robert got up to the deck, he caught up to her, held her arm and asked again, 'Did ya not hear me?'

In one swift movement she pulled her knife and held it to Robert's throat. 'Do not presume too much because of last night! Now, you can call me Captain Girlington!' She spoke with authority and bluntness, gone was the charismatic, alluring voice.

She stared into his eyes fiercely. 'This parchment is a warrant for your arrest on suspected thievery and signed by the Aldermen of Leeds. If you're caught, you'll be tried and you'll hang!'

Robert swallowed slowly and glanced down at the blade at his throat then up into her eyes. 'DO IT!' he demanded.

Girlington could feel the eyes of her crew upon her; they stopped what they were doing and waited. She smiled, as did her crew, then withdrew her knife and put it back in the scabbard. Her crew continued readying for sail.

Ursula's steps were purposeful as she strode past Robert, a tempest of emotions swirling within her. He took a steadying breath, watching her retreating figure before following suit. As he approached the entrance to the cabins, the security watch, a silent guardian of the ship's inner sanctum, interposed himself with a steely resolve.

The security watch who was standing next to the entrance to the cabins, stepped in front and put his hand on the handle of his knife.

Robert went to take a step around him.

The watch took a step in the same direction and barred his entry.

Robert heard a cough from behind. He turned around and Beaman was standing there.

Beaman's reassuring cough broke the impasse, a signal that diffused the tension like a gust of wind dispersing storm clouds. With a subtle gesture, Beaman extended his hand, a silent invitation to leave the brewing conflict behind. Robert hesitated for a moment before relenting, his shoulders slumping as he turned and followed Beaman's lead.

The journey back to Ye Olde Black Boy was a muted procession, each step carrying the weight of unanswered questions and unresolved emotions. They entered the familiar tavern, its atmosphere a stark contrast to the tempestuous sea of emotions that had roiled within them mere moments ago.

Beaman pointed to an empty table then called out to a rather stout middle-aged lady, 'Go 'ave a seat, lad. Wife, bring us ale!'

The drink arrived, a symbol of solace in times of uncertainty, and Beaman took a long swig before addressing Robert's pensive silence.

'I suggest you be on yer way, lad. Come now, let me buy ya an ale and put ya on yer way. Ya horse is loaded and waitin' fer ya.'

Beaman took a swig of his ale, and put his huge forearms down on the table. 'Don't take it personally; ya best to forget 'er now.'

'But I love her.' Robert's voice wavered, his heartache laid bare in his gaze as he recalled the tender moments they had shared.

Robert frowned… *Forget her? But I love her!* He dropped his chin sadly. Beaman's laughter rumbled through the air, a response that held a touch of amusement and a hint of sage wisdom. 'Ah, lad, matters of the heart can be a treacherous sea to navigate. Sometimes it's best to let go and set sail for new horizons.'

'And Wilding?'

Beaman sniggered. 'Oh, don't you worry about 'im, we'll take 'im ta sea and put 'im in Davy Jones' locker. Cause ya no more bother.'

As the conversation continued, the weight of the truth began to settle within Robert. The revelation about Wilding's fate sent a chill down his spine, a stark reminder of the perilous world in which they all resided. The tide of emotions ebbed and flowed, carrying him through a sea of introspection as he wrestled with his own demons.

Beaman skulled the rest of his ale and plonked the tankard down on the table. 'Come now, let's get you on yer way.'

Robert followed Beaman out into the courtyard. Three crewmen loaded the pack horse with the wool Ursula had promised.

Still melancholy, Robert attached his saddle bag and mounted his horse. 'When you see her, tell her I will return in two months with the cloth and her horse.'

Beaman smiled sympathetically. 'I will. Safe journey, Robert.'

As Robert rode away, the courtyard fading into the distance, he couldn't help but reflect on the unexpected twists and turns that had brought him to this point. The truth was a complex tapestry, woven with threads of loyalty, sacrifice and untold secrets. And only Beaman, the keeper of hidden knowledge, knew the full extent of the arrangement Captain Girlington had made, a single condition that would forever shape the course of their destinies.

Only Beaman knew the arrangement Captain Girlington made with her father. 'One condition,' she agreed to before he would allow her to captain *The Pearl*.

Under no circumstances was she to promise herself to any man while still aboard *The Pearl*. He always blamed himself for his wife's death. Being a superstitious soul, he was adamant the bad luck which affected him would not be passed to any other. He made her swear and she did.

Beaman, Edwin and Horace watched Robert slowly canter out of the courtyard, pulling the horse holding the sack of wool behind him.

'Do ya think he'll be back?' Horace asked.

'He seems like a good lad, but not if he's smart.' Beaman wandered back into the tavern.

The trio returned to the familiar warmth of the tavern, the scent of ale and the hum of conversation enveloping them. Beaman's eyes flicked toward the corner table where Captain Girlington sat, her form a picture of quiet contemplation. Without hesitation, he approached her and took a seat opposite her, a silent understanding passing between them.

The air was heavy with unspoken words as Beaman allowed her the space to gather her thoughts, his patience a testament to the depth of their bond. Ursula's fingers traced the rim of her ale tankard, her gaze unfocused as she wrestled with the conflicting emotions that churned within her.

Beaman was silent and waited patiently before speaking. 'Ya know, ya can't keep going on like this. You'll have ta settle down sometime – kids, nice 'ouse.'

She ignored him and took a swig of her ale.

Beaman wasn't insulted by her silence as it was a conversation they had many times before. 'Surely, you've got enough stashed away by now so you don't need ta keep doin' this.'

Ursula was frustrated. 'Don't know if I'm ready and besides, I really don't know what all the fuss is about getting married and being at sea.'

Beaman's eyes bore into hers, a silent understanding passing between them. He leaned forward, his voice lowered to a hushed murmur that only she could hear. 'You know how superstitious yer father is. He just doesn't want ya endin' up the same way as 'im – old and alone.'

Her frustration palpable, Ursula took another swig of her ale, as if seeking solace in the bitter liquid. 'But the sea's in my blood. It's not fair he should place such demands on me.'

Ursula shook her head in defiance, 'But the seas in my blood, it's not fair he should place such demands on me.'

Beaman's voice softened, his words carrying the weight of years of friendship and shared history. 'Yer father just wants the best fer ya. He told me ta keep an eye on ya, and I'll uphold that promise until the day I die.'

Girlington gazed down at the table sadly.

'Did ya like 'im?' Beaman asked.

'Of course, or else I wouldn't invite him for dinner.'

'Mmmmm, said he'd be back in two months with the cloth, what will ya do then?'

Ursula's eyes held a glimmer of uncertainty, a reflection of the crossroads that lay before her. 'I suppose… I'll have to decide whether to seize the opportunity for change or continue sailing these uncharted waters.'

Beaman's weathered hand reached across the table, resting atop hers in a gesture of support. 'Whatever path you choose, Captain, I'll stand by your side, as I always have.'

And as the tavern bustled around them, their shared understanding and unbreakable bond served as a silent testament to the ties that bound them together – bonds forged by the sea, by duty, and by the unspoken promise that neither of them would ever truly be alone.

'Now what about the thief-taker?' Beaman asked quietly.

'We will take him to sea. He threatened to slit my throat, so better make a point of it.'

Beaman's face was flushed with anger. 'Did he now? They will be his last words!'

Girlington whispered, 'We'll do it off Spurn Point, strong tides will take him away, we can't have him drifting back to shore. Too many questions will be asked if he's working for the alderman.'

☆

Back in her cabin, Captain Girlington opened the strongbox to look at the sapphire. It was gone! *Damn him all to hell!*

The provisions loaded, Captain Girlington stood on the foredeck watching Beaman order to sail.

On the foredeck, Beaman's voice sliced through the night like a blade. His orders were met with swift and practiced action as the crew scurried to obey. The sailors knew the importance of their task – to carry out the captain's will without hesitation.

'HANDS ALOFT TO LOOSE THE FORE TOP. MAIN TOP. FOR TOPM' STAYS,' Beaman yelled.

'HANDS ALOFT TO LOOSE THE FORE TOP. MAIN TOP. FOR TOPM'ST STAYS, I MATE,' called out Edwin.

Seamen scattered and climbed the shrouds.

Beaman bellowed, 'LAY AWAY.' His voice echoed once more, a rallying cry that brought the crew back to the present moment. Their mission was far from over, and the crew knew that their unity and skill were crucial in carrying out the rest of their plans.

'ON DECK!' Horace stood on the foot rope and untied the hitch.

Beaman peered up and bellowed, 'ALOFT! MAIN TOP LOOSE TO THE BUNT!'

'READY CAPTAIN.' Beaman gazed over at the captain.

The captain nodded her head. 'LET FALL MATE!'

Beaman glanced at the captain and bellowed, 'Aye captain, LET FALL!'

The crew on the deck were at their stations ready to haul.

Beaman called out, 'MARRY UP YOUR GEAR!'

The sails were pulled taut and the main topsail set, Beaman watched for the captain's signal.

Captain Girlington called out to Beaman, 'ALL HANDS TO BRACE AROUND.'

'Aye, Captain, ALL HANDS TO BRACE AROUND!'

The Pearl cut through the waters of the Humber past Salt End then catching the wind they navigated south towards Spurn Bight. They sailed east through the gap at Spurn Point then out into deep water.

The captain glanced at Beaman and directed her eyes toward the ladder leading to the hull.

Captain Girlington stood at the helm, her steely gaze fixed on the horizon. Beside her, Beaman stood vigilant, his weathered face etched with a blend of resolve and anticipation. The time had come to deliver their justice to the thief-taker who had dared to cross their path.

As the ship navigated through the narrow gap at Spurn Point, a signal passed between the captain and Beaman. A silent understanding that it was time to execute their plan. Girlington's eyes flicked toward the ladder leading to the hull, a gesture not lost on Beaman.

With a synchronised effort, the crewmen hauled Wilding's limp body onto the deck, his bindings preventing any struggle. The thief-taker was dishevelled, his appearance a stark contrast to the arrogance he had once displayed. Horace's bucket of water brought Wilding to a groggy state, his senses returning just enough to comprehend his dire situation.

Edwin picked him up underneath the arms.

Wilding was unsteady on his feet. He dropped to his knees. His hair was wet and drooped over his face. His chest was scarred and the congealed blood dried around his mouth and chin.

Beaman pulled him up with his bindings. 'Come on, boyo, won't be too long now and it'll all be over.'

Horace tied a rope around his ankles and another to his bindings. Crewmen from both the port and starboard side pulled him to the stern. They sat Wilding on the edge with his feet dangling over.

Beaman yelled at the crew, 'LAY AWAY!'

Wilding fell into the water with a splash.

The crewmen started walking toward the bow pulling the rope behind them along the port and starboard side of the ship. Wilding's body was dragged along the keel.

The rest of the crew cheered then ran to both the port and starboard sides of the vessel. They could see the sea turn red.

The crewmen kept pulling and pulling then they felt resistance and stopped.

Beaman noticed what was happening and helped them pull. The rope went slack.

Captain Girlington watched as the frayed end of the rope appeared over the bow.

Beaman stared at Captain Girlington. 'Barnacles sliced it, he must a' got caught up!'

The captain's eyes met Beaman's, a shared understanding passing between them. The sea had granted Wilding a temporary reprieve, a chance to cheat death once more. As the frayed end of the rope dangled over the bow, the crew stood frozen, grappling with the unpredictable currents of destiny.

In that moment, *The Pearl* became a vessel not only of vengeance but of uncertainty, its crew caught in the ebb and flow of fate's relentless tide. The thief-taker's escape left a bitter taste, a reminder that even the best-laid plans could be thwarted by forces beyond their control.

☆

As Wilding was pulled into the water, he took a deep breath. He wasn't as near to unconsciousness as they thought. He moved his body around and took up the slack. He gripped the barnacles on the keel with his feet to slow his movement, then rubbed his bindings on the barnacles frantically. Once freed he swam dolphin-like over to the rudder.

Wilding's head burst through the surface of the water; his chest felt like it was about to burst; he took deep breaths and looked above. His feet stung and there was a cloud of blood around him. He took another deep breath and dove down to untie the bindings around his ankles. The water was cold and he shivered. It took several times before the bindings came loose.

Wilding's survival instincts propelled him onward. He dove beneath the water once more, his body moving with aching determination. The ship sailed away, its sail catching the wind, and Wilding watched it retreat into the distance. His muscles screamed in protest, yet he pressed on, his resolve unbroken.

Hours stretched into an agonizing eternity as he kicked, every movement fuelled by sheer willpower. The peninsula loomed in the distance, a beacon of hope that kept him focused despite the torment that wracked his body.

He floated there for a while, catching his breath then focused west and could see the peninsula about three miles away. He turned on his back and started kicking his feet. A trail of blood followed him through the water as he went. Every few minutes he would stop and float to see if he was going in the right direction.

It took six hours to float back to Spurn Point. When he crawled onto the beach he collapsed, the blood from his feet awash in the sand and small surf.

The sun was going down, when he finally woke and he grimaced from the sting on his feet. He gazed down and caught sight of a small crab feeding on the skin dangling loosely from his foot. He grabbed it quickly and shoved it in his mouth chewing and crunching it.

Hands trembling, he grabbed his ankle and turned his foot. His feet were red raw punctured and grazed, with shreds of skin hanging loosely like long, white bands of white seaweed. He ripped pieces of cloth from his undershirt and tied it around his feet.

As the sun dipped below the horizon, casting long shadows across the beach, Wilding's eyes flickered with newfound resolve. He may have narrowly escaped the clutches of death, but his journey was far from over.

Wilding tried to stand but it was excruciatingly painful and he collapsed onto his knees in the sand. He crawled over to a piece of driftwood and used it to help him stand. He limped up the dunes to the tree line, wincing with each step.

He had a loathing for Robert Rushworth and his slut like no other and vowed revenge. First he would wait until his feet healed then return to Leeds to find Rushworth's brother. *He would know where Robert's gone.* If he couldn't get the necklace, he could still earn the reward for capturing the thief who took it.

In an effort to shield himself from the cold and unforgiving sand, Wilding pulled leaves and fashioned a makeshift shelter around him. He cocooned himself within the foliage, seeking refuge from the harsh elements as he drifted into a restless sleep. His dreams were tainted by visions of his impending revenge, a storm that raged within him even in his slumber.

The next morning, he awoke to the distant sounds of childish laughter and sat up. He squinted and peered down on the beach and could see a Puritan man and two children digging in the sand for Periwinkles. They each held a wooden bucket and a small spade.

'HELP!' Wilding called out, 'HELP!'

They couldn't hear him above the sound of the surf coming in so he waited between breaks and shouted again, 'HELP!'

Finally, Isaiah lifted his head, 'Did you hear, child?'

The children stopped what they were doing and scanned the beach, 'Tis comin' from over there, Father.' They started running over to where they heard the call come from.

'Children, come back!' Isaiah raced after them.

They stopped at the top of the dune and were motionless just staring.

When Isaiah arrived, he stood beside them putting his arms around them protectively. They gazed suspiciously at the stranger.

Wilding pleaded, 'Please help, me feet, I can't stand!'

Isaiah took a step toward him. 'What are ya doin' all the way out 'ere?'

Wilding replied hesitantly, 'Fell overboard, swam back ta shore and cut me feet on barnacles.'

Isaiah bent down and tried to remove the bloodied cloth from Wilding's foot. 'Where ya from?'

'Boarded in Hull.' Wilding groaned as Isaiah removed the bloodied cloth from one of his feet.

'Looks nasty, we better get ya back to camp so I can tend to those cuts. Tis not far.' He was suspicious of him but couldn't leave him out in the open injured and cold. It would be an un-Godly thing to do. It was a sandy beach and no barnacles for miles. He wondered how he cut up his feet.

Wilding used his driftwood stick to help him stand and as he did, scowled from the pain.

‘Here, let me help you.’ Isaiah put Wilding’s arm around his neck. He helped him down to the hard sand.

Wilding’s eyes met Isaiah’s, a silent acknowledgment of their fragile alliance. As they began the journey back to the camp, their footsteps marked the beginning of an unexpected partnership forged by necessity and circumstance. The path ahead was uncertain, fraught with challenges and suspicions but for now, Wilding found himself leaning on the unlikely kindness of a Puritan stranger.

‘We have a small hut down the beach, come here ta collect the Periwinkles. We ‘ave a horse and cart we can get ya back as far as Skeffling on the morrow.’

Wilding limped along the beach for about half a mile, then up into the dunes. He could see the small hut. The children ran ahead.

Isaiah called out after them, ‘Jobe, stoke and feed the fire, son.’

Jobe kept running and called out, ‘Yes, Father!’

The small hut nestled within the dunes provided a semblance of shelter and respite. Wilding’s weakened body was eased onto the straw mattress, his face etched with a mixture of pain and gratitude. He watched as Isaiah bustled around the small space, a sense of urgency underlying his actions. The Puritan’s stern demeanour did little to mask his concern for the injured stranger.

Isaiah helped him in and plonked him down on the rolled-out straw mattress. ‘Sit here fer a minute and I’ll take another look at those feet. Fern, boil some water and put the fish knife in the coals.’

Isaiah looked at his children with pride. ‘My children, Jobe and Fern. Jobe is the oldest. We come ‘ere each week collect Periwinkles and God willin’ fish when they’re bitin’.’

‘Could I ‘ave some water and if ya got anything to eat…’ Wilding asked.

‘Of course, we’ll cook up some fish.’ Isaiah’s face turned serious. ‘But let’s get something straight: yer no sailor. I seen ya hands, smooth as a baby’s bum and ya didn’t cut those feet on barnacles round ‘ere.

So, keep yer business to yerself. We'll feed ya and take ya ta Skeffling but then yer on yer own. Fern, how's the water comin' along?'

Wilding grumbled, 'Yer, right. I ran in with some pirates. They tried to keelhaul me, but I escaped.'

Wilding's story of encountering pirates rolled off his tongue, a half-truth that sought to paint a desperate picture. Isaiah's scepticism remained, his suspicions lingering like a shadow, but his commitment to aiding the injured man was unwavering.

He helped Wilding lay down with his feet towards the fire. His son stood behind and held a candle nearby so his father could see. He turned away when he saw the bottoms of the stranger's feet.

Isaiah frowned as he undid the bandages and lifted the flaps of skin from the soles of his feet. 'Fern, go the beach and get some sea water. We'll use it ta clean the wounds. Jacob, get the jug of Brandy from my bag.'

Jobe put the candle down, retrieved the ceramic jug and gave it to his father who took a large swig then gave it to Wilding. 'Take a good swig 'cause this is gonna hurt.'

Wilding took another swig then gave it back. He lifted the largest piece of skin to reveal the muscle and ligaments exposed. There were still pieces of shell and barnacle imbedded in the heal of his foot. He gently removed them with his fingers and a small, sharp knife.

Isaiah tried to put some of the skin back over the wounds but it was wrinkly and soft and didn't match the lacerations. 'Fern, pass me the knife from the fire. Jobe, give 'im yer belt to bite down on.'

He carefully took the handle from her while Jacob placed his leather belt in Wilding's mouth.

The air grew tense as Isaiah readied the hot iron, the anticipation hanging heavy in the air. The scent of burning flesh mingled with the crackling of the fire, and the small space seemed to close in on them. Wilding's grip on the leather belt tightened, his knuckles white as he braced himself for the searing pain.

The first touch of the iron sent shockwaves of agony through Wilding's body, his screams muffled by the belt clenched between his teeth. Isaiah's unwavering hand held the iron steady, determination etched across his features. The ordeal was a test of endurance, a battle between pain and survival.

'Is he dead, Father?' Jobe whispered.

'No, just out to it, probably best fer 'im. Fern, heat the knife again.'

Isaiah took another swig of Brandy then bandaged the foot with a piece of cloth then gently placed his foot down on the mattress.

'One down, one to go.' He followed the same routine removing the barnacle and shell fragments. He gazed at his chest and noticed the whip marks and then the rope marks on his wrists and ankles.

When Isaiah was finished, he bandaged the foot and then put Wilding's hands together and bound his wrists. 'He'll be out to it for most of the night, but just in case.'

☆

The night air was thick with tension, a palpable sense of foreboding that clung to the walls of the small hut. Jacob and Fern's eyes shot open, their senses instantly alert to the guttural sound that tore through the silence. Their bodies tensed as they beheld the nightmare before them – Wilding perched atop their father, a small knife glinting in his hand.

☆

Wilding applied more pressure and pushed deeper. 'Shhhhhh, Father, it will soon be over. Sleep now.'

There was a gargling sound coming from Isaiah's throat as he tried to call out, then the blood streamed down the sides of his neck. His hands went limp. The jugular was severed and blood bubbled with his last breath.

The room was consumed by chaos, a cacophony of terror and desperation that seemed to reverberate through the very walls. As Jobe disappeared into the night, Fern followed suit, her footsteps a whisper against the earth as she fled from the nightmare that had descended upon their lives.

'FATHER!' Jobe screamed again. 'NOOooo!' He ran out into the darkness.

Wilding cackled, showing his grey teeth. He turned the handle of the knife inward and cut the bindings around his wrists. He then undressed the father and sitting on the floor, put on his clothes which were in much better condition than his. He took off his black open sided shoes and carefully slipped them on and did up the leather laces. He felt in his pouch and there were a few shillings, enough to get him a room and some grub back in Hull. He wiped the blade on his old undershirt and placed it back in the sheath and stuck it down the inside of the back of his breeches. Finally, he tried Isaiah's black felt hat and placed it proudly on his head.

The sun was just starting to come up when he limped to the horse and attached the cart. He climbed up onto the seat and took the reins in his hands and called out, 'Jobe, Fern, come out. I will not hurt thee, I want the horse and cart, tis orl. Come out and I will take ya home, I swear it.' The lie hung heavy in the air, a testament to the depths of his depravity.

Wilding approached the lighthouse and ignored the lighthouse keeper waving from the top. He kept his eye out on the track along Spurn Road as it was low lying flat land and it would be easy to spot them.

As the cart rolled forward, leaving the hut and its horrors behind, the echoes of betrayal and malevolence lingered, a chilling reminder of the sinister path that had been forged.

After he passed, the lightkeeper looked down at his feet where Fern and Jobe were cowering and quietly sobbing.

Wilding continued along, enjoying the smell of the sea breeze with not a care in the world. Along Spurn Road he went, turning west on Weeton Road then passed through the tiny village of Skeffling and smiled.

The sun was going down when he arrived back in Hull. He rode the horse and cart through the archway of the William Hawkes, tide the horse up in the courtyard and limped in with his driftwood walking stick.

The publican greeted him, ‘You’ve done yerself an injury. Will ya be wantin’ a room? Come, sit at the table.’

‘Fair enough, yes, I’ll take a room, some grub and ale,’ Wilding replied.

The publican returned with the ale and put it on the table with some bread and cheese.

Meanwhile, Wilding tried to listen in on the conversation of the two men sitting at another table.

‘Aye, couldn’t understand where the smell was comin’ from,’ one of the men began, his voice a blend of intrigue and trepidation. ‘Then found ‘er under the bed in one of the rooms.’

Wilding’s heart quickened. The mention of the mysterious scent and the discovery of the servant girl under the bed stirred a hunger for answers deep within him. He subtly edged closer, ensuring his eavesdropping remained inconspicuous.

‘Servant girl they said, from Leeds,’ the other man chimed in, his voice tinged with sympathy. ‘Tried ta find ‘er mistress but she was long gone.’

The words hung in the air, their implications shrouded in uncertainty. Wilding’s mind raced, weaving webs of conjecture and possibilities.

The publican directed him up the stairs to the last room on the left so Wilding grabbed his ale and took his time climbing up the stairs. He made his way along the hallway, opened the door and went inside. He lit the candle.

Sitting on the bed, he took out his knife and began to cut his beard. Piece by piece, the whiskers fell on the floor in front of him. He started by cutting chunks, then using the sharp edge to cut closer to the skin. He finished by cutting his long hair piece by piece, then shaved his head until he was completely bald.

It was starting to get late and he was tired, so he took his tunic and shoes off. He inspected the bottom of his feet; the blood oozed through the bandages.

He laid down and went to sleep. In the embrace of sleep, Wilding surrendered to the currents of mystery, his mind a canvas for the story yet to unfold. The winds of fate whispered their secrets, and he, now a willing participant, was poised to listen.

CHAPTER 13

Warning Danger

The next morning, Wilding woke early, put the breast collar, harness and bridle on the horse, attached the cart and departed. He headed for Leeds following the river Ouse for a while before stopping off at Selby. It took most of the day to get to Leeds and he pulled up outside the Nags Head.

The early morning light filtered through the window casting a warm glow upon the worn wooden tables and the familiar faces that gathered within. Wilding's arrival was met with a mixture of curiosity and familiarity, a quiet acknowledgment that he was a man of purpose. The driftwood walking stick, a constant companion, bore witness to his journeys and trials.

With a determined gait, Wilding made his way to his usual table, a sense of anticipation stirring within him. As he settled into his seat, Smythe, a man marked by scars both visible and unseen, approached with a hushed urgency. His scarred hand trembled slightly, a silent reminder of the paths he had walked.

The new barmaid, a fresh face in the familiar surroundings, appeared with pewter tankards of ale, her presence a reminder that life flowed forward even as secrets and vendettas echoed through the past.

'No trinkets?' Smythe was expecting the usual assortment of silver and lace.

'No, I been away. The Rushworth brother, where is he?' Wilding asked.

Smythe rubbed the numbness in his hand. 'Oh, him and Rosie left, shacked up in a cruck house on this side of the river. She's with child and doesn't come around anymore. He's workin' at a fullin' Mill. What do ya want 'im fer?'

Wilding looked frustrated. 'Tis Rushworth, bastard got away in Hull. I caught 'im and the necklace then ran into a spot a' trouble.'

With a nod of understanding, Smythe rose from the table, his scarred hand lingering on the edge. 'Watch yer back, Wilding. The shadows have eyes, and the echoes of our past have a way of catching up.'

Smythe looked away, sniggered and looked back. *I imagine, where his limp came from. Bastard deserves everything he got and there's more to come, believe me, there's more to come, son of a bitch.*

☆

The sun cast a warm, golden glow upon the village of Millford, even as evening drew near. John Rushworth, a burly man with calloused hands and a weathered face, had just finished a long day's work at the Mill. He wiped the sweat from his brow and turned his gaze toward the river, lost in its gentle rhythm. Among the figures strolling up from the Mill, he spotted a familiar face, one that didn't sit well with him.

John never liked Wilding and was hesitant to his approach. 'Mr Wilding, what brings you down ta the river?'

Wilding frowned. 'I'm trying ta find ya brother, 'ave ya seen 'im?'

'No, just up and left, didn't even say goodbye, no idea where he went,' replied John.

Wilding stroked his chin. 'Mmm, home… where, lad?'

John felt uneasy. 'Why are ya lookin' fer 'im, Mr Wilding?'

'Just 'ave some coin fer 'im.' Wilding pulled out the pouch he stole from Isaiah and poured some coin into his hand and showed John.

'Knowing my brother, he could be anywhere,' John replied, not trying to give away too much information.

Wilding took a step closer. 'Smythe said you were from the west, where exactly?'

John paused and looked at Wilding suspiciously. 'Northwest… near Halifax.'

'Where exactly, lad?' Wilding smiled falsely.

John dropped his chin, 'Haworth.'

'I know people in Haworth from the army. I've been meaning to get up there to see 'em. Maybe I can kill two birds with one stone. Well, I better let ya get 'ome, give me regards ta Rosie.'

'Will do, Mr Wilding.' John kept going and after a while turned to see if he was still there; he was gone. He shook his head and kept going.

Later, sitting at the table, John told Rosie, 'Robert's in danger.'

Rosie turned from the cauldron. 'What sort of danger?'

John replied, 'It's Wilding, he's after 'im, stopped me on the way 'ome, want's ta know where he's gone.'

Rosie shook her head. 'Well, do ya know?'

John looked down. 'Aye, I know, I'd say he's gone back ta Haworth. I told him; you know I told him but he wouldn't listen. He said one more job. Well sounds as if it were one job too many,' John lamented.

Rosie put her hand on John's shoulder. 'What are you going ta do?'

John placed his hand on Rosie's. 'Well, there's not much I can do, can't leave you 'ere alone with the baby on the way. If there was only some way I could get word to him, warn him.'

Rosie smiled. 'There is: pigeons. We'll go to the church in the Briggate tomorrow. Send a message to the church in Halifax. They can get word to Robert in Haworth.'

John looked up at her. 'You are smart as you are, pretty wife.'

St Johns was a magnificent building with ashlar stone and a grey slate roof. On each side of the church were four-light perpendicular windows, with five-light windows at the east ends.

Rosie waited at the large open oak door. John walked inside and was in awe of the elaborately carved screen across the nave and the aisle. There was similarly detailed carving on the wall panels, the pews and the pulpit.

A lone clergyman knelt at one of the pews in silent prayer. His eyes closed and his hands clasped together tightly.

John walked up to him. 'Pardon me, your grace, I was told I may be able to get word to my brother in Haworth.'

The clergyman remained quiet his eyes closed and his hands clasped.

John turned to look at Rosie and shrugged his shoulders.

Rosie gestured for him to continue.

John tried again, 'Pardon me, your grace…'

The clergyman interrupted, 'Amen.' He got up from the pew.

'Your grace, I heard I may be able to get word to my brother in Haworth. Tis urgent! His life may depend on it.'

The clergyman introduced himself as the rector of St Johns, Samuel Pigett, 'I will speak to the vicar. What message would you like to send?'

'The message is for Robert Rushworth of Haworth. Just say:

DANGER, WILDING APPROACHES

He'll know what I mean.' John gave the rector ten pence for his trouble.

In the face of danger and uncertainty, a plan had begun to take shape, and a renewed determination ignited in John's heart. As the stars emerged in the ink-black sky outside, he felt a surge of gratitude for the woman by his side, a partner in both love and strategy. Together, they would find a way to safeguard Robert, even in the shadowy depths of danger that threatened to engulf their lives.

CHAPTER 14

The Ducking Stool

Robert stayed north of Leeds and Bradford and continued along Harden Road towards the Crossroads then headed west along Haworth Road. As he rode, he reached back and felt the sapphire sewn back in his tunic.

He peered across the green pastures and the moors beyond. The silence and the remoteness were a welcome change from the city. He was not in a rush; he closed his eyes and raised his nose, breathing in the fresh air.

It had been years since Robert had left his family's home and ventured into the bustling city. He had always felt a sense of restlessness and a desire to explore beyond the familiar landscapes of his upbringing. But now, as he stood in front of his childhood home once again, the memories came rushing back.

The two sisters were playing outside. Mirtle saw the horses coming up the hill and called out, 'MA, SOMBODY'S COMING.'

Isabel stepped outside. She put her hand up to shield her eyes and squinted to try to see who it was. 'It's Robert. Oh, William will be so pleased.'

Robert reined in the horse and jumped off and embraced her, 'Isabel, tis so good ta see ya.'

'Oh, Robert, look at you with yer fancy clothes and the horses. Morwen and Mirth, say hello to ya cousin Robert.'

Robert crouched down and embraced them both. 'You two, you've grown sa much. Isabel, where's Da?'

'Went in ta village with Tommy, shouldn't be too long. Come in, ya must be tired from yer journey.'

Inside, the cozy cottage seemed smaller than he remembered. The warm scent of freshly baked bread filled the air, a comforting aroma that brought a smile to Robert's face. He took a seat at the wooden table, his eyes wandering around the room, taking in the details that hadn't changed over the years.

Isabel bustled around, setting out plates and pouring mugs of tea. Mirtle and Morwen curiously peeked at Robert from behind their mother's skirts, their eyes wide with curiosity and excitement.

'Tell us 'bout the city, cousin Robert,' Mirtle piped up, her young voice filled with eagerness.

'Aye, tell us 'bout all them tall buildin's and carriages,' Morwen chimed in.

Robert chuckled, a warm feeling of nostalgia washing over him. 'Well, it's quite different from this quiet countryside, I'll tell ya that. The city is bustling with people, and there are buildings that reach up so high, they seem to touch the sky. Carriages race through the streets, and there's always something happening.'

The children listened intently, their imaginations running wild as they tried to picture the distant world Robert was describing.

As they chatted and caught up, the front door swung open, and in walked William, Robert's father. His eyes widened in disbelief as he took in the sight of his son sitting at the table.

☆

Reaching the cottage, Tommy and William heard the uncustomary sounds of horses around the side of the cottage. 'What's this then?'

He glanced at Tommy then went to the door, lifted the latch and stepped inside.

William was shocked and confused as a well-dressed man with his back to him stood and turned. 'Daa!'

'Robert? Is that truly you?' William's voice trembled with emotion as he crossed the room in a few swift strides and enveloped Robert in a tight embrace. Tears welled up in his eyes as he held his long-lost son.

‘Aye, Da, it’s me,’ Robert replied, his voice choked with emotion. ‘I’ve missed ya.’

The room seemed to fill with a mixture of joy, relief, and a hint of sadness. The prodigal son had returned, bringing with him tales of the outside world and a renewed appreciation for the simple pleasures of home.

As the family gathered around the table, sharing stories and laughter, it was clear that this reunion marked a turning point in their lives. Robert had returned not just to the place he had left behind, but to a newfound sense of belonging and connection that he had been searching for all along.

‘Father, I’ve got somethin’ fer ya.’ He pointed behind.

‘What’s this then?’ William and Tommy turned to see the large mound of wool sitting at the side of the spinning wheel.

‘Tommy, William… Robert’s a trader!’ Isabel exclaimed excitedly. ‘He wants us to ‘ave this fine wool, God luv ‘im!’

The smile on William’s face was gone.

The room fell silent as the weight of Isabel’s words hung in the air. The tension in the cottage was palpable, like a storm gathering on the horizon. The revelation of Robert’s newfound trade had stirred something within the heart of William, something that went beyond mere scepticism.

Isabel stepped forward. ‘William, why, tis a gift and there’s four tods of it outside.’

‘Mmmm, trader ay?’

Isabel watched her husband closely, her eyes pleading with him to see the potential in Robert’s proposition. She knew that their family’s fortunes were at a crossroads and this fine wool could be their ticket to stability once more.

Robert stood there, bewildered. ‘But, Father, there’s no shame! I simply buy wool from those who can’t get to market and sell cloth to clothiers who can. Tis no different to what ya do in Halifax.’

'TRADERS ARE THE ARSEWORMS OF THE MOORS! They pray on the poor shepherds and boost prices more than tis worth!'

'Tis a fable, Father, am I not doin' a service buyin' from those who can't get to the cloth market in Leeds?'

William continued to examine the wool, his rough hands caressing its fibres as if trying to divine its true worth. His mind raced, torn between tradition and the promise of something new. He was a man deeply rooted in the old ways, a shepherd whose hands had guided countless flocks over the moors. Yet, the world was changing, and the allure of prosperity whispered to him like a siren's song.

Finally, after what felt like an eternity, William's eyes met Robert's. A flicker of uncertainty danced in their depths before determination settled in. He let out a long sigh and looked at Isabel.

'I'll admit, the thought of tradin' does sit uneasy with me, Robert. But times are changin', and we can ill afford to ignore opportunities that come our way. This fine wool… it could be our salvation.'

Isabel interjected, 'William, the coin from the cloth would come in useful and we could afford to pay our lease, fines and more, tis "fine" wool from Lincolnshire!'

'Fine wool, ya say?'

'Aye, tis fine wool from Lincolnshire,' Robert stated proudly. 'Brought it up here fer you to spin and weave. I'll take it back to Hull and export it fer a good profit.'

William separated it and rubbed it between his fingers. 'Well, yer right there, tis fine wool! Where did ya get it? Be honest, lad.'

Robert took a step forward confidently. 'Hull, it was gonna be put on its way to the Baltic. This wool, tis not like the long staple around here. If we spin it and weave it, I can take it south and sell it fer a handsome sum. Pay the lease and more! There are four tods of it outside, should get twenty or twenty-one pounds profit. It'll be worth ten times the price of yer kersey!'

'A handsome sum,' said Tommy. 'We could pay the rest of the fines!'

Robert's heart swelled with a mix of emotions – pride, relief and a renewed connection with his family. He had taken a risk in revealing his trade, uncertain of how they would react. But in this pivotal moment, he saw the threads of change begin to weave a new path for them all.

'And the horses?' William asked.

Robert shook his head. 'Da, I been working for two years now, bought the army horse from a Roundhead soldier who needed the coin. The other belongs to a friend.'

This was happening all over, those who were once rich were now poor and those with the trading spirit were becoming rich. There was a new middle class emerging.

'Da, ya can't sell wool to the Flemish anymore. I been buyin' wool in Lincolnshire and putting it out, then I take the cloth to Hull and export it to the Baltic fer double the price. They pay a pretty penny fer it there fer clothes fer the rich.'

Robert looked at Tommy for support. 'Help me out here, I paid fer the wool and brought it up 'ere, I thought you'd be pleased! Think what ya could do with the money!'

Isabel's eyes shimmered with tears of joy as she hugged both her husband and her son. 'Thank you, Robert. You've brought us a chance to turn our fortunes around.'

Isabel glared at William with contempt then softened her gaze as she peered back at Robert, she smiled. 'Robert, ya should be congratulated on ya success.'

Isabel held out her hand. 'Robert, please sit down and I'll get ya some supper, ya must be starvin' and what tales ya must 'ave.'

'William, Tommy, please sit down, let Robert rest a while before ya continue yer inquisition.' Isabel placed the earthenware ale jug on the table.

She turned to stir the pottage in the cauldron. 'I'm sorry, Robert, we don't have much.'

‘Well… we’ll ‘ave ta change that, Isabel, let’s go to market tomorrra’.’

William looked at his son suspiciously, even a little jealous his son had accomplished what he couldn’t. ‘Robert, yer mother and I gave you life, God rest her soul. If I find out any of this wealth has come from dubious means. Well…’

‘Oh, William, please, give it a rest, we haven’t seen the lad fer two years.’ Isabel spooned pottage into a wooden bowl and placed it in front of Robert.

William relented, ‘Okay, okay, Isabel. So what news ‘ave ya from your travels, and yer brother, what da ya know of yer brother?’

Robert finally felt at ease. ‘John works at a fulling mill in Leeds, loads cloth on the pack horses, before they take it to Hull. I see ‘im whenever I’m back there. He ‘as a wife now and she’s with child. Married Rosie, a girl from London.’

William held onto every word. ‘A child?’

Robert smiled at his shock. ‘Gonna name him Thomas after yer father if it’s a boy and Lucy if it’s a girl.’

William croaked and swallowed away the sentimental knot in his throat. He gazed down sadly reminiscing then looked up with pride and excitement.

Isabel smiled and placed freshly baked bread on the table then poured them all ale. She put her hand on William’s shoulder to comfort him.

‘He’ll come home soon but probably better off where he is at present.’

‘Come on you lot eat up and drink for we need ta welcome home Robert in the proper way.’ She sat beside Tommy and bowed her head as did the others. Tommy said grace.

‘O Christ our God, bless the food and

drink of your servants, for you are

holy always; now and forever. Amen.’

They all dug into the bread, slurping, drinking and listening to Robert's tales of Leeds and Hull. They all laughed when he told them about Brewster.

'It was a tough time when we first got there, lost our money, stolen right out of me tunic. We were going to come home again but got a job in a tavern makin' brew.'

'The tavern keeper put us up in his cellar until we could get on our feet.'

'John got a job at one of the fullin' mills on the river.'

'You should see Leeds, never seen such a place, and the houses, traders' houses made from stone and brick with slate roofs. So many people of all kinds, rich and poor livin' side by side.'

They all listened intently to Robert's stories until William piped in, 'And the coin fer the wool, where did ya get it… must of cost yer soul?'

'Da, like I told ya, I been workin' hard for two years.' Robert felt bad about lying to his father but knew it was for the best. He also knew his father was wise.

Isabel glimpsed at Robert then back at William. 'Oh, William, leave the poor lad, let 'im rest, he's only just got 'ome. From memory, you were no angel when you were 'is age!'

'Aye, but I wasn't dishonest, nor was me da or his before 'im!'

Robert thought back to what seemed like a lifetime ago now, he dared not tell his father how he really acquired the wool. He also knew if his father found out about his recent adventures, he would probably turn him in. *T'would finish everythin'.*

It was late when Robert finished telling his stories. He yawned loudly.

The last couple of days were hectic and he hadn't slept well because of the thoughts of Ursula, Wilding and the necklace.

Tommy peered at Robert. 'You look tired but before you go to bed, we also 'ave some news; young Will has been offered an apprenticeship at the manor.'

Robert glanced up. 'At the manor?'

Tommy wore a proud look on his face. 'Aye, he started muckin' the stables and they asked him ta stay on at the mill. Tis only small, two looms and six wheels but gives him a start.'

Robert peered at Will, who just arrived home, and smiled. 'Good on ya Will, an apprentice.'

Will smiled proudly. 'I'm leavin' tommora mornin', they've told me I 'ave ta stay at the mill.' Will looked down with a dreaded anticipation.

The next morning Will left, he turned to take one last gander at the cottage where he was born. He could still see his mother, father and Robert standing near the door waving.

Uncle William wasn't the emotional type so went back inside to continue combing the new wool.

Will continued climbing up Marsh Lane. The roadside cruck houses once a hive of activity were empty and derelict. The thatch, old and damp, fell through the roof trusses leaving them exposed to the elements. He peered down into the green valley. Most of the Silver Birch and Oak trees once there were gone, cut down to make way for the herds of sheep now grazing.

Will thought about the discussion with his family the previous night.

☆

The fire crackled in the hearth, its warm glow casting dancing shadows on the walls of the cottage. William and Tommy sat in their familiar high-backed chairs, puffing on their pipes with a sense of companionship that transcended words. The room was steeped in a mixture of comfort and melancholy, the anticipation of change hanging heavy in the air.

Will carefully added another piece of dried peat to the flames, coaxing it to catch with a gentle breath. He settled on a stool between his father and uncle, his gaze fixed on the flickering embers. It was a moment of quiet reflection, a pause before the impending journey that lay ahead.

William and Tommy sat down at the wooden, high-backed chairs near the hearth. They both took puffs on their pipes slowly and methodically.

Will placed another piece of dried peat on the flame and blew on it to catch, then sat on the stool in front of the hearth between them.

Uncle William, his face etched with lines of wisdom and experience, broke the silence with a voice that carried both gravitas and tenderness.

'You know, Will, every step you take in this world leaves a mark, a mark that tells a story of who you are. As you embark on this new path, remember that you're not just leaving behind a place, but you're taking with you the lessons and love that have shaped you.'

He took another contemplative puff on his pipe before continuing. 'This opportunity, son, it's a chance for you to forge your own path, to make your mark in a world that's waiting to be explored. But amidst the uncertainties and challenges, always hold onto the values that have been instilled in you. Be strong, cherish kindness and forgive yourself when you stumble.'

Will nodded, his eyes absorbing the wisdom of his uncle's words. He felt a mixture of excitement and trepidation about the journey ahead. Leaving home, even if it was just up the road to the manor, felt like a significant step into the unknown.

Uncle William took another puff. 'Most importantly, walk honourably with yer head held high and don't forget your beginins.'

Will whispered. 'I… I can't believe I'm leaving; I know it's not far to the manor but still, tis the thought of it, seven years is a long time away from home!'

Isabel could hear Will talking, she smiled, shuffled over and placed her hands on his shoulders affectionately. She gave him a peck on the cheek. 'I love you, son.'

Tommy watched her do it and smiled. ‘Come on, luv, don’t get all soppy now. He’s only movin’ up the road!’

‘Aye… I know, but still doesn’t make it any easier, me boy, all grown up and leavin’ home. He’s the centre of me life and always will be. When he was young, I was the rock in his life, now I’m older, he’s the rock in mine, and I’ll miss ‘im so!’

Isabel could feel the lump growing in her throat and the tears building in her eyes. She turned away and went back to the table, wiping her eyes with her apron.

In the midst of bittersweet farewells and heartfelt embraces, the embers of departure ignited a fire of determination within Will. He realised that stepping out into the world was not a farewell to his roots, but a continuation of the legacy his family had built. The journey ahead was an opportunity to honour his beginnings while embracing the future with an open heart.

And so, in that small cottage nestled among the moors, a new chapter began. The spinning wheel hummed with renewed purpose, as the family worked together to transform the fine wool into something greater. As the threads of change intertwined with tradition, the future remained uncertain, but there was a newfound hope that carried them forward.

CHAPTER 15

The Apprentice's Oath

The chill of uncertainty hung heavy in the air as the village of Haworth woke to a new day, a day that would mark a significant turning point in the lives of many, including young Will. The specter of Milton Killsin, the overseer of the poor, loomed over the community, his stern mandate to remove the youth from the relief rolls and thrust them into employment casting a shadow of unease.

Will's parents were not happy about it, but they knew if they didn't allow him to go to the mill, then they could be denied relief.

Milton Killsin, a figure of authority with a heart seemingly untouched by empathy, held the power to reshape the destinies of the village's youth. His stern countenance and unyielding demeanour sent a clear message – compliance or consequences. In a time when the lines between privilege and poverty were starkly drawn, his dictates were law.

And so, within the hallowed walls of the village vestry, a pact was made. Tommy, with a heavy heart and a heavy hand, signed the indenture that bound young Will to Jasper Calamy, a mill owner who had been assigned his share of pauper apprentices. The quill scratched across the parchment, etching a contract that sealed Will's fate as an apprentice, a fate that would see him toiling away in the heart of the mechanised world.

As the ink dried on the page, the vestry minutes captured the moment, an unassuming record of an arrangement that held the weight of generations. It was a dance of survival and subsistence, a negotiation between the past and the present.

Killsin had the power to apprentice any child fourteen years of age. Parish farmers, tradesmen, shopkeepers and factory owners were expected to each take a share of the pauper apprentices in Keighley unless they paid the fine for 'not' taking one.

Tommy drew his 'X' on the indenture and the agreement between Jasper Calamy and Tommy Rushworth noted in the vestry minutes by the vicar.

Reaching Weavers Hill, Will peered westward to the lush green hills intermittently divided by rows of trees which missed the chop of the woodcutter. The grey flat-bottomed clouds drifted across the sky casting shadows on the pasture. He could hear the slight trickle of the beck behind as it meandered its way down the valley.

Will eventually reached the manor; it was the biggest house on the road with its stone walls and grand hall. The manor formed the administrative centre of the village and surrounds.

As he stood on the precipice of his new life, Will held onto the words of his father, the lessons of his mother, and the wisdom of his uncle. The embers of their love and guidance would accompany him on this daunting path. With determination burning in his eyes, he took a deep breath and set his gaze forward, ready to face the challenges that lay ahead.

He moseyed nervously up the drive and around the back to the kitchen and knocked on the door.

Moments later, the door opened, it was Mr Griswold. He stood there in his black felt hat and doublet with its bright, white laced ruff and cuffs.

Griswold stepped out and quickly closed the door behind him. 'Alright lad come with me!'

Will followed him out towards the barn then past it to another building recently constructed. He could tell by the newly thatched roof and freshly lime washed walls. As they got closer, he could hear the continual Rap! Trap! Rap! of a loom.

Griswold marched quickly and Will took long strides to keep up. He pushed Will through the door. 'Here ya go, Mr Dodds, here's another one fer ya.'

There were three spinning wheels and a hand loom in the small mill, all manned by apprentices like himself albeit a bit older. They all glanced up from their wheels when Griswold stepped inside.

The apprentices' eyes followed Will as he was led to the back of the shed, curiosity and amusement dancing in their glances. The older one among them, a wry grin playing on his lips, regarded Will with a mix of appraisal and mischief.

The olfactory symphony of this mill was a testament to its purpose. The dominant aroma that enveloped the senses was that of raw and processed wool. Raw wool carried with it an earthy, almost primal scent, a reminder of its origins in the lush meadows and pastures of Yorkshire. Yet, there was more to it; the very essence of the wool, the lanolin, whispered faintly in the air, offering a gentle, slightly greasy undertone.

Wool preparation demanded an array of cleaning agents. The air bore witness to this choreography of scents – a blend of soapy and herbal fragrances.

Carding and combing, the intricate dance of wool fibers being aligned and prepared, created a rhythmic cadence. Spinning wheels, tirelessly turning wool into yarn, lent a soothing hum to the air. Mr Dodds turned and glared at Bobbly and the others so they immediately dropped their eyes and became more expedient in their spinning and weaving.

The oldest checked out Will while he mechanically threw the shuttle back and forth. He grinned mischievously.

'Come on, you, out the back!' Mr Dodds pushed Will toward the back of the shed. 'Okay, Mr Griswold, I'll sort 'im and get 'im ta work! We'll get 'im settled in quick smart.'

Mr Dodds turned his gaze toward Will, a mixture of scrutiny and evaluation in his eyes. The weight of this moment settled upon them, the loom's lament a symphony of possibility and challenge. Will took a deep breath, his gaze steady, and the mentor and apprentice exchanged a silent understanding.

Will's heart raced as he followed Mr. Dodds through a small wooden door. The new environment felt both unfamiliar and laden with expectation. He clutched his linen market bag, the meagre contents serving as a tangible connection to his past.

Mr Dodds climbed the ladder and Will followed. Upstairs, there were three box beds and a small table with stools. A Bible was placed on the top of the table. The roof was exceptionally low so both Mr Dodds and Will stooped to stop from hitting their heads on the trusses.

Mr Dodds looked Will up and down. 'Right, you'll share a bed with one of the younger boys. Bobby, bein' the oldest, gets 'is own. Put yer bag there, come down and we'll get ya to work.'

Will nodded, his bag clutched tightly in his hand. He placed it on the designated spot, a silent acknowledgment of his place in this new realm.

Mr Dodds spoke as he walked toward the ladder. 'Now listen 'ere, if ya want to last, stay out of trouble, keep yer mouth shut. You'll get food, lodgin' and six pence a day. Ya work from dawn till dusk, muckin' out the stables, cleanin' sweepin' the mill and any other jobs Mr Griswold or I asks ya to do. You're never to be seen at the front of the 'ouse unless ya got work ta do there! If ya found in the ale house, you'll get a whippin', if ya swear, you'll get a whippin'. Only time yer allowed in the kitchen is at mealtime, one meal each day at eleven bells. If ya caught cavortin' with kitchen maids, you'll get a whippin'. If ya caught stealin', fightin', missin' church or not readin' the Bible... you'll get a whippin'.'

As they descended the ladder, Mr Dodds outlined the rules of survival in this unfamiliar domain. His words were like a litany of expectations, a code of conduct that carried the weight of consequence. Will listened intently, his heart sinking with each stipulation, the reality of his situation crystallising before him.

Will dropped his chin. 'B-but sir, I can't read.'

Mr Dodds's sharp glance bore into him. 'Well, that's somthin' we may 'ave to rectify, aint it!'

Mr Dodds continued, 'Now, one of the other apprentices is on his last year, so if ya play yer cards right you might take over a wheel. Only if Bobby leaves to be a journeyman. Yer allowed out after dusk fer an hour and before dawn fer an hour, but if the sun beats you then ya get a whippin'. Yer either in the mill or in ya lodgin'. Oh and by the way, the doors are locked at night so if you got any ideas about sneakin' out, I'd rethink em' or else you'll get a whippin'.'

Mealtime is at eleven bells, so we got a bit a' work to do before then, now 'urry up or else…!'

He turned his back to Will.

Will whispered, 'Yeah, I know, I'll get a whippin'!'

The speech concluded, a heavy silence settled in the air. Mr Dodds turned away, leaving Will to absorb the weight of his responsibilities. Will watched him for a moment before he finally took a deep breath and accepted his fate. He wasn't sure how he would survive this new reality, but he was determined to try.

Seated on the edge of a box bed, Will tested the straw mattress under his weight, his fingers tracing the coarse fabric. The room was sparse, but its simplicity held a promise of rest and respite. He unpacked his meagre belongings, a small reminder of the world he had left behind.

At the bottom of the ladder, Mr Dodds was waiting for him and handed him a broom. 'I'm sure ya know 'ow to use one of these.'

The other three apprentices smirked as they continued their spinning. Already thinking of practical jokes to play on the newcomer.

Will peered around, it was dusty and the noise coming from the loom was deafening.

Rap! Trap! Rap!

The mill hummed with purpose, a symphony of industry that reverberated through the wooden beams and machinery. Three shutters stood ajar, allowing the cool breeze to filter in and offer respite from the stifling atmosphere. At the far end of the building, a small hearth radiated warmth, its heating stone a testament to the meticulous care that sustained the delicate process of combing and weaving.

Will started to sweep, each stroke accompanied by the weight of his uncertain initiation. He could feel the gaze of the other apprentices, their eyes like probing instruments measuring his competence and determination.

Mr Dodds stood and watched him for a while, then ambled back to a table near the hearth where samples of wool and cloth were placed. He sat and wrote in a large black leather-bound journal.

Mr Dodds picked up his whipping stick he kept on the table in front of him. He strolled down the front of the loom inspecting the width and length of the cloth and the thickness of the yarn on the wheels. He then returned to his table and jotted down some figures.

Time flowed like an unyielding river, carrying them through the hours of toil. It wasn't until the distant bells of Saint Michael's tolled their solemn chime that the spell was broken, announcing the arrival of a new phase in their relentless routine.

Mr Dodds slapped his journal shut. A figure of authority, he commanded their attention, and the air grew tense with anticipation.

The apprentices stopped their spinning and quickly stood out in front of the spinning wheels. One by one, they fell into formation, a testament to the structured hierarchy that governed their existence. Will didn't know what to do, so he just waited motionless, broom in hand.

Bobby, the eldest, gestured for him to come and stand next to him.

Will leaned the broom against the wall then strolled over.

Mr Dodds stood waiting for him to do so, then turned to march out the door. The boys followed him one after the other, first Bobby, then Will and the other two behind. After the boys left, he turned and locked the door.

The boys lined up outside in single file Bobby at the front, then Will then the two others. They waited for Mr Dodds to get to the front of the line then followed him.

As they marched toward the manor, the boy behind Will tugged on his shirt and ran so he was lined up in front of him. A moment later the other boy did the same so Will followed up the rear. Silently, they marched past the barn and up to the door of the kitchen. As they got to the door, Bobby the eldest, hurried past Mr Dodds, lifted the latch and opened the door for him to step through. The other boys followed.

The large trestle table stood at the heart of the room, a place of convergence where disparate lives intertwined for the duration of a shared meal. Mr Dodds, the overseer, anchored one end, while the housekeeper, Mrs. Stuart, held court at the other. A dance of hierarchy and camaraderie played out, as the two kitchen maids and the four apprentices gathered on either side, their places demarcated by pewter bowls and mugs of ale.

The anticipation in the air was palpable, a mixture of hunger and anticipation as the kitchen maids bustled about, orchestrating the symphony of sustenance.

Will noticed Margaret from church, she stirred the cauldron in the hearth and began to scoop its contents into a large ceramic bowl. Seeing this, Mr Dodds and Mrs Stuart sat as did the others.

Margaret went around the table and scooped the contents of the ceramic bowl into each plate starting with Mr Dodds, Mrs Stuart then the apprentices and kitchen maids. When she finished serving, she sat in her spot opposite Will. They bowed their heads in unison while Mr Dodds said grace.

The kitchen maids peeked slyly at Will and the apprentices watched the kitchen maids peek slyly at Will. The only one who didn't was Margaret who kept her eyes closed tightly in prayer.

Will looked at Margaret. The kitchen maids stared at him, smiled and then one of them whispered something to the other.

Will picked up his pewter spoon and glimpsed down into the bowl. He stirred the contents and felt large pieces of potato and onion and, low and behold, a small piece of lamb.

The others greedily broke bread and dipped it in slurping down the broth. Will picked up his piece of bread and slyly tucked it into his tunic for later. Bobby noticed.

There was little sound around the table except the scraping of metal against metal as they all tried to spoon the last of the runny liquid. Mr Dodds broke off another piece of bread and wiped up the remnants in the pewter dish.

The others watched on, hungrily wanting more, but dared not ask.

After the meal was finished, Mr Dodds took out his clay pipe and lit it, 'The pottage was extremely tasty today, Mrs Stuart!'

'Why thank you, Mr Dodds! You are too kind.'

The aeromantic smell of the British grown tobacco with its rich, deep pungent smell filled the room.

Mrs Stuart closed her eyes and lifted her nose taking in the sweet, spicy aroma. 'Mr Dodds, the smell of your tobacco is divine.'

The apprentices skulled their ale, stood and went outside. Will followed, leaving the kitchen maids to tidy up and Mr Dodds and Mrs Stuart to pass the time of day.

Mr Dodds looked at the pipe in his hand. 'Aye, tis a special blend from down south.'

Margaret took the bowl from in front of Mr Dodds. Her presence a constant undercurrent in the room, deftly cleared the bowl from in front of Mr Dodds. The housekeeper's observation did not go unnoticed, her whispered assessment a reminder of the harsh judgments that permeated their world.

Mr Dodds looked Margaret up and down. 'I see ya 'ave another, what's 'er name?'

'This one, young Margaret,' Mrs Stuart whispered, 'I think she's a bit slow.'

Margaret heard but didn't flinch as she was used to the putdowns and subjugation directed at her regularly. Her resilience, honed by years of enduring the cruelty of others, held her steady even in the face of such dismissive scrutiny.

Although the work on the manor was hard, Will took an interest in it, and especially in the horses. The horses were fine well-bred animals and received every care and attention from him. His hands worked with a quiet reverence, a testament to the bond he was forming with these creatures of grace and power.

The first night brought a jarring awakening for Will, a brutal initiation into the unspoken rules of their shared realm. The attack was swift and merciless, the linen bag over his head, the blows to his body, and the cruelty of the act etching a painful lesson into his memory.

'Hmoof!' Will clutched his stomach and couldn't breathe; the wind knocked right out of him.

Bobby punched him again. 'This is what happens if you ever tell on us!'

Will rolled onto the floor groaning, clutching his stomach and breathing heavily trying to get his breath back.

Bobby picked up Will's tunic, found the piece of bread and started breaking it handing pieces to the others.

By the time he was breathing normally, the candle was blown out and the apprentices were already back in bed. Will's gaze traced the ceiling as he lay in bed, his mind swirling with a mixture of anger, confusion, and determination. The darkness above seemed to mirror the shadows that seemed to be closing in around him.

When Will wasn't in the stable he spent most of his time in the small mill. He swept the floor, got water for the other apprentices, cleaned shoes and ran errands for his grace.

The overseer, Mr Dodds was a tough task master and had no qualms about using the whipping stick if one of the apprentices slackened off.

Night after night, the apprentices gathered for their mandated Bible readings, a ritual that felt both sanctimonious and oppressive. Mr Dodds's stern gaze watched over them as they stumbled through the words, the sting of his reprimands punctuating the sacred verses. Will's hands bore the brunt of his inadequacy, red and sore from the strikes, a testament to his struggles in the realm of letters and faith.

On one occasion Bobby was drunk and caught by Constable Pigshells in one of the ale houses. He was escorted back to the manor, stripped naked, hung by his thumbs and lashed twenty-one times by Mr Dodds. The other apprentices were forced to watch. Will looked away.

The apprentices were sly young men and were always trying to trick Will into parting with his food. They were vain and lazy and often stole extra food when Mr Dodds and Mrs Stuart weren't looking. If anything went missing, they would blame it on Will who would get a whipping.

The other boys spent their off time discussing the kitchen maids and providing descriptions of the carnal acts they would perform if given half a chance. They often spoke of Shrove Tuesday, the only day apprentices were allowed off to partake in activities normally forbidden, such as cockfights and ball games.

Besides the odd whipping, Will settled in quite well, he learnt how to sound out words from the Bible. He still liked to race home to see his parents and quite often arrived back after dusk and took the beating while the other lads watched on smiling.

Mr Dodds would wait for him at the entrance to the mill. He stood there, arms folded, whipping stick in hand.

'Are ya not getting sick of these hidings, lad? You know the rules.'

'I'm sorry, Mr Dodds!' Will glanced down apologetically.

'Righto, where do ya want it?'

Will stood in front of him and turned. He scrunched up his face waiting for the first strike. He heard Mr Dodds behind him and heard the whipping stick slice through the air with a whoosh and felt the sting on the backs of his legs.

Will scrunched his face up and waited for the second contact, he heard the whoosh again sensing its imminent arrival then felt it.

Amidst the trials and shadows, Will's spirit remained unbroken. The small acts of resistance, the silent bonds formed in the stable, and the moments of stolen solace were the embers of hope that he clung to. In the heart of the manor, where the boundaries of servitude and survival blurred, Will's journey continued, a chapter in a story of resilience and the enduring pursuit of a brighter dawn.

CHAPTER 16

Shadows of Accusation

Robert heard a noise outside.

'Tommy Rushworth, it is I, John Pigshells, the church warden and the baliff come to see if sabbath is being followed in the proper way.'

Those sitting around the table were surprised. William stood. 'Ere, ya can't come in 'ere unannounced, it aint proper like.' William's voice trembled with a mixture of indignation and caution, a plea for propriety in the midst of an abrupt and unwelcome intrusion.

Pigshells rolled his eyes. 'We've got orders from his grace and the minister to ensure all Sabbath holy ways are followed.'

The three men ducked their heads and stepped inside. The bailiff held a parchment in his hand. 'I've been asked to deliver this message by his grace Jasper Calamy. Tommy, a presentment has been made to the court leet, regarding the death of Mr Killsin's pig.'

Alarmed, Tommy took a step out from the trestle table. 'Fer the death of his pig, what rot, I 'avn't been anywhere near 'is pig!'

Milton Killsin looked at Isabel menacingly. 'No, not you – your wife, Isabel Rushworth!'

Fearfully Isabel stood in shock. 'Me, I avn't done nowt, 'ave nothin' to do with 'em.' Isabel's shock was palpable as her innocence was called into question, her voice a desperate protestation against the accusations that threatened to upend her life.

The warden explained, 'I'm afraid this seems to be the problem; Milton has accused you of un-Godly like ways and as a result he has reason to believe it has caused evil to fall upon his land and the death of his pig.'

William stood protectively. 'Absurd, Isabel wouldn't hurt a fly, I dunno about a pig. What evidence have you?'

'All in time, William. Isabel is to appear at the court leet in a fortnight. Please ensure she is present,' the bailiff demanded. He provided Tommy with the parchment and left through the door.

The parchment, a physical manifestation of Isabel's impending trial, was a stark reminder of the forces at play beyond their control. The summons to the court leet held the promise of justice but also the threat of dire consequences that could further shatter their already fragile existence.

Milton Killsin stayed momentarily then snickered before turning and walking out the door.

John Pigshells remained momentarily. 'I'm sorry, Tommy, there was nowt I could do.' Dejected, he walked through the door and closed it quietly behind him.

Alarmed, and saddened, Isabel plonked herself back down on the stool and wept. *I could be fined, end up in the stocks or worse. Then we'll never pay the lease fines. Milton Killsin, he's behind all this! Bastard!*

Tommy went to her and placed his arm around her shoulder, 'Do not worry yourself, wife! Milton Killsin has it out fer us. Ya can't be punished fer something ya havn't done!' The gravity of the situation, the potential fines, public humiliation, and the looming specter of the stocks, hung like a heavy cloud over their hopes.

As the door closed behind the departing figures, the room was left to its silence, a quiet space where the echoes of accusation and uncertainty reverberated. In the midst of the gathering shadows, the Rushworths found themselves standing at a crossroads, facing a trial that would test their bonds, challenge their convictions, and reveal the depths of their resilience.

☆

The court leet was held inside the Kings Arms and all who were tenants, copyholders and freemen were obliged to be present. Those absent were fined tuppence. The twelve jurors were already chosen by house row and accepted their oath provided by the bailiff and kissed the Bible.

The bailiff called out, 'HEAR YEE, HEAR YEE, the court leet is now in session and will be presided over by his grace, Justice of the Peace, Jasper Calamy. Presentments with respect to matters of local concern will be offered and the rules of natural justice will be applied. God bless you all!'

The twelve jurors sat at two long trestles placed on either side of Jasper Calamy. Their faces etched with determination and gravity. Witnesses, complainants and informers stood nearby, their collective anxiety underscoring the seriousness of the proceedings.

The bailiff cleared his throat and directed his gaze to the jurors and justice, 'With a commanding presence, the bailiff began to present the cases that hung in the balance. There are presentments fer three citizens yer grace.'

The bailiff continued, 'The first for Nicholas Taylor for twenty-three assaults, gambling eleven times and striking a constable and a barkeep.'

The night watchmen and constable brought in the first defendant. He was shackled and forced into a high-backed chair in front of the jurors. The bailiff and the constable stood either side of him to ensure his cooperation.

He had a rugged and weathered appearance in the courtroom. His attire was simple and worn, reflecting the hard life he likely led. He had a scruffy beard that had seen little care, and his hair was unkempt and greying at the temples. His face bore the lines of a life filled with hardship, violence and thievery.

His voice was coarse and filled with a thick, working-class accent, a testament to his humble origins. His outburst in the courtroom revealed a fiery temperament, suggesting he had likely faced many struggles and confrontations in his life. His words were laced with a strong sense of defiance and anger, as if he had grown accustomed to fighting.

As he stood there, his body language exuded a sense of stubbornness and resentment, with clenched fists and a scowl on his face. His outburst against John Pigshells demonstrated a deep-seated grudge and a willingness to speak his mind without reservation, even in this formal setting. He stood. 'I 'aven't assaulted anybody and if I did, they deserved it! Lyin' bastard son of a whore. John Pigshells is a dirty fuckin' cheat!'

The excited babble of the crowd filled the room. Most were cackling and smiling at the defendant's antics as he tried to push the constable and bailiff away.

John Pigshells punched the defendant in the stomach.

'Hmoof.' Taylor bent over, gasping for air a momentary dance of agony and surprise.

'No respect for my office, your grace.' The room fell into an uneasy silence, the echoes of the strike reverberating through the space.

The justice banged on the table with his gavel. 'QUIET, QUIET or else I will clear the court, BAILIFF!'

The heavy-set bailiff lifted his hands to quieten the crowd. 'QUIET!'

The crowd hushed.

Justice Jasper Calamy's gaze remained fixed, his role as the final arbiter of justice clear in the gravity of his expression. The proceedings hung in the balance, a delicate dance of accusation and defense that would ultimately be shaped by the collective judgment of the jurors.

Calamy stood. 'What say you, jurors?'

They whispered among themselves, then one stood. 'I was in the Kings Arms the night he thumped the barkeep 'cause he wouldn't fill his tankard. Made a right nasty mess of 'im he did.'

Another stood. 'Aye, and I were there the night Pishells and Taylor were playing cards. Taylor gave 'im an 'earful then thumped him!

Admittedly, the constable gave some back and the two of us helped lock 'im up.'

Jasper Calamy raised his hands. 'And what say you to these charges, Nicholas Taylor?'

Taylor stood again and pointed at the two jurors. 'You wait ya FUCKIN' ARSEWORMS, I'll 'ave ya guts fer garters! AND YOU PIGSHELLS YOU FUCKIN CHEATIN' BASTARD. I'LL BE COMIN' FER YA! You mark me words, I'll be comin' fer ya.'

John Pigshells smirked and pushed down on his shoulders to seat him.

The courtroom crackled with energy as Nicholas Taylor's outburst reverberated through the space, his accusations and profanities echoing against the walls. Defiance hung in the air as his words, fuelled by rage and desperation, clashed with the stern authority of Jasper Calamy and the assembled jurors.

One of the jurors stood and yelled over the hubbub of the onlookers. 'YA GET WHAT YA DESERVE, NICHOLAS TAYLOR, YA BEEN WARNED UMPTEEN TIMES!'

The justice banged down on the table with his gavel. The crowd quietened in readiness. 'In light of these accusations, I have no option other than to sentence you. Nicolas Taylor, you are to be stocked for six hours on the following three Saturdays. May God bless you and help you see the error of your ways! Take him away, bailiff!'

The defendant stood yelling and struggling under the constable's grasp. 'Leave me be, I done nowt. DONE NOWT, I SAY! You two sons of whores, yer finished, finished I tell ya! PIGSHELLS YER NOT GONNA GET AWAY WITH THIS, YOU THIEVIN' BASTARD!'

The crowd jeered as the bailiff and John Pigshells led him away. They parted as the defendant resisted and kicked over chairs and tables on the way.

Outside, Pigshells took out his thick stick and clobbered him on the back of the neck. 'Hmumf.' Taylor slumped and they dragged him toward the lockup.

The excitement of the crowd increased as the entertainment continued.

A few moments later, the constable and bailiff returned.

The bailiff raised his hands for all to be quiet. 'Justice Calamy, the next presentment is fer Henry Tussler, who by his own admission did last Sabbath grind grain outside his lodgin'.'

His physical presence carried an aura of humility and simplicity. His gait was measured, reflecting a lifetime of labour and experience. His attire was plain and practical, a reflection of a life lived in an age when extravagance was a luxury few could afford. His garments bore the marks of wear and tear, telling the story of countless days spent toiling in the fields for others.

Henry's most striking feature was his eyes – beady and bewildered. They held a glint that revealed a soul unaccustomed to the spotlight of attention. Those eyes seemed to harbor a sense of wonder and vulnerability, as if they had seldom gazed upon the world beyond the confines of his everyday existence. In the dimly lit courtroom, they betrayed a mixture of curiosity and apprehension, as though he had been plucked from the obscurity of his life.

His weathered face bore the lines of time and experience, etched deep by trials and tribulations. Though he may have been a simple man, his lowly countenance suggested a reservoir of simple wisdom acquired through hardships and challenges.

Henry Tussler's life had been shaped by the simplicity of his surroundings. As he faced the scrutiny of the courtroom, he seemed both out of place and yet profoundly human.

His dirty brown frayed linen shirt revealed his skinny arms and grubby hands. Patched leggings came to his knees, no shoes or hose, his feet dirty and calloused. White whispers of hair curled down the sides of his face from beneath his grey woollen hat. His white, unkept beard stained from the dried dung tobacco he smoked.

His attire, offered a glimpse into a life marked by toil and struggle. Yet, his smile, though tinged with confusion, held a warmth that radiated from within, a testament to the resilience that defined his existence.

Amidst the cacophony of voices that clamoured for justice, a chorus of compassion rose in defence of the unassuming figure. 'POOR OLD 'ENRY, LET 'IM GO!' His wife called out from the back of the room.

'Poor old 'enry wouldn't 'urt anybody, let 'im go!' bellowed another.

'Let the poor old buggar go!' The crowd followed suit calling out their frustration and sympathy for the old man.

The justice raised his hand to quieten the crowd, 'What say you, Henry Tussler?'

Henry stood nervously his back bent over, from the cracks in his spine, his voice, though quiet, carried the weight of honesty as he explained the circumstances that had led him to grind grain. 'I'm sa sorry, yer grace but I 'ad ta grind me grain on the Sabbath 'cause there was no wind day before and we 'ad no bread!'

Jasper Calamy smiled a flicker of understanding. 'Henry Tussler, do you not know it is against God's laws for any to be working on the sabbath and is punishable by a day in the stocks?'

Henry didn't care. 'Rather a day in the stocks than a day wi' no bread, yer grace.'

The crowd found his forthrightness amusing and laughed out loud. 'GOOD ON YA, 'ENRY! HAHA. HAHA. HAHA.' Laughter, borne from a place of camaraderie and appreciation for his candidness filled the room. The collective mirth, a testament to the resilience of the human spirit, wove a tapestry of connection amidst the divisive proceedings.

The crowd hushed as the Justice of the Peace stood and paused in thought. 'As there was a lack of wind preventing the grinding of grain, this court finds you innocent of the presentment and you are free to go, Henry.'

Henry stayed seated. 'Yer grace, I'd rather go back ta the lock up, grubs good in there, there's even meat in the pottage, better than the wife's.'

At the back of the crowd, Henry's wife looked on, rolling her eyes. 'Silly old buggar!'

His grace smiled. 'Henry, you are free to go. Bailiff, please escort Henry out. Oh and bailiff, see Henry gets some grain and meat from the kitchen to take home.'

The crowd cheered. 'Gew on, Henry, off ya go back ta ya grinding and ya diggin' HAHA.'

The crowd erupted. 'HAHA.'

'HAHA, on ya Henry.'

'HAHA.'

Henry scurried through the parting crowd who patted him on the back as he made his way toward the door and out. His wife was waiting outside.

He couldn't understand what all the fuss was about. He was used to spending time in the lock-up or the stocks on successive weekends for one reason or another.

The bailiff stood. 'Yer grace, the next presentment is fer Isabel Rushworth who has been accused of placing a spell on her neighbour's pig.'

The air in the tavern grew charged with tension as the bailiff's proclamation hung heavy in the room. The villagers, familiar with the Rushworth family's steadfast character, were taken aback by the accusations levied against Isabel. Murmurs and whispers filled the space, weaving a tapestry of disbelief and scepticism.

The murmuring in the room got louder for all in the tavern new the Rushworth's to be a fine hard-working family and Isabel to be kind and gentle.

She adorned her Sunday best.

Her auburn hair flowed like liquid gold, framing her face in a radiant halo. She wore a cream-coloured linen shift with a beige collar which folded diagonally about her neck. Long sleeves tightened at the wrist then puffed out to accentuate her long slender fingers. She wore a dark brown bodice dyed in tea and a dark brown, wrinkled ankle length skirt which she lifted with one hand as she gracefully sat on the chair.

Jasper Calamy stood. 'And who makes this presentment against Isabel Rushworth?' His voice held a measured calmness, a judge presiding over the uncertainty that gripped the room.

Milton Killsin stepped forward through the crowd. 'It is I, Justice Calamy,' he declared, his voice carrying the weight of his grievance.

'Ahhh Milton Killsin, and why do you bring this presentment forward against Isabel Rushworth are they not your neighbours?'

'She placed a spell on my pig!' Milton stated.

The crowd's collective voice rose in a cacophony of protest, a testament to their unwavering support for Isabel, a woman they had seen grow from girlhood into a beacon of kindness and compassion. The crowd, knew Isabel since she was a girl, booed and jeered their discontent.

'BOOOOO, LET 'ER GO!'

'LET 'ER GOOO!'

'ISABEL WOULDN'T 'URT ANYBODY!'

The justice banged on the table with his gavel. 'QUIET, QUIET or else I will clear the court, BAILIFF!'

The bailiff lifted his hands to quieten the crowd. 'QUIET!'

The crowd hushed.

Isabel's gaze remained steady, her eyes a pool of tranquil resolve amidst the storm of accusations. Isabel shook her head worriedly. 'I aint done nowt, yer grace, just keep to me self and care for the family best I can.'

The room fell into a hushed silence, the weight of Isabel's words hanging in the air. For in that moment, the villagers realised that the heart of their community was under threat, not from a bewitching spell, but from the erosion of trust and the rise of suspicion.

Jasper Calamy's stern gaze pierced through the smoky tavern air, his voice resonating with authority. 'And Milton Killsin, what evidence have you, then? Isabel Rushworth responsible for the death of your pig? Come now, let reason guide our deliberations.'

Milton, a man driven by simmering grievances and a longing for a resolution, stumbled over his words, his voice quivering with a mixture of trepidation and accusation. 'It's them, Justice, they… they 'ave strange ways, always laughin' and disrespectin' the sabbath.'

I've seen her doing strange things in the vegetable garden. She sings and see's things on early summer mornings, I see 'er standin'… and watchin' the sun come up.'

The crowd leaned in, caught between fascination and scepticism, as Milton's tale took a darker turn. 'One morning, I went into the barn and my horse, bathed in sweat, had been ridden. I nailed a horseshoe over the door for protection.'

His voice grew more resolute, eyes narrowing as he painted a picture of malevolence. 'I'm sure she wished me a bad wish, and this befallen on my pig.'

I also did see a hen crow on the fence and as everybody knows a whistling maid and a crowing hen are fit for neither God nor men. Tis evil I say, EVIL!'

Milton's inner thoughts betrayed his true intentions, a calculated scheme to rid the village of a family he deemed troublesome. Milton thought to himself, *This'll get rid of them.*

Isabel, however, was not one to be silenced. Rising from her seat with an air of defiant resolve, she retorted, 'I aint done nowt, your grace! Tis 'im, always starin' and peerin over! Can't go anywhere without his beady little eyes following me around!'

All in the tavern laughed.

'HAHAhahah.'

' HAHAhahah.'

' HAHAhaha.'

'MAYBE YA SHOULD SPEND MORE TIME TENDIN' TO YA PIG AND LESS TRYIN' TO TEND TO OUR ISABEL,' yelled somebody from the back of the room.

'AYE MORE SWINE 'N LESS PRIME, YA OLD FOPDOODLE!' Robert Ferguson bellowed.

'HAHAHA.' The crowd erupted with laughter.

The jurors sitting beside Calamy fought to hide their amusement.

'ORDER, ORDER!' the Justice bellowed.

'BOOOOO, LET 'ER GO!'

'BOOOOO!'

'I KNOWN ISABEL SINCE SHE WAS A GIRL. SHE'S NOT CAPABLE OF SUCH A THING!'

Jasper Calamy knew what Milton Killsin was up to. The justice banged on the table with his gavel to bring order to the room. 'Milton Killsin, are you saying what I think you're saying?'

'YES, YOUR GRACE, tis true, we all know women are tempted by the Devil!'

The room hushed, the weight of his statement lingering like an unspoken challenge. In the face of mounting prejudice and fervent beliefs, Jasper Calamy's task had become not only to uncover the truth behind these accusations but also to confront the deeper shadows that danced within the hearts of the villagers.

Tommy pushed in front. 'SHE'S DONE NOWT, YER GRACE! He's just makin' it up, wants me land!' Tommy hurried over and stood beside her.

Justice Calamy stood and called out, 'Is the minister present?' He called out, seeking the voice of reason and divine guidance amidst the chaos.

Arthur appeared. 'Yes, I am, your grace!'

'Minister, what say you about this presentment? Is it possible there is evil in our midst?'

Jasper Calamy knew to ask the question or else the vicar would send letters to the rector in Bradford.

The minister paused while he glanced at Isabel and Tommy. Though he had earned his newfound position and recognition, a darker motive gnawed at him, fuelled by the shillings he received from the likes of Milton Killsin. As the silence lingered, he chose his words carefully, knowing that his response would have far-reaching consequences.

The minister called out, 'PEOPLE OF HAWORTH, we need to take the threat of the Devil's work seriously! The antichrist has but twenty years in which to win, convert and torture mankind, so we must be ever vigilant!'

Tommy reacted protectively. 'NOOOooo, me wife 'as done nowt, you leave 'er be!' He took a step toward Milton Killsin aggressively.

The constable and bailiff stepped forward and grabbed Tommy's arms.

He tried to wrestle free. 'ISABEL!'

'LEAVE HIM BE!' screamed Isabel! The uproar within the tavern swelled like a roaring tempest, the cacophony of voices reaching a crescendo of hollers and jeers. Jasper Calamy's commanding presence cut through the chaos, his raised hands a beacon of authority. 'QUIET! Let the minister speak!'

The minister, Arthur, stood at the precipice of a choice. A choice between pursuing truth and yielding to the currents of manipulation that threatened to drown reason. As his eyes darted across the faces of the crowd, he was well aware of the role witchcraft accusations played in maintaining control, a sinister check on anti-Puritan behaviour. Accusations against a few could serve as a chilling deterrent to others who dared to question the established order.

'The presence of the devil is in our community! God will protect his servants and keep them out of harm's way; therefore, it is my proposition… that Isabel Rushworth… be…' Arthur glanced at Milton Killsin. 'Examined!'

Arthur scanned the room. 'We need the assistance of master Matthew Hopkins to assist in this presentment. Please step forward, your grace, and I thank you for your speedy arrival.'

The crowd parted as a tall, grey, bearded Puritan made his way slowly to the front.

He took off his hat and politely bowed to the justice and the jurors. 'Matthew Hopkins, at your service.' He spoke very posh with the soft dialect of a southerner.

The crowd hushed.

Two men standing behind Tommy started to whisper to each other. ''Ere, I've 'eard of 'im, he's a witch finder! Goes about the country findin' witches and hangin' 'em if he proves 'em guilty.'

Tommy, hearing this, tried to free himself from the bailiff's' grasp, then John Pigshells put the shackles around his wrists.

'JOHN PLEASE, LET ME GOOOooo!'

'Sorry, old friend, it's fer yer own good.'

The crowd pushed forward, shoved and hollered their disapproval, the women shrieked and pleaded for Isabel's release.

'BOOOOOoo, LET ER GO!'

'BOOOOOoo!'

'BOOOOOoo!'

The bailiff stood and took out his large iron mace holding it high for all to see, 'TAKE ONE STEP CLOSER, AND SOMEBODY'S GONNA GET IT! STEP BACK! STEP BACK, I SAY!'

The crowd went silent.

Isabel watched in dismay, her heart pounding with a mix of fury and helplessness. The tendrils of intrigue and manipulation had woven a complex tapestry, ensnaring her family and the very fabric of their community.

The tavern's atmosphere had grown almost unbearable in its anticipation as Justice Calamy's voice cut through the stillness. 'And how do you intend to carry out this examination, Master Hopkins?' The room's focus shifted to the enigmatic figure of Matthew Hopkins, his presence a palpable reminder of the weight of impending judgment.

Hopkins' smile seemed to dance upon his lips, a calculated gesture that hinted at a deeper knowledge. 'The accused will be asked to say the Lord's Prayer, and if she can do so without interruption, then she should be free to go.'

Calamy knew what Killsin was up to and this was how he could set Isabel free. 'Very well, Isabel Rushworth, do you agree?'

Isabel cleared her throat. 'Of course I can, say it every sabbath in church!'

'PROCEED!' yelled the justice.

The crowd remained quiet; you could hear a pin drop.

Tommy watched on nervously.

Isabel cleared her throat and began. 'Wee fatheur which art in 'eaven, hallowed be thy name. Thy kingda cum, thy will be done on Earth, as it is in 'eaven. Give us this day our daily bread…'

Isabel stopped, forgetting mid-sentence and struggled to speak the words.

The minister and the justice frowned and peered at each other questioningly then at master Hopkins.

He smiled. 'Isabel, please continue.'

'An' forgive our debts…. as we forgive our debtors… an' lead us not into temptation, but deliva us from evil for thine is the kingdom, an' the power, 'n t' glory, for ever. Amen.'

The crowd murmured.

Isabel and Tommy's eyes met. They both waited for the justice to speak.

Hopkins bowed and leant across the juror table and whispered.

All in the room waited nervously in anticipation.

The jurors conferred amongst themselves, their heads bent in deliberation. Jasper Calamy turned to his fellow jurors, a silent consensus passing between them.

The justice cleared his throat. 'Mr Hopkins?'

'The results are inconclusive! You must be further examined.'

The room seemed to hold its breath as the weight of those words settled upon Isabel, a chilling reminder of the precarious path she now tread.

The crowd's jeers reverberated, a dissonant chorus of frustration and anger. 'BOOOOOooooo, LET ER GO!' The villagers' voices rose, an impassioned plea for mercy that reverberated through the room.

Mr Hopkins now knew he would get paid his fifty shillings. He gestured for his assistant to come over. 'Stearne you know what to do!' The transaction was set in motion, the gears of a sinister mechanism clicking into place.

Isabel stood. 'NOOOoooo, leave me be!' Her voice pierced through the turmoil, a desperate cry for freedom.

Tommy tried to wrestle himself away from Pigshells and the bailiff.

Pigshells held firm. 'Come on, Tommy, she'll be fine. No harm will come to 'er, or else there will be a reckonin', I swear it!'

She took a step backward in defiance.

Hopkins grabbed her hands roughly and placed them on the table in front of Calamy. 'Come now, woman, don't struggle! It'll all be over soon.'

Stearne approached from behind, his movements rough and calculated. He tore at the fabric of her dress with an almost predatory urgency, exposing her back to the cold, unforgiving air of the tavern.

Isabel's breath caught in her throat, her defiance giving way to a sense of vulnerability.

The crowd fell into an eerie silence, a collective anticipation that hung like a heavy fog. Stearne's gaze fixated upon Isabel's back, his inspection methodical as he sought the elusive mark, the sign of the devil's touch.

He smiled and reached into his leather doublet and pulled out a witch pricker. It was a metal, pointy, sharp instrument used to pierce the skin. A witch would be insensitive to its puncture.

Seeing this, Tommy thrashed about and punched the constable knocking him over a table. He tried to free himself from the bailiff's grasp and almost did until Pigshells clubbed him across the backs of the legs.

Tommy slumped forward onto his knees. He growled angrily between clenched teeth, 'LET ME GO!'

The tavern's air crackled with tension as the unfolding scene bore witness to the lengths one man would go to secure his ambitions. Milton Killsin's insidious words slithered into Tommy's ear, a venomous whisper that carried a choice wrapped in a chilling promise. 'Come now, Rushworth, lest ya be named the witch's familiar. Leave yer land and all will be forgiven. I can end this right now!'

Pigshells heard him. *So tis true, he is after his land, the pig fucker! Nowt I can do now though. Isabel the poor lass. For her sake I must let this run its course.*

Tommy resisted again, knocking off Milton's hat, in the melee, to reveal his bald white head and whispery strands of hair.

Isabel screamed as Stearne pushed the pricker into her lower back then pulled it out and pushed it into the area just above her shoulder blade. She screamed again with the pain and started to sob.

The two wounds did not bleed. He continued to push the pricker into her back. 'TOMMY!'

The marks left small red welts in her skin but there was no blood.

'ENOUGH!' bellowed Jasper Calamy.

Hopkins turned to him. 'If there is no blood then we are too late, the devil has had his way with her. There is another way to be sure… by sacrament of baptism.'

'Continue.' Justice Calamy's voice held a sombre resignation, the gravity of their predicament weighing heavily upon him.

The sinister plan unfurled, a twisted ritual that sent shivers down the spines of those present. Hopkins' words dripped with a chilling determination. 'If she were a witch, water would reject her body and prevent her from submerging. She will be taken to the ducking pond, bound, and dropped into the water. If she floats then it is confirmed, she is a witch and may God have mercy on her soul!'

'NOOOooo, me wife has done nowt, you leave 'er be, she aint no witch!' Tommy head butted the bailiff and tried to wrestle free.

This hurts me more than its gonna hurt you, Tommy, Pigshells thought, then hit him on the back of the neck.

The constable supported Tommy's limp body to the floor. When he came around, he escorted him out of the tavern. He whispered, 'I'm sorry, Tommy. You 'ave ta let things be fer the moment. Trust me, there'll be a reckonin' and Killsin will get his!'

Stearne's grip on Isabel tightened, unyielding as he led her through the crowd and onto the bustling Main Street. Her struggles were futile against his strength, her voice a resounding plea that pierced the night. 'Let go of me! We've done nowt. 'Tis Milton Killsin who's started all this. LET ME GO!' Her cries echoed like a lament, a testament to the turmoil that had enveloped her world.

In the midst of it all, Milton Killsin slithered away, a smug smile playing upon his lips. The knowledge of his impending victory, of the land that was all but within his grasp, fuelled his arrogance.

He glanced down noticing the metal witch pricker Stearne had dropped. He picked it up and examined it closely. The sharp point was menacing and he lightly placed his thumb on the tip to feel it. He applied more pressure and felt the sharp tip go back into its barrel. The sharp point retracted.

He frowned. *Of course,* he thought. *No blood! Now they won't have any other choice but to vacate the property, not after this ordeal. I warned them!*

Killsin started on his way home. *Seems the extra coin to get Hopkins was well worth it.*

The crowd staggered out of the Kings Arms turning right into Main Street and down past the Fleece Inn to the manor. They continued down Sun Street and across the field to the ducking pond. As they got closer, the rambunctious fervour of the crowd increased as did Tommy's anger and pleas of innocence.

The path led them to the ducking pond, an eerie site shrouded in darkness. The crowd's fervour intensified as they approached, the tension palpable and electric. Isabel's heart raced as the weight of her situation pressed upon her, her struggles a battle against the relentless currents of fate. Stearne ripped her kirtle further and sat Isabel down on the wooden stool, binding her ankles to the legs.

The moon's pale glow cast a spectral luminescence over the scene at the ducking pond. The cold, oppressive air hung heavy with a sense of foreboding.

The crowd collected around the pond, their torches shining a light on the edge of destiny. They yelled their disfavour, 'BOOO!' 'LEAVE 'ER BEEE!' 'LET 'ER GO!'

The ducking stool was attached to a long wooden beam with a fulcrum at its centre which, when turned would extend the stool out into the middle of the pond. The bailiff and Stearne pulled on a large chain attached to the end which raised the stool from the ground.

'Pigshells, ya know she's no witch, unshackle me!' Tommy continued to grapple with him.

William rushed over to Justice Calamy, removed his felt hat and bowed submissively, 'Sir, I believe there are shenanigans afoot. Would you please 'ave mercy?'

Calamy was undeterred as he knew to keep order he was to keep his power over the people.

Hopkins butt in, 'There has been evidence of supernatural misconduct and she must be tested! We must rid the community of sinners and those who do not uphold Puritan values.'

William pleaded, 'But, yer grace, respectfully, surely there is no crime against singin' an whistlin'. Let me take 'er place, I beg you.'

Calamy's frustration seeped through, his sympathy for Isabel at odds with his duty. 'The law is the law, and the jurors have made up their mind. Now leave me!' The finality in his words silenced any hope of reprieve.

Tommy waited for Pigshells to relax then shrugged him off and ran over to the stool and leant down in front of her. 'Isabel, do not fret. Just before yer 'ead gets close to the water, 'old yer breath and release small bubbles. The water is cold and yo'll be in shock. Ya must not panic, stay calm and wait fer 'em ta bring you up again!'

Terrified, Isabel said nothing, turned and peered into Tommy's eyes, she whispered, 'Tell Will I love 'im.'

Pigshells marched over to Tommy and lifted him up, 'Come on, mate, don't make this any 'arder than it already is.'

'YER GONNA BE ALRIGHT, JUST DO AS I SAID!'

The bailiff and Stearne grabbed the chain and put their weight on it then manoeuvred the beam so the chair was suspended over the pond.

Isabel screamed, 'I'm innocent, let me BEEEeeee!'

The bailiff and Stearne let go of the chain and the stool crashed into the water submerging Isabel. She lifted her head and took deep breaths before she went under.

Tommy watched Isabel struggling beneath the surface. 'Come on, Isabel, calm thyself,' he whispered. Isabel's struggles became less panicked.

It seemed like an eternity.

The crowd started to yell, 'LET 'ER UP! LET 'ER UP!'

They pulled down heavily on the chain which lifted the beam and the chair out of the water slowly.

Isabel coughed and spluttered water, shaking her head to remove her hair from her eyes. She continued to cough and spit and opened her eyes, trying to blink the water from them.

Tommy with a panicked expression on his face.

'TOMMYYYYY!' Isabel groaned.

Master Hopkins stepped forward and bellowed, 'ISABEL RUSHWORTH, DO YOU PLEAD GUILTY AND ADMIT YOU'RE IN LEAGUE WITH SATAN? CONFESS NOW AND YOU WILL BE SPARED THIS DISCOMFORT.'

All knew if she confessed she would surely hang.

Isabel coughed, and tried to speak, weakly she yelled, 'I'VE DONE NOWT!'

Master Hopkins nodded at Stearne, who once again let go of the chain allowing the chair to crash to the surface of the water and submerge.

The crowd sympathised with Isabel.

'LET 'ER UP!'

'LET 'ER UP!'

'LET 'ER UP!'

Tommy also yelled her innocence as he watched the small bubbles of air break on the surface of the water.

I don't think she can take much more of this. Hold on Isabel, hold on luv. William dropped his chin and shook his head from side to side. He glanced at Tommy who was beside himself with fear.

Mr Hopkins nodded at the bailiff and Stearne, who pulled down on the chain and lifted the stool back out of the water. Isabel was spent.

Tommy yelled at Calamy, 'YER GRACE, YA MUST STOP THIS, I'M PLEADIN' WITH YA, PLEEEASE!'

Master Hopkins stepped forward and waited for Isabel to stop coughing and spluttering. 'Isabel Rushworth, do you plead guilty and admit you're in with the devil? Answer truthfully and all this will stop!'

Coughing and spluttering then breathing heavily she hacked up some water and whispered, 'Please sir… I'm…'

The crowd booed.

'LET 'ER GO, SHE'S NO WITCH!'

'YER LET 'ER GO!' another bellowed.

Hopkins once again nodded at the bailiff.

Tommy was petrified. 'She won't last another dunkin!'

Sun Street was cast in an eerie glow as the scene at the ducking pond unfolded. Just as hope seemed to waver on the edge of despair, a sudden commotion broke through the night's tension. Across the street, a figure appeared, running towards the pond with an urgency that seemed to resonate with the very air.

'WAIT! WAIT! I WAS WRONG, LET HER UP, LET HER UP!' Milton Killsin's frantic cries pierced the night, a stark contrast to his previous smug demeanour.

Master Hopkins and Jasper Calamy both appeared shocked.

Jasper Calamy stood from his seat and put his hand up. 'STOP! Bring her up!'

Calamy stepped toward Hopkins. 'Release her until we investigate this matter further!'

William dove into the frigid water and swam down to Isabel who was shaking and struggling from the pressure in her lungs. Large bubbles of escaping air came from her mouth.

She saw William and started to shake her head from side to side in a panic. Her long hair waved slowly in the current.

William grabbed the rope bindings and pulled on them, loosening them enough for her to slip her feet through.

Isabel expelled one last slow release of bubbles and went limp before him. The chair started to slowly rise, and William pushed up on it until Isabel's head was above the surface of the water.

Pigshells and Tommy ran over and helped the bailiff and Stearne pull down on the chain and swing the boom back onto dry land.

'JOHN, Take the shackles off, HURRY, DAMN YA!'

Tommy ran to Isabel, yelling, 'ISABEL! NOOOOoo Isabel!' He lifted her and placed her gently on the wet grass.

He gently moved the wet hair from her face and grabbed her shoulders, shaking them urgently. 'Isabel… Isabel… ISABEL!'

He shook harder. 'Isabel come back to me.' A tear started to pool in the bottom of his eyelid and his voice quivered. 'Isaaaabel.'

But as the truth of Isabel's state became apparent, a storm of emotions overtook Tommy. His grief transformed into a searing anger, a fire that blazed with intensity. His eyes locked onto Milton Killsin, hate and retribution shining in their depths. 'You… you bastard! You did this! You son of a whore!' His voice was a venomous hiss, the words a bitter indictment of the man who had wrought this torment upon them. Tommy glared at Milton with hate and retribution in his eyes, he whispered.

Tommy stood slowly, glaring at Milton with revenge in his eyes. He took a step toward him, his fists clenched, and his teeth bared. Milton put his hands up defensively and took steps slowly backward.

Isabel jolted and coughed. Water and vomit gushed from her mouth. She groaned and coughed again, turning on her side she continued to gag, cough and expel water and saliva.

'ISABEL!' Tommy turned and slowly sank to his knees besides her. 'ISABEL, are you orlright, my luv? ISABEL? Thank the Lord.' He placed his hand on her arm lovingly.

Isabel's struggles began to subside, her coughs and gags gradually giving way to ragged breaths. Through the haze of her pain, she heard Tommy's voice, his touch a lifeline that anchored her to reality. She opened her eyes, a faint glimmer of consciousness returning as his face swam into view. 'Tommy? I love you, Tommy.' Her words were a fragile confession, a beacon of love that pierced through the darkness.

Milton Killsin removed himself, moving backwards quietly through the circle of spectators as they glared at him loathingly.

CHAPTER 17

Whispers in the Shadows

Earlier in the afternoon Milton Killsin arrived home from the court leet feeling pleased with himself. The plan worked. *I'll have that land soon, very soon.*

As evening draped a cloak of darkness over his home, an unexpected and unwelcome presence shattered his sense of triumph. A figure materialised in the dimly lit room, its features obscured by two holes cut into a piece of fabric that draped over its head. The ghostly appearance of the intruder sent a chill down Milton's spine, his bravado faltering in the face of this unknown adversary.

'Don't move!' The intruder demanded. His voice was a low, menacing whisper, the command hanging heavy in the air. Milton's hands shot up instinctively, trembling as fear clutched at his heart.

'Ya won't get away with this!' Milton's voice wavered, a desperate attempt to assert control in a situation that was quickly spiralling out of his grasp.

The intruder took a step forward and placed the tip of the barrel of his pistol against Milton's back. 'Won't I now, and what da ya intend ta do about it?'

Milton stuttered and looked at the intruder with his peripheral vision. 'Th...the... Justice of th...the Peace and the magistrate are known to me, they will 'ave you hanged!'

He pushed Milton in the back and he stumbled awkwardly through the door. 'Now then, SIT DOWN!' He pushed him again. Milton's legs gave way beneath him, and he found himself seated on a chair, his heart pounding in his chest.

Milton grunted. 'Me wife, she will return soon with friends, you'll be outnumbered. If you leave now, I won't tell anybody!'

'Don't be absurd, you fool!' The intruder growled.

Milton sat on the chair and stared nervously at him. 'God will punish you, comin' into people's homes tis a treacherous act!'

The intruder kept the pistol pointed at Milton; he crept around the back of the chair and tied his wrists together. He then took a piece of linen from the kitchen and shoved it in his mouth.

Suddenly the door opened, and Milton's wife came in. 'Milton, are ya home?' Startled, she dropped the basket she was carrying and put her hands to her face. 'MILTON!'

'Mmmmmfff.' Milton mumbled.

'Ahhhh, we been waiting fer ya misses! SIT THERE!' the intruder demanded!

Shocked, she lifted her grey kirtle and scurried over to sit on the stool.

The intruder's voice, a low and ominous murmur, sent a shiver down Milton's spine as he leaned in close, his words a chilling reminder of the stakes at hand. 'Now, while I wait here with yer misses,' he whispered, the threat implicit in his tone, 'yer gonna go and stop the vicious use of the duckin' stool.' The weight of the demand hung heavy in the air, a command laced with a promise of dire consequences should it be ignored.

Milton stubbornly resisted. 'Tis probably too late; she's already gone!'

He undid the twine binding Milton's wrists, grabbed him by the back of the collar and lifted him up, pushing him toward the door. 'Well then, you better hurry!

'Remember, I'll be watching and if ya don't want ta come back to find her throat slit, you better do as I say!'

Mrs Killsin's panic was palpable, her eyes wide with a mixture of terror and helplessness. She watched as her husband scurried down the hill towards Sun Street, her heart aching with worry for both his safety and her own.

Milton scurried down the hill towards Sun Street. He continued to turn and glance back sheepishly checking to see if he was being watched.

The intruder crept over to Mrs Killsin and tied her hands and feet to the chair. He lent down slowly and whispered, 'Ya tell anybody about my visit and I'll come back, da ya hear!' The fear that settled in her chest seemed to tighten its hold as she nodded, a silent acknowledgment of his power over her.

The intruder looked around. 'Now where's the coin? Where da ya hide it? Nice big 'ouse like this, ya must 'ave coin about. Tell me or else you'll lose an ear!'

'Tis in the ceramic jar there in the corner.' She pointed to the corner of the kitchen.

Keeping his eyes pointed in her direction he smashed the jar on the stone floor.

'Now you 'ave the coin, let us alone!' Mrs Killsin pleaded.

He picked up the five gold guineas and put them in the pouch in his long coat. He took another cloth from the cooking area and placed it in Mrs Killsin's mouth.

The room seemed to hold its breath as the intruder moved toward the indicated spot, his actions a haunting reminder that danger could strike from the shadows at any moment.

☆

Tommy helped Isabel to her feet, she was cold, wet, pale and exhausted, 'Come on, luv, let's get ya home.'

Tommy put his arm around her and supported her as she staggered away. She was weak and her undershirt clung to her body.

The ordeal at the ducking pond had left her cold, drenched and drained, her body trembling with exhaustion. As they moved, a compassionate woman from the village stepped forward, draping a cloak around Isabel's shoulders to shield her from the chill. 'There you are, luv. Keep ya warm until you get to your hearth. God bless ya,' she offered, her gesture a small glimmer of kindness amidst the darkness.

Tommy pulled the cloak together in the front and braced her as she stumbled. She continued to cough and hack up water and vomit which tasted acidic in her throat her body wracked by the remnants of her harrowing experience.

Robert followed behind. 'Ya orl right, Isabel? BASTARDS will pay fer this!'

Robert turned to see Milton Killsin talking with the bailiff and Jasper Calamy. The last thing he noticed was Milton Killsin being led away.

As they arrived at the bottom of the hill to their cottage, Isabel stopped to get her breath. 'Tommy I can't go any further.'

'Tis orl right, wife.' Tommy bent down and placed his arms behind Isabel's knees, lifter her up and carried her up the hill.

She placed her head on his shoulder and closed her eyes.

Tommy kissed her on the head and allowed her to snuggle into his neck.

Robert stormed ahead to open the door as Tommy carefully guided her through.

William quickly grabbed the mattress and unrolled it on the floor next to the hearth.

Tommy carefully placed her down and covered her with the woollen blanket, wiping her hair from the front of her face. 'The poor love, she's already asleep,' whispered Tommy.

'What are we gonna do?' Robert asked.

'Slow down, nephew, these are funny times, we don't wanna be causin' ourselves more trouble with the bailiff. We all know who's behind all this.'

'The last thing I saw when we left was 'im bein' taken away.'

'Where did ya get it?' Robert stared at the pistol sitting on the mantle. He strode over and picked it up. 'Powder's damp.' Robert realised he said too much, smiled and put the pistol back down.

'Don't you be getting any ideas.' Tommy stared at Robert. 'And how is it ya know sa much about such things, nephew?'

'The city can be a dangerous place, Uncle.'

The events of the day had left an indelible mark on their lives, but amidst the darkness, a glimmer of unity and resilience shone through.

☆

As the cottage fire crackled and cast its warm glow upon the makeshift bed where Isabel lay, a scene unfolded elsewhere. Tommy remembered the old musketeer at Tadcaster, all those years ago.

'What's wrong, lad? Never put yer eyes on a musket before? Gew on, pick it up if ya wish; what's your name?'

'Me name is Tommy, Tommy Rushworth.'

Tommy was embarrassed and felt like he'd been put on the spot. 'No, yer grace, but thanks fer offerin'.'

'Gew on, Tommy Rushworth,' the musketeer picked up his musket and offered it to him.

Tommy took it in his hands uncomfortably. 'What if it goes off?'

'No chance lad; the pan's empty, and I'm holding the match cord. See here?' The musketeer blew on the match cord and the tip became red.

Tommy took the musket; it was heavy, solid wood and metal. He remembered how the soldier fired and hit the clay jug back in Bradford. He stood at the edge of the faggot and pointed the barrel down the road towards York.

The old man pushed the barrel higher with his finger. 'Gew on, lift the barrel higher, one foot back.'

Tommy felt its weight. 'It's so long, heavy, heavier than I imagined!'

Henry grinned. 'Aye, has ta be lad, to bust a lead ball through the breastplate.'

☆

William glanced at Robert and could sense his son's innocence was gone.

'Da, I 'ave ta go out fer a bit, won't be long.' He took his cloak from the nail beside the door and put his hat on. He opened the door.

Will came racing up. 'MA!' Will's face was red and flushed, and he was panting heavily from his panicked run from the manor.

Tommy heard him enter and turned. 'Tis alright son, she's sleeping,' Tommy whispered, 'Don't worry yerself she'll be okay.'

'Da, I didn't know, I raced down here as soon as I 'eard, kitchen girl from the manor told me. What 'appened?'

'Milton Killsin presented her as a witch, and the court leet ordered the testin'.'

Will bent down and put his hand gently on her forehead, 'The BASTARDS ARE MAD, Ma, a witch, NOOOoooo. It's not fair Da, we gotta do somethin'! They can't get away with this!'

'Will, CALM DOWN! These be strange times lad and we live in 'em! Nowt we could do, anyway she's 'ome now and restin' quietly. Best you be back to the manor before ya get another hidin'.'

'Okay, Da but tell 'er I'll come and see her tomorra!' Will bent down and gave Isabel a gentle peck on the cheek. 'I luv ya, Ma. You sure she's gonna be orlright?'

'Yes, son, she'll be fine tomorrow, she just needs rest.'

Lifting the latch, Will went outside into the chilled evening. The sun was already setting and he knew Mr Dodds would be waiting for him.

As he approached the Mill, his steps grew heavier, a sense of impending doom settling in his chest. He knew what awaited him, the harsh sting of the whipping stick, a cruel reminder of his helplessness in the face of authority.

When he got back to the Mill there he was, whipping stick in his hand slowly tapping his thigh. 'Are ya not getting sick of these hidings, lad? You know the rules.'

‘I’m sorry, Mr Dodds!’ Will dropped his gaze, knowing what was to come.

Mr Dodds raised the stick.

Will turned and would normally scrunch up his face, but still angry about his ma, stood defiantly waiting for the first strike.

He heard the whipping stick slice through the air with a whoosh, felt the sting on his back. Will waited for the second blow.

‘Whoosh!’

‘Whoosh!’

‘Whoosh!’

Mr Dodds struck again and again. He rested, breathing heavily from his exertions. He leant over. ‘I ‘eard about ya mother. Sorry lad.’

With each strike, Will stood tall, his defiance a testament to his strength and resolve. The pain was sharp, but he refused to let it break him. As the whipping stick fell once more, Will’s gaze remained steady, a spark of determination flickering within him. He would endure, he would fight, and he would stand strong for his family and the truth they held dear.

After the last ‘whoosh’, Will stood up straight; the recent events hardened him. The ‘whippin’ didn’t hurt anymore. Will’s gaze met Mr Dodds’, a fiery determination replacing the fear that had once gripped him. He squared his shoulders and lifted his chin, his voice unwavering. At that point the boy became a man.

Mr Dodds whispered to him, ‘Will, Mr Griswold ‘as a special job fer ya to do tomorra. In the morning, go to the stables and start mucking them out and wait.’

Will took a step toward the door and was pulled back by his tunic. Mr Dodds, knowing the other boys were listening, made sure he seemed impartial. ‘And don’t be late again ‘cause next time, I won’t be sa kind!’

Will stood tall and strolled inside the mill and up the wooden steps as if nothing happened.

The other boys sat up from their beds to watch him by the light of the candle. They snickered.

Will stopped in his steps and looked slowly at each of them one by one. A silent warning. His gaze steady and unwavering. His silence spoke volumes, a warning that needed no words. In the midst of their smiles, they fell silent under his piercing stare.

Mr Dodds called up from downstairs. 'Right, you lot shut it!'

They all heard Mr Dodds stomp across the wooden floor and close the door behind him locking it from the outside on his way out.

Will undressed down to his undershirt and climbed into the box bed beside the other boy, who took far more of the bed than he needed.

Will elbowed him in the ribs, pulled his blanket over himself and closed his eyes.

Bobby blew out the candle.

Will tried to sleep but couldn't, worried about his mother. *Bastards are gonna pay for what they did!*

With a heart full of resilience and determination, Will drifted into a restless slumber, ready to rise to whatever challenges awaited him in the light of the morning. The village may have been shrouded in shadows, but Will's spirit burned brightly, a beacon of hope and defiance against the trials that sought to extinguish it.

CHAPTER 18

Unravelling Deceit

The atmosphere in the Kings Arms was tense as Milton Killsin sat on the stool, his eyes darting nervously between the stern faces of the justice and jurors. John Pigshells, the bailiff, and the constable stood by, their expressions a mix of curiosity and scepticism. The room had hushed, the earlier raucousness replaced by a heavy anticipation.

Now you'll cop it, ya fucker, thought John Pigshells.

Calamy frowned. 'Now, Milton Killsin, you understand a false presentiment is a serious matter. Would you mind explaining what has been going on.'

Nervously, Milton gazed down hoping they would believe him, he whispered, 'Intruder, came into my house, tied us up, threatened to slit my wife's throat if I didn't stop the ducking.'

A ripple of disbelief swept through the room, followed by murmurs of scepticism from both jurors and patrons who had remained at the tavern. Milton's story seemed far-fetched, and some couldn't help but chuckle at the audacity of his claim.

Jasper Calamy leaned closer. 'Did I hear you correctly, intruder? Don't be absurd man!'

There was a mummer from the jurors and what was left of the earlier patrons who were further inebriated and less vocal.

'Come now, Mr Killsin, surely you don't expect us to believe a housebreaker came to your house.'

Some of the jurors, by this time, were full of ale and they started to chuckle with disbelief.

'Mr Killsin, the punishment for false presentment at the court leet is four weekends in the stocks!'

Killsin looked up. 'But, your grace, it's true. My wife can prove it. Your grace, it's true, I swear it!'

Calamy frowned in disbelief. 'Your wife?'

'Yes, he tied her up and told me he would cut her throat if I didn't do as he asked.'

'Constable, go to the Killsin house and bring Mrs Killsin here at once!'

'Mr Killsin, to be honest, I don't know what to believe anymore. First you claim Isabel Rushworth is a witch; she is clearly not. Now you claim an intruder, broke into your house! This all sounds somewhat fanciful.'

Milton's mind raced as he fought to keep his composure. He had hoped that by pointing the finger at an intruder, he could escape the consequences of his deceit. But now, facing the scrutiny of the court leet, he realised he might have played his last card. The room held its breath, awaiting the arrival of Mrs Killsin.

A few minutes later, the constable marched in with her; she was out of breath and red faced from the quick climb up the hill.

'Are here we are, Mrs Killsin, thank you so much for coming at this late hour. Your husband tells us you were terrorised by an intruder, a footpad.'

'Wha… what, your grace?' she replied nervously as the jurors watched on.'

Calamy re-phrased his question. 'An intruder came to your house and threatened you?'

Milton Killsin stared at his wife, puzzled. 'Tell them dammit!'

Mrs Killsin felt a lump form in her throat as the weight of her husband's accusation settled upon her. The room seemed to close in around her and her mind raced to find an explanation, then she remembered the intruders threat.

'Intruder? With all respect, your grace, I don't know what yer talking about.'

A ripple of whispers spread through the jurors and the crowd, each exchange fuelling the growing sense of intrigue. The situation had taken an unexpected turn, and it was clear that Mrs. Killsin's response had cast doubt on her husband's story.

The jurors whispered to each other as did the onlookers who by now were enjoying the entertainment. They enjoyed seeing Milton Killsin squirming like a worm.

John Pigshells smiled. *Hahahah, try and get out of this one, you old bastard!*

'I see!' Justice Calamy whispered to the juror on each side of him then signalled for the bailiff.

Jasper Calamy turned his gaze to Milton Killsin. 'The court leet charges you with false presentment and sentences you to six weekends in the pillory. When not in the pillory, you'll spend time in the lock up. '

Milton glared at his wife angrily, 'WIFE, TELL THEM THE TRUTH! I'm innocent, I tell you! WHAT HAVE YOU DONE? TELL THEM!'

Mrs Killsin gazed at the ground sadly then watched the bailiff put shackles on her husband. 'I'm so sorry, husband! Milton?'

She thought about the last thing the intruder whispered, *Ya tell anybody about my visit and I'll come back, da ya hear? I'll be back and all you know will be gone.*

'Bailiff, take Mr Killsin to the lock-up and in the morn, have him placed in the pillory for all to see.'

Milton Killsin's face turned ashen, the weight of his deceit and the consequences of his actions crashing down upon him. His attempt to manipulate the court had unraveled before his eyes, leaving him exposed and facing a harsh punishment.

'Mrs Killsin, you are free to go! This court leet is adjourned may God have mercy on your soul!'

Jasper Calamy knocked the table with his gavel and stood as did the jurors.

The bailiff lifted Killsin by the arm from the stool and escorted him out the door.

Calamy went outside and climbed in his carriage.

The jurors and remaining patrons filed out of the Kings Arms. They slowly made their way off in different directions toward home.

When Griswold arrived, Master Calamy was still awake and sitting by the fire, so he sat down in the chair opposite.

Griswold watched the flickering flames, allowing Calamy the space to gather his thoughts. He knew that the events of the day had stirred something within the justice, something that required consideration.

Calamy picked up the pewter goblet from the small table beside him and gulped.

He thought about the day's events and felt guilty about what happened to the Rushworth woman.

Calamy knew the minister used the fear of the devil to entice locals to his sermons, but he thought today was going too far. *Milton Killsin is behind all this. What if she died? There would have been a reckoning. The magistrate would have been involved. What if this had got back to Lileburn?*

Jasper broke his gaze from the fire and glanced at Griswold. 'Well?'

'Your grace, I've received word from Sergeant Wilding.'

'Wilding, what now?' Calamy asked abruptly.

Griswold continued, 'He is coming to Haworth. Your grace, I should remind you, he was of great service to us in the war. His er... special talents came in very handy at the time.'

Jasper Calamy shook his head, weariness etched into his features. He took the last sip of his wine, the liquid warming him from the inside out. 'I don't want to know,' he said with a sigh, his voice tinged with exhaustion. 'Spare me the details. The less I have to do with Wilding, the better. Keep him out of my sight.'

‘I received news from York today,’ said Griswold. ‘New laws have been passed in Long Parliament focusing on abuses within the cloth-making industry. They are calling for inquiries into all matters of embezzlement and illegality.’

Calamy leaned back in his chair, his fingers drumming thoughtfully against the armrest. ‘We need someone we can trust to oversee these inquiries lest we lose everything.’

‘I believe Milton Killsin about the intruder, your grace. This intruder, could he and the highwayman be one and the same?’

Calamy considered the connection, his thoughts spinning. ‘It’s an intriguing possibility, Griswold.’

Griswold leaned in, his voice lowered. ‘Allow me to handle Milton Killsin. I can arrange for his release and ensure his cooperation. A small sum of coin to the bailiff should smooth the way.’

Calamy’s expression shifted, a mixture of contemplation and concern. ‘Griswold, my reputation is at stake. I cannot be seen as directly intervening.’

‘Your grace, this is a discreet matter. No one need know of your involvement.’

☆

Mr Griswold rode his horse to the lock up, the bailiff heard and opened the door to his house which adjoined.

The bailiff held his lantern which cast shadows over the stone wall. He meandered over and took the reins of the horse so Griswold could dismount. ‘Mr Griswold, what are ya doin’ ‘ere this time a’ night?’

‘I need to speak to Milton Killsin.’

The bailiff yawned. ‘Well, it’s very peculiar given the circumstances, I was just about ta go ta bed.’

Griswold handed the bailiff a parchment. ‘Please read this, it’s from Justice Calamy. It pardons Milton Killsin due to new evidence.

‘His grace also asked me to give you this, a token of his gratitude for the mix up.’ He handed over two shillings.

The bailiff gladly took it, never one to pass up extra coin.

‘Right, you are then,’ the bailiff took the keys from his belt.

He placed the oil lantern on the log outside and peered through the barred opening and unlocked it. ‘There’s somebody ‘ere ta see ya!’

‘Bailiff, would you be so kind as to give us a moment?’ Griswold stepped into the dark cold room.

With a panicked voice, Milton Killsin stood from the dirty mattress on the floor. ‘Mr Griswold, you’ve got to get me out of here. I’ve done nowt except what you told me ta do!’

‘Keep yer voice down, man! You’re the one who wanted them off the land, I was merely suggesting a convenient way ta do it.’

‘Get me outta here!’ Milton demanded.

‘Hold your tongue, you are free to go and his grace has agreed to your position as inspector of wool. You will be sworn in and provided with your seal. This will be very convenient for our plans.’ He lifted the lantern so he could see Killsin’s face.

Milton was surprised. ‘Inspector of wool?’

Griswold whispered, ‘There’s one other thing, you may remember John Wilding. He is on his way up here and is not to be trusted.’

‘John Wilding?’ Milton’s memories from his army days came flooding back. A man known for his brutality and cruelty, Wilding had been feared by Royalist sympathizers. He had inflicted terror and pain without mercy, showing no restraint even in the face of surrender. He had a barbarous inhumanity of the worst kind. There was rumour of torture and hacking of poor wretches and often enacted his fury on dead men. He knew no limit, slashing at soldiers who surrendered or hanging them and carving off their skin with his knife. He never gave fair quarter or mercy.

After the war, Wilding was arrested and sent to Lord Fairfax for trial. He was later pardoned and released after a plea from Jasper Calamy at the behest of Griswold.

As Griswold and Milton continued their conversation in the cold confines of the lock-up, a sinister alliance was taking shape: one that held secrets, power, and dark intentions. The path ahead was paved with deception and manipulation, with the lives of innocent villagers hanging in the balance.

CHAPTER 19

Unexpected Reactions

The morning sun peeked through the small windows of the mill, casting a warm glow on the activity within. Will's awakening was punctuated by the sharp crack of Mr. Dodd's whipping stick on the wooden bed frame.

'Come on, you lot, up ya get. There's work ta be done. The cloth won't weave itself! You got twenty minutes ta do yer constitutionals and get to it. Rushworth, after breakfast yer to slop out the stables.'

'Aye, Mr Dodds.' He wiped the sleep from the corners of his eyes then rushed outside to wash his face in the horse trough. The water was cold and it shocked him into wakefulness.

Bobby and the others were slow to rise.

Will lit a candle and went into the storeroom under the stairs. He took three skeins of yarn for the loom.

Mr Dodds watched, a rare smile gracing his lips. 'Good lad,' he acknowledged, though his tone remained gruff.

Will stretched the warp between the two parallel wooden boards. He bound the bulk yarn and wound it around the board at the end of the loom then thread it through the heddles. Then, taking each individual thread from the warp he attached it ensuring the threads were separated in the raddle. He took the skein and wrapped the yarn around the shuttle horizontally from one end grove to the other. Having done this several times, he was now becoming quite proficient.

They all listened for the bell of Saint Michael of all Angels. The bell rang four times and on the last, the boys started spinning and weaving.

Mr Dodds sat at his desk, writing in his ledger.

Will rushed over to the sorting table and started to separate the wool delivered yesterday into its various grades and thicknesses.

He took some sorted wool and placed it on the carding board and began to comb it, repeating the process several times. Eventually a light, airy fibre was left. This was then set aside for spinning which the younger boys did. It took three spinning wheels to keep the loom operating; the boys would get a whipping if it ran out.

'Will, take the kersey outside to the vat and start the fullin' and be quick about it or else you'll miss breakfast,' Mr Griswold warned.

Will rushed to the other end of the table and picked up the undyed kersey and took it round the side of the building. He unfolded it, placing it in the large vat of urine. Taking off his boots he stepped in and started stomping.

The stale urine had an acidic, putrid smell and made him gag and cough when he took a breath. He tried to keep his head up and swiped at the flies attracted to his efforts. He continued to stomp pushing down the cloth if it was not submerged.

The colour of the urine began to change colour from a clear liquid to a cloudy yellow as the oils and lanolin seeped from the cloth.

Two hours later, Will stepped out of the vat and carried the cloth to the drying frame. He pulled it taught so it dried in the breeze.

While Will was washing his feet, Mr Dodds appeared at the door. 'Come, Will, tis almost breakfast!'

They all heard the bells of Sanit Michael of all Angels toll.

The looms went silent.

Will ran inside and stood at the end of the line with the other boys. Mr Dodds strolled through the door outside. The boys followed him one after the other, first Bobby, then the other two then Will.

Mr Dodds turned and locked the door behind him.

They waited for Mr Dodds to get to the front of the line then followed him. They marched past the barn.

Will grabbed the shirt of the lad in front and pulled him back, stepping forward to take up his new position.

His bedmate let out a grumble of protest, but Will was undeterred.

As they got closer to the kitchen door, Bobby ran past Mr Dodds, lifted the latch, and opened the door for him to go through.

The other boys followed.

Bobby put his foot out to trip Will.

Will easily stepped over it.

Bobby noticed the other boy following at the back; he punched him in the arm.

Margaret was at the window washing plates and noticed Bobby's foolishness.

The boys filed in, taking their seats with a mix of exhaustion and hunger evident on their faces.

Mrs Stuart was waiting. 'Ah, Mr Dodds, how are ya on this fine mornin?'

The large trestle table in the middle of the room was set for eight. Mr Dodds stood at one end and the housekeeper, Mrs Stuart, stood at the other.

Margaret stirred the cauldron in the hearth and began to scoop its contents into a small ceramic bowls.

Mr Dodds and Mrs Stuart sat.

Margaret served Mr Dodds and Mrs Stuart. She served the apprentices starting with Bobby. She could sense Will's attention, so she glanced at him and smiled. In doing so, she took her eyes off the bowl and spilt it into Bobby's lap.

'ARRGH! ARRGH!' Bobby stood quickly trying to pull the hot, wet breeches away from his skin. 'You dew-beater, look what you've done!'

Mrs Stuart was startled by the commotion and the other two apprentices started laughing, one of them hysterically.

Margaret dropped the ceramic bowl and it smashed on the ground; she stood back, her hands at her face, embarrassed, she raced out the door.

Mrs Stuart glared at the other kitchen maids. 'Well, don't just sit there. Get 'im something to wipe his breeches!'

Will bent down and started picking up the pieces of ceramic then went outside and over to the bench where Margaret was sitting.

She was bent over with her face in her hands, weeping.

'Are ya orlright?' Will sat down beside her. 'It was only an accident, don't worry yerself.'

Margaret looked up and smiled. 'I'm not worried; he deserved what he got. I saw him try to trip you.'

Will's eyes opened wide. 'Hahahah, yer cheeky, you'll end up in all sorts a' trouble.'

Mr Dodds appeared at the back door. 'WILL, COME IN'ERE AND FINISH YER BREAKFAST AND BRING 'ER WITH YA!'

'COMIN', MR DODDS.' Will stood quickly. 'Come, Margaret, before we both get a whippin!'

Will put his hand out toward Margaret who was taken back by his presumptuous gesture. She reached up slowly and grabbed his hand.

He pulled her from the bench and pulled her toward the kitchen door. They were both smiling.

'Will, stop!' She giggled.

Margaret managed a small smile, a glimmer of hope returning to her eyes. In that moment, amidst the shards of broken ceramic and the weight of their responsibilities, a bond between them grew.

As they neared the door, they slowed, wiped the smiles from their faces and entered.

Mrs Stuart was quite annoyed as they all waited for the two to be seated. When they were, they all closed their eyes and bowed their heads in unison while Mr Dodds said grace. All except for Will and Margaret who peeked at each other.

'Almighty God, the eyes of all

look to you, and you give them their

food at the proper time. Bless the

earthly bounty you have provided

now before us. Let these nourish

and strengthen our frail bodies, that

we may better serve you;

through Jesus Christ. Amen.'

'*Amen,*' they repeated.

Will saw one of the kitchen maids nudge the one sitting beside her as she noticed Will smile at Margaret.

Mrs Stuart, an annoyed look on her face, said, 'Margaret, soon as ya finished ya can start clearin' the table and doin' the washin' up. Don't think the broken dish isn't comin' out of ya pay!'

Will kept his eyes on his plate to save her embarrassment.

But Bobby, ever eager to assert himself, saw an opportunity to regain some semblance of control. 'You watch what yer doin' next time!' he declared, his tone a mix of arrogance and condescension.

Will's jaw clenched, his fingers tightening around his fork as he fought the urge to respond with anger. The tension between the two boys had been simmering for a while and Bobby's smug demeanour pushed Will's patience to its limit.

Bobby lifted his chin and made a mocking clicking sound with his tongue, a gesture that was meant to belittle Will. It was a subtle provocation, a challenge.

With a deliberate exhale, Will slowly pushed his chair back and stood up. He met Bobby's gaze, his expression a mix of determination and restraint.

As the seconds ticked by, Will and Bobby held each other's gaze, the tension between them reaching a boiling point. It was a battle of wills, a clash of personalities, and the outcome was uncertain.

Mrs Stuart cleared her throat, breaking the silence and defusing the situation. 'Enough of that, both of ya. Back to work now, and no more nonsense.'

The atmosphere in the kitchen was palpably tense as the aftermath of the incident unfolded. Will's attempt to comfort Margaret had not gone unnoticed, and the knowing glances exchanged between the kitchen maids indicated that their interaction had not escaped their attention.

Mr Dodds sensed the uneasiness in the room. 'Come now, it was an accident, no 'arm done. Eat yer grub so we can get back to work all of ya!' He took out his pipe. 'Fillin' as usual, Mrs Stuart, thanks muchly.'

'Yer quite welcome, Mr Dodds, would ya like more?' Mrs Stuart always appreciated the compliment.

'No, Mrs Stuart, I've eaten me fill, better get back to work. Come on you lot, back ta the mill!'

Will and the apprentices stood, still chewing on the last of their bread then went outside giving their thanks as they did.

Mr Dodds walked through the door. 'Will, you go to the stables, the rest of ya, we got cloth ta weave.'

Will watched them march down the path to the mill; he shook his head at the ridiculousness of the ritual.

'Pssssst, Will!' It was Margaret, 'Quickly, take this.' She held out her hand and there was a shiny red apple in it. 'I 'ave ta go before I'm missed.' She turned, lifted her kirtle and ran. She waved then disappeared inside the kitchen door.

Will watched her, then glimpsed at the apple. He gave the apple a shine on his tunic and took a bite, smiling as he continued toward the stables.

He went around the side of the stable and retrieved the wheelbarrow and pushed it through the stable door. The white mare reared up and put her head over the half door to greet him. He gave her the rest of the apple.

CHAPTER 20

A Sinister Pact

Mr Wilding pulled up outside the Black Bull.

He paid for a room and limped upstairs. He could feel his feet healing as the skin was peeling and they started to itch. There were places where the skin was very thin and pink, but he assumed this would heal in time. *Better than the alternative,* he thought.

He was pleased with his new appearance; his bald head gave him a more menacing look. He thought for a moment. *Not even Robert Rushworth would recognise me now.*

A few moments later there was a knock at the door.

'Who is it?' he called out, taking his knife from the back of his breeches.

'Boy from the tavern, tavern keeper said you wanted me ta deliver a message.'

Wilding opened the door. 'I want you to go to the back door of the manor and ask for Mr Griswold. When you see him, I want you to say this: "I'm 'ere and stayin' at the Black Bull. Meet noon tomorra." 'Ave ya got it?'

The boy repeated, 'Aye, I'm 'ere and stayin' at the Black Bull. Meet noon tomorra.'

Mr Wilding placed a penny in the hand of the boy and closed the door.

In the dimly lit corner of the Black Bull, Mr Griswold and Mr Wilding huddled together, their whispered conversations shrouded in secrecy. Each time the barmaid approached to refill their mugs, their voices hushed to a barely audible murmur, the weight of their discussions heavy in the air.

Mr Griswold stared at Mr Wilding; he was unrecognisable. Gone was the long hair, beard and bushy sideburns. He wore new clothes and there was coin in his pouch.

'I've been hunting Robert Rushworth for some time; I followed him to 'ull then 'ere. He 'as something belonging to me! I also 'ave a warrant fer his arrest. Tis important he not know I'm 'ere.'

Curiosity piqued, Griswold's eyebrows raised. 'How is it that you know him?'

Wilding thought about the first time he met the brothers. 'I know Robert Rushworth and his brother from Leeds, we 'ad dealin's.'

Griswold leaned in closer. 'Well, since he arrived he's been throwin' coin around. When he returned, he brought two sacks of fine wool with him.'

Griswold's eyes gleamed with intrigue and he leaned in further, his voice dropping to a conspiratorial level. 'There might be a way to turn this situation to our advantage, for both of us.'

Wilding took another swig of ale. 'Where do the Rushworths live?'

'Live at Hall Green, his cousin Will Rushworth is an apprentice at the manor mill.'

Mr Wilding thought. *How am I gonna get Rushworth back to Leeds? If he gets an inkling I'm here, he'll run fer it and I'll never find him.* 'Tell me what you know of the Rushworths.'

Griswold continued, 'They're freemen with lifehold on Calamy's land from before the war.'

'Lifehold?'

'Yes, you remember Milton Killsin? He wants them off so he can lease it for his herd.'

'If they leave, Calamy can charge rack rents and earn more from it.'

'Fuckin' Calamy! He doesn't need the money!'

‘The Rushworths couldn’t afford the rent until Robert turned up with fine wool. If they weave it and sell it, they’ll be able to afford the lease fines and we’ll never get rid of them.’

‘So what do ya want me ta do?’

Griswold’s eyes bore into Wilding’s, his voice a low, calculated whisper. ‘Mr Killsin is now the local “inspector of wool”. He can refuse to stamp the sacks. If we acquire the wool, Mr Dodds can spin it and weave it. Sell it before anybody’s the wiser.’

In the concealed depths of the Black Bull, the conspiratorial conversation between Mr Griswold and Mr Wilding took on a darker, more strategic tone. Their minds were set on a plan that danced on the precipice of danger, an alliance forged in the shadows.

Wilding’s expression was a mix of scepticism and intrigue. ‘But Dodds… Are you certain he can be trusted?’

Griswold’s smile was sly, confidence radiating from his demeanour. ‘Rest assured, Dodds will comply. I hold the reins at the manor and I can make his life unbearable if he chooses not to cooperate. He knows better than to cross me.’

Wilding looked around nervously. ‘Mmm, maybe we can, kill two birds with one stone. If they don’t have wool, they can’t pay their lease and Calamy can turn them off. You give me the cloth and I’ll sell it in Leeds and we’ll split the profit.’

Wilding’s fingers drummed thoughtfully on the table, the pieces of their plot falling into place like a malevolent puzzle. ‘Indeed, a lucrative venture that serves both our interests. But remember, Griswold, I want Rushworth. Once he’s in my grasp, then we can seal this sinister pact.’

Griswold nodded in agreement, his gaze unwavering. ‘Rest assured, Mr. Wilding, I will arrange the stage for your grand entrance. Rushworth will be delivered to you, and our partnership will solidify.’

☆

They left when they heard the bells for prayer in the distance. The cold morning air brushed against the faces of the Rushworths as they walked along Sun Street, heading toward the church for Sunday prayers. The weight of uncertainty hung heavy on their hearts, the shadows of their troubles casting a pall over what should have been a serene moment.

Tommy escorted Isabel, he spoke quietly, 'We know why Killsin wants the land. He's bought more sheep and needs more land to feed 'em. He'll take over our land if we can't pay.'

Tommy continued, 'Fer all we know, Jasper Calamy might be behind the whole thing! We don't pay rack rents and if there was a new tenant, Calamy could increase it. Rack rents would be much higher than the lease fines.

☆

Wilding watched them climb up Sun Street then came out from the woodland. He jumped over the dry bap wall and marched along it up the hill toward the cottage. 'ANYBODY HOME,' he called out. '*Silence?*'

He entered the cottage; it was a typical one room weaver's cottage with a small hearth. A wooden trestle sat in the middle of the room close to the fire. The room had a low ceiling and thick oak beams supported the loft above. Two wooden straight-backed chairs sat on either side of the hearth. The spinning wheel and loom took up much of the space. A wrought iron trammel hook with a small black cauldron and a ceramic curfew sat in the hearth.

Wilding climbed the ladder and peered at the sleeping area. Straw mattresses, pillows and the toilet bucket.

He climbed back down and went outside. Going around the side to the enclosure, he saw the sacks of wool stacked up against the wall.

I wonder if the fucker has a bill a' sale? If he didn't, Wilding knew theft of the sacks would have him swinging from the end of a rope. *Profit from the wool would be better in my pocket. No, best keep this quiet.*

He reached in and grabbed a piece of the fleece; it was soft, fine and would fetch a tidy penny.

If he could get the cloth to Hull and get the reward for Rushworth, he'd pay back The Company who he knew were desperate to find him.

Wilding crept over to Robert's horse and rubbed it on the rump. He peeked inside Robert's saddle bag for the necklace. *Nooo, his slut has taken it with her.* He examined the inside, carefully looking for hidden pockets.

Frustrated, Wilding proceeded around the back of the cottage, then crossed the field to the Killsin's cottage.

Entering through the front door, he poured himself an ale, sat down at the tall back form, in front of the fire, and waited.

Milton Killsin's eyes widened in shock as he felt the cold edge of the knife pressed against his throat. He froze, his heart pounding in his chest. The familiar face of John Wilding leered at him from behind and he realised that the past had finally caught up with him.

'Wilding! What in the devil's name are ya doin' here?' Milton's voice trembled, a mixture of fear and anger in his eyes.

Wilding's grip tightened on the hilt of the knife, his voice dripping with menace. 'I think you know damn well what I'm doin' here, Killsin. You've got somethin' that belongs to me.'

Milton's mind raced, his thoughts a whirlwind of possibilities. He swallowed hard, his throat dry. 'I don't know what yer talkin' about!'

Wilding's lips curled into a sinister smile, his eyes narrowing. 'Don't play dumb with me, you rat. I'm talkin' about that coin you took from me after we dealt with those Royalist sympathisers.'

Milton's heart sank as he realised what Wilding was referring to. It had become a haunting reminder of the darkness that had consumed his life. 'I ain't got it anymore, Wilding. I spent it long ago.'

Wilding's grip loosened slightly, his brows furrowing in suspicion.

Wilding's gaze hardened, his voice a low growl. 'You expect me to believe that?'

Milton's heart pounded in his chest and he knew he was on thin ice. 'It's the truth, Wilding. I had to make ends meet after what you put us through.'

A tense silence hung in the air as Wilding contemplated Milton's words. The room felt stifling, the fire crackling in the hearth the only sound.

Finally, Wilding let out a derisive laugh, the sound cutting through the tension like a blade. 'Well then, it looks like you owe me, Killsin. You're gonna help me out with a little job, and maybe I'll spare your sorry hide.'

Milton's heart sank further, his mind racing to find a way out of this impossible situation. He was trapped between the devil he knew and the devil he didn't.

'And what if I refuse?' Milton's voice held a defiant edge, his eyes narrowing.

Wilding's grin widened, his voice a low whisper. 'Then, my friend, I'll make sure that necklace ain't the only thing missin' from your life.'

'I have a message from Mr Griswold.' Wilding reached into his tunic, brought out a clump of fleece. He handed it to Milton.

Milton took the fleece. 'Mmm, nice, haven't seen wool like it in a long time.'

'The Rushworths own two sacks of it and we're gonna take it before they have a chance to weave it. Milton, Griswold will 'ave it weaved, then I'll take it to Leeds where a colleague of mine will finish it. Then to Hull!'

'Wilding? Take it? There's a hefty punishment, we could all end up on the end of a rope,' Milton Killsin warned.

'Milton, you are the overseer in these parts, no one will suspect you and besides, he doesn't have a bill of sale, I'm sure of it.'

Milton Killsin was blinded by greed. 'Well, if they don't have the wool, they won't be able to afford the lease fines and Calamy will have reason to get rid of them.'

‘I’ll take it to Leeds so it can be measured and stamped by a colleague of mine just in case I’m stopped by the land-waiter.

‘Bring the constable and request a Bill of Sale and when he can’t, take the wool.’

Wilding stood and went to the door and opened it as Mrs Killsin was making her way up the path. ‘Missis Killsin!’ He doffed his hat and strolled past her.

She stepped inside the house. ‘Milton, who was the strange man?’

Milton wore a sheepish look on his face. ‘An old friend, Mr Wilding, we served together in the war.’

Mrs Killsin gazed at him. ‘How come you’ve never spoken of him before?’

‘It’s never come up! Stop fussing, woman!’ Milton was angered by her interrogation.

Milton went outside to see where Wilding was. He peered at William Rushworth and Tommy digging through the sack of wool separating it. He watched for a while until he noticed Tommy cease what he was doing and fix his gaze across the paddock. Milton put his head down and went inside.

CHAPTER 21

A Battle of Wills

Will heard the bells of Saint Michael of All Angels toll. Bobby and the others stopped work and stood in front of the loom. Mr Dodds closed his ledger and stood. He strolled outside and the boys followed him. Mr Dodds locked the door. The other boys raced off to their respective houses, all except Bobbly who was an orphan, and proceeded to the Kings Arms.

Will ran down Main Street toward home, he went through the gate then rushed up the hill toward the cottage.

William and Robert hauled a mixture of manure and human excrement from the pile out to the field. They hauled load after load then spread it while Tommy dug it into the rocky soil. Pulling a cart of manure through the sloping field was back breaking work.

'How's ma?' Will asked as he raced past and lifted the latch on the door, quickly stepping inside.

As Isabel gazed into the crackling fire, her mind was a swirl of emotions. The events of the past days weighed heavily on her heart, and the shadow of suspicion that had fallen upon her still lingered. She couldn't shake the feeling of injustice, the fear of being accused and the uncertainty of what the future held for her and her family. Isabel sat back in her chair, her eyes fixed on the mesmerising flames as if they held the secrets of her newfound strength.

Two days had passed since she had faced the ordeal that would forever change her life – surviving the dreaded ducking stool. It was an event that had threatened to drown her, both in the icy waters of the pond and in the suffocating grip of societal judgment. But Isabel had emerged from that watery abyss not weakened, but tempered like a blade in the forge. Will rushed over to her and knelt beside her. 'Ma… You orl right?'

Isabel turned her head slowly to gaze at him. 'My boy,' she said with a quiet, croaky voice while gently caressing the side of his face.

The sparkle in her eyes was returning. ''Ere luv, you sit and I'll get ya some supper.'

Isabel went to stand. Will put his hand on her shoulder. 'No, Ma, I can get it, you sit here and rest.'

'I do feel a little tired.' She sat back in her chair and stared back into the flames remembering what happened two days prior.

Outside, the fading light of the day cast long shadows on the walls of the cottage. The wind whispered through the trees, carrying with it a sense of hope and resilience. Isabel's eyes remained fixed on the flames, her thoughts a mix of worry and determination.

☆

Isabel noticed Milton Killsin ogling her whenever she went to the vegetable garden. At first, she would wave. When he saw this he would put his head down and continue his chores. He made her feel uncomfortable.

She would often speak to Mrs Killsin at the market or on the odd occasion they passed each other on the way to the village. She was an amiable, friendly lady and she liked her.

One afternoon Thomas, William and Robert went into the village and Will was away at the manor. Isabel was tending to the chicken eggs in the coup, turning over their eggs and ensuring they were warm enough.

She turned around to make her way out of the coup and was shocked to see Mr Killsin standing there at the entrance. Isabel's heart raced as she tried to maintain composure in the face of his unsettling presence. The afternoon sun cast long shadows around them, creating an eerie atmosphere that mirrored her growing unease.

Startled, Isabel brought her hand to her chest. 'Mr Killsin, you gave me a fright!'

'Sorry, Mrs Rushworth, or can I call you Isabel?' he asked with sarcasm.

She scurried nervously toward the door. 'Isabel is fine.'

Mr Killsin did not move and blocked Isabel's departure. 'You can call me Milton.'

She felt uneasy. 'Right ya are, Milton it is then.' Isabel forced a smile and dropped her chin as she crept closer to the door.

Once again Milton did not move. 'You know I been watching you poking around the garden, I can give you some seed if you wish.'

Isabel glanced at Milton's face; it was shiny and flushed and a drop of perspiration was dribbling down his face from beneath his hat.

'So kind of ya. We'd be happy to take it if ya can part with some.'

Milton took a handkerchief from his pocket and wiped his face. 'It's not a problem, us neighbours watch out for one another, now don't we?'

Feeling very scared, Isabel took a step to the side to get past Milton but he moved and once again blocked her. 'Yes we have ta help each other, for instance, if I give you seed…'

Milton raised his hand and touched the top of Isabel's hand softly, the one she was carrying the egg basket with, he continued, 'Then… there might be some things you can do for me. Firstly, you must convince your husband to move off this land. You must go to the city; this is no life fer a pretty girl like you. In the city there's work, everybody's movin' there!'

Isabel's instincts told her to escape this uncomfortable situation, but she couldn't allow herself to show fear. She took a steadying breath and met his gaze with determination. 'Mr Killsin, I don't appreciate the way you're involving yourself in our affairs. We've lived here peacefully for years, and we won't be bullied into leaving.'

Milton's face reddened and he took a step closer, invading her personal space. 'You should think twice, Isabel. Your family might find themselves in a dire situation if you don't cooperate.'

'Mr Killsin this is our home, and nobody will turn us off!' She took a step backward. 'Mr Killsin, I must go, me husband and the rest will be back very soon!'

‘Come now, don’t give me that. You know as well as I, they’ll be at the Kings Arms swilling ale. You’re right, I have been watching, be a good hour before they get back I’d say.

‘Justice of the peace wouldn’t like it if he knew they were still drinking and gambling behind closed doors. The lot of them could end up in the lock up. I might be just the person to tell him unless you provide me with favours occasionally.’

Isabel took a step forward.

He didn’t budge so she tried to brush past him, but he was too fat. ‘Please, Mr Killsin, please! LET ME PASS!’ Isabel’s heart pounded against her ribcage, her breath coming in shallow, panicked gasps.

The weight of his threat hung heavy in the air, suffocating her like a thick fog. She knew what he was insinuating, the ugliness he was demanding from her and the helplessness she felt clawed at her insides. But Isabel wasn’t one to be easily subdued. Her mother’s stories of resilience and her father’s unwavering sense of justice surged through her veins, fuelling a flicker of courage within her.

He grabbed the egg basket and flung it; the eggs broke on the ground behind.

He took a step forward. ‘I can make things extremely easy for you and yer family or exceedingly difficult, it’s up to you. Now come here and give it to me, give us a kiss, SLUT, and all will be well. I’ve seen you selling your wares to the men at market.’

Frightened, Isabel took another step backwards. ‘Please, Mr Killsin, STOP THIS!’

Milton put out his arms and grabbed her, pulling her closer. ‘Now, come on, you know you want it. I see you waving at me all the time. My wife’s not home and we have all the time in the world!’

He pulled her close and began to kiss her on the neck repeatedly. Milton then put his face down onto the top of her breasts plumped up above her bodice.

‘MR KILLSIN, NO! STOP!’ Isabel lifted his chin and tried to wrestle free.

'Come on now, stop struggling.' Milton pulled her closer to him and he kissed her on the top of the breast again. 'Mmmm, mmm, mmm. Come, Isabel, don't be like this…' He held her tight against him with one arm, then reached down and tried to lift her kirtle.

'LEAVE ME BE!' Isabel pushed down her kirtle then lifted her knee into his groin.

'Humph erggh, YOU WITCH!'

Milton fell to the ground, clutching his groin. 'You'll pay for this, arrrgh, you'll pay, I swear! YOU BITCH! YOUR DAYS IN HALL GREEN ARE FINISHED! DO YOU HEAR ME, FINISHED! ERGGH!'

Isabel stepped over him and ran out of the chicken coup, glancing back to see if he was still on the ground. She ran around the front of the cottage and went inside, putting the bolt on. She peeked through the door and a few minutes later saw him bent over and limping back towards his cottage.

She sat on the form near the door and began to weep. *I can't let Thomas and William see me in this state.*

Isabel wiped her eyes with the back of her hand. *What ta do... if Tommy finds out about this... he'll kill 'im then end up on the end of a rope. No, I'll say nowt... and carry on as if nothin' happened... won't tell nobody.*

Isabel went to the water bucket and poured some into the ceramic bowl, then rinsed her face and took the linen towel to dry it. She pinched her cheeks and squeezed a blueberry to colour her lips. She tried to put what transpired out of her mind but couldn't.

A few minutes later Isabel took a deep breath, undid the bolt, lifted the latch and went outside. She watched Thomas, William and Robert coming up the hill and tried to compose herself before they arrived home. She gazed over at the Killsin's cottage to see if she could see him.

☆

Will disturbed her thoughts. 'Ma.... ma... MA! I 'ave ta go!' Will quickly bent down and gave her a kiss on the cheek. 'Ma, are you gonna be alright?'

'Of course, gew on, off ya get before Dodds gives you another hidin'. I'll be fine, don't you worry.' Isabel forced a smile.

She never told Tommy or the others what happened for fear of retribution. She knew if Tommy found out he would take matters into his own hands. It was one thing for him to try to get the land, but another if he found reason to have Tommy taken into custody or worse.

The weight of her secrets bore down on her like a heavy stone, threatening to crush her spirit. She knew she had to be strong, not just for herself, but for Tommy and their future. The danger that lurked in the shadows was real and she couldn't afford to let her guard down.

As the days passed, Isabel went about her chores with a sense of urgency, her mind constantly racing with thoughts of what could happen if her secrets were revealed. The cottage, nestled on the outskirts of the village, provided some semblance of isolation, but she couldn't shake the feeling that danger was closing in.

CHAPTER 22

Threads of Opportunity

Jasper Calamy inspected the parchment, his brow furrowed in concentration. 'Robert Rushworth?'

'Son of William Rushworth from Hall Green, been away in Leeds they say,' replied Griswold.

Calamy was curious. 'And how on Earth did one of the Rushworths get enough coin to purchase fine wool?'

'I don't know, your grace, he just showed up out of nowhere. Has two horses!'

Calamy's lips curved into a half-smile, a mixture of bemusement and suspicion dancing in his eyes. 'Two horses, you say? How does a family barely able to pay their lease become wool traders overnight? There's more to this than meets the eye. You must investigate this further, Griswold. Make inquiries at the tavern, see if anyone knows anything about this sudden wealth.'

'I've done one better, your grace, and acquired the services of John Wilding who you may remember was quite useful to us in the past.' Griswold did not let on about the circumstances of their agreement.

'What? Wilding? My God man, I am the Justice of the Peace and my name must remain honest and untarnished.'

Griswold bowed respectfully, concealing the true nature of his arrangement with Wilding. 'Of course, your grace. I assure you, he will work discreetly and his involvement will be known only to us.'

With a dismissive wave of his hand, Calamy allowed Griswold to depart on his mission. As the steward strode purposefully across the stone floor and into the kitchen, Calamy's thoughts churned. The Rushworths' sudden rise in wealth was a mystery that begged to be unravelled.

The kitchen bustled with activity, and Griswold's presence commanded respect from the staff. The household members stood up as he entered, a display of deference that acknowledged his authority.

'Please sit. Mr Dodds, when you've finished would you mind stepping into the parlour. Mrs Stuart, please have tea brought in?' He turned and went back into the hall then into the parlour.

'Aye, Mr Griswold, I'm finished. Bobby, here's the keys, the lot of ya get back ta work, and no dawdling on the way!'

Bobby stood obediently. 'Oh, no, Mr Dodds, course not! Wouldn't dream of it.'

When Mr Dodds went through the kitchen door, Bobbly smiled cheekily. 'Come on we'll 'ave time fer a good smoke before he gets back.'

'Margaret, take tea into the parlour for Mr Griswold and be quick about it and mind ya don't spill it, tis very dear!' Mrs Stuart rolled her eyes.

Margaret scurried over to the shelf and took some tea from the caddie. She went to the cauldron in the hearth and scooped boiling water out with a ladle and poured it into a cup to heat it. Taking the tea pot, she put the tea into it then poured in the boiling water. She delicately placed the teapot and the cup onto a pewter tray.

Amidst her task, Margaret felt the weight of someone's gaze upon her. She blushed, her cheeks tinged with a rosy hue. She dared not meet the eyes of the person watching her – Will, one of the apprentices in the kitchen. His presence was a secret source of fascination and trepidation, a forbidden alliance she could ill afford.

Margaret had a natural beauty that radiated from within. Her eyes, the colour of fresh spring leaves, were a vibrant shade of green that seemed to reflect the world's lushness. Freckles dotted her porcelain complexion, like constellations scattered across a canvas of alabaster. The freckles were a charming contrast to her fair skin, and the fire's gentle caress had left a delicate rosy hue on her cheeks. Margaret pushed the door open with her shoulder and shuffled out then knocked on the door of the parlour. When she entered, both Mr Dodds and Mr Griswold were sitting in front of the fire opposite each other. The air was thick with an unspoken tension, a sense that important matters hung in the balance.

'Can't you ask Will?' Mr Dodds inquired, his voice a low rumble that resonated within the room.

Margaret's ears perked up as she caught fragments of their conversation. Hearing Will's name, she became curious. She attempted to linger in the room, her feet seeming to take on a mind of their own. She yearned to catch more of their hushed exchange, to glean insight into the cryptic conversation that seemed to revolve around the enigmatic Robert Rushworth and the strange circumstances of his sudden affluence.

Griswold saw Margaret and whispered, 'I'd rather not, Mr Dodds, it might arouse suspicion. If Tommy Rushworth got wind he'd go to the magistrate.'

Margaret heard them mention Robert's name and was curious; she tried to delay leaving the room.

Margaret placed the tray on the side table. 'Would ya like me ta pour, Mr Griswold?'

He frowned at her. 'No, leave it seep a while, that will be all.'

Margaret left through the door and closed it slowly behind her. She paused for a moment, listening.

'Aye, I'll ask around see if anybody knows anything else about him,' Mr Dodds remarked.

Back in the bustling kitchen, Margaret found herself amidst the flurry of activity. The clatter of dishes and the hum of conversation surrounded her, but her mind was elsewhere. She wanted to share the tidbits of information she had overheard, particularly with a certain someone who had piqued her interest.

'COME ON, GIRL, what's wrong with ya? Don't take long ta pour tea, now help the others and clean up, we 'aven't got all day!'

Feeling embarrassed for Margaret, Will stood and took the ceramic plate to the washing bucket where she stood with her back to him. As

Will crept up behind her, he peered around to see if anyone was watching and nudged her with his elbow.

Startled, Margaret turned to find Will standing beside her. His eyes held a glimmer of mischief, a shared understanding passing between them. He nodded toward the door, silently urging her to join him in a brief moment of escape.

She managed a small smile in return, her fingers brushing against his as they exchanged the ceramic plate. The touch sent a shiver down her spine, a tantalising promise of secrets yet to be revealed.

With a surreptitious glance around to ensure no prying eyes were upon them, Will slipped through the door, Margaret following closely behind. As they stepped into the cool air outside, their breaths mingled with the sense of anticipation hanging between them.

'Meet me at the abandoned stone cottage before dusk,' Margaret whispered, her voice barely audible. She met Will's gaze, her eyes shining with a mixture of excitement and trepidation.

Will's expression was a mixture of suspicion and curiosity, his brow furrowing slightly. He hesitated for a moment before nodding in agreement. With a final, longing look, they parted ways, each returning to their duties with newfound purpose.

In the hours that followed, the estate continued its usual rhythm, unaware of the secrets and whispers that circulated beneath the surface. Margaret and Will's clandestine meeting loomed on the horizon, a meeting that held the promise of answers to questions they had yet to fully comprehend.

In the evening the bells of Saint Michaels tolled, Will made his way home to see his mother. A few moments later he heard Margaret running to catch up.

The sun was starting to go down.

Margaret was out of breath. 'Will, hffff, gasp, Will, hffff, gasp, I 'eard Mr Griswold and Dodds chattin' about yer family. They mentioned Robert.'

'Aye, he's me cousin, just come 'ome from Leeds.'

‘I ‘eard Mr Dodds say he’s gonna make enquiries about ‘im. There’s somethin’ dodgy goin’ on, I can feel it.’

‘Quick, get off the road. There’s somebody comin’.’ Will grabbed Margaret by the hand and they rushed off the road. They hid behind the cottage.

As the day waned, the sun cast a warm glow upon the village, and a farmer’s horse-drawn cart ambled its way up Main Street. In the midst of the fading light, Margaret leaned against the old stone wall, her long blonde hair dancing in the gentle breeze.

As he stood there, watching her, Will felt a mixture of awe and shyness. The beauty that Margaret possessed seemed to cast a spell on him, making him momentarily forget himself. He felt a flutter of discomfort at being alone with her, as if her presence held an enchantment that made him acutely aware of his own insecurities.

But there she was, leaning against the weathered stone wall, the embodiment of grace and charm. Will’s heart raced as he tried to gather the courage to approach her, his shyness battling against his undeniable attraction.

‘Come on, let’s go before we’re seen. Mr Dodds will ‘ave my guts fer garters if he hears we been out ‘ere alone!’

‘Wait, what are ya gonna do?’ Margaret asked.

Will looked worried. ‘Tell me da, see what he says! Come on, I better go, you be careful goin’ ‘ome!’

‘No chance, I aven’t got a home,’ Margaret quipped.

‘What da ya mean?’

Margaret was saddened. ‘They got me out of the alms house in Bradford, me ma died giving birth and don’t know who me da was.’

‘I’m sorry,’ Will said sympathetically.

Margaret smiled. ‘Tis alright, rather be ‘ere than in the alms house! Besides, Mrs Stuart took me in or else his grace would ‘ave been fined ten pounds.’ She ran off. ‘Bye, Will, see ya tomorra.’

‘Bye, Margaret.’ Will picked up the pace so he could be back to the manor before dusk. He jumped over the wall and noticed the chimney chugging smoke and candlelight peeking through cracks in the shutters.

The loom was quiet.

Will went inside; his father sat on a form where Isabel was sitting and put his arm around her. ‘Da, what’s goin’ on?’

In the dim candlelight Tommy started to recount what Isabel told him, ‘Milton Killsin cornered ya ma, told her to convince us to move ta the city.’

Isabel left out the other part of their ‘discussion’.

‘Move to the city, why would we want to? This is our home.’

The wool lay before them, a testament to their hopes and dreams, its pure whiteness a canvas for the future they sought. The cottage was alive with anticipation, the crackling fire casting dancing shadows across the room. The sound of laughter and conversation filled the air as the family gathered around the table, a simple reprieve from the struggles that had burdened them for so long.

Tommy’s weathered hands ran over the smooth strands of wool, his fingers tracing the path that would lead them to a better life. His eyes met Will’s, the spark of excitement mirrored in both their gazes. It was as if the wool held within it a promise, a chance to break free from the cycle of poverty and oppression that had gripped their family for generations.

It was beautiful clean white wool, not the kind Will was used to working with. It was scoured and the sweat locks, short wools and matted pieces were removed.

Will’s face shone with excitement. ‘But where did he get it?’

‘Robert wants us to spin and weave it so he can take it back and export it. We can use the profit to pay the lease fines.’

‘Oh, grand, Killsin will never get us off now!’

But even in their moment of triumph, a shadow loomed on the horizon. The tale of Robert's sudden wealth had spread like wildfire, whispered in hushed tones among the villagers. It was not long before those whispers reached the ears of the estate's watchful overseers.

Milton Killsin, a man as cunning as he was ruthless, had built an empire on the backs of the struggling villagers. He held their futures in his hands, his every move calculated to ensure his grip on power remained unchallenged. As news of the mysterious wool and Robert's newfound prosperity reached him, a sinister smile played upon his lips.

'Da, I got somethin' ta tell ya. Margaret, maid at the manor, heard Mr Dodds an' Mr Griswold talkin' about Robert. Seems Mr Griswold is curious about where he got the coin and the wool.'

Tommy shook his head in disbelief. 'Ta be honest, doesn't surprise me. Robert comes 'ome with all this fine wool and 'orses, course people are gonna ask questions.' *There'll be consequences.*

Will rose to his feet, moving to open the door. In walked William and Robert, their presence commanding attention. The two men made their way to the water bucket, cleansing their hands in a ritual of camaraderie.

Will joined them at the table in front of the fire while Isabel placed wooden mugs and bowls on the table. She poured ale into the mugs which they all drank with relish. Acorn bread which she baked earlier was placed on the table and she ladled pottage into their bowls.

After the meal, Isabel herself sat down, savouring a well-deserved portion of pottage and acorn bread. The room was alive with a sense of shared purpose and family bonds, a refuge from the complexities of the world outside.

'I better be on me way. Bye, Ma.' Will kissed Isabel on the cheek and rushed through the door.

'See ya tomorra, Will.' Isabel smiled with affection.

William frowned.

'Robert, seems you've stirred up a bit of interest at the manor. Will's friend heard 'em talkin' about you.'

'Not against the law ta buy wool!' Robert replied defiantly.

Tommy raised his eyebrows. 'You start livin' above yer station and people are gonna start askin' questions.' He warned him about the unspoken shadow of class difference.

William, however, offered a different perspective. 'Tommy, I used to think the same as you, but really, why shouldn't we be able ta earn coin the way others do? Seems there are rules for some and different rules for others,' he mused, his words challenging the established social norms.

'William, it's the way of the world.' Tommy's voice held a note of resignation, a sense of surrender to the established order.

William shook his head. 'Tommy, we're supposed to be freemen, how are we free?'

'I 'eard Calamy let Killsin go free,' claimed Tommy disappointedly. 'And to make matters worse he's been appointed overseer and wool inspector in the parish.'

Isabel's eyes flashed with a fire ignited by indignation. 'It's NOT RIGHT!' she declared, her voice carrying a resolve that seemed to echo through the room, a declaration of defiance against a world that sought to subdue their spirit and stifle their dreams.

The small cottage seemed to hold its breath as the weight of whispered revelations hung heavy in the air. Tommy's voice broke the silence, his words laden with a mixture of frustration and determination.

'John Pigshells told me there were things I didn't know, but he wouldn't say what, so they couldn't hold him.'

William's response was swift and heated, his voice seething with disgust. 'BASTARD! He deserves to be taken before the magistrate fer what he did!'

Tommy replied, 'Pigshells told me there were things I didn't know, but he wouldn't say what, so they couldn't hold him.'

'I agree! Tommy what can we do?' Isabel asked.

William focused his eyes on the scratches in the table then whispered, 'Pigshells told me he 'eard Milton Killsin threaten Tommy to leave the land or else. He's gonna take care of it he said. The presentment was all a sham to get scare us into giving up the tenancy.'

Tommy, Isabel and Robert stared at him.

William spoke louder. 'They're trying to force us out, Calamy, Griswold, Killsin, I bet they're all in it together!'

'Fear not, Isabel, were not done yet!' Robert stood and pulled his cloak around his shoulders. He lit the candle in the lantern and went outside, closing the door behind him.

After making his way around the side of the cottage, he made his way into the covered enclosure and started brushing his two horses. They were good mares strong and quick.

A few minutes later Tommy came into the enclosure. 'What are you going to do?'

'He can make all the enquiries he wants.' Robert glanced up. 'All ya need ta know is if we sell the wool fer a shillin', we'll make six shillins' profit per tod and more if we spin, weave and finish it. I'm sick of the rich getting richer and the poor getting poorer.'

Tommy frowned inquisitively. 'Robert, where did ya get the wool?'

Robert smirked. 'I dunno what everybody is so worried about, I been buying wool in Hull before its loaded onto ships to the Baltic. Friend of mine is in the export business.'

William came around the corner. 'What are you two up to? Come on, give me a hand we'll split the tods and start spinnin' skeins tomorra. You know what, we should take some of it and sell it on Weaver's Hill. We could get enough to buy grain and eat well for once. Take it to an old friend of mine, ask fer Calico.' His voice carried a note of urgency, a reminder of the risks they faced. 'Don't forget, or else they'll slit yer throat.'

The room seemed to buzz with energy, the weight of their newfound plan hanging between them. In the midst of uncertainty and adversity, a glimmer of opportunity had emerged – an opportunity to reclaim their agency, to turn the tide against the forces that sought to control them.

As they finalised their pact, the lantern's flame flickered in the lantern, casting dancing shadows upon the walls. The room was imbued with a sense of purpose, a shared determination to challenge the status quo and seize the chance for a better future.

With their minds set and their actions aligned, the trio exchanged glances, each face reflecting a mix of anticipation and courage. The challenges ahead were formidable, but they were united in their belief that their efforts could weave a tapestry of change, one thread at a time. And so, as the night stretched on and the fire's embers burned low, they embarked on a path that would test their mettle, challenge their limits, and ultimately define their legacy in a world where threads of opportunity were woven amidst the intricate fabric of their lives.

As the first light of dawn painted the sky in hues of pale pink and gold, Tommy and Robert were already stirring, their determination propelling them into action. The horses were saddled and laden with their precious cargo, and with a shared purpose, the two men set out on their journey. They led the horses down the hill then up Marsh Lane and Sun Street and tuned left on Weavers Hill.

Down the hill they went, horses' hooves clattering on the cobbled path. Along Marsh Lane and Sun Street they rode, the morning air crisp against their skin. A left turn onto Weaver's Hill marked the entrance to a place steeped in both industry and intrigue. It was a ghetto of small cruck cottages one on top of another with one purpose, to spin and weave wool at the lowest price. The inhabitants were a law unto themselves and didn't care where the wool came from or who it belonged to. There was always trouble there and most kept away even the constable, for a fee.

Here, the air was thick with the scent of wool and the hum of looms, the cacophony of industry echoing through the narrow streets.

The inhabitants of Weaver's Hill were a breed of their own, united by a singular purpose: to spin and weave wool at the lowest possible cost. The rules that governed the rest of society seemed to hold little sway here; the people were driven by survival and profit, unconcerned with the origins of the wool that passed through their hands.

Halfway up the street was Spinners Way and it was here where put outs were negotiated with traders, well those who dared to go there. A narrow path amidst the chaos, held a particular significance. It was the place where deals were struck, where wool changed hands, and where the delicate balance of power was negotiated.

There was a shrill whistle from somewhere, an alarm.

Tommy got off his horse and led it up the cobbled lane with Robert riding slowly behind, curiously gazing in the doors at the looms in full motion.

The cottages were a patchwork of ramshackle structures, their residents emerging to assess the strangers who had invaded their territory. Skeletal children with snotty noses and bare feet played in the streets, their laughter a stark contrast to the hardships etched on their faces.

They were extremely poor families; a young girl sat on a wall coughing uncontrollably and her sister consoled her grey bearded father. He could not stop coughing blood into a piece of linen.

Skinny, half-starved dogs yapped at the newcomers, their mangy fur a testament to their struggle. Old men, once proud broggers now reduced to poverty, whispered secrets to one another, their voices carrying the weight of a lifetime of hardship.

The street itself was a canvas of squalor, filled with half barrels of stale urine and young girls stomping and fulling cloth. The stench of industry mingled with the acrid tang of decay, a sensory onslaught that left no doubt about the harsh realities of life in this corner of the world.

Snotty-nosed, barefoot boys rolled the hoop of a barrel down the cobbled street chasing after it.

The small chimneys chugged grey smoke from the fires which heated the combs.

Numerous half barrels of stale urine lined the street with skinny, young girls stomping and fulling cloth. They swiped at the flies buzzing around them and coughed when they swallowed one.

The skinny, mange ridden street dogs barked at the strangers and destitute old former broggers whispered to each other.

Wooden tenter frames sat outside each house stretching and drying the crisp white cloth in the sun.

Tommy was not used to dealing with these people as his family always spun and dealt with wool honestly.

All in the district knew Spinners Way offered the cheapest price for their work. They also held the reputation for acquiring wool which was not theirs, stretching cloth and mixing in poorer staple. They were also had ways of exporting wool by night away from the eyes of inspectors and custom's tidewaiters.

The families of Spinners Way lived this life for generations and their dubious history was full of stories of cut throats, hedge thieves and tuft pickers. Many of their kin, over the years, met the three-legged mare or the Halifax Gibbett. It was considered one of the pitfalls of the job and only their mothers mourned their passing.

At the top of the hill was a small stone house, more ambitious, sturdier and higher than the rest with three stone steps leading up to the open door.

Waiting outside the entrance was a figure that commanded attention – a hulking presence with a physique that seemed moulded from the very earth. His tunic hung open, revealing a barrel-shaped chest covered in a thick mat of hair. The tattered breeches and bare feet spoke of a life lived on the fringes of society, a world apart from the gentry and the polished veneer of the manor.

He watched the strangers make their way up the middle of the road the large man's gaze followed their every move, his scrutiny a palpable weight that settled upon them. His gaze lingered on each tod of wool, assessing their worth and perhaps the motives that brought them to this perilous corner of the world.

He turned around and disappeared inside the darkness of the house.

Robert walked to the bottom step and waited for Tommy. 'Come on let's sell this wool and get out of 'ere!' He could feel eyes on them and felt uneasy.

A young boy meandered up and took the bridle of the two horses while Robert and Tommy climbed up the steps. They stood at the entrance and peeked inside; it was dark then Tommy saw and heard a candle lit.

'Come inside, my friends.' A deep raspy voice emanated from the darkness.

With a shared glance, Robert and Tommy ascended the steps, their hearts pounding with a mixture of anticipation and caution. They stood at the entrance, their eyes adjusting to the darkness within as they tried to discern the figure that beckoned from the shadows.

'I am Robert Rushworth and this is my uncle Tommy. We don't want to leave our wool outside.'

'I know who ya are. Don't worry, it won't be touched!' The man's voice held a gravelly tone, a mixture of authority and familiarity. 'BOY, BRING THE FINE WOOL INSIDE AND LET ME 'AVE A LOOK. Sorry about the darkness, but I 'ave guests and they're still resting.' He smiled. 'I'm Jack Calico, my friends call me Calico and my enemies call me the biggest, meanest bastard that ever walked the moors.'

'How do ya know we've got fine wool?' Tommy asked.

'You'd be surprised what I know, now come sit, be my guests.'

Tommy was intimidated by the man but he and Robert went over and sat on the form near him. As they settled, the young boy reappeared, bearing a tray of ales. The transaction was swift and soon, leather jacks were in hand, raised in a toast to health.

Their host raised his jack. 'To yer health.' He chugged it down in one gulp then forced a loud prolonged burp that reverberated through the room.

Tommy and Robert looked at each other uneasily. A candle on a bedside table illuminated the scene, its dim glow casting an eerie aura upon the room. A mixture of odours hung heavy in the air, stale ale, urine and an undercurrent of intimacy that seemed out of place amidst the rugged surroundings.

Robert was surprised by the nature of the house; there was an embroidered drapery hanging down the wall which was out of place in such surroundings. A large four poster bed sat beneath it with two naked women lying asleep. Their legs were entangled and their hair dishevelled. The stuffy room smelt of stale ale, urine and sex. There was a bedside table with a candle almost burnt to the wick and three pewter goblets and a black glass bottle.

The young boy brought a tod of wool in and put it in the middle of the room. He glanced at his master who nodded. The boy placed it at his feet.

The room seemed to hold its breath as Calico's gaze lingered on the tods of fine wool. His large hands reached down, fingers working the wool between his palms as if seeking some hidden truth within its fibres. The act was deliberate, measured, and carried an air of expertise that left Robert and Tommy both intrigued and wary.

Calico stared at them. 'Tis fine wool, you 'ave two sacks of it. I would be careful leaving it unsupervised in the enclosure at the side of your cottage.'

Tommy glanced at Robert quizzically wondering how this man knew so much. The revelation about the enclosure by their cottage caught them off guard, reminding them that Calico was not just an observer but held a knowledge that reached beyond the surface.

In a deep raspy voice, he uttered, 'Not much in Keighley that I don't know.'

'Is that so? That's a bold claim,' replied Robert.

'I know people have been making enquiries about Robert Rushworth. I also know that Tommy Rushworth can't pay 'is lease and is soon to be turned off by that bastard Jasper Calamy.'

The bombshell dropped with a weight that left them speechless. 'I also know that there's a stranger in town from Leeds who's been meeting with Archibald Griswold in secret.'

The shock of the revelation left Robert and Tommy momentarily stunned, their minds racing to process the implications. A stranger from Leeds, secret meetings with Griswold – it was a puzzle with pieces that did not yet fit together.

As the silence hung heavy in the air, Calico's gaze seemed to bore into their souls. 'Now, I assume you've come 'ere wanting ta sell these tods, but I ask ya, what are ya gonna do with the rest?'

Tommy's eyes flicked to Robert and back to Calico, his voice resolute. 'We're goin' ta spin and weave it!'

Robert's response was swift, his resolve unyielding. 'Then take it to The Haven and export it to the Baltic. We need the money…'

Calico's smile was a cryptic interplay of wisdom and intrigue, his chest swelling with a sense of power. 'Let me guess… to pay your lease and fines… Good plan,' he mused, his voice holding a mixture of admiration and amusement. Then came the pivotal proposition that would change the course of their lives. 'But 'ow would ya like ta triple yer money?'

The room seemed to hold its breath, the gravity of Calico's words settling upon them like a cloak of possibility. Their futures were poised on the precipice of transformation, a decision that could lead them down a treacherous path or catapult them toward untold wealth. Calico's proposal hung in the air, an invitation to navigate the intricate threads of trade, ambition and secrecy that wove through their lives.

Calico paused. 'I also know that there's a stranger in town from Leeds who's been meeting with Archibald Griswold in secret.'

Shocked, Robert frowned at Tommy then at Calico alarmingly. 'From Leeds?'

'Would you like ta triple yer money?' His words hung in the air, a proposition that shimmered with temptation.

He continued, 'I'll 'ave me people spin the wool and add just a touch of somthin' else, it'll be so smooth ya won't even notice. Then some others will weave it, so tight that ya won't see the difference between the weft and the warp.'

Tommy and Robert were intrigued. 'Go on.'

'After the fullin', me special ones, will shear it so smooth that Cromwell himself will want a pair a' breeches from it. Others will beat it and stretch it and then we'll groom the cloth and shear it again. What was once a yard will become three. What say you?'

The allure of Calico's offer was undeniable, a chance to navigate the blurry edges of legality and dive into the depths of trade that thrived beyond the manor's gates. Robert and Tommy exchanged a meaningful glance.

Tommy shook his head. 'We just want ta sell these four tods, so that we can buy some grain and be on our way.'

In the dim light of Calico's chamber, the tension hung heavy as his gaze narrowed, scrutinizing Robert and Tommy. His contemplative expression was disrupted by an unwelcome disturbance, the moan of one of the women who stirred from her slumber on his bed. Calico's growl cut through the room, a sharp rebuke that silenced the disruption.

'SHUT UP!' His words reverberated with a force that demanded compliance and one of the naked women, seemingly unperturbed by the harshness, reached for the goblet on the nearby table. She downed its contents in one gulp, a rattling cough punctuating the act. The display of nonchalance only deepened the enigmatic aura that surrounded Calico's domain.

His eyes shifted back to Robert and Tommy, his voice holding a hint of concession. 'Tell ya what I'll do, bring the sacks to me, I'll 'ave it spun an' woven down the street quick as a spit, then I'll 'ave the cloth taken to 'ull. No excise, no taxes, no worry and for all this I will only ask 'alf the profits.'

'But if we spin and weave it and transport it ta Hull, we'll get all the profits!' Robert replied.

'Aye,. but the roads between 'ere and 'ull are long and dangerous and who knows what highwaymen and footpads might be waiting fer ya? Then you'll end up with nowt!'

'I tell ya what I'll do, I'll keep these tods and I'll give ya a pound a tod so ya can eat well. I'll send me men down to fetch the sacks tomorra and we'll go fifty-fifty, keepin' in mind that I take all the risk and there's nowt fer you.'

Robert peered at Tommy for advice then back at Calico. 'But 'ow do we know that you'll keep yer 'alf a' the bargain. Can we 'ave some time to think about it?'

'Aye, ya can, but don't think too long, the stamps on that sack 'ave been painted over so the quicker tis spun and woven the better.'

As the early morning light filtered through the grimy windows of Calico's rundown cottage, a sense of unease settled over the room. The air was heavy with the weight of secrecy and danger, as if the walls themselves were conspiring to keep hidden truths from prying eyes. Calico, a weathered and enigmatic figure, had just handed Robert a small piece of parchment, a simple action that set off a chain of events that would forever alter the course of their lives.

'Bring the sacks 'ere tomorra.' Calico smiled. 'To show you good faith there is also this.' He reached over and gave Robert a small piece of parchment. 'One of my men shot down a messenger pigeon the other day.'

Robert opened it up and stared at it, 'What does it say?'

Calico couldn't read either but he took it to the vicar. 'It says,

DANGER, WILDING APPROACHES.'

Robert's face was painted with fear. The room seemed to grow colder, the ominous message casting a pall over their conversation. Robert's face contorted with fear, his mind racing to piece together the puzzle that had suddenly presented itself.

'Who is Wilding?' Tommy interjected, his curiosity getting the better of him.

Robert tried to dismiss his question. 'It's nothing, just a message from me brother that's all.'

Tommy let it go, not wanting to say anything else in front of Calico.

Calico called for the boy and in a deep decisive voice ordered, 'TAKE IT DOWN THE STREET!'

The boy ran in and grabbed the tods, quickly taking it out the front door. A moment later he grabbed the others from the horse.

‘Now, if ya don’t mind, I should get back ta business, ya can see yerselves out.’ Calico stood and took off his sleeveless tunic as if to emphasise his point. The air of mystery had not dissipated; if anything, it had intensified.

Outside the cottage, a new day was dawning, casting a soft, golden hue upon the quaint village. The air was alive with the sounds of life, birdsong mingling with the distant hum of activity. The gravity of the message seemed to fade against the backdrop of the ordinary, leaving the trio’s encounter with Calico shrouded in uncertainty.

Tommy was the first to step out into the daylight. Robert followed but paused and turned around to see Calico drop his breeches. He climbed onto the bed with his guests. Feeling his presence, they woke and reached out for him quietly moaning in anticipation.

Little did they know, the enigma of Calico and the ominous message were but the first threads in a tapestry of intrigue that would lead them down a path they could never have foreseen.

When they went outside, the boy was holding the bridle of their horses. They took the bridle and led them slowly down the cobbled street. Robert glanced across; their tods of wool were already unpacked and two young men were combing it with heated combs.

CHAPTER 23

What Stolen Goods?

The morning sun cast a warm glow over the quaint Rushworth cottage, painting the scene with a deceptive sense of serenity. But within the hearts of those gathered, a storm was brewing, and the arrival of Mr Killsin and the constable only intensified the tension that hung thick in the air.

Mr Killsin and the constable arrived at the Rushworth cottage with Mr Wilding's cart. William watched them drive up the hill and called out to Tommy and Robert, ''ERE! We got trouble.'

The constable stopped the cart outside the cottage. The constable and Mr Killsin jumped down from the cart.

'William, as you've probably 'eard, Mr Killsin is the overseer in this area and wants to see the wool you recently acquired.'

Robert left the enclosure. 'What's the problem, Da?'

'They want to see the wool!'

Milton Killsin looked around. 'Please let me see your bill of sale for the wool, William?'

William exchanged a hesitant glance with Robert, uncertainty clouding their expressions. 'Bill of sale?' he echoed, his voice tinged with doubt.

Robert glared at the constable. 'No I don't, didn't think I'd need it all the way up 'ere. It was a gift. I can get one, but it may take some time.'

'A gift?' Mr Killsin remarked. 'They're bringin' in statutes, all wool must be stamped and have a bill of sale when bought and sold. Wool sacks need to be stamped and any cloth must 'ave the weavers mark.'

Mr Killsin strode into the enclosure and looked at the sacks. 'Stamps been painted over. I'm afraid we'll have to confiscate this wool until you can provide a bill of sale!'

Robert stepped forward. 'No ya don't, tis my wool!'

John Pigshells stepped in front of him and winked apologetically. 'Robert, we have ta take it until you can provide proof a' purchase. Sorry mate.'

The constable and Milton Killsin picked up the sacks and loaded them on the back of the cart.

William, Robert and Tommy watched with a mix of frustration and helplessness, their arms folded in a silent protest.

As the last sack was secured on the cart, the trio stood united, a sense of camaraderie born from shared adversity binding them together. The cottage, once a sanctuary, had become a battlefield, and the choices they made in the face of this unjust predicament would set the stage for a struggle that would test their resolve and reshape their destinies.

Killsin pulled himself up onto the cart, as did the constable. With a click of his tongue, they rode the cart down the hill and out into Marsh Lane.

William, Robert and Tommy watched them go.

Fucking cunts. Robert vowed revenge.

'What now,' said Tommy sadly. 'We're finished.'

William went back into the cottage.

Robert and Tommy watched the cart disappear then followed him inside.

In the midst of the tangled emotions that swirled like a tempest within the Rushworth cottage, a glimmer of understanding passed between father and son. Robert's smile, though tempered with uncertainty, sought out William's gaze. 'Da, do ya know Jack Calico?'

William's own grin was tinged with a knowing edge, a glimpse into a world of secrets and connections. 'Yea, 'course, everybody knows Calico. That's why I sent ya up there.'

'Why didn't you tell me?'

'As soon as I saw the stamps painted over, I knew that there was somethin' dodgy. Calico's the only one round 'ere that can take care of that. We been mates fer years.'

'How do you know him?'

'Calico's been wheelin' and dealin' his whole life and made a fortune. Son, whoever ya bought that off, it wasn't their's ta sell and if ya ever lie ta me again, you would 'ave wished ya hadn't.'

Robert dipped his head and whispered to his father apologetically. 'I'm sorry, Da.'

'Anyway, enough about that, what Calico 'ave ta say?' William asked.

Tommy butt in, 'Asked us if we wanted to triple our money, let 'im spin, weave it and take it ta Hull.'

William laughed. 'Haha, still up to 'is business, I thought he might say that. What did ya say to 'im?'

'Da, we sold 'im the four tods and told 'im we'd think about it.'

'Haha, think about it? You two will be lucky if yer not sent to the gibbet fer thievin'!' William shook his head.

Tommy stood impatiently. 'Well, there's nowt we can do now, wools gone!'

William's mind churned as he considered their options, his eyes narrowing in thought. 'Look, go back ta Calico. He'll already know what's 'appened. He'll know what ta do.' His voice carried a note of reassurance, a glimmer of hope amid the storm. 'Seems you 'ave a partner, son.'

The weight of William's words settled over them. Father and son stood united, bound by a shared history and a future that was now inexorably intertwined with the enigmatic figure of Jack Calico. In the face of adversity, a new path had emerged, one that held both uncertainty and promise.

Under the morning sun's gentle embrace, Robert and Tommy rode their horses along the well-trodden path to Weavers Hill, a sense of determination radiating from their every stride. The air was pregnant with anticipation, and as they reached their destination, a figure emerged from the shadows, a wry smile playing at the corners of his lips.

Jack Calico was waiting for them. 'SEEMS YOU'VE FORGOTTEN SOMETHING.' He called out.

They got off the horses and left them for the boy following Calico up and inside his cottage. They peered around, the same two women were laying on the bed naked.

'Wool's been taken,' claimed Robert.

Calico was disappointed. 'Aye, I know, seems you should 'ave taken my offer sooner.'

'Why didn't ya tell us ya knew me father? It was him who told us ta come see ya.'

'How is Willy?' Calico's tone shifted, the familiarity of their shared history evident in the affectionate nickname. 'I've known yer father since we were both lads with one hand down the breeches and one finger up the nose.' He chuckled, a twinkle in his eye.

Calico's attention turned to his goblet, taking a swig before bellowing, 'BOY, MORE WINE!' The boy scurried to fulfill the command, a silent witness to the unfolding drama.

'Da's orl right, gettin' along. The trips back and forth to the markets are takin' their toll. And now this!' Robert's voice carried the weight of the challenges that had beset their family.

'Orl right, look, seein' as yer da's an old mate, I'll help ya get yer wool back, but if we do, we split the profits fifty-fifty.'

Robert glanced at Tommy, back at Calico then nodded. 'Okay then.'

‘Orl right first thing we ‘ave ta do is find out where the bastards ‘ave hidden it. They’ll take it to Calamy’s mill so it’ll be somewhere nearby.’

‘We may be able to find out, me cousin Will works there.’

Calico smiled. ‘Oh aye, I ‘eard. He’s taken a liking to one of the pretty young kitchen maids there.’

And with that, a pact was sealed, an alliance forged between a trio of determined souls. The cottage, witness to secrets and negotiations, seemed to pulse with an energy that foretold of a journey yet to unfold. The road ahead would be perilous, fraught with challenges and uncertainties, but as Robert, Tommy and Calico stood united in that moment, they were bound by a shared purpose that would see them through the darkest of days.

☆

The atmosphere was charged with an undercurrent of tension as Mr Killsin reined in the horse-drawn cart, his unease palpable. ‘I feel very nervous about all this, I must say,’ he admitted, his voice betraying a mix of apprehension and uncertainty.

Waiting in the drive of the grand manor was Mr Griswold, a figure of authority who wasted no time in joining them. With a swift jump, he settled into the cart, his purpose clear and unwavering. ‘Drive down to the mill and offload there,’ Mr. Griswold instructed, his voice carrying the weight of urgency. ‘The sooner we get it spun and woven, the sooner we sell it.’

Mr Killsin whipped the back of the horse with the reins. As they arrived outside the mill, Mr Dodds came out to greet them.

‘What do ya ‘ave there, Mr Griswold?’

Griswold jumped down from the cart. ‘Mr Dodds, this wool needs to be kept in a special place if you get my meaning. It also needs to be spun and woven as soon as possible.’

Mr Dodds meandered up to the back of the cart and took a sample of the wool. ‘Mmm, this is good wool, where did ya get it?’

'Let's just say it was acquired locally,' he replied, the unspoken implications hanging in the air like a veil of secrecy.

'I aint seen wool like this in years! This aint from around 'ere. Short staple! I'll get one of the boys ta come offload it.'

It started to rain.

Mr Dodds yelled, 'WILL, STOP WHAT YER DOIN AND GET OUT 'ERE. Unload that wool and get it inside before it gets wet.'

'Yes, Mr Dodds.' Will began to unload the back of the cart. With each load of wool that he transported into the mill, suspicion and contempt glimmered in his gaze as he stole glances at Mr Killsin atop the cart.

'What are you starin' at, boy?' Killsin growled.

Mr Griswold stood in front of him at the entrance. 'Will, I hear you've a visitor at home.'

Despite his best efforts, a hint of unease flickered across Will's features. 'Aye, me cousin is stayin' with us,' he responded, his voice carrying a note of guarded reserve.

Mr Dodds called out angrily. 'Come on, Will, get a move on then back inside with the others!'

Will reacted to his command just as Bobby arrived to give him a hand. They both took two tods at a time and stacked them inside beside the wall.

As the cart was emptied, Mr Killsin retreated into the shroud of darkness, his enigmatic presence a constant reminder of the unseen forces at play. Mr Griswold's voice broke through the air, cutting through the tension with an urgency that hung heavy in the damp air. 'Mr Dodds, leave whatever you're working on and get the short staple finished as soon as ya can.' The weight of his words bore witness to a task of utmost importance. 'Oh, and don't forget, let's keep this one quiet.' With a conspiratorial wink, he turned and sauntered away.

'Aye, it'll be worth a tidy penny once finished.'

He went back inside. 'Come on, you three, change the skein. Get moving on the short staple as quick as ya can. Will, start pullin' open the sacks and sortin' the wool.'

Bobbly sat back at the loom and continued weaving but couldn't take his eyes off the new wool.

Mr Dodds saw him. 'Bobby, dunna worry about the new stuff, you get back to work, get that kersey finished.'

The next morning the apprentices took one of the tods of wool each and sat behind their spinning wheel. They set up their bobbin and started roving to catch the starter thread. They stretched the length of the fibres and overlapped the starter yarn. Turning the wheel by hand they created tension in the yarn. The starter yarn twisted into the wool roving. They then started pushing down on the treddle slowly at first being careful to ensure the wool was a consistent thickness.

Mr Dodds instructed the other apprentice to show Will how to spin and he became quite proficient. 'Careful, Will, remember not too thick or too thin.'

'Aye, Mr Dodds.' Will smiled with pride knowing his master was pleased with his efforts.

Mr Dodds turned to Bobby on the loom. 'Bobby, 'urry up.'

'Aye, Mr Dodds.' Bobby could sense that he was out of favour since Will arrived.

Later in the day, Will arrived home to find Tommy and Robert gone, but knew that as the sheep were missing. *They probably took them into the moors to feed.* A few moments later, their faint whistles and the 'bleat' and 'baa' of the small herd coming down the track behind the cottage could be heard.

Will opened the gate and the sheep entered the enclosure with a sense of familiarity. But a heavy realisation settled over him as he gazed upon the empty space that should have been filled with wool. Tommy's voice cut through the quiet, his frustration evident. 'Tis all gone, every tod, taken by the constable and Milton Killsin. Said we didn't have a Bill of Sale. God knows where it is now.'

Will's frown deepened, a sense of indignation creeping over him. 'I know where it is,' he admitted, his voice tinged with a mix of guilt and discomfort. 'Milton Killsin was at the manor today, dropped off a whole load of fine wool to Mr Dodds.'

Robert shook his head in disapproval.

Tommy was frustrated. 'Those bastards, we need that wool!'

Robert turned to Will. 'What are they doing with it?'

Will looked uncomfortable as if he did something wrong. 'We just took it inside; Jemoin and I were spinnin' it all afternoon.'

☆

The air inside the mill was thick with tension as Will returned, his heart racing in his chest. His eyes darted around the room, searching for any sign of the precious wool that had vanished. Climbing the stairs, he found the other apprentices seated around the table, absorbed in their reading of the Bible. Mr Dodds, the figure of authority, sat with his ever-present whipping stick, a constant reminder of the discipline that awaited any misstep.

'Mr Dodds, the wool?'

The stern mill overseer met his gaze with a measured look, his tone steady. 'Tis orl right, lad. We'll only bring out enough fer the day ta work on. Now, you take the good book and continue.'

Will took his turn. '*For God sa loved t' world, an' he gev 'is only begotten son, so whosoeva believeth on 'im should not perish, bur 'av eternal life.*'

'Very good, Will, yer improvin'. Now, the lot of ya, tomorra's gonna be a long day so ta bed with ya.' He blew out the candle and climbed down the stairs.

Will heard the main door to the mill close.

Bobby got out of bed and crept over to Will's bed. He leant over the edge and put his hand over his mouth. 'This is a message from Mr Griswold, if ya sa much as whisper where the wool's gone, yer gonna cop it.'

Before Will could react, Bobby's fist struck with surprising force, connecting with his stomach. The impact stole his breath, and he doubled over, clutching his abdomen, struggling to regain his composure. As quickly as the encounter had begun, Bobby retreated to his own bed, a haunting reminder of the shadowy forces that loomed over him.

☆

The next morning, Will rose early before dawn and rushed home; the family were already up and weeding the barley.

He ran over to his father. He was out of breath and panicked. 'Da, the wool, tis gone!'

Robert strolled over. 'What da ya mean it's gone?'

'It was there, now it's gone!' Will tried to catch his breath. 'Mr Griswold turned Bobby onto me. He said if I told anybody about the wool, I'd cop it!'

'Da, I know where they're hiding it. Behind the hay bales in the hidden store of the barn.'

Robert's expression shifted from confusion to understanding, his mind racing to process the implications of this newfound information. He glanced at Tommy, a sense of gratitude and reliance passing between them. 'Will, go back to the mill and carry on as if nothing has happened. Bobby won't bother you anymore.'

☆

Will's heart raced as he sped through the streets, a sense of urgency propelling him forward. Sun Street unfolded before him as he darted down the drive of the manor. He reached the barn, his breath coming in rapid bursts, and quickly moved around its perimeter. Climbing the hay bales, he peered over, his heart nearly stopping as he caught sight of a flickering candle's glow and the murmur of voices.

Will could hear Bobby's voice. 'It was here, I swear, sacks of wool ready fer spinning and weaving.'

‘Well, it’s not ‘ere now is it!’ Mr Griswold dropped his chin and shook his head.

Will’s heart pounded in his chest as he strained to hear the conversation, every word sending a shiver down his spine. He needed to go before he was discovered, and with a sense of urgency, he clambered down the hay bales and raced back to the mill.

Upon his return, Will threw himself into the task of sweeping, his movements swift and automatic. He needed to appear as if he had been there the entire time, his heart still racing from the tension of eavesdropping on the clandestine conversation.

Mr Griswold walked up to the Black Bull. He made his way up the stairs and knocked on the door. ‘Wilding, it’s me,’ he whispered.

Wilding held the handle of his knife that protruded from the back of his breeches and opened the door slightly to check the identity of his visitor. He opened the door and closed it quickly after Griswold entered.

‘It’s gone, the fine staple, it’s gone!’ Griswold looked concerned.

‘What da ya mean it’s gone?’ Wilding growled.

Griswold shook his head. ‘It was hidden away, they were only takin’ out enough each day ta spin. Dodds and a boy went to get some more and it was gone.’

‘Who?’ Wilding asked with concern.

‘It has to be the Rushworths!’

Wilding held out his hand and gestured for his guest to sit at the chair beside the window. He sat opposite on the rusty old bed. ‘The Rushworths, this family is turnin’ out to be more trouble than they’re worth.’

Griswold checked out the room it was small and sparce with wooden floorboards, wooden walls with panels that overlapped and a small window. Daub was pushed into small cracks in the walls to prevent drafts. A worn timber table sat beside an uncomfortable looking iron framed, wooden bed with a grimy, worn straw mattress. A wicker chest with its lid open sat on the floor at the bottom of the bed devoid of any possessions. In the corner there were two triangular shelves; a small almost spent candle sat on the top shelf. Leaning against the side wall sat a small bench with a ceramic washing bowl and basin which hadn't been emptied in some time. There was a toilet bucket in the corner with a contemptable aroma emanating from it.

Wilding's gaze remained fixed on the outside world, his mind churning with thoughts and plans. 'Mmm… I think it's time I met up with Robert Rushworth and got me self back ta Leeds,' he mused aloud, his words laced with a sense of urgency.

Griswold's features tightened, a cloud of worry settling over his brow. 'And what about the wool? If it is Rushworth that has it, we can't allow him ta sell it and make the payment on the lease.'

A flicker of determination crossed Wilding's eyes as he met Griswold's gaze. 'You leave that to me, but know that if I retrieve the wool, then you are in my debt. Agreed?'

Griswold's response was swift and unequivocal, his voice tinged with resignation. 'Agreed!' With those words, the terms were set, a pact forged in the midst of uncertainty and danger.

As Griswold departed, his footsteps echoing against the ground, the weight of their arrangement settled heavily upon him. The looming shadows of secrecy and deceit stretched out before him, a reminder that danger lurked in every corner of their world.

Back at the manor, Griswold's purpose was clear as he headed toward the mill, his resolve unyielding. The scene that greeted him as he arrived was one of stark contrast. Bobby emerged from the mill, his appearance marred by the brutal aftermath of a confrontation. His eye was blackened, his lip split, and his shirt torn and stained.

Griswold's eyes rolled with a mix of exasperation and frustration, a silent commentary on the chaos that seemed to trail behind him. He held his tongue, understanding that words could offer little comfort in the face of the danger that surrounded them.

CHAPTER 24

The Tides of Defiance

It was almost midnight when Calico, his two men, Robert, William and Tommy crossed the moor from Dimples Lane and made their way to the manor. They left the horses just on edge of the woodland and snuck up to the barn.

They followed Will's directions and climbed up the bales of straw. When they got to the top, Tommy lit the candle in the lantern and looked over. He could see the small gap between the straw and the wooden wall. He peered down and noticed the small set of iron bolts sticking out of the beam which Will described to him. Tommy clambered down.

When he was at the bottom, he felt around for the panel. It moved so he lifted it out.

Shedding light on the room's contents, Tommy couldn't believe his eyes; there were sacks and sacks of corn. Also, numerous sacks of wool.

He peered around wiping cobwebs away. He noticed their wool up against the far wall.

He rushed over and felt it just to make sure it was theirs. *Yes it's ours, so, so, soft.*

Tommy went back to the opening in the wall and a rope was dropped down to him. The others took a hold and one by one they pulled the sacks up.

Tommy lifted the lantern and gaped. *Bastard engrossers, fuckin' Calamy and Griswold. This is what's causing the dearth, not bloody witches and spells.*

He stared up into the darkness waiting for the rope to be dropped down again.

Tommy grabbed one of the sacks of corn and brought it over tying it to the rope. The others felt the tug and were surprised by the weight.

When they got it to the top, they felt through the hessian bag and could feel what it was.

William eyed Robert and Calico in the darkness, shrugged his shoulders and undid the rope.

Tommy put the panel back and climbed back up.

They took four tods each and Calico threw the sack of grain over his shoulder. They clambered down the bales of straw and made their way quickly and quietly back to the horses.

They loaded the sacks of wool and west through the woodland and back to Dimples Lane. Then they followed that south to Hanging Gate.

'Fiitin' name fer this road, ya know yer face the rope if ya get caught movin' wool at night-time,' Calico whispered.

They travelled further south then turned right on Marsh Lane and left on Moorehouse lane toward the old Hargreaves Cottage. William led one of the horses and the others followed.

The old, dilapidated cottage brought back memories from when he was a young man. He remembered…

The cottage was lit by the fire at the chimney and impromptu oil burners placed in positions of advantageous illumination. The warm glow cast dancing shadows across the room, creating an ambiance that felt more like a refuge than just a dwelling. The cottage, with its layered stone and mud walls, stood as a testament to the strength of generations past, its thatched roof sheltering its inhabitants from the elements.

A sense of coziness enveloped the space, contrasting sharply with the cold uncertainty that often lurked beyond its walls. It was a sanctuary, a place where the burdens of the outside world could be temporarily set aside. The crackling fire in the hearth emitted a gentle warmth, and the aroma of burning wood mingled with the faint scent of herbs, creating a tapestry of scents that spoke of comfort and familiarity.

The chimney stood as a symbol of both sustenance and connection. Its path allowed the smoke to escape, carrying with it the stories and conversations that filled the room. Around the hearth, family and friends gathered, their voices interweaving in a symphony of shared experiences and laughter. The fire was not just a source of heat; it was the heart of the cottage, the nucleus around which life revolved.

A hay crib stood at the end of the cottage, a testament to the labours of the land and the sustenance it provided. Cordoned off by a small wall, it held precious fodder for the ox, the three lambs, and the inquisitive cow that helped herself to the hay on offer. The animals, loyal companions of daily life, found solace and nourishment within these walls, their presence a reminder of the intricate bond between humans and the earth.

Nearby, a large half barrel brimming with water awaited the thirsty animals. It was not just a vessel for hydration; it was a communal space, a hub of life where creatures both two-legged and four-legged quenched their thirst. John Hargreaves, a man of hearty character, was known to dip his head in the barrel after a night of merrymaking, an act that never failed to elicit chuckles from those who witnessed his antics.

As evening settled in, the chickens and rooster were safely tucked away for the night. They scratched at the fresh straw that lined the floor, searching for sustenance in the form of unsuspecting maggots. Their small, bustling movements added a touch of animation to the tranquil scene, a reminder of the circle of life that encompassed both the mundane and the miraculous.

In the heart of this cottage, stories were woven like the threads of an intricate tapestry. Conversations echoed off the walls, laughter filled the air, and the flickering fire cast its benevolent light upon the faces gathered around it. The cottage was more than just a physical space; it was a vessel of memories, a repository of shared experiences, and a haven of belonging.

As they took in the sights, sounds, and smells of this cherished place, a sense of gratitude washed over those who stood within its walls. The cottage stood as a testament to endurance, resilience, and the unbreakable ties that bound them together. In a world filled with uncertainty, it was a constant, a sanctuary of warmth and light that beckoned them home, a place where they could find solace and strength to face whatever challenges lay ahead.

Now John and Margaret Hargreaves were gone and all that remained were memories.

The thick wooden trellis holding the thatch sagged under the weight of years, its weathered form bearing witness to the passage of time. Within the confines of the old cottage, memories lingered like whispers of forgotten tales, and amidst the decaying structure, a hidden haven awaited discovery.

William's mind wandered back to the past, retracing the steps of another era. He remembered the crawl space beneath the gravel and dirt, a subterranean chamber that John Hargreaves had dug out in times long gone. It had served as a sanctuary for sustenance and secrets, a refuge for survival in times of adversity. Now, that same space held the promise of safeguarding a new treasure – a cache of wool that carried with it the hopes and aspirations of those who sought to challenge the forces that sought to oppress.

William convinced the others that this was the safest place to keep the wool for a few days until it could be taken to Calico.

Tommy used the flint and steel to light the candle in the lantern and gave it to William who kicked the dirt and gravel around searching for the leather handle of the door. He lifted it slowly allowing the dirt and gravel to slide off. Holding the lantern, he turned to climb down the ladder.

Reaching the bottom, he swiped away the cobwebs with his hand and bent down allowing his eyes to focus in the darkness. There were three beams holding up a wooden subfloor. It wasn't high enough to stand but it was large enough to store the wool.

One by one, the others passed down the tods of wool, their hands exchanging silent vows of determination and resilience. William stacked the bundles along the stone wall at the back of the chamber, each tod a symbol of resistance, each fibre a testament to the indomitable spirit that had brought them to this pivotal moment.

He climbed back out and closed the door. The others pushed the dirt and gravel back over the door again.

Calico's voice lingered in their minds, a promise of future action. Three days they would wait, three days until Calico and his companions would return to retrieve the wool and continue their mission. The plan was set, the threads of fate interwoven, and as they went their separate ways, a sense of purpose pulsed through their veins.

Robert's journey to Leeds loomed on the horizon, the weight of cloth as significant as the secrets it carried. In the shadows of the cottage, as stars blinked overhead and the world slept, a new chapter in their shared story began to unfold. The old cottage, a keeper of memories and a witness to history, stood steadfast, its walls imbued with the echoes of whispered conversations and whispered hopes.

And so, under the cover of darkness and within the embrace of hidden chambers, the legacy of defiance and determination continued to thrive, ready to be passed down through the ages, a beacon of hope for all who dared to challenge the tides of oppression and injustice.

☆

The next morning arrived with a foreboding chill that seemed to settle over the Rushworth cottage. Milton Kilsin, the constable, and the bailiff returned, their presence casting a shadow over the tranquil landscape. As the family toiled in the barley crop, the ominous arrival disrupted their tasks, prompting them to pause and approach the unwanted visitors.

The family stopped what they were doing in the barley crop and went up to greet them.

Isabel's voice carried authority as she called out to her daughters, Morwen and Mirth, instructing them to retreat inside the cottage.

'Oh, Ma, do we 'ave to?'

'Daughters, do as yer told!' The exchange between mother and daughters was a poignant reminder of the ever-present need to shield innocence from the harsh realities of the world.

The constable reined in the two horses and allowed Milton Killsin and the bailiff to jump down from the carriage. John Pigshells jumped down and racked up the horses with the halter and tied them to a tree.

Milton glared at Tommy. 'As a representative of Lord Protector, Oliver Cromwell, Customs House and the guard of the staple, I've been authorised to search this area for stolen wool.'

Isabel's gaze bore into Milton Kilsin, her eyes brimming with a mixture of disgust and defiance. Beneath the surface, she held a truth she dared not speak, a truth that could unravel the carefully woven threads of deceit that had shrouded her family. The venomous words she held at bay simmered just beneath her composed exterior, a promise of retribution that lingered like a storm on the horizon. *One day, Milton Killsin, you will pay.*

Milton Killsin eyeballed her. 'Ahhh, Isabel Rushworth, I hope that you are in good health and my wife sends her regards.'

Isabel's memories of his touch and his invasive presence flooded her senses, a nauseating reminder of a past she wished she could erase. She shuddered at the memory, her gaze never leaving Milton's eyes as they locked in a silent battle of wills.

Isabel fumed. 'Mr Killsin, yer wife is a kind soul and I hope that one day you will see fit to applaud her ways. Yet, I fear that day is a long way off owing to yer presence 'ere this mornin'.'

Tommy Rushworth, a pillar of strength and protection, moved to stand by his wife's side, his presence a silent reassurance. He whispered urgently, his words a balm to her seething anger. 'Quiet, wife, yer gonna make things more difficult than they already are.'

Isabel's temper was momentarily quelled, her gaze softening as she fixed her eyes on her husband's.

Tommy fixed his gaze on Milton Killsin with an expression of hatred.

Milton blew his nose in a hankie. 'And Tommy Rushworth, have ya not come by that wool we took from ya? If yer give it up, yer family and home will be spared the indignation of a search and all will be forgotten.'

Tommy's response was laced with a hard edge, his voice a quiet assertion of his resolve. 'Milton Killsin, me house is open to ya... search... then be off with ya!'

Isabel stepped toward the door. 'Morwen, Mirth come 'ere, me loves.' She stood behind them and guided them out of the way.

Milton Kilsin knelt before the young girls, his demeanour shifting to one of feigned charm. 'Ahhh, you two, you've grown so much, almost women in yer own right. As fine as yer mother,' he cooed, his words dripping with condescension.

He glanced up at Isabel smugly. 'You should keep your eyes on these beauties, make sure they're safe. Wouldn't want anything to happen to them now, would we?'

John Pigshells, a compassionate observer to the scene, met Isabel's gaze and offered a subtle wink, a reassuring gesture that whispered of protection and safety.

Protectively, Isabel pulled her daughters closer to her and glared at him angrily. 'Why don't ya leave us in peace!'

Killsin smiled. 'Tommy... yer wife has a fiery temper and needs cooling. I suggest you dose the flame before she ends up on the ducking stool again.'

Tommy's hands clenched into fists, his knuckles white with suppressed rage. The suggestion of his wife's past humiliation ignited a fury that threatened to consume him. His voice, a growl barely contained, resonated with raw anger. 'Killsin, you've come 'ere for a purpose. I suggest you and yer bailiff tend to it and leave!'

'Your land ya say, I believe this land belongs to his grace and I believe it would be in everybody's best interest if you packed yer belongings and left. Tommy Rushworth, nobody wants you here.'

William glanced at Tommy, he could tell he was holding his raging anger back and was proud of his nephew for having so much restraint.

He thought for a moment and considered the memories of his own older brother Thomas, Tommy's father. He had passed some time ago, but he could see similar traits. *He has a quiet strength like his father and the nut didn't fall far from the tree. God I miss me brother, he'd know what to do.*

William thought about his own son and he could tell things were different. *As a child, Robert always tried to find the easy way unlike his brother John who was a hard worker, softer and much more like his mother Lucy.*

He thought back to the time when they were children playing ball outside and even then, he could tell what men they would become. John would always try to play fair and not hurt his brother; however, Robert, if he knew he was going to lose would cheat or fight.

Milton's command shattered William's reverie, a harsh reminder of their predicament. 'SEARCH IT!'

John Pigshells and the bailiff marched into the cottage. John Pigshells and the bailiff, embodiments of Killsin's authority, moved into action. Pigshells ascended to the loft, while the bailiff probed the animal enclosure with a pitchfork. Each movement, a violation of their privacy, stoked the fires of resentment that simmered beneath the surface.

Pigshells feigned checking the chimney then climbed into the loft, 'Nothing up 'ere.'

The bailiff went around the back, opened the gate to the animal enclosure, and started stabbing the small mound of hay with a pitchfork. Satisfied there was no wool, he went back outside.

Milton's frustration boiled over, his voice dripping with impatience. 'Tommy, I'm giving you a chance to come forward and tell us where the wool is. If you're honest with me, we can forget about all these unpleasantries and all will be as they were.'

Tommy remained silent and stared at him with contempt.

'If you are found in possession of the wool or even know of its whereabouts, then I can't help you. You and your family will face the full brunt of the law.'

Tommy raised his eyebrow but remained steadfast.

'Surely, you wouldn't want Isabel and William jailed. And of course, these young ones would be taken away and placed in the alms-house.'

The threat hung in the air like a storm cloud, casting a shadow over the Rushworth family. Tommy's eyes flickered toward Isabel and their daughters, a silent promise of protection and determination. 'And you, Milton Killsin, what makes ya think we had anything to do with your stolen wool? Wool ya stole from us in the first place!'

Killson frowned. 'I'd be very careful with yer words, Tommy Rushworth, my patience will only go so far.'

William's heart swelled with pride for his nephew, who stood unwavering against the tide of authority. He could sense Tommy's restraint slipping, the tempest of anger and defiance threatening to engulf him. The stakes were high, and the clash of wills between Tommy and Killsin marked a pivotal moment that would ripple through their lives and shape the course of their destiny. As the tension hung heavy in the air, the Rushworths stood united, a fortress of resolve against the onslaught of power that sought to break them.

Milton Killsin and the other two got back on the carriage, turned the horses and rode back down the hill toward Sun Street. Pigshells waved comically from the back of the cart.

☆

Under the shroud of darkness, the clandestine operation continued to unfold. Robert, William, Calico and his two men, bound together by a shared mission, returned to the old Hargreaves cottage. The dim light of a lantern pierced the night, revealing the hidden cache of wool that had been carefully stowed away. As William climbed down the ladder into the secret chamber, his heart pounded with a mixture of anticipation and trepidation. The tods of wool were passed up, one by one, a symbol of their defiance against injustice.

Robert and Calico quietly bid farewell. They led the horses along Moorhouse lane, north along Dimples Lane then cut across the woodland to Weavers Hill.

Three of Calico's men were waiting for them at the edge of the woodland where they unloaded the horses.

Robert whispered, 'I'll meet you here in five days.'

Calico nodded. 'Five days.'

Robert and William led the horses back to Dimples Lane where they mounted them and trotted home. As they arrived back at the cottage, the low light from the fire was emanating from the gaps in between the shutters. Robert lifted the latch, the scene that awaited them inside was far from what they had expected. Robert pushed open the door and froze, his heart pounding as he took in the chilling tableau before him. Wilding, a sinister figure, holding a knife to Isabel's throat.

'AH, ROBERT, long time no see. We've been waiting fer ya.'

Isabel's eyes had tears and she sat there on a stool, Morwen and Mirth whimpering at her feet.

Robert gawked at Tommy who was bound and gagged. Motionless, his eyes grew wide as he glanced up at William with fear.

Robert turned to Wilding and growled, 'Leave them be?'

'You 'ave a beautiful family, Robert, 'specially these three country roses.' He grabbed Isabel's hair roughly. Wilding taunted, his voice dripping with malice. The realisation of their vulnerability hit Robert like a physical blow.

William's voice wavered with a mix of fear and fury. 'What's wrong, Robert?' He stepped inside, his eyes widening as they fell upon the terrifying scene. 'What? BLOODY HELL! WHO ARE YOU?'

Isabel screamed as did Morwen and Mirth who started crying uncontrollably. 'MAaaaaaa!'

She glanced at Tommy who struggled and strained against his bindings and tried to scream although it was muffled by the gag.

Robert remained calm. He took a step forward and his voice became deeper. 'Leave them be.'

William noticed a side to his son he hadn't seen before. *Who is he? So confident, so calm.*

'The necklace damn ya ta HELL!' Wilding snarled.

'Girls, take yer mother up into the loft.'

'Now ya 'ave me, ya need not threaten me family any further.' Robert muttered.

The room seemed to pulse with tension, each heartbeat a testament to the high-stakes battle of wills that raged within its walls.

William heard and grunted with confusion.

Wilding smirked. 'They don't know… ya 'avn't told 'em!' His words carried a venomous weight, revealing a sinister truth that sent shockwaves through the cottage.

'My name is John Wilding and I 'ave been hired by the Alderman of Leeds, his Lordship Thomas Metcalf, to take yer son back ta hang. Yer son 'as been an awfully baaad boy and has taken property that don't belong to 'im.'

The revelation struck like a thunderbolt, the gravity of the situation sinking in like an anchor. William's gaze shifted from Wilding to Robert, disappointment etched on his features. He couldn't help but recall his own troubling dream, the unsettling vision that had haunted his sleep. *Is this going to play out like my dream? No, God help me.*

Robert's voice, heavy with regret, confirmed the truth. 'Tis true, Father, he has the right to take me.'

Wilding brandished a parchment, a warrant that held the power to tear their world asunder. 'I have a warrant for his arrest or the person suspected of thieving the necklace. Oh, and I have a witness.' His satisfaction oozed like poison as he relished his upper hand.

Robert's anger ignited, his voice a seething growl. 'SMYTHE, yer talkin' about Smythe!'

'Aye, it took some convincin', but I finally got it out of 'im.' Wilding remembered the damage he done to his hand. *It was worth it.*

Wilding knew he was with the upper hand. 'Now, there's two things I need from ya ta spare yer family any more displeasure. The wool you have and the sapphire necklace. Give 'em both ta me and we can spare yer family and be on our way back ta Leeds.'

Robert's retort held a note of bitter sarcasm, he mumbled, 'You know as well as I do, the captain has it, and by now probably sold and spending the coin somewhere in Europe. Do ya really think I'd keep it on me knowing you were hunting me?'

Wilding thought about his pact with Griswold. 'Where's the wool?'

'I 'ave no idea. Killsin, the overseer, took it not a week ago. I didn't have a bill of sale.'

Wilding's impatience grew, frustration fuelling his desperation. 'Where's the wool?' Wilding squinted in disbelief. 'Don't lie to me!'

Robert eyed him and frowned. 'Now do ya not think if we had the wool, would we not be spinnin' and weaving it as quick as we could? If you don't believe me search the cottage.'

Wilding grew more inpatient. 'Turn around and face the wall and any funny business and I'll slit his throat!' He pointed to Tommy.

A tense standoff ensued, the room a battlefield of wills and intentions. William, torn between his protective instincts and the grim reality, felt a helpless rage building within him. 'LEAVE HIM BE!' William protested and took a step toward Wilding.

'OH, SHUT IT, OL' MAN!' Wilding's words were a venomous hiss, his knife a deadly extension of his will. He pointed his knife in his direction.

William stopped, he stood motionless. As Robert faced the wall, his fate sealed by circumstances beyond his control, William's heart ached with helplessness. His words, a desperate whisper, held a promise of hope. 'We'll get ya outta this son.'

Amidst the turmoil, a tragic farewell played out between father and son. Robert's voice trembled with regret, his eyes meeting William's with a depth of emotion too profound for words. 'Stop, Da, my fate is sealed. I'm sorry, Father.'

Wilding tested the bindings. 'No point in struggling, ya won't get out of them. More ya struggle, tighter they'll get.' He escorted him outside and attached a long rope to his bindings.

'A condemned prisoner gets one request, at least let me say goodbye to me family.' Robert's plea hung in the air, a testament to his love and determination.

William's footsteps echoed behind them, a silent vigil that bore witness to the unfolding tragedy. A whispered promise escaped his lips, a pledge to save his son from the noose that threatened to tighten around his neck.

Robert fell back. William dropped to catch him. 'Take it ta Smythe, Nags Head, Leeds.'

Robert whispered, 'Take it ta Smythe.'

Isabel cut Tommy's bindings, Tommy's fingers trembled as he grasped the pistol on the mantle, his heart pounding with a mixture of fear and determination. The memories of the Musketeer's gift flooded back, a relic from another time that now held a life-altering purpose. He raced up into the loft, the dim light casting eerie shadows as he rummaged through his belongings, seeking the musket ball and powder that lay hidden away. The weight of his actions hung heavy in the air, a choice that could alter the course of their lives forever.

With the pistol, powder and shot in hand, Tommy burst outside, only to find that Wilding had already vanished, his retreating figure a cruel reminder of the powerlessness that plagued their situation. William's steady presence at his side offered a much-needed anchor, a reminder that recklessness could cost them dearly.

William put his hand against Tommy's chest. 'Now's not the time. If anythin' happens to him now on our land we'll all face the full brunt of the law. We'll lose everything. Patience nephew, patience.'

William took the pistol from him and put it back on the mantle, 'Mirth, Morwen, ya can come down now, he's gone.'

Isabel's disbelief hung heavy in the air, her voice a mix of sorrow and confusion. 'Robert, a thief I don't believe it!'

'I don't know me own son,' William lamented, the weight of his words conveying the depth of his concern and uncertainty. 'Now, we wait until Calico has finished weaving the cloth then I'll set off fer Leeds.'

'Robert whispered something to me. He said take it ta Smythe.'

William paused and stared blankly at Tommy. 'He wants us ta go ta Leeds. I remember him talking about Smythe and the Nags Head. He said see Smythe. And… he said "take it", but TAKE WHAT?'

'Take what?' Tommy was confused.

William thought for a moment. *Take it?... Take it?* 'What the bloody hell does he mean by "it"? Hold on, hold on, it… it… it? He doesn't mean the cloth, no it's something else.'

William's face lit up. 'The necklace, that's "it". He still has the necklace… and… I think I know where he's hidden it.'

'But why would he still 'ave it?'

'Cause he's a cheeky buggar, come on.'

Tommy charged toward the door. 'I'll come wi' ya.

William paused and turned, his gaze shifting to Isabel, who offered a smile of reassurance amid her own worries. 'GO, get our Robert back, we'll be orlright,' she insisted, her love and strength a guiding light in the darkness.

They peered up at their mother worriedly, then watched their father and William grab their cloaks and depart through the door.

Mirth and Morwen ran to the door and watched them mount the horses and ride down the hill to Sun Street.

CHAPTER 25

The Jewel of Hope

Tommy laid eyes on the moon as he rode along. It was a waxing, gibbous moon. He looked through whisper of cloud making out the small spots. They appeared cold and moist and he knew they were responsible for the morning dew.

When they arrived at the edge of the woodland, Calico and his two men were waiting.

'I'm sorry ta hear about Robert!' he whispered.

Calico's men loaded the cloth onto the two horses and walked back in the direction of Spinning Way.

Calico stayed. 'What now?'

William spoke with fearlessness. 'I 'ave to go to Leeds ta get me boy back. Jack, fer old time's sake, please keep an eye on the cottage, Isabel and the girls.'

Calico gazed at William and put out his hand. 'Of course my old friend, now God speed. Get Robert back and if you ever need me, send word.'

William and Tommy led their horses back through the woodland to Dimples Lane.

William stood there in silence for a moment, 'We 'ave ta go to the Hargreaves cottage.'

'What fer?' Tommy was bemused, 'William, let's get out of 'ere before the darkness breaks.'

William ignored him and trotted down Moorhouse Lane. Tommy shrugged his shoulders then trotted after him.

☆

Outside the Hargreaves cottage, William reined in his horse and waited for Tommy to catch up.

'Hold onto this.' William handed Tommy the reins of his horse and dismounted. He ripped a piece of linen from his undershirt and walked over to a Scots Pine. Breaking off a two-foot branch, he wrapped the cloth around the top. Dipping it into the sticky resin which escaped from the bark he placed it on the ground and used his flint and steel to light it.

Tommy tied up the horses and followed him into the gutted cottage. William found the leather strap and pulled on it. The dirt, crushed stone and dirty thatch slid off. Tommy held the trap door while his uncle climbed backwards down the small ladder.

Tommy watched the flickering torchlight dance across the rugged features of his uncle's determined face. There was an air of urgency, a tension that hung heavily in the damp, musty air of the cottage. The events of the past days had pushed them to the edge, and now, within the ruins of the Hargreaves cottage, a hidden clue beckoned them onward.

William knelt, moving the torch before him as he peered around. He noticed some disturbed dirt over near the far wall and crawled over to it. Wiping away the dirt, he felt a small linen bag; he pulled it out then noticed a glint out of the corner of his eye. He paused and placed the torch down.

Tommy climbed down and crawled over to William who he could see him digging around. 'William, what is it?'

As the torch illuminated the small linen bag that William had discovered, Tommy's heart quickened. The bag seemed innocuous enough, a simple piece of fabric tied with a frayed string. Yet, in this world of secrets and uncertainties, even the most ordinary of objects held the potential for revelation.

William felt around in the hole. He pulled another smaller linen bag out and brushed off the dirt. Untying the knot, he reached inside.

Tommy knelt, staring, mouth open in wonder at the brooches, jewellery and trinkets William held in his hand. They said nothing, William tied a knot then handed it to Tommy.

William picked up the torch again and ripped some of his undershirt, wrapping it around the torch bringing it to a brighter flame. He gave it to Tommy and once more reached down into the hole feeling yet another small linen bag. Lifting it up he once again, untied the knot.

He dangled it in front of the flame. They were both speechless.

A blue sapphire, it was a magnificent piece, swirling jewels, a painted opaque enamel bow. They admired it until the torch's flame started to dwindle.

'This can save Robert!' William asserted. 'Gimmie the bag.' William took the torch then put the Sapphire in the bag and slipped it into his tunic. He started crawling over to the ladder. 'Come on Tommy, let's get out a' here.'

Their fear was renewed. They were transporting cloth worth more than fourteen shillings under the cover of darkness. Now in their possession, was stolen goods belonging to the Alderman of Leeds.

'Oh well, you can only lose ya head once,' William mumbled. He rolled his eyes.

They climbed out, mounted their horses and continued down Moorhouse Lane toward Oxenhope. When they got to the Lamb Inn, they followed Denholm Road then headed north to avoid the nightwatchmen.

Just outside Bradford they stopped and rested the horses in a ravine to hide the light from their fire. They unloaded the cloth from the horses and removed the saddles and horse blankets using them as protection from the damp ground. After William lit the fire, they sat leaning against the saddles warming themselves.

'Why da ya think he did it, William? The necklace.' Tommy was baffled.

'Who knows... God knows, he always lived in the light of his brother. Suppose it was his way of proving himself and getting ahead. He was always a spirited lad and so competitive. Always had to win the ball, shear more sheep, run faster, jump higher. Always out to impress, now where's it's got 'im? The young fool!'

Tommy listened to William's sombre words. 'I remember me da tellin' me about somebody else in the family like that.' He smirked.

Now uncle, 'How we gonna get 'im back?'

William was stumped. 'Haven't quite figured it out yet. We'll head to the Nags Head in the morn' besides we should find John first. We'll get there before them, should take 'em an extra day on a cart.'

William laid down, leaned his head against the saddle, turned over and covered himself with a blanket.

Tommy laid there for a while staring into the flames. 'Girlington, Uncle. Captain Girlington. If we can find him, if we can uncover the truth from his lips, we might be able to prove Robert's innocence.'

A thoughtful expression crossed William's face and he nodded slowly. 'Aye, Tommy, you might be onto something. We'll need to gather information, find out where this Girlington might be, and how he's connected to all of this. But we must be cautious, for the shadows are deep, and danger lurks at every turn.'

The fire burned low, its embers casting a faint glow upon their faces as they exchanged silent vows. The journey ahead would not be easy; they were up against powerful forces, entwined in a conspiracy that reached far beyond their understanding. But they were not alone. Their determination, their resilience, and the glimmering sapphire that now rested in their possession, would guide their path.

As the flames dwindled, casting a blanket of darkness over the ravine, William's voice cut through the silence. 'Rest now, lad. Tomorrow, we begin our search for Captain Girlington, and with him, we'll uncover the key to Robert's salvation.'

Tommy tried to o sleep but his mind was too active and he worried about Isabel and the girls. He wondered how Will was going at the mill. '*Must be hard fer him.*'

Will was tall and strong like a man but still owned the mind and sentiment of a boy. Tommy remembered the night he was born and how proud his father Thomas was. *God I miss him.*

☆

In the midst of the rain-soaked night, as flames licked at the hearth and the world outside seemed shrouded in darkness, a new life emerged. Will Rushworth, a tiny yet determined being, took his first breath in a cottage filled with both chaos and joy.

Tommy stood there, soaked to the bone, his heart swelling with a mix of awe and pride as he beheld his wife and their newborn son. Isabel's exhaustion was evident, but her eyes radiated a fierce love and a profound connection to the new life cradled in her arms. The cries of the baby, once an anxious wail, had softened into the contented rhythm of nursing.

The tavern erupted in cheers, the collective voices of the patrons echoing the celebration of a birth – a birth that symbolised hope, resilience, and the unbreakable bonds of family. Thomas Rushworth, a man of few words, could hardly contain the tears that welled up in his eyes as he embraced his son. It was a moment of pure joy, a rare respite from the tumultuous events that had unfolded.

As the tavern resounded with merriment, the rain continued to fall outside, a gentle reminder that life carried on, unfazed by the struggles and triumphs of its inhabitants. Tommy's gaze lingered on the faces of those gathered around him – the supportive friends, the proud family members – and his heart swelled with a profound sense of gratitude.

In the days that followed, life settled into a rhythm once more. The cottage was repaired, the fire rekindled, and the Rushworth family adjusted to the presence of their newest member. Will Rushworth, snugly wrapped in his blankets, nestled against his mother's chest, became the heart of their home.

Isabel's strength and resilience shone through as she cared for her son with unwavering dedication. The trials and tribulations of their recent past seemed to fade into the background as they revelled in the simple joys of a growing family. Lucy, Agnes, and the rest of the village rallied around, providing support and sharing in the joyous occasion.

As the weeks turned into months, young Will thrived under the loving care of his parents. His bright eyes and curious expressions brought laughter and warmth to the cottage, a constant reminder of the future they were forging amidst the challenges of their time.

Tommy often found himself gazing out at the horizon, pondering the mysteries that lay beyond, contemplating the legacy he would leave for his son. The events that had unfolded – the theft, the fire, the secrets – served as a reminder that life was unpredictable, that darkness and light were forever intertwined.

But in the midst of it all, there was love. Love that transcended hardship, that bound them together as a family, and that fuelled their determination to overcome whatever obstacles lay ahead. Will Rushworth, a symbol of that enduring love, represented a new beginning, a fresh chapter in the story of their lives.

And so, under the watchful eyes of the saints, amidst the backdrop of a small village in the heart of England, the Rushworth family found solace, purpose, and a renewed sense of hope. The winds of change continued to blow, but within the walls of their cottage, a flame burned brightly – a flame that could not be extinguished, for it was fuelled by the unbreakable bonds of family, the resilience of the human spirit, and the enduring power of love.

☆

As the first light of dawn began to paint the sky with its muted colours, Tommy and William emerged from the damp ravine. Their breath misted in the cool air as they quickly gathered their belongings and prepared to continue their journey to Leeds. The urgency of their mission loomed over them, driving away the remnants of sleep and uncertainty. Tommy rubbed the sleep from his eyes and re-adjusted his tunic. He pushed his dark hair off his face and rubbed his face into wakefulness.

The grass around them was wet from dew and mist still collected in the ravine. The fire turned to ash through the night and Tommy shivered. He pushed William in the back and listened to him groan. 'William, we should make way, wake up.'

Tommy stood and kicked what was left of the fire around then picked up his blanket and went over to the horse. 'We better move if we wanna get to Leeds before 'em.'

William sat up but still appeared groggy and confused. He remembered the events of the previous evening which sprouted some urgency. 'We 'ave ta get ta Leeds, should only be another few hours.'

William saddled his horse then draped the cloth over its hind quarters gently feeling its softness. *Calico and his people did a grand job, cloth's fine and you'd never know there was long staple mixed in. Already fulled, washed and stretched, so difficult to tell how many threads. I'm sure tis a hell of a lot longer than if we weaved it at home. His people can comb and work the wool so even the long staple seems soft. Must be a good twenty pounds worth of cloth 'ere maybe more. Ten-pound fer Calico and ten fer us, plenty ta pay the lease fines and more. Should set us up with some wheat grain fer next season as well.*

Tommy placed the pad on his horse then the saddle with leather covered arches. When he finished saddling his horse he picked up the cloth and draped it over its hind quarters and noticed the fake weaver's mark at the top and smiled. *You'd never tell and hopefully nor will the aulnager.*

Tommy tightened the billet strap, untied the halter from the tree and climbed up. Moving the reins to the right he followed William up and out of the ravine.

CHAPTER 26

Pursuit of Truth

Leeds came into view, its buildings rising against the horizon, a blend of old and new, tradition and progress. The town's bustling energy greeted them as they entered its streets, guiding their way toward the heart of the town. It was a place of opportunity and danger, a place where secrets were traded like currency, and alliances were forged and broken with a mere whisper.

The Briggate unfolded before them, a chaotic tapestry of life and livelihood woven through narrow lanes and bustling streets. The air was thick with the mingling scents of fresh bread, the acrid tang of butchery, and the pungent smoke of taverns. The clamour of voices, the cacophony of animals, and the hurried footsteps of passersby created a symphony of urban existence that was both intoxicating and overwhelming.

They rode across the bridge over the river and past the burgage plots. They passed the tofts, made of timber, very compact and close together.

Tommy and William guided their horses through the labyrinthine alleys, their senses bombarded by the sights and sounds of the bustling market town. The narrow lane ways revealed glimpses of hidden lives – sick children, old women, hovels barely standing, and the hustle of merchants peddling their wares. Dogs darted past, pigs rooted in the muck, and chickens scratched for sustenance. It was a raw and unfiltered portrait of life, a vivid contrast to the tranquillity of their rural existence.

The more well to do residents owned upper stories which hung over the road shielding the butcher shops below. A woman emptied her chamber pot from the upper window and it splashed just in front of William's horse spooking it.

Above Kirkgate end stood the Moot Hall, in front of which were the stocks and pillory; the inhabitants scowling at the passers-by who threw rotting vegetables left from the previous market.

At the front of the building, above the road was a niche, home to a statue of Queen Anne. She stood watch over the Shambles.

Butchers threw guts, and buckets of blood into the street runnel where mange dogs slurped and fought over offal.

Eventually they found the Nags Head at the corner of Commercial Street and Albion Place. The wooden sign hung from the wall above it.

They led their horses through the arch at the side, tied them up then went inside. The tavern welcomed them with a cacophony of voices and the warmth of camaraderie. The scent of ale, wood smoke, and human sweat hung in the air, creating an atmosphere that was both inviting and brimming with stories. The barmaid's gaze met theirs, her expression indifferent yet expectant.

The tavern was a busy, loud place full of the rich and the poor. There was a large fireplace and numerous round and rectangular wooden tables. A large oak bar topped with an ale barrel and numerous pewter and wooden mugs was the centre point. It always attracted both the best and the worst traders, rogues and vagabonds. Those who wanted more and those who didn't.

A large wrought iron candle chandelier hung from the ceiling; wax drips dripped down the length of it fashioning a wax sculpture. Small oil lamps rested on most of the tables, the grey acrid smoke floated up to the wooden beams above.

A man sat at a round table near the window and he glanced up to see the two strangers. His hand was bandaged, he rubbed it carefully and grimaced.

They meandered up to the bar. The barmaid turned to them. 'What can I do fer ya?'

'Just an ale, if ya don't mind. We're looking fer a bloke by the name of Smythe.'

She put two ales on the bar in front of them. ‘Smythe? Never ‘eard of no Smythe.’

‘The man sitting by the window called out to the barmaid. ‘BRING US AN ALE, GERTIE!’

She hurried over with the tankard. ‘Two strangers lookin’ fer ya.’

Smythe looked up curiously. ‘Try and find out where they’re from.’

Gertie returned to the bar. ‘Why you lookin’ fer ‘im?’

William scanned the tavern. ‘He was some assistance to my sons John and Robert some time ago. I just wanted to thank him.’

Gertie looked over at Smythe; seeing this, Tommy and William plodded over to him. ‘You must be Smythe.’

‘Depends, who’s askin’.’

Smythe didn’t know them so was immediately on edge. ‘So what brings ya to Leeds, work? Women? Song? Or ‘ave ya come ta make yer fortune like the rest?’

Smythe glared at Tommy, the younger of the two men, and placed his hand on the hilt of his knife.

It wasn’t the first time somebody came hunting for him from the old days, but like the last one who tried, he hoped it wouldn’t have the same outcome.

These days his methods were far simpler and did not attract as much attention. Just a few drops of the white sap from the Little Apple of Death in their brew.

What came next wasn’t pretty. Tightness of the throat, burning sensation in the stomach and death would occur soon after.

The patrons in the tavern, turned a blind eye and usually helped take the body out the back and into the courtyard to be thrown in the river later at night.

‘I am William Rushworth and this is my nephew Tommy, I believe you know my sons John and Robert. Just wanted to thank you for lookin’ after them.’

‘Hahah oh, why didn’t ya say so? Come, why don’t ya join me? Sit I’ll ‘ave the woman bring ya some grub. GERTIE!’

With warm smiles, William nodded in acknowledgment of Smythe’s offer, and the two of them settled into the seats across from him. The barmaid, Gertie, was summoned with an exclamation that could have awakened the entire tavern, and soon enough, their table was adorned with tankards of ale and a haphazard array of bread and salted lamb.

Tommy and William were ravenous so they broke bread and chewed on it hungrily.

‘We ‘avn’t eaten in a couple a days, come all the way from the Pennine.’ Tommy coughed as a piece of bread went down the wrong way.

‘Likeable lads, John and Robert. John comes in ‘ere regular like.’ Smythe relaxed.

Tommy washed down the bread with a gulp of ale. ‘Robert... Robert Rushworth...’

William interrupted, ‘Is in a bit of trouble for thievin’.’

Tommy leant forward. ‘Robert told us to come ta Leeds and find you!’

Smythe took his hand off his knife. ‘By God, well you’ve found me!’

He smiled and called out to Gertie, ‘COME ‘ERE, WOMAN, THIS IS JOHN’S DA AND...’

Tommy cut in, ‘Cousin!’

The barmaid got excited. ‘Noooooo couldn’t be, John will be so pleased ta see ya. He works at the fullin’ mill but should be home after dark. You know he’s married now! Rosie, used to work ‘ere. She’s with child.’

‘Yes, Robert told me, can’t wait to see them. We’ll stay ‘ere until dark, do ya know where they’re shacked up?’ asked William.

'Aye, John and Rosie moved to a small house on the south side of Kirkgate, corner of the Briggate, just before the river. If you see Leeds Bridge you've gone too far.'

'More about that after,' Tommy whispered. 'Smythe, we 'ave pressin' matters involving Robert. We hoped you could help us.'

William placed the bag of jewellery on the table and Tommy quickly put his hat over it.

Smythe frowned curiously. 'Tis alright in 'ere.'

Tommy removed his hat and Smythe lifted the bag and untied the knot. He took out the smaller bag and peered inside at the jewellery, his eyes lit up with wonderment. 'My, my you 'ave been busy.'

'Not us, Robert!' Tommy exclaimed.

Smythe picked up the smaller linen bag, opened it and fixed his eyes inside, he was gobsmacked. He quickly put the bag of jewellery and lace in his tunic. He put his elbow on the table and open hand to his forehead, 'Don't want anything to do with it?' *If I get caught up in this and bring unwanted attention to myself, I'm finished.*

'He told us to bring it to you,' stated Tommy.

Smythe shook his head in frustration. 'A thief-taker, Jacob Wilding, 'as been scouring the countryside hunting for it, there's a ten-pound reward for information leading to the culprit or culprits who stole it.' *Silly buggar, why didn't he do what I told him?*

'It belongs to the Alderman's wife! You 'ave ta get out of 'ere. I can get rid of the other trinkets fer ya but not the necklace,' Smythe whispered. ''Ere, ya can 'ave it back.'

Tommy stared at Smythe. 'And do what with it, can I give it back?'

Smythe laughed. 'There's things about the necklace you don't know and don't want to know. I don't want anything to do with it. Noo, yer better off doin' what I told Robert, take it ta Captain Girlington in Hull.

'Look, come back in a week and I'll 'ave coin fer the other trinkets, but this ya can take it with ya.' Smythe gave the small bag back to William.

Tommy leant forward and whispered, 'Wilding has already arrested Robert and is bringing him here for trial, we 'ave ta help him.'

Smythe leaned back, his demeanour shifting to a more serious tone. 'It won't be without its challenges, but I'll do what I can to set things in motion. We'll need to move discreetly, gather some information, and tread carefully.'

Tommy and William exchanged a glance, their determination unwavering. 'We're grateful for your help, Smythe. Whatever you need from us, we're ready.'

'Not much chance, they'll hold him in the lock up at Moot Hall until they can transfer him to York Castle. He'll sit in judgment at the quarter assizes in front of a judge from London. If convicted, he'll spend some time in York Castle prison before visiting the Three-Legged Mare.'

William perturbed, dropped his eyes sadly. *My dream, was it foretold?*

Tommy gazed at Smythe curiously. 'The Three-Legged Mare?'

'Aye, gallows at York. Tyburn stands on three wooden pillars thus its name. Thought I was gonna end up there once. Drawn by horse and cart from the prison sittin' on me own coffin with a noose around me neck. The crowd cheerin' and booin' as if it were a celebration. Watchin' me bein' disembowelled and quartered while I watched. Brrrrrr, sends cold shivers down me back!'

Distressed, Tommy glanced at William then back at Smythe. 'We 'ave ta do something! Smythe can you not help us?'

'Errrg, yer complicating me life, I retired from all this!' Smythe frowned.

'Look, I heard from an old mate Captain Girlington took a liking to yer son Robert. We need to send a message to the captain. You go to Hull quick as ya can. Go to Ye Olde Black Boy in the Haven.' Smythe disappeared for a moment then returned, 'Ask fer Beaman give him this.'

Smythe handed Tommy a small piece of parchment but as he couldn't read he stared back at him.

Smythe read with urgency, 'It says:

SELBY, COME QUICK!

ROBERT IN TROUBLE

BRING CREW

S

Mention my name, now go!'

Smythe followed William and Tommy out into the courtyard to find their cloth was no longer strapped to the horses. 'OUR CLOTH!'

'Bloody Brewster's been up to it again, never ya mind, I'll get it back. I've told 'im before about liftin' round 'ere! Thievin' bastard!'

Tommy and William mounted their horses, turned then trotted off through the archway and out into the street.

William called out to Tommy. 'We'll stay at John's place tonight and leave early in the morning.'

Smythe went back inside and sat back down at the table all the while thinking about what could be done.

Smythe glanced up as the door opened. 'Brewster, bring the bloody cloth back and get yer things. We're goin' on a little trip.'

Brewster worked for Smythe for years until they both retired to Leeds. Brewster was cunning and mischievous but totally loyal to Smythe. They had been through much together in the old days.

And so, in the heart of the Nags Head, amid the raucous melodies of camaraderie and the whispers of secrets, a new alliance was forged

– one that would prove pivotal in the fate of Robert Rushworth and the Rushworth family.

CHAPTER 27

Bonds of Family and Determination

William and Tommy rode down the Briggate, it was lined with shops, offices, workshops and houses both grand and humble. Some had three-storeys with a projecting upper storey.

There were beggars and bitches with protruding ribs, elongated nipples and sad eyes. The widowed and fatherless children created by the war just existed with sorrow and no pension.

They passed The Pack Horse Inn with its Templar Cross and the small alley ways leading to the yards behind.

Tommy and William waited at the corner of the Briggate and Kirkgate as Gertie instructed. There was a throng of people walking up from Leeds Bridge from The Queens Mill. As the crowd started to disperse, they saw him meandering along, head down the weight of the world on his shoulders.

William jumped from his horse and handed Tommy the reins then walked toward him. 'JOHN!'

John looked up slowly and smiled, he walked faster. 'Da, what the blazes are ya doin' 'ere?'

William embraced him. 'Son, it's so good ta see ya!'

John noticed Tommy and waved. He started walking toward him. He put his forearm up to his mouth. 'KHOFF! KHAK! KHAK!'

Tommy dismounted his horse and put out his hand.

John shook his hand tiredly. 'Well, I'll be blowed… the whole family's… AHEM… here. KAFF! KAFF!'

'You orl right son?'

'Da what are ya doin' 'ere? AHEM!'

William's face turned serious and he lowered his voice. 'Robert's been arrested by a thief taker. He's brought him here to Leeds. If found guilty he'll hang!'

John's face creased with worry. 'I warned him, even sent a message to him. KHOFF! KHAK! KHAK! I d… don't know if he got it. AHEM!'

'He got it John, but there was nothing we could do,' Tommy replied, saddened by the predicament. 'This thief-taker threatened the family. Robert was forced to go with him.'

John shook his head. 'I warned him to stop his ways. AHEM! But he just kept saying one last job, WOULDN'T BLOODY LISTEN. KHOFF! KHAK! KHAK! AHEM! Come, let's not talk anymore about it here. You must be tired from your journey and there's somebody I want you to meet. AHEM!'

They led the horses down Kirkgate then turned right on Call Lane and headed to a row of working-class houses. The houses were small with one privy for every four.

As they strolled by, gong farmers were collecting night soil from a privy and scavengers were busy removing waste from the streets. After being dug out, the solid waste was removed in large barrels, which were loaded onto a horse-drawn cart. The liquid waste drained away.

William and Tommy were now used to the foul odour of the city but the sight of the gong farmer climbing from the pit, covered up to his waist in excrement was too much.

There were disconnected streets at right angles to Calls Lane. It was a mishmash of small houses, walls, alleyways and hovels.

They passed Cloth Hall Street then went down a lane to a row of cottages crammed into courts behind large tradesmen's grandiose houses. The tiny courtyard was cobbled with no vegetation and little daylight.

They hitched the horses and removed the saddles. They followed John through a tunnel under the first floor of the building and up to the door.

A very pregnant Rosie was waiting and opened the door for them. 'Husband, yer late, I was starting to get worried.'

'Rosie AHEM! We 'ave guests, me da and Cousin Tommy come 'ere all the way from Haworth. KHOFF! KHAK! KHAK! AHEM!'

'Oh, what a wonderful surprise, 'ow do? You must be tired, please sit down and rest; I'll get ya some grub.'

The small cottage was filled with a mixture of weariness and determination as the Rushworth family gathered. The low ceiling and close quarters seemed to amplify their shared concern for Robert's fate, while also fostering an atmosphere of intimacy and shared purpose.

The house was about thirteen-foot square with a stone ground floor and an upper story bedroom. The ceiling was very low and one could touch it with an outstretched arm. It was small and sparsely furnished, there was a large chopping block in the corner, a wooden chest along the wall and a small water barrel beside the hearth.

William and Tommy sat on stools at a small trestle table in the middle of the room. A small fire sat in a hearth recessed into the far wall. It did just enough to take away the chill.

'Congratulations on the bairn, Rosie. Robert told us you were with child,' said Tommy.

'Tis very exciting, just wish it would 'urry up.' She put her hands on her hips and tried to hyperflex the pain away in her back.

As they sat around the trestle table, Rosie's kindness and hospitality were a balm to the weary travellers. The aroma of fresh bread and the taste of ale provided a comforting contrast to the harsh realities they faced in Leeds. The flickering firelight cast dancing shadows on the walls, creating an almost surreal backdrop to their urgent conversation.

John joined them at the table. 'Now tell me what's 'appened to me brother.'

William recounted the story of how Robert arrived one day with horses and fine wool. Then how the thief taker had shown up out of nowhere, accosted the family and arrested Robert and said he was taking 'im ta Leeds.

Tommy looked frustrated. 'We couldn't do anything this thief-taker possessed a parchment from the alderman.'

Tommy reached into his tunic. 'There's also this.' He placed the emerald necklace on the table.

Rosie's eyes widened with both surprise and concern as the emerald necklace was placed on the table. She leaned in to examine the intricate craftsmanship, her fingertips brushing the cool surface of the jewels.

'Where did ya come by this, if I may ask?' Rosie inquired, her voice hushed as if speaking too loudly might shatter the fragile hope that now lay before them.

'It was part of the goods Robert had with him when he arrived,' William explained. 'We reckon it's worth a fair sum, and we're hopin' it might be enough to secure his release or at least buy us some time to figure things out.'

John's brow furrowed as he examined the necklace, a mixture of awe and concern clouding his expression. 'It's a beautiful piece, no doubt about that. But it's also a dangerous one. If Wilding or the alderman find out we've got this, it could bring even more trouble down on us.'

John declined to tell his father about Rosie's previous profession.

William picked up the necklace and put it in his tunic. 'No fear, Rosie, we leave early on the morn' to Hull. We're to meet a fella called Girlington, Captain Girlington. Your friend Smythe told us he may be able to help us.'

'Hahah Ol' Smythe, KHOFF! KHAK! KHAK! don't know what would have 'appened if we hadn't met him when we got ta Leeds. AHEM! Put us up, fed us. Then I met Rosie.'

They chatted until late, John telling them about his job at The Queens Mill. 'Yeah, tis hard work but it's honest. Twelve-to-fourteen hour days, six days a week. Leeds isn't a bad place, AHEM! They reckon a third of England's cloth exports come through 'ere now. More and more move 'ere every day.'

'Tommy looked at John's pale and weary face. 'So what do you do there, nephew?'

Loading cloth off boats and onto corves , loading and emptying the racks and sometimes cropping. The pounding of the cloth by the big mallets is deafening. A far cry from the silence of the moors. I often miss home and the solitude. How's Isabel and the children?'

William and Tommy dropped their gaze.

'Da, what's wrong, tell me!'

'Isabel, Morwen and Mirth are fine, but…'

'But what?' John's face was painted with worry.

Rosie could tell all was not okay. She crept over and put her hands on John's shoulders caringly.

'The fines for the lease, we can't pay 'em! Calamy raised 'em, we 'ave a month to pay 'em or else Milton Killsin takes over the lease.'

'AHEM! Da, we been on the land fer generations, what about the lifehold?'

Tommy cut in sadly, 'We'll lose it if we can't pay the lease fines within the month. He's also raised the rack rents; most have been turned off or fled.'

John shook his head. 'AHEM! Da, what can I do? KHOFF! KHOFF KHAK! KHAK! AHEM!'

'Nasty cough ya got there, son.'

'He's been coughing and spluttering fer a while now. Come on love, let's get you up ta bed. Early mornin' tomorror.'

John reached out and placed a reassuring hand on Rosie's, his eyes conveying a silent message of gratitude and love. 'We'll need to be cautious and strategic. We can't draw too much attention to ourselves, but we can't let fear paralyse us either.'

'Go on son, get yerself ta bed and rest. Besides, there's not much ya can do, you need to stay 'ere and look after Rosie and the bairn. Tommy we should get some sleep we've got a long day tomorra.'

'Yer right.' Tommy stood, grabbed his horse blanket and saddle, near the door, and put it down in front of the hearth. William followed suit.

John slowly climbed the stairs to the bedroom. 'Night, Da. Night, Tommy.'

Rosie followed closely behind. 'Night, Mr Rushworth. Good night, Tommy. See you in the morning. KHOFF! KHOFF KHAK! KHAK! AHEM!'

'Good night. Rosie, you can call me William or Da, whatever takes yer fancy, lass.'

She smiled appreciatively.

After they left, Tommy whispered, 'William, what's with John's cough?'

'Mill fever, he really needs to rest.'

The next morning, they were all up before the sunrise. Rosie roused the fire and stirred the pottage. John crept down the stairs and sat at the trestle. He looked weary and older than his years. William and Tommy joined him.

They all slurped their pottage in silence coming to terms with the start of another day. Then John stood. 'Da, Tommy, AHEM! I 'ave ta go, or I'll lose a day's pay if I'm late. It was grand ta see ya. KHOFF! KHOFF KHAK! KHAK! AHEM!'

'Go son, go.' William and Tommy also stood and bid farewell to him. 'Rosie, we must go also.'

She put a shawl around her shoulders and followed them out into the small, cobbled courtyard. She shivered in the cool morning breeze.

After saddling his horse, William walked over hugged and kissed Rosie on the cheek. 'Look after yourselves, Rosie, and know there is always a warm bed fer ya up at home. Please make sure ya look after me boy and me grandson or granddaughter.'

'Ya don't need ta worry about William... Da.' She smiled gratefully.

Tommy mounted his horse then nodded with affection. 'Bye Rosie.'

Trotting down the lane, they ducked their heads as they went through the archway. Riding toward Halton Moor then Selby Road, it would take them two days to get to Hull. They chose to travel just north of the Humber River.

The crisp morning air held a sense of anticipation as William and Tommy rode side by side along the winding path. The weight of their mission hung heavy on their shoulders, but there was a newfound determination in their hearts. The previous night's discussions had forged a plan, and now they were on the path to putting it into action.

The landscape around them began to transform as the first rays of sunlight painted the horizon. Fields stretched out in all directions, their dew-kissed grasses glistening like precious gems. The sound of their horses' hooves echoed through the quiet countryside, a steady rhythm that matched the beat of their resolute hearts.

They rode in silence for a while, each lost in their own thoughts. The road stretched out before them, winding its way through quaint villages and open fields. Occasionally, they passed fellow travellers – farmers tending to their fields, traders making their way to market, and families going about their daily routines.

As the day wore on, they stopped at a small village inn to rest their horses and break their fast. The innkeeper, a stout and friendly woman, served them a simple meal of bread, cheese and ale. The warm hearth crackled in the corner, casting a cozy glow across the room.

'We've got to be careful, Tommy,' William said in a low voice as they ate. 'We can't let anyone know about the necklace or our plans. The wrong person could bring everything crashing down.'

Tommy nodded, his gaze flickering to the emerald necklace hidden beneath his tunic. 'Aye, I know. We'll have to watch our words and keep our intentions close to our chests.'

After their brief respite, they continued on their journey, the road leading them through changing landscapes and changing weather. The skies darkened as clouds gathered overhead, and a fine mist began to fall, adding a sense of urgency to their ride.

By the time they reached Hull, the sun had set, and the city was shrouded in twilight. The bustling port town was alive with activity as ships arrived and departed, and traders hurried to unload and load their cargo. The salty scent of the sea mingled with the cries of seagulls, creating an atmosphere that was both familiar and foreign.

They made their way to a modest inn near the docks, where they secured lodging for the night. The innkeeper, a grizzled man with a friendly demeanour, greeted them warmly and showed them to their room.

As they settled in for the night, Tommy couldn't help but feel a mixture of anticipation and apprehension. The plan was set in motion, and their journey had brought them to the doorstep of uncertainty. But as he lay in his bed, staring up at the ceiling, he knew that the determination and unity of the Rushworth family would see them through whatever challenges lay ahead.

Tomorrow, they would set out to find Captain Girlington and uncover the truth behind the emerald necklace. The road ahead was fraught with danger and intrigue, but with their resolve unshaken and their hearts set on justice, they were ready to face whatever obstacles came their way.

☆

When Wilding's cart arrived in Leeds, he was exhausted. Robert even more so from the occasional thumping. Wilding drove the cart to Moot Hall then took Robert inside where the bailiff was waiting.

'What's this then,' asked the bailiff who was a rather large rotund man with a lot of keys hanging from his belt.

'Robert Rushworth, arrested for thievery, here's the warrant signed by the alderman.

Finally, the reward. It was all Wilding could think about.

The bailiff took the parchment and recognised the alderman's seal. 'Come on you, this way.'

The bailiff took Robert's other arm and marched him down the stone floor which echoed with each step. They took him to the back of the building where it was dark and gloomy. There were two holding cells with two men in each. The cells had a large oak door strengthened with Iron bolts from top to bottom and a barred opening.

The bailiff unlocked the door and pushed Robert inside. The walls were thick; a toilet bucket was recently used. Three thick, iron rings were attached to the wall above a bench, two of which were occupied.

The bailiff put a set of iron shackles on Robert's wrists than attached him to the remaining ring. He sat down while Wilding undid the bindings on his wrists and unwound the long rope around his arms and chest. The bailiff left the cell and Wilding followed.

'What now? How do I get my reward?' Wilding was exuberant knowing he could now pay back the company.

'Nothin' to do with me, you need to contact Alderman Metcalf. Let him know ya 'ave ya man. He'll arrange fer him ta sit at the next assizes court, next quarter session in York. There he'll be tried. If he's found guilty, he'll hang, and then you'll get your reward.'

'Hold on, I was hired to catch him, not hang 'im!'

'Like I said, nothin' to do with me!'

Robert sat there on the bench, next to the other inmates, tired and beaten.

He heard their conversation outside, so did the other two inmates.

Robert took a deep breath and dropped his head, gazing into nothingness.

☆

Wilding made his way out the front entrance and glanced back at the building. He jumped back up in his cart and with a flip of the reins headed toward the Nags Head.

The Briggate was becoming more and more congested with people escaping the rural areas further north. The streets were full of good men, bad women and… The Beast.

Wilding, feeling a sense of accomplishment, took a deep breath knowing he wouldn't have to hide from the 'Company' any further.

He drove his horse and cart to the Briggate at the corner of Commercial and Albion.

Strolling across the courtyard and into the tavern, he sat down at his normal table. He looked around suspiciously. Gertie brought over an ale and plonked it on the table before him.

Smythe was tending to his brew, so didn't notice his arrival.

Gertie went to the bar coughed and as he turned, she glanced in Wilding's direction.

Smythe scurried over and sat opposite just like normal. 'Any trinkets for me?'

Wilding picked up his ale and skulled it. 'ANOTHER!'

Wilding glared at Smythe. 'Room?' He growled.

'Aye just as ya left it.'

Smythe tried to act normal but inside he was seething from the pain and suffering Wilding inflicted. *He'll get his just deserts soon, very soon, mark my words,* he thought to himself.

Wilding skulled the second ale, put a shilling down and headed off to his room. He opened the door, took off his boots, laid down on the bed and fell asleep.

☆

It was still dark when he woke, so he grabbed the strong box, went downstairs and waited for Smythe.

Smythe acted none the wiser. 'Ya got it back, the necklace?'

'No, the sapphire is long gone, split in a hundred pieces by now, I'd say. This is just the strong box, but it'll be enough to convince the alderman and the judge.'

'So, you've got a ten pound reward comin', gotta be happy.'

'No, course I'm not happy, Rushworth sits in a cell at Moot Hall waitin' to be taken ta York. I don't get me reward until he's sentenced to hang.'

Smythe snickered falsely. He hid the uncomfortable feeling in his stomach.

After an ale and a noggin of pottage, Wilding departed. He strolled past Moot Hall, up Lands Lane and reached Upper Headrow. Making his way up the path of the huge red brick building. He used the roaring lion, iron door knocker on the large, panelled oak door.

The door opened and a servant girl, with a lit candle, greeted him. 'Can I help you?'

Wilding took off his hat. 'Jacob Wilding to see Alderman Metcalf.'

The servant girl looked him up and down. 'Just wait here a jiff… moment.' She tried hard to extinguish the commonness of her speech.

She closed the door to keep the cold out.

A minute later the door opened. The alderman peered around to see if anybody was about. 'Mr Wilding, come in!' He quickly closed the door.

Wilding entered a magnificent receiving hall with polished oak stairs and an ornate carved banister leading up to the second floor.

'Please, Mr Wilding, this way,' the alderman ushered him into the parlour. He turned up his nose at his sweat and body odour.

'Mr Wilding, if you wouldn't mind, in future could you please come to the back door, I wouldn't like anybody knowing our business.'

'Of course, yer grace. My apologies,' he grumbled.

Rich tradesmen like the alderman dressed in expensive coloured wool and linen. His breeches were made of the finest black linen and came to just above the knee. His red garters came to the knee and were buckled. He wore a patterned waistcoat with many buttons reaching down to his thigh. His shoes were blue with painted red heels. He also wore a dark blue woollen coat and he held a tricorn hat with a gold cockade. He smelt of floral, spice and musk.

The alderman spoke well with the King's English. 'Now then, what do you have for me, I see you have my wife's strong box.'

'Aye, I have the strong box and the thief who stole it, but sadly not the necklace, which I bet is currently bound fer Europe.'

'Disappointing,' said the alderman. 'Mmm, and the man responsible?'

‘Robert Rushworth, yer grace, currently in the lock up at Moot Hall.’

‘Well, I suppose it’s something. Shame about the necklace though, my wife will be devastated.’

Wilding tried to look distressed. ‘Aye, tis, sir, tried me best went all the way ta Hull but it was too late, the ship already sailed with the sapphire on it.’

‘And this Robert Rushworth, who is he and where’s he from?’ He squinted to emphasise his curiosity.

‘From the northwest yer grace. Place called Haworth. I went all the way up there to get him. Terrible, cold place. Inconvenience it was.’

The alderman was disgruntled. ‘Very well, I will make presentment to the York court of assize for the next quarter session.’ He walked toward the door.

‘Beggin’ yer pardon, yer grace, there was the issue of the reward. Ten pounds I believe it was.’

The alderman chuckled, a wry smile playing on his lips. ‘Patience, my dear man. The wheels of justice turn slowly, but they do turn. Rushworth will face trial at the quarter sessions in York, and if found guilty, you shall have your reward. In the meantime, please accept this as a token of my thanks.’ He placed half a crown in Wilding’s hand.

The alderman went over to the small table beside an elaborately embroidered chair, lifted a small bell and rang it. ‘Betsy, would you please show Mr Wilding out? Oh and Betsy, the back door if you please.’

Wilding could not help but notice the rich fabrics, lacquered furniture, tapestries, paintings and miniatures in the room. *Worth a bloody fortune,* he thought.

Betsy took Mr Wilding through the kitchen to the back door and opened it for him. ‘There ya… you go, Mr Wilding, you have a good night.’

Once out the door, Wilding opened his clenched fist and glanced at the coin. 'Cheap fuckin' bastard, half a crown erghh, all fer half a crown.' *Would a' been better off breakin' in there me self.*

He strolled down the side of the house and kept going for a while before turning back to stare at the house. 'Back door 'ey, I'll give 'im back FUCKIN' door, grrr.'

Back on the bustling streets of Leeds, Wilding's frustration grew. He knew he was entangled in a web of power and deceit, and he was determined to come out on top. With a newfound resolve, he headed back to the Nags Head, his mind racing with plans and schemes to secure his future.

Little did he know, his actions had set in motion a series of events that would impact not only his own fate but the fate of the Rushworth family and the elusive truth behind the emerald necklace. As the pieces of the puzzle began to fall into place, the tangled web of secrets, lies, and ambitions would soon unravel, revealing a shocking revelation that would change everything.

☆

The days in the holding cell seemed to stretch endlessly for Robert and Palmer Johns. The anticipation of their impending journey to York Castle Prison weighed heavily on their minds. The hours passed slowly, marked by the echoing footsteps of the guards and the distant murmur of activity beyond the thick stone walls.

Robert gazed up at the ceiling from his hammock which was stretched across the seven by thirteen-foot cell. The ceiling was bright white and arched; the rising light came in through a deep recessed, angled and barred window.

As the sun's feeble light filtered through the barred window, Robert sat on the bench, lost in thought. His mind was a tumultuous whirlwind of regret, fear, and uncertainty. He wished he could go back in time, undo the choices that led him to this point. The emerald necklace, once a symbol of desire and ambition, had now become a heavy burden that threatened to crush him.

There was a shelf which held the hammocks and blankets in the daytime. The toilet bucket's contents fouled the air. The marks of previous inmates were etched into the stone wall, small vertical lines used to count the number of incarcerated days.

I hope my father managed to move the cloth. If they could get the cloth to Ursula, they would have enough coin to pay the lease fines. He also hoped they could put two and two together. If they hadn't then they were finished and he would swing from a rope.

The idea of the short drop terrified him; he'd seen one in Bradford. Constriction and pressure on the neck then panic. The face becomes engorged with blood. Burst blood vessels on the face and in the eyes. Eventually, a loss of consciousness and jerky body movements until the end. Then the tongue protruding. He shivered with fear.

Palmer Johns, the seasoned inmate with a weathered face and a dark past, had been a source of reluctant companionship during their confinement. His coarse humour and stories of the outside world provided some respite from the suffocating atmosphere of the cell.

'Oye, Rushworth, you've been sittin' there like a mournin' widow. What's eatin' at ya?' Palmer drawled, leaning against the cell wall.

Palmer let out a gruff chuckle. 'Aye, we've all got a tale to tell, don't we? Life's a fickle mistress, she is. Takes ya down roads ya never thought you'd travel.'

Robert nodded, his gaze dropping to the floor. 'I never meant for things to turn out this way. It was just one job, one chance to make enough coin to save my family.'

Palmer's gaze softened, a glimmer of understanding in his eyes. 'Aye, desperation can drive a man to do things he never imagined. But remember this, lad – it's the choices we make that define us, not the circumstances we're born into.'

Eventually, Robert was taken before the magistrate in Leeds where he was questioned by local law officers, the sheriff and petty jurors from the area. The Alderman, Thomas Metcalf, described the necklace and Wilding corroborated Robert's possession of the item.

Smythe tried to help by bribing the magistrate, as he did many times before, but as the theft involved the alderman's property he was refused.

Robert was arrested on 'suspect' of a felony and the failed interrogations by court officers, the magistrate's only option was to bind him over to the next York Assizes quarter sessions. Here he would be questioned in front of a judge and jury from London.

We'll get ya outta this son. Robert thought about the last words his father spoke to him.

He figured this would be difficult now for he knew once he got to York Castle Prison, leaving was almost impossible. He tried not to think about it.

Robert remembered the night with Ursula, his first time, and she made it so special. He remembered her green dress and the pearls and the pure opulence of the silver, but she sparkled more than all. He remembered her fragrance, the softness of her skin, the smell of her hair as it drifted across his face.

His thoughts were disturbed by the echo of the bailiff's boots stomping towards the cell.

The bailiff banged his day-stick on the barred opening of the doors to both cells trying to rouse the occupants. 'Come on, you lot, up ya get. It's a beautiful day.'

One of the occupants of the other cell yelled out, 'GO FUCK YERSELF!'

The bailiff banged on the opposite door again. 'You, ya dopey buggar, you'll be spendin' the day in the pillory out front, now come on get a move on.'

He grabbed a hold of the huge collection of keys dangling from the key ring on his belt and put one of them in the lock and opened it. 'Come on, ya old bastard, do ya penance and be off with ya.'

The old bearded, toothless man with the shredded breeches and torn undershirt climbed out of his hammock. 'Oh… but bailiff ya keep the best of accommodation, I'll be so sad to leave. GO FUCK YERSELF!'

Robert and the other men got out of their hammocks, folded them, and put them on the shelf with their blankets.

The bailiff grabbed the old man's arm. 'We'll see if ya so jovial and spirited after a day in the pillory. Let's see if we can quieten yer tongue and keep ya off the grog fer a time.'

'Fuck off.'

Robert glanced at his cell mate's brown complexion, very much marked from the pox. His cheek bones were broad, his face thin.

'I'll be joinin' ya in York, Sabbath tomorra they'll cart us off the next day.'

CHAPTER 28

To the Haven We Go

Tommy and William arrived at the Haven in the late afternoon having spent the previous night on the side of the road.

The docks were a mile of merchant's store houses, divided by narrow lanes running down to the wharve's edge. The ships were anchored three abreast. The river was a mass of masts and ropes.

The Haven dock master held an axe ready to cut adrift any ship who didn't follow his wishes, all except *The Pearl,* which came and went as she pleased.

Some ships anchored mid-river and without wharve space unloaded their cargo onto shallow draft Humber Keels. Tide waiters stayed on board checking goods against manifestos until holds were emptied.

Tommy and William made their way down High Street. Eventually finding Ye Olde Black Boy, they rode into the courtyard.

The horses were panting, sweating heavily and white froth dripped from their mouths.

Tommy and William took off their saddles, bridles then led them over to the trough to drink then tied them up.

They went into the tavern and conversations went silent. Tommy felt uncomfortable. All eyes were on them, including the frowning red-haired monster of a tavern keeper who stood there wiping a pewter tankard.

He was a bald, heavy-set man with large silver earrings dangling from both ears. A long, thick, red moustache which was platted and dangled down his chest. The sleeves of his tunic and shirt were cut off emphasizing his muscular upper arms born of years spent in the rigging.

William took out the parchment Smythe had given him and rested his forearms on the bar. He leaned forward and whispered, 'We 'ave a message for Captain Girlington.'

Beaman put the tankard down on the shelf and made his way closer to the bar to stand in front of William threateningly. 'Do ya now? Seems ya may have come to the wrong place. No Girlington 'ere.'

William was about to say something until Tommy nudged him with his elbow and gestured for him to peek behind. William could see with his peripheral vision. There were five crewmen most with their hand on the knife hanging from the belt. They were dirty and ragged and wore gaudy jewellery, rings, ear pendants, pearls and cut off slops.

Two of the sailors standing behind, grabbed Tommy by the shoulders of his tunic.

Tommy began to panic. 'I 'ave a message to give to Captain Girlington about Robert. We don't want any trouble, we just need to find Girlington, Smythe sent us,' claimed Tommy.

'STOP, LET 'EM BE!' the barman yelled.

The seaman let go and returned to their tables.

Tommy handed over the parchment.

Beaman smiled. 'Smythe? Why didn't ya say so?'

Tommy and William heard distinctive steps coming from the back of the room.

'Clomp!'

'Clomp!'

'Clomp!'

'Clomp!'

Beaman turned away and poured two tankards of ale while the group of crewmen parted like the Red Sea and allowed the captain to stroll through.

Tommy and William turned around.

‘Come with me.’ Captain Girlington walked toward the door.

Tommy gawked at her, shocked. ‘Yer… a…’

Girlington turned and stepped toward the door. ‘Are you going to give me the message or not?’

‘Of course, misses.’ William gave it to her.

‘Captain to you!’

She took her hat off to reveal her wavy dark hair tied at the back with blue ribbon. Her high cheekbones and long lashes a tribute to her beauty and downplayed with the scruffiness of her robe.

Tommy still couldn’t take his eyes off her as he watched her read the message. He could smell a faint whisper of wildflowers or herbs, reminding him that beneath the rugged exterior lied a captivating spirit of freedom and adventure.

Girlington gazed at William and Tommy curiously. ‘Beaman, ready the crew, were going to Goole. If we leave now, we’ll catch the high tide.’

‘Aye, Captain.’ He whistled and the five crewmen reappeared and followed Beaman out the back door.

‘Come with me!’ Girlington followed.

William and Tommy glanced at each other, shrugged their shoulders then followed her. She marched down High Street toward the docks.

Out of breath, William called out to her. ‘Beggin’ yer pardon, Captain Girlington, but are we not ta Leeds?’

She ignored him and continued. By the time they arrived at *The Pearl* Beaman was on-board shouting orders at the crew.

The five men from the tavern were the officers of *The Pearl.* The tavern keeper, Beaman, was the first mate. The other four, quartermaster, sailing master, gunner and boatswain and all loyal to

Captain Girlington. The cook, the most experienced seaman preferred to spend his time in the galley.

The ship was a Sloop with two masts, it held a gaff sail stretching from the mast to the back, and two jib sails.

The rigging allowed a Sloop extreme manoeuvrability to sail when the wind was coming from the starboard or port side of the vessel. This allowed *The Pearl* to tack quickly and sail the curls and bends of the river.

'HANDS ALOFT TO LOOSE THE FORE TOP, MAIN TOP, FOR TOPM'ST STAYS,' Beaman bellowed.

'HANDS ALOFT TO LOOSE THE FORE TOP, MAIN TOP, FOR TOPM'ST STAYS, I MATE,' the crew called back.

Various seamen scattered and climbed the shrouds with urgency.

'LAY AWAY,' yelled the first mate.

'ON DECK!' The crewman standing on the foot rope untied the hitch.

Beaman peered up. 'ALOFT! MAIN TOPLOOSE TO THE BUNT! Ready, Captain!'

Captain Girlington nodded her head. 'Let fall mate!'

Beaman peered up. 'Aye, Captain, LET FALL!'

The crew on the deck were at their stations ready to haul.

Beaman called out. 'MARRY UP YER GEAR!'

The sails were pulled taut and the main topsail set, Beaman peered at the captain.

Captain Girlington called out to Beaman, 'All hands to brace around first mate.'

Beaman peered around the ship. 'Aye, Captain, ALL HANDS TO BRACE AROUND!'

The shantyman called out, 'OUR BOOTS AND CLOTHES ARE ALL IN PAWN.'

The crew broke into song.

'Go down you blood red roses, go down
And it's mighty draughty around Cape Horn.

Go down you blood red roses, go down.'

The Shantyman sang loudly,

'OH YOU PINKS AND POSIES.'

The crew continued singing in time to the pulling of the ropes,

'Go down you blood red roses, go down

It's round Cape Horn we've got to go
Chasing whales through ice and snow

Oh my old mother she wrote to me
My darling son come home from sea

Oh it's one more pull and that will do
For we're the bullies to kick her through.'

The Pearl sailed out into the Humber then catching the wind, navigated west towards Black Toft.

The salt marsh on both sides of the river were home to hundreds of fouls like the Marsh Harrier which wheeled and tumbled over the reedbeds looking for small mammals and frogs. Its high pitched 'Kek!' 'Kek!' 'Kek!' filled the ears of all who listened. Flocks of Avocet used their long bills to probe the mud and repeated a high pitched 'Kleet,' when a ship approached.

The marshland emptiness was interrupted by the occasional white sail of an easterly bound ship. The sinking silvery sun sparkled on the water and going against the tide, waves slopped against the bow.

William stood on the aft deck behind Captain Girlington. He took off his hat and stepped forward. 'Beggin' yer pardon, Captain, but why are we not ta Leeds?'

She spoke quietly and politely. 'They will take him to York. We will sail to Selby then board *The Courage,* a flat-bottomed Humber

Keel and hopefully get to York before them. William, your son is in good hands.'

'Then what, we can't break 'im out of York Castle Prison,' stated Tommy irreverently.

Captain Girlington frowned. 'There are things we do not know. You are welcome to make your own way if you wish.'

Tommy's feeling was she knew more than she was letting on. He was impressed with her accent; it was the King's English, polite and proper. He returned to stand beside his uncle; having never been on a ship before they were fascinated by what transpired before them.

There were fifty crewmen hauling rope, climbing the shroud lines and standing on footropes forty feet in the air unfurling sails.

The Pearl sailed north along the river Ouse as far as Goole, thirty miles west of Hull. The *Pearl* often used this as an unloading port to avoid the excise and duties tax in Hull.

Goole was an isolated, rural farming area and hidden inland port. If you knew the right people, like the captain, one could offload goods onto a Humber Keel.

These small flat hulled ships were designed to work in water ways which were only three feet deep. They could carry forty to fifty tons of cargo inland on the small estuaries, for the agreed fee and a box of imported wine.

Captain Girlington held a long-time partnership with the captain of *The Comrade* and so did her father. When they came upriver, he and his son would lift anchor immediately and join them mid-stream.

One advantage of the design of the Humber Keel was the ability to sail remarkably close to the wind, which was essential on the narrow waterways to Selby and further inland.

The Comrade was very manoeuvrable and stable because of the pair of leeboards and the small topsail which was used when they navigated westerly.

Captain Girlington ordered the anchor to be dropped and the sails to be furled as they would be anchored for a while. The crew went about their duties hauling rope and bringing up the sails to tie them off. All this while singing:

'Oh, blow the man down, bullies, blow the man down!
To me way-aye, blow the man down.
Oh, Blow the man down, bullies, blow him right down!
Give me some time to blow the man down!

As I was a-walking down Paradise Street,
To me way-aye, blow the man down.
A pretty young damsel I chanced for to meet.
Give me some time to blow the man down!

She was round in the counter and bluff in the bow,
So I took in all sail and cried 'Way enough now.'

I hailed her in English, she answered me clear,
'I'm from the Black Arrow bound to the Shakespeare.'

So I tailed her my flipper and took her in tow,
And yardarm to yardarm away we did go.

But as we were going she said unto me,
'There's a spanking full-rigger just ready for sea.'

That spanking full-rigger to Glasgow was bound;
She was very well manned and very well found.

But soon as that packet was clear of the bar,
The mate knocked me down with the end of a spar,

And as soon as that packet was out on the sea,
`Twas devilish hard treatment of every degree.

So I give you fair warning before we belay;
Don't never take heed of what pretty girls say.'

They made good time and Selby, with a good wind, was only another two hours away.

The captain strode to the port side of the aft deck and gazed across the river to *The Comrade* which was making its way toward them. She could see her father standing on the bow. She neglected to wave but smiled.

Tommy meandered over and stood beside her; he peered across at *The Courage*. 'William, ya may want ta come and see this.'

William climbed up to the edge of the bow and stood there squinting. 'Is that…?'

Girlington glared at William, paused then growled, 'Captain Smythe to you, sir.'

His appearance was different; his clothes were changed he wore a tri cornered hat of desirable felt and a fashionable blue coat and white ruffled shirt. What was most distinctive was the bright white cravat beneath his chin and the thigh high boots. He wore a wide black leather belt diagonally across his chest which held his weapons, two pistols and a cutlass hung from his waist.

Beside him stood the old man from the Nags Head, Brewster, in full seaman's garb; a red dirty cap, stockings, blue and white shirt, cotton waistcoat and cotton slops.

'Well, I'll be buggered.' William looked down and shook his head.

The Courage came up beside and Beaman's lads threw gatling hooks to bring her alongside. They placed a long, thick oak plank between the two ships.

As Captain Smythe made his way across, the crew, fifty of them, stopped what they were doing and stood tall. He slowly climbed to the aft deck.

Captain Girlington was waiting for him at the top of the stairs.

When he got to the aft deck, he turned around, dipped his hat. He noticed Beaman, paused, then turned and climbed the steps to the sterncastle and the captain's cabin.

Captain Girlington marched toward the door as the boatswain hurried to open the door then stood tall beside it. Captain Girlington followed, then Beaman, Tommy and William.

Once inside the cabin, Captain Girlington removed her hat and rushed to Smythe and kissed him on the cheek then whispered, 'Daddy, it's so good to see you. I've missed you so much.'

Tommy looked confused. He raised his eyebrows, glanced at William, and silently mouthed, 'Daddy??? WHAT???'

Captain Smythe hugged her and held her close; he smiled contentedly. 'It's so good to see you baby girl, I've missed you too. It's been too long.'

Beaman watched on silently.

Captain Smythe glanced at him. 'There will be time for pleasantries later but now, it's a difficult time and we must discuss the situation and make plans.

The captain walked up to Beaman and put his hand out. 'It's good to see you, my old friend.'

Beaman smiled with affection, shook the captain's hand with respect. 'Tis good ta see ya, Captain Smythe. It's been a long time.'

There was a knock at the door; Beaman opened it.

Brewster stepped inside. 'Captain Smythe, *The Courage* is almost ready to up anchor.'

Smythe was pleased to be back at sea. 'Aye, quartermaster.'

Beaman marched out and closed the door quietly behind him.

Girlington went back to a large oak storage chest which sat underneath the ship's windows which spanned the width of the room. She lifted a panel and took out a thick glass blue bottle of imported wine and filled silver goblets that Captain Smythe placed on the table.

He pulled out a chair and sat. 'Please sit, tell me, what news you have?'

William, Tommy and Ursula sat down at the table. Tommy and William noticed the different façade from what they saw in Leeds. He seemed much bolder and more self-assured. Even his accent changed and gone was the Yorkshire phonetic notation. It was replaced with the pronunciation of r's and characteristics of proper English.

William recounted what happened in Haworth. 'He just showed up out of nowhere, put a knife to me throat and threatened to kill Isabel and the children if we didn't cooperate. When Robert came home he arrested him fer theft. He bound him, put him on the back of a cart and took him away. We followed him ta Leeds and we met you.'

'Mmm.' Captain Smythe rubbed his hand where the blade penetrated and felt the large pink scar with his thumb and middle finger. 'We must let this play out.'

'PLAY OUT and let me son hang?' William was disturbed by his words.

'William, I understand your frustration, but I cannot say too much because the walls have ears. Let me say this, all is not as it seems.'

'WHAT DO YA MEAN?'

'WILLIAM! Calm yourself, trust your son and I'm asking you to trust me.'

Ursula watched her father rub the scar. 'Daddy, what happened to your hand?'

'Don't worry, daughter, bit of a disagreement among friends.'

Tommy reached out and put his hand on William's shoulder. 'All will be well. We need to trust them, Uncle.'

William took a deep breath, he reached into his tunic and pulled out the small bag, reaching in he lifted it out and dangled it for all to see, 'Then there's this…'

Everybody's eyes lit up as they marvelled at the precious blue stone which glinted in the candle light.

Captain Smythe stared at Ursula. 'The necklace?'

Ursula looked down. 'Robert said it was too dangerous, said it was his problem and was worried about tide waiters searching the ship.'

'Gentlemen, would ya leave us, I need to discuss some pertinent issues with my daughter.'

'Of course,' said William now feeling guilty about his outburst. 'You must 'ave catchin' up ta do.' William followed Tommy out the door to the aft deck.

Captain Smythe never kept anything from his daughter and filled her in on details. 'You must keep this to yourself Ursula.'

'They'll take Robert to York Castle Prison for the quarter Assizes to be tried in front of a judge and jury.' Captain Smythe rubbed the scar on his hand again. 'Mr Wilding is indebted to me, and I intend to repay him twofold. We need to make sure he never seeks retribution.'

Ursula remembered the night with Robert and the honest and gentle way in which he treated her. She found him to be far different from the other men she'd been with. She liked his smile, his boyish charms, and the way in which he peered into her eyes. She thought about him on the voyage to the Baltic and the way in which they parted company so abruptly. *I feel so guilty, I shouldn't have treated him so.*

Captain Smythe held Ursula's hands in his. 'We must use the court to our advantage if we are to see young Robert free.'

'What do you mean, Father?'

☆

Outside, William and Tommy watched Beaman and the rest of the crew unloading the cargo brought from Europe and the Baltic. There were barrels, and sacks of all sizes full of wine, copper, spices, wood, and dyestuffs to be distributed to all parts of the country.

William scoffed. 'Imagine that old Smythe a ship's captain, who'd 'ave thought?'

William nodded. 'I think there is much more to Captain Smythe than meets the eye, did ya not notice the respect the crew gave him when he came aboard?'

CHAPTER 29

Shadows of Desolation

Robert heard the turning of the key in the lock and glanced up to see the bailiff's unshaven face through the barred opening in the door.

Palmer then proceeded to carve something into the stone wall beside the graffiti of others.

I have never been to a hanging, not yet. PJ

Robert thought it very strange.

'Come on you two, there's a cart waiting outside fer ya.' The bailiff watched as the warder placed shackles on them once again and ushered both out of the cell and down the corridor.

They were led past the old man still in the pillory, a group of children were giggling and calling out things. They peppered him with rotten fruit left over from the last market.

Both Robert and Palmer were pushed up wooden steps and into an iron cage on top of a cart. It wasn't tall enough to stand so they both kneeled.

The driver and his companion locked the gate and put the wooden steps aside. They both jumped up into the front of the cart and with a flip of the reins, trotted off in the direction of York. Two soldiers on horses escorted them, their halberds glistening in the sun, in the sun.

'I know these roads,' said Palmer. 'They are not friendly, and it will take a good five hours to get there but at least it's a break from the monotony of the cell.'

Robert heard Palmer but did not answer, preferring to peer through the bars at the thieves, paupers, prostitutes and beggars flooding the streets. He wasn't proud of his past, but these people convinced him his life was a lucky one despite his current situation. He wished he'd listened to his brother.

Outside, the world was alive with activity, but Robert felt detached from it all. As he was led to the waiting cart, he couldn't help but cast a last glance at the Moot Hall, where his journey through the wheels of justice had begun.

The journey to York Castle Prison was long and arduous, the cart bumping along uneven roads and rutted paths. Robert's mind was a jumble of thoughts – memories of his family, regrets, and the uncertain future that awaited him. He wondered if his father and Tommy had managed to sell the cloth, if Ursula was safe, and if justice would truly be served.

They travelled northeast along York Road; it was a bumpy ride and more like a track than a road. The muddy ruts and bumps caused by frequent rains were suitable for packs of horses carrying cloth but totally unsuitable for a four-wheeled cart.

At the side of the road the land was wooded and dense. *The perfect place to holdup a stagecoach,* Robert thought to himself. Often the driver and his companion would get off the carriage and assist the horses up the hill.

Palmer asked if he could assist.

The driver and his companion smiled cheekily. 'Haha, no Palmer tis best you stay where you are. This area is well known fer the shenanigans of footpads and highwaymen. Best you stay safe and out of harm's way lest you miss your Tyburn jig.'

Aye, taken many a jewel and half-crown from around here. Palmer smiled.

'Once we gerr ta t' Old Red Lion a' Whinmoor tis orl downhill,' said the driver who awaited their stop thirstily.

☆

Tommy and Beaman had been waiting at the Old Red Lion for most of the day when they saw the wheeled cart and cage pull up outside. They knew to get to York they would come right past but thought themselves even more blessed when they stopped.

Tommy could see Robert sitting in the cage desperate and despondent.

The driver reined in the four horses. ‘‘Ere you keep an eye on them and I'll go get us an ale.'

The driver jumped down from the cart and strode inside the tavern with one of the soldier escorts.

There was a stagecoach in, on its way to Leeds, so it was busy, all accept two small, square tables by the window. Beaman and Tommy sat at one of them. If anybody tried to sit at the other, Beaman would stand and glare at them menacingly until they moved.

Robert watched the driver look around and saw him notice the empty table. He made his way over to it and sat down. ‘Good day ta ya.'

‘Better day than what they're ‘avin by the looks of it,' said Beaman investigating the caged cart outside.

The barmaid wandered over with a tankard of ale and put it down on the table in front of the driver, he lifted it up and said, ‘Good cheer to ya.'

Beaman and Tommy clinked tankards with the driver. ‘Health and happiness.'

The driver skulled the ale and was about to stand.

‘Where ya takin' ‘em, York Castle?' Tommy enquired.

‘Aye, the two of ‘em ta' meet with the three-legged mare, one fer thievin' and one fer stealin' ‘orses. Silly buggar confessed in a letter to his brother.'

‘Mmmm can't be too careful on the roads these days, bloody highwaymen, and footpads! Listen can I buy you and yer mate a brew fer doin' the job ya do?' Tommy reached into his pouch and took out some coin.

'Temptin' but I better be off, can't leave me mate out there on 'is lonesome fer too long besides tis his turn ta drive, also he's a bit slow if ya know what I mean.'

Beaman stood and towered over the driver, 'But we insist, won't take long I'll get ya mate one.'

The driver peered out the window at his mate and the two soldiers then sat back down again. 'Oh alright, if you insist.'

Tommy tried to spot the barmaid, but she was busy taking jugs of ale to the other side of the tavern. 'This is a quiet ol' argument this, I'll go an' get 'em me bloody self!'

Tommy stood and strode to the counter and asked the barkeep for four more ales.

He went back to the table. ''Ere ya go, give this one to ya mate.'

The driver called over the barmaid and instructed her to take the tankard outside to his companion and he watched her out the window.

His mate smiled simply, lifted the tankard in a gesture of good will, and drunk it down with relish.

'He seems happy enough now,' said the driver.

'Do ya think it would be alright if we travelled with ya as far as York, safer in numbers, ya know what I mean.'

The driver thought about it momentarily. 'I don't see why not tis all downhill from 'ere and besides, we could use the 'elp if we do get stuck again.'

Beaman chugged his ale, glanced at Tommy then smiled. 'Come then let's make way.'

The driver marched over to the cart and jumped up as his mate slid across to the driver's seat. the two soldiers mounted their horses as did Beaman and Tommy.

They both trotted over, Tommy winked at Robert who was astonished to see him and Beaman. He held back his exuberance.

They continued northeast along York Road, one soldier in front of the cart and another behind; Tommy and Beaman followed up the rear.

They continued down Micklegate toward the gate of the walled city. Apart from the odd house or cottage there wasn't much development. Inside, suburbs were recovering from the war.

As they crossed the Ouse, Robert peered along the river, barges were dragged along by horses on uneven, muddy tracks. Fully loaded Humber Keels made their way under the one high arch to the merchant warehouses of York with their cargoes of silks, satins and fine wines.

The walled part of the city was eight hundred yards along the riverbank divided by Micklegate and the Ouse Bridge. There were five arches with one central one being more then seventeen feet high. The top of the bridge was crowded with houses and shops. Saint Williams Chapel was at one end and the Council chamber beside it. The city jail was beneath.

The more serious criminals like Robert and Palmer, were interred in York Castle prison to await trial.

They passed through the Micklegate Bar into the city of York with its lion head carvings and its severed heads hanging on pikes from the turrets.

The driver slowed as a shepherds herded sheep through the gate in front of them.

On the other side there were small houses all crammed together. Pitched wooden rooves and heavy, ornate, vertical, wooden beams. Some were closer to the street and others were in urgent need of repair; the wattle showing through the daub. Most had mullioned windows both upstairs and down and large stone chimneys chugged grey smoke.

Across the way, Robert could see fields, crops and established gardens. They continued past the church and went across the Ouse Bridge, the only way into the other part of the city.

As they got to the other side, they could see Clifford tower sitting on a huge grassy mound. They turned south down Clifford Street and the tower got closer and larger, closer and larger.

The keep was situated on a huge, raised area and accompanied by a high walled bailey; this was then surrounded by a deep ditch and palisade.

The military garrison was still present in the castle, and it was one of the most defended, still a symbol of Parliamentary strength and power over the Royalists.

Robert could see cannon jutting out from the gun placements and soldiers on guard at the top. 'I've never seen anything like it before.'

They were stopped at the Tower Street gate then allowed entry after the captain of the guard received a parchment from the driver.

The wheeled cart creaked to a halt as the driver and his mate dismounted to attend to their horses and make final preparations. The journey had been relatively uneventful, but the walls of York Castle, where Robert would soon be confined, were a stark reminder of the confinement that awaited him. He glanced at Tommy and Beaman, grateful for their presence, yet keenly aware of the trials they had yet to face.

The driver followed the escort along Tower Street then reined in the horses at the gate leading through the bailey wall. Six soldiers were lined up on either side of the cart then escorted them to the far side of the grounds.

There was the Grand Jury House, great hall, a lesser hall with a chapel adjoining, Court of Justice and gaol. Ladies and gentlemen were milling around outside and watched the caged cart as it rattled by with its escort.

Outside the gaol the driver and his 'simple' companion jumped down trying to put on a persona of importance having delivered their prisoners. The driver put the steps down and climbed up to unlock the gate.

Robert and Palmer stepped down awkwardly, stiff and sore from the journey. The six-man escort turned to the front and escorted them to the gaol door.

As they approached the large wooden door, a bearded face appeared at its barred opening. The door opened with a whine to allow them entry. Robert was ushered into a dimly lit chamber. The air was damp and cold, a stark contrast to the warmth of the world outside. As he stood there waiting, the reality of his situation set in once more – he was at the mercy of the justice system, a pawn in a game he had little control over.

Both Robert and Palmer shuffled along in their shackles, dried blood could be seen on their wrists and ankles where the shackles dug in.

Once inside, the bailiff closed and locked the door behind them. There were two soldiers standing at attention with their halberd beside another iron bolted door.

The bailiff unrolled the two parchments the captain of the guard gave him. He inspected them then glanced up at Robert and Palmer who were standing in front of him. After writing something in his large black ledger, a warder led Robert and Palmer through the door, then down some wooden stairs.

'Errgh, the stench.' Robert put his shackled hands to his mouth and nose as did Palmer. There was an unpleasant, mouldy odour filling the air due to dampness and poor ventilation. Filth from poor sanitation, decaying organic matter and prisoners' body odour added to the stench.

'Don't worry, you'll get used to it,' said the warder with a smile.

It got darker and the dampness and the stench got stronger as the stairs turned from wood to stone.

The jailer was waiting for them at the bottom.

There were oil lamps situated along the corridor, recessed into the stone wall, which lit the way. The stone walls were wet and shiny from seepage.

Waiting for his eyes to adjust, Robert squinted in the poor light. The jailer led them along the corridor beside the cells.

He stopped and fumbled around with his keys on his belt. Finally, finding the right one, he put it into the lock and turned it with a clink. Pulling the barred door open with a squeal, he put his hand to his face to shield his olfactory senses.

The jailer grabbed Robert's wrists, unlocked his shackles then bent down to unlock the ankles while the warder looked on. He stood, pushed Robert through the door opening then closed and locked the heavy oak door behind him.

'This one, he's special, aren't ya, mister Johns? Tends to escape, so he's to 'ave a cell all on 'is lonesome. Besides, he might 'ave ta go to London fer trial so I'm told. Quite famous our Mr Johns, haha.'

Robert heard the shuffle of Palmer John's shackles as he was taken down the corridor to another cell.

Time in the suffocating darkness of the cell stretched on, each moment dripping with a sense of hopelessness and despair. Robert found himself trapped not only by the cold, stone walls that surrounded him, but by the weight of his own regrets. As the days turned into a seemingly endless procession of misery, he clung to the memories of his past, the faces of his loved ones, and the glimmers of hope that had carried him this far.

These were holding cells; they were packed and Robert was taken aback by the human misery and despair. The fetid air clung to his skin, a constant reminder of the squalor he now inhabited. The cell was a breeding ground for suffering, a place where the destitute and the condemned mingled in a sea of shared anguish. The prisoners, each a victim of their circumstances, fought for scraps of sustenance and a semblance of dignity. Amidst the chaos, Robert stood against the urine-stained wall, his body aching, his mind numbed by the relentless onslaught of human misery.

The room was full of tired moaning occupants. *The wretches of Yorkshire,* he thought. Thieves, murderers, political prisoners and debtors all awaiting trial, execution, or very rarely, release.

The cell was small and cramped. Prisoners were often pushing and arguing over one thing or another. There were men, women and two children crying at the foot of their mother.

The filth knew no bounds and with no waste removal, the buckets in the corners of the cell were full of human excrement and other unimaginable contents. The stone floor was damp and wet from the recent rains and flooding. There was no light 'cept what shone through the small, barred opening from the oil lamp outside.

The stale air was consuming and the coughing, hacking and crying sent shivers down his spine. He heard the forced excretions, nausea and vomiting of cell fever. There was no room to lie or sit so Robert folded his arms and stood with his back to the closest urine-soaked stone wall.

He stared at a body lying at his feet, it was a naked old grey-haired man, his clothes removed by others. The was a rash all over his chest and his eyes were staring blankly upwards.

Robert nudged him with his foot but there was no reaction. He nudged him again, still nothing.

There was no sleep and Robert felt stiff and sore from the journey the previous day. He lost all concept of time but guessed it was a new day when he heard the jailer open the door.

An old woman held a large wooden spoon and a metal pot which the prisoners were attracted to like flies to toilet buckets on a hot summer day.

The arrival of the oatmeal brought both a fleeting relief and a poignant reminder of the depths to which humanity could sink. As the old woman's meagre offering was distributed among the desperate prisoners, Robert's stomach churned with hunger. He watched as people clamoured for their share, their hands outstretched, their eyes hollow and desperate. And yet, even in their own suffering, the collective instinct to survive prevailed.

Once served they fought through the others to find a space to squat and devour their meal. They savoured every mouthful licking their dirty stained fingers clean.

Robert watched as the woman split the oatmeal and placed it into the hands of her two crying children. She went back to get more but the door was shut in her face by the jailer.

She banged on the door repeatedly. 'Fer me children, more, please some more!'

She dropped her head and began to sob, limping slowly back to her children who were finished.

One of the children rushed at her, hugging her legs. 'When are we goin' 'ome, Mother?'

'Soon my dears, very soon.' She bent down and pulled both the children close to her.

The old woman appeared twice a day and on her second appearance, hunger forced Robert to lunge at her. He fought for his position, holding out his hand through the crowd of people standing in front of him.

He went back to his spot against the wall and greedily ate half his oatmeal being sure to leave a small portion for the woman.

This routine occurred two more times. He calculated he was inside for three days. On the fourth, the jailer and the warder entered, marched over to the old man, picked him up and dragged his body from the cell.

Robert thought the jailer was going to lock the door again, when he stopped and turned. 'Rushworth, Robert Rushworth!'

'Yes, tis me!' Robert wandered through the crowded cell toward the door.

The jailer put the shackles back on his wrists and on his ankles. 'Come with me,' he grumbled.

Robert shuffled down the corridor toward the stairs and followed the warder up toward the light.

When they got to the top, the warder peeked through the barred opening.

The bailiff unlocked the door to let them into the room from whence his ordeal begun. Robert shielded his eyes with his hand.

The warder went back down the stairs and left him in the company of the bailiff and two soldiers. Robert was escorted outside, two other soldiers stood on either side of him. They marched toward the Court of Justice to the Grand Jury House.

The weight of the upcoming trial bore down on Robert's shoulders, a constant reminder that his fate lay in the hands of the courts. As he awaited his turn to face justice, he found himself reflecting on the events that had brought him here the choices he had made, the paths he had taken, and the consequences he now had to confront.

The Assize Court buzzed with anticipation, a microcosm of society gathered to witness the unfolding drama of justice. Robert stood in the centre of it all, the weight of his fate hanging in the balance. He cast his eyes upward, searching for a familiar face among the sea of spectators, but the crowd's reaction was far from what he had hoped for. Laughter, jeers and obscenities rained down upon him from the questionable characters who had come to mock his misfortune. Then he noticed John, his weary eyes meeting Robert's with a mixture of hope and uncertainty. Their silent exchange conveyed a shared understanding. Robert was shocked by the noise coming from the gallery above.

'GUILTY!' 'GUILTY!' 'HAHah.'

'HANG THE BASTARD!'

'GUILTY!'

'LOOKS AS GUILTY AS THEY COME!'

The Assize Courts attracted a large part of the populace of York both in support and denial of the accused. They expressed their views on the innocence or guilty of the prisoner. It was entertainment.

Robert looked up at the retches who wanted to decide his fate before the trial even started.

He was marched over to the bar, which held a mirrored reflector above him allowing light from the window to shine on his face. This provided a better view of his facial expressions.

Judges sat on the other side of the room. Two sets of six jurors sat on either side of him, mostly yeoman except for one gentleman as far as he could tell. At a large table below the judges, sat the clerks, lawyers and writers who took notes on the proceedings.

The judge stood the gallery went quiet.

The clerk stood and read the indictment. 'Number 343, Robert Rushworth indicted for the burglary and theft of a sapphire necklace at Red Hall in Leeds.'

'Robert Rushworh, how do you plead guilty or not guilty?'

Robert stared up into the gallery and behind the wooden railing hoping to cast his eyes on his father or Tommy. Nervously, he resisted saying anything and gazed back at the judge.

With each passing moment, Robert's resolve grew stronger. He stood before the judge, no longer just a defendant, but a seeker of justice in his own right. The courtroom's attention was now focused on him, his determination to uncover the truth casting a light into the darkest corners of the case.

Growing impatient, the judge leaned forward. 'Robert Rushworth, may I remind you a deliberate failure to plead, will result in "Peine forte et dure".'

Mr Huddleston explained what it meant.

Without a second thought Robert called out, 'NOT GUILTY!'

The questionable characters in the gallery laughed in hysterics and called out obscenities and verdicts until the judge warned them to be quiet.

'Very well. Mr Huddleston, call your first witness.'

'The prosecution calls his grace, Alderman Thomas Metcalf.'

Robert watched the alderman approach from behind the wooden railing and strolled slowly up the aisle. He stepped up into the witness box facing him.

'Please state your name and occupation,' said the lawyer.

'I am a tradesman in cloth and current alderman of Leeds residing at Red Hall.'

The judge leant forward. 'Alderman Metcalf, could you please deliver your testimony for the court.'

‘It was on the morning of Tuesday 13th April when my wife and I were woken by a servant girl only to find the top draw in our chest of drawers open. We both quickly rose ourselves and went to the drawer; the strong box in which we held the sapphire among other trinkets was gone. I immediately sent the servant girl to find the constable and report the theft.’

‘Later that day, I employed the services of a Mr Wilding to find the whereabouts of the necklace and return it. I also made a presentment to the sheriff and the justice of the peace for a warrant for the person suspected of taking the necklace. This was given to Mr Wilding to aid him in the capture of the culprit.’

‘Alderman Metcalf, are you sure the necklace was in the drawer before you retired for the night?’

‘Yes, because the strong box in which it is held, is opened by my wife each night for her to deposit her jewellery. The sapphire was present before we retired.’

‘Can you please describe it?’ The judge asked.

‘A beautiful piece with French enamel, swirling jewels, a painted opaque enamel bow and the dark blue sapphire. It’s worth about two hundred pounds.’

‘And the servant girl, how do you know she didn’t take the necklace?’

‘Lizzie has been with us for many years and I suspect if she were the one to take it, would have disappeared immediately, not stay within our employ. I also searched the house, including her quarters.’

‘Alderman Metcalf, have you met with the prisoner before?’

‘I have not!’

‘Then how did the prisoner know of the necklace?’

‘I assume he didn’t but may have chanced upon it.’

‘Surely, your grace, you, Mrs Metcalf or the servant girl would have heard the intruder come into the bedroom.’

'No, my wife was staying with her sister and Lizzie stays down in the servant's quarters in the basement.'

'Robert Rushworth, how did you know about the necklace?' The judge fired the question at Robert, trying to catch him off guard.

Robert thought for a moment. 'Your lordship, I know nowt about a necklace. If it was me who stole the necklace and flogged it, then why are me family, as we speak, being tuned off our land at Hall Green?'

The judge leaned across to the clerk and whispered, 'Hall Green, what is this Hall Green? Find out!'

The clerk immediately left the court then returned a short time later and gestured for the judge to come closer so he could whisper, 'Jasper Calamy.'

The judge was curious about Robert's statement, 'Mmmm, I've heard of this Jasper Calamy. He's been buying up land up north.'

The jurors whispered amongst themselves, and the gallery became rowdy and boisterous until the judge stood.

'Alderman, you can step down.'

The alderman peered at Robert, stepped down from the witness box, strolled back down the aisle and continued to the other side of the railing.

The journey from the depths of the holding cell to the heart of the Assize Court had been a tumultuous one, a rollercoaster of emotions and revelations. And now, as the trial continued, Robert stood at the precipice, ready to confront the mysteries that lay ahead. The shadows of doubt and despair that had haunted him were slowly giving way to the light of truth, guiding him on a path toward vindication.

CHAPTER 30

Unravelling Deceptions

The next day, Robert was once again led into the courtroom and up into the dock.

The judge stood. 'Mr Huddleston your next witness.'

'JACOB WILDING.'

Robert gazed at Wilding as he plodded down toward the witness box. He was holding the valuables box taken from Robert's room.

'Please state your name, occupation and place of residence for the judge.'

'I'm Jacob Wilding, currently live at the Nags Head in Leeds.'

The judge focused on Wilding. 'Mr Wilding, could you please explain how you are connected to this crime.'

'Aye, I was 'ired by the alderman to get his necklace back and the culprit who stole it.'

'So, you are employed as a thief-taker?'

'Yes, yer grace.'

'Can you please explain how you apprehended the prisoner and the circumstances surrounding the theft of the sapphire necklace?'

'I found the empty valuables box in his room at the Nags Head.'

'Whose room?'

'Robert Rushworth's room.'

'Please continue.'

'Well, old Smythe told me he went to 'ull to sell it, so I followed 'im there, but I was too late he'd already flogged it.'

'And how do you know this?

'He told me!'

'Told you?'

'He said he gave it to a ship's captain to fence overseas where it wasn't so noticeable. He fled, so I followed him and took him into custody and brought him back ta Leeds. Now I come 'ere ta get me ten pound reward.'

The gallery became boisterous again calling out, some of the women suggesting illicit ways he could spend the reward.

The judge called out, 'ORDER, ORDER IN THE GALLERY OR ELSE I WILL HAVE YOU REMOVED!'

The judge looked down at his clerk. 'Take the box from Mr Wilding as evidence.'

The judge looked on curiously. 'I see. Now, Mr Wilding, when you say "he", who exactly are you referring to?'

Wilding pointed at Robert. 'Him, over there! Who do ya think?'

'Mr Wilding, just answer the question. Mr Wilding, did you ever see the necklace in his possession?'

'No, well, yes, found the empty box, but I know he thieved it. Smythe told me.'

'Oh, and how?' asked the judge.

'In my profession ya often 'ave ta deal with the culprits on the other side of the law and he's one of 'em.'

'Mr Wilding, have you yourself ever been in trouble with the law?'

Wilding paused. 'Yeah, once.'

'Could you please tell the court what for?'

'Liftin' wool from the boats in the Humber, but I got off.'

There was commotion in the gallery and the jurors turned to whisper to each other.

'I see, and how do you know the prisoner was in possession of the necklace?'

Wilding felt nervous about his admission of theft. 'He told me he gave it to the captain.'

'Captain?'

'Yeah, captain of a ship bound fer Europe.' Wilding started to become frustrated with the questioning.

'Do you have anything else you would like to add, Mr Wilding?'

'Yeah, HE'S A THIEVIN' BASTARD!' He pointed at Robert. 'HE SHOULD HANG FER IT!'

The noise and commotion in the gallery got louder and rowdier.

'THANK YOU, Mr Wilding, you can step down.'

'Mr Huddleston?'

'URSULA ARLINGTON.'

Robert was shocked to see her sashaying down the aisle. She wore the green velvet dress, with shiny light green ribbon and decorated with white glass pearls. The collar and sleeves were decorated with bright white lace and her hair was pushed back off her face all except two ringlets. They dangled down the side of her face. She had applied red lip colour to her lips and cheeks.

'Please state your name and place of residence for the judge.'

'Ursula Arlington, Portishead, Somerset.'

'You are a long way from home, Ms Arlington.'

'Yes, your honour, I was born into a wealthy family so spend my time travelling England with my two servants. Those things make death less formidable and your future state more happy.'

'Ms Arlington, please explain how you know the defendant.'

Ursula smiled then looked embarrassed. 'We were lovers!'

'Please repeat what you said, loudly, please, Ms Arlington.'

'We'—she smiled—'WERE LOVERS!'

'LUCKY BASTARD,' yelled a man from the back of the gallery.

The gallery erupted with laughter.

Another called out, 'COOR… I'D GIV' 'ER ONE.

'ONE? I'D GIVER 'ER TWO, HAHAHhahaha.'

'HAHAHAhahaha.' All in the gallery – men, women and children – were in hysterics.

The jurors whispered to each other, trying to keep a straight face.

The other judges on the panel turned to each other whispering and nodding.

'Order… ORDER! ORDER!' The judge sat forward.

Ursula spoke confidently in her best English. 'The prisoner couldn't have taken the necklace because on the night of Monday the 12th of April. He was with me in my bed chamber.'

The courtroom erupted again. The judge banged his fist on the bench to bring order and silence to the courtroom.

'Ms Arlington, are you sure?'

'Yes, very sure. I wouldn't forget a special night, Judge.' Ursula blushed then gazed at Robert and smiled coyly.

A woman from the gallery yelled out, 'YOU LUCKY BITCH, IF ONLY I COULD BE SA LUCKY!' She slapped her snoozing husband on the back of the head. He was startled awake. He was still dopey and unimpressed.

The gallery erupted. 'AHAHAHahaha.'

'Order… ORDER!' The judge became impatient.

Wilding stood up angrily clenching his fists seeing his reward slipping out of his hands. He went to storm back down the aisle, but two soldiers stood in front of him.

'SHE'S A LYIN' WHORE. SHE'S THE ONE WHO FENCED IT!'

The judge held up his hands. 'SERGEANT. Mr Wilding, please have a seat until we can get to the truth of this matter.'

'Fenced it, Mr Wilding? You testified Robert Rushworth gave the necklace to a ship's captain. Ms Arlington does not look like a ship's captain to me.'

'SHE'S THE CAPTAIN OF THE PEARL!'

Wilding still struggled until a third guard came over and they ushered him over to a chair against the side wall.

Wilding tried to stand. 'SHES LYIN'. I TOLD YA!'

'MR WILDING, please quiet yourself or else I will have you removed from the court.'

'Thank you, Ms Arlington, you may step down.'

She glanced at Robert in passing and went to the back of the room.

The judge glanced at Mr Huddleston. 'Please continue.'

'MARY KELLY!'

Robert stared down the aisle and watched a woman scurry towards him and he gasped. It was the streetwalker, Rosie's girl. *I'm finished!*

The clerk stood. 'Please state your name, address and profession for the court.'

'I am Mary Kelly.' She whispered of no fixed address 'And I… er… perform… services for… certain… gentlemen.'

''OW MUCH YA CHARGE, LOVE?' a man yelled from the back of the gallery.

The gallery erupted. 'HHAHAHAHAHAH!'

'ORDER, ORDER,' yelled the judge. He smiled at Mary. 'I'm sure the court understands your meaning, Ms Kelly. I understand you saw the man running from Red Hall with this valuables box on the night of April 12th.'

Mary sat forward uncomfortably in her chair. 'Oh, yes, Judge. Plain as day.'

The courtroom held its collective breath as Mary Kelly began to recount her version of events. Robert's heart raced, his mind grappling with the sudden appearance of a witness who seemed determined to seal his fate. He watched Mary's hesitant gestures, her discomfort evident as she recounted the night of April 12th.

Mary's voice quivered as she spoke. 'I… I saw 'im, yer honor. Runnin' from Red 'all, 'e was, clutchin' that box tight. I was on me way, I was… workin', you know. Saw 'im from a distance, I did.'

Wilding smirked triumphantly, exchanging confident glances with Mr Huddleston. The gallery seemed to relish Mary's testimony, their laughter and jeers reverberating throughout the room.

Wilding sighed with relief and glimpsed at Robert who appeared concerned, and rightly so.

The judge turned to the witness. 'Ms Kelly, can you please explain to the court what you saw?'

'Well, I was standing at the corner of Boar Ally that leads down to the Shambles with a couple of other sisters. Suddenly, I see this rumper rushin' toward us. I put on me best face and called out to 'im. He ignored me and ran past, t'was the last I saw of 'im until today.'

The judge looked over. 'And the valuables box you see there, was he carrying it?'

'Oh yes, yer grace, I remember it well, couldn't understand why somebody was carryin' valuables around at that time o' night. Streets are dangerous at night, ya know. Anythin' can happen to ya. I remember just last week…'

The judge interrupted her. 'Now, Ms Kelly, can I call you Mary?'

'Oh, course, yer grace, ya can all me what ya like and when ya like but it aint free!'

The gallery broke the silence again erupting into a mob of laughing lunatics.

The clerks and jurors tried hard to hold back their smiles.

The judge hollered, 'ORDER, ORDER, ORDER, I TELL YOU!'

The gallery quietened to whispers.

The judged smiled patiently. 'Now, Mary, is the man you saw in this room?'

'Oh, yes, yer grace.'

'Can you point to him?' the judge asked.

Robert stared at her, he could feel his heart pounding and he blinked slowly; it seemed as if time slowed. He gazed into the gallery to see if he could see Ursula, but it was too dark. He gawked at the witness then dropped his gaze waiting for the final nail to be put in the coffin…

The judge was starting to get annoyed. 'Mary, can you point to the man who you saw running away from Red Hall.'

Mary could hear the frustration in the judge's voice. 'Yeah, course, that's 'im, over there!'

Robert looked up slowly, expecting her to be pointing at him.

She pointed right past him to Wilding who was sitting on the chair against the wall.

Wilding stood and wrestled with the soldiers trying to restrain him. 'THEY'RE LYIN, ALL OF 'EM, CAN'T YA SEE? FUCKERS ARE LYIN'!'

The judge glared at him. 'Bailiff, please restrain Mr Wilding. If there are any further outbursts, please have him removed.'

The two soldiers held him while the bailiff placed a set of shackles on his wrists.

The courtroom went quiet.

'Ms Kelly, are you absolutely sure it wasn't the prisoner, you recognised?'

'On my bloody oath, yer judgeness! If it was 'im I'd remember 'cause he's a looker, mmm, oh yes I'd remember him orlright.'

The gallery erupted again. 'AHAHAHahaha.'

The judge leaned over and smiled. 'Ms Kelly, Judge or your honour, if you please. You can step down now.'

Mary stepped down and sashayed down the aisle, but stopped halfway, turned, waved, then blew the judge a kiss.

'HHAHA…HAHA…HAHA!' The clerks and jurors coughed their laughter away.

The judge could feel the redness in his face and banged his fist on the desk. 'ORDER! If there is one more outbreak, I will have the court cleared.'

The judge stared at Mr Huddleston. 'Any more witnesses?'

'CAPTAIN SMITH?'

The courtroom's tense atmosphere hung thick like a storm cloud, heavy with anticipation. As Captain Smith, stepped forward, a collective hush fell over the onlookers. The door opened at the back; it was dark so Robert couldn't see but heard slow footsteps then he recognised him.

It was Smythe but gone were the captain's garb and he'd used an alias for obvious reasons.

Smythe's entrance was a spectacle in itself. The room seemed to hold its breath as he removed his hat and executed a graceful bow before the judge. The extravagant attire he donned exuded an air of both opulence and intrigue. The detailed description of his attire painted a vivid picture of a man who had reinvented himself, assuming an identity that was both grandiose and enigmatic.

Robert and Wilding exchanged bewildered glances, their minds racing to process this unexpected turn of events. As Smythe took the witness stand, his natural wig and clean-shaven face added to his mystique.

He made his way slowly to face the judge, took off his plumed felt hat and with a sweeping arm movement bowed in front of him.

He wore a large, bright white lace collar and gold embroidered sleeves with lace cuffs. A blue piece of satin crossed his chest diagonally and was tied at the side of his waist. He wore a large gold belt buckle and red breeches adorned with gold-coloured buttons spaced down the side of his legs. The breeches were tied below the knee with a frayed gold guilted garter and expensive leather boots were folded down at the knee.

The courtroom went quiet except for the murmurings of the jurors.

The clerk stood. 'Please state your name and place of residence.'

'I am Captain Smith of *The Pearl*, retired to Leeds some four years now to tend to my investments.'

Robert and Wilding stared at Smythe wondering where he picked up the posh southerner's accent.

Wilding whispered under his breath, 'Investments? Is that what he calls it?'

The judge turned to him. 'Captain Smith, I understand you know the prisoner?'

'I do, he was in my employ in Leeds for some time in a tavern I own.'

The judge was curious. 'Can you vouch for him?'

With the precision of a seasoned actor, Smythe recounted his association with Robert, highlighting his commendable qualities as a hardworking and honest man.

Yet, it was the revelations about Wilding that set the room abuzz. Smythe's recounting of the altercation, the stolen jewels and Wilding's sinister plans painted a vivid tapestry of deceit and betrayal. The tension heightened as Wilding's outbursts punctuated Smythe's testimony. The courtroom seemed to hold its breath, teetering on the precipice of chaos.

'It has been testified Robert Rushworth fenced the necklace to a captain bound for Europe.'

'I know nothing about it, Judge, my first mate takes care of *The Pearl* these days.'

'I also understand you know of Mr Wilding?' the judge asked.

Smythe rolled his eyes. 'Oh, yes, he's been staying at the tavern for some years now.'

'And can you vouch for Mr Wilding, is he a man of integrity and honour?' the judge asked.

'Your honour, I am the owner of a tavern, what tenants do in their private lives is no concern of mine just as long as they pay their way.'

'I understand you made a presentment to the magistrate in York. I also understand you disagreed with Mr Wilding, and he caused you harm.'

Wilding became more and more agitated.

Smythe rubbed the scar on his hand. 'Yes, it was some time ago now, he showed up at the tavern with jewels. Said he was going to fence them at the docks in Hull most especially, a blue sapphire necklace.'

Wilding stood. 'LIES, ALL OF IT LIES, FUCKERS, CAN'T YOU SEE WHAT THEY'RE TRYING TA DO!'

'SILENCE!' the judge called out.

Smythe continued, 'He also said he was hired by Alderman Metcalf to find the sapphire at any cost. He said he would fence it and report to the alderman it couldn't be found. He was worried he would be found out if he tried to fence it in Leeds, so he took it to Hull.

'Mr Wilding also told me he would go after the prisoner and blame the entire ordeal on him then collect the reward. He asked me where the prisoner was but when I couldn't tell him, he became incredibly angry and stabbed my hand with his knife. I have the scar to prove it.' Smythe held up his hand.

'JUDGE, YA CAN'T BELIEVE 'IM, THEY'RE ALL IN IT TOGETHER, CAN YA NOT SEE IT!'

Wilding started to wrestle with the two soldiers. He headbutted one who fell back. The other soldier smashed him with his halberd. He grunted and flopped into the chair.

The judge became frustrated. 'For goodness sake, Bailiff, would you please escort Mr Wilding to the gaol block.'

'NO... NO... NO YA DON'T. LET ME GO!' Wilding laughed in troubled hysterics. 'HAHAHAH!... NOOOO... YER ALL FUCKED! JUST YOU WAIT, I'LL SLICE YOU UP!'

Wilding thrashed around trying to free himself. They wrestled with him down the aisle and he stopped in front of the alderman and his wife. 'ALDERMAN, PLEASE TELL THEM THE TRUTH! TELL 'EM, PLEASE TELL 'EM!'

The alderman and his wife ignored him as the guards pushed him forward and out the door.

The judge shook his head in disbelief. 'Captain Smith, do you know the whereabouts of the necklace now?'

'Oh no, your honour, the last time I set eyes on it was when Mr Wilding brought it to the tavern.'

'Thank you, Captain Smith, you may step down.'

Smythe strode calmly and confidently to the back of the room and went through the door, down the corridor and outside. He smiled as he watched the three soldiers and the bailiff struggle with Wilding across the courtyard to the gaol. He still pleading his innocence.

The judge turned to the jury. 'Gentlemen of the jury, it is time for you to deliberate. Foreman?'

The foreman stood and went over to the six jurors on the other side of the dock, bent over and heard their plea then returned to stand in front of his seat. 'Your honour we feel we can deliver a verdict without leaving the room.'

'What say you?'

'We find the prisoner, NOT GUILTY, Judge.'

The judge stood. 'It is my declaration the prisoner Robert Rushworth be RELEASED!'

'Mr Huddleston, can you please prepare an indictment for Jacob Wilding for nocturnal burglary, assault and perjury?'

Mr Huddleston stood and bowed. 'RELEASE THE PRISONER!'

Some of the gallery claimed Robert as one of them, they cheered and applauded. Others booed and jeered, knowing they were going to miss out on a good hanging.

The bailiff escorted the prisoner out of the dock, down the steps and undid his shackles. Robert rubbed his wrists. He stood there then glanced at the judge, not knowing what to do or say.

'You are free to go, Robert Rushworth.' The judge waved him away, then called the clerk, 'How many more?'

The clerk glanced down at his ledger. 'Ten, your honour.'

The judge rolled his eyes, thinking of the merriment and indulgence he would be shown by the Sheriff of York after the day's business was concluded.

Robert marched down the aisle and followed the alderman and his wife out the door. Outside, William, Tommy, Smythe and Ursula were waiting for him.

Ursula sauntered toward him in her beautiful dress, said nothing but wrapped her arms around him, squeezing him tightly. He nodded at Smythe then held out his hand to Tommy who shook it lovingly.

He stepped in front of his father, who stood there holding back the emotion not knowing what to say or how to react. He grabbed Robert and pulled him closer to him, and whispered, 'My son, we'll talk about this at home.'

CHAPTER 31

A Dangerous Gambit

Captain Smythe's gaze swept over the ancient castle's towering walls as he adjusted his coat, a transformation from the refined manner he had earlier adopted. The polished veneer of formality gave way to the rugged cadence of his true self. Captain Smythe was disturbed. 'Come on, this place is makin' me nervous, let's get back to *The Courage.*'

Tommy and William gazed at him curiously.

'Ya don't sail the seven seas fer a lifetime without pickin' up a few tricks.' Smythe smiled, winked then meandered over and put his arm up to escort Ursula out of the castle.

He whispered to Ursula, 'Look at us, will ya? Proper couple a' dirty beaus, ahh, ya ma would be sa proud. That was the first and last time I'll ever be in court, mark my words.'

Ursula leaned into her father's arm affectionately, a daughter's love and admiration evident in her eyes. 'I love you, Daddy,' she whispered, bestowing a tender kiss upon his weathered cheek. The bond between them was unbreakable, forged through countless adventures and trials. 'So, what do you think of him?'

Smythe put his hankie to his lips and coughed once again feigning the posh accent. 'Who my dear, to whom do you refer?'

She laughed. 'Daddy, you know who… Robert!'

'My dearest, I think 'e would make a fine addition ta the family, but remember our agreement. Ya must give up *The Pearl* if ya want to 'ave a family.'

Ursula glanced up at him. 'I think it's time, Daddy!'

Her father frowned. 'Orlright then… hold on a bit, 'as he asked ya?'

‘Not yet.’ She smiled. ‘But he will, hahaha. Oh, Daddy, I’m so happy.’

On the horizon, *The Courage* awaited their return, a steadfast companion on the sea of life. The crew shifted seamlessly between ships, their familiarity with the rhythms of sailing evident in their efficient preparations.

The Courage sailed back down the Rover Ouse and they boarded *The Pearl* which the crew readied and started rigging for departure.

With the Pearl’s rigging underway, Captain Smythe emerged transformed, the persona of the seasoned seafarer once again taking command. Clad in his ‘seaworthy attire’, he stood tall upon the aft deck, the embodiment of maritime authority.

‘Mr Beaman, ready to up anchor?’ Smythe’s voice carried across the deck, a proclamation of readiness.

‘Aye, Captain!’ Beaman’s response echoed back, resolute and unwavering.

Smythe’s confidence emanated like a force of nature. ‘Very well, ‘UP ANCHOR! Come on, let’s get home.’

The command reverberated through the crew, setting a cascade of actions into motion. Beaman’s voice rose above the din, rallying the hands to their duties, each step executed with the precision of a seasoned team.

As sails unfurled and lines were drawn taut, the ship stirred to life beneath the hands of skilled mariners. Smythe’s eyes surveyed the scene, a mixture of nostalgia and fulfillment welling within him. Beaman’s thoughts mirrored his captain’s sentiment, the sight of Smythe taking charge reminiscent of days long past.

‘Captain on board again, like the old days,’ Beaman mused, his heart swelling with a sense of unity.

The main topsail billowed with wind, the ship’s response to the efforts of the crew resounding with a powerful grace. Beaman’s gaze never left the captain, his anticipation palpable as the final step approached.

‘Captain,’ Beaman called out, his voice carrying a blend of readiness and respect.

Smythe met his first mate’s gaze, a shared understanding passing between them. ‘Beaman, all hands to brace around!’

‘Aye, Captain!’ Beaman’s command reverberated, and the crew moved as one, adjusting the sails to catch the wind’s embrace.

As the ship began to respond to their ministrations, Smythe turned his attention to Tommy and William, his expression a mixture of pride and camaraderie. ‘We ‘ave good wind, won’t take us long to get back.’

The voyage ahead was filled with promise, the sea a canvas upon which their destinies would be painted. Together, Captain Smythe, his crew, and *The Pearl* embarked on a journey that held the allure of uncharted waters and untold adventures, guided by the steadfast bond of family and the unyielding spirit of the open sea.

Robert and Ursula retired to the captain’s cabin, where the cook filled a metal bathtub. Robert undressed and stepped in while Ursula undressed behind the screen.

The warm water in the metal bathtub enveloped Robert’s body, soothing his tense muscles as he recounted the intricate plan to Ursula. Steam curled in the air, adding an almost mystical quality to the cabin. Ursula’s eyes held a mixture of concern and admiration as she listened to her husband’s tale.

‘How did you know I was working for the alderman?’ Robert asked.

Ursula stepped out from behind the screen with nothing on but a woollen towel which covered her breasts and reached down to just above her knees. She shook out her hair and it cascaded down the sides of her face.

Ursula smiled. ‘I didn’t until I saw my father in Selby and he explained how he was asked by the alderman to find somebody he could trust.’

Ursula’s touch was gentle as she continued to dab Robert’s chest with the damp flannel. Her fingers lingered, tracing the lines of his skin, a silent reassurance amidst the uncertainty of the dangerous path they had chosen to tread.

'Robert, it's a perilous game you played,' Ursula remarked softly, her voice a delicate whisper in the intimate setting of the cabin.

'Wilding got what he deserved,' replied Robert.

'The *company* are not the sort of people to get on the wrong side of and ruthless when it comes to debts owed and loyalty lost.' She nodded in understanding, her fingers pausing for a moment before resuming their soothing motions.

'Well, better 'im than me!' Robert splashed his face with the warm water.

Ursula sat on the side of the bed. 'When the alderman and his wife are involved, it requires a little more, shall we say resourcefulness.'

'My father and I have dealings with the *"Company"* for some years now and they call on us to deal with those difficult situations, oh and to move opium when required.'

She sat down beside the bath and picked up a flannel, dipped it in the warm water and began to dab Robert's chest gently. While doing so, she listened to his account of the time when he first met the alderman.

☆

The night air was thick with tension as Robert stood before the imposing entrance of the alderman's house, his heart pounding in anticipation of what lay ahead. The moonlight cast eerie shadows on the cobbled path, and a sense of foreboding hung in the air like a shroud. He had been called upon, summoned into a world of intrigue and danger, his fate now intricately linked with the alderman's clandestine ambitions.

Robert was called to the back door of the alderman's house in the dead of night. He was taken to the parlour where the alderman and Smythe were waiting.

As the door swung open, revealing the dimly lit interior of the parlour, Robert's gaze was immediately drawn to the figures seated within. The alderman, a man of authority and influence, rose from his chair, a formidable presence that demanded respect. Beside him stood Smythe, his easy smile belying the gravity of the situation.

'Robert.' Smythe's voice was warm, a stark contrast to the tension in the room. 'Allow me to introduce Alderman Metcalf.'

Robert inclined his head respectfully, his mind racing to grasp the significance of this unexpected meeting. 'Yer grace, pleased to make yer acquaintance,' he greeted with a bow, his curiosity piqued by the mysterious encounter.

'Please to meet you. Smythe tells me you may be able to be of some assistance to me and my associates. What we are asking needs some level of secrecy.'

'Please call me Robert.' He glanced at Smythe curiously. *How the hell does Smythe know the alderman? No wonder the charlies won't go near 'im.* Robert frowned.

The alderman continued, 'The gentleman of note is a former Parliamentary henchman, he was of some service to us once, buying wool on loan on our behalf.

'We also caught Jacob Wilding stealing the same wool back from our ships. At the time, we contacted authorities and he was caught red handed and jailed.'

The alderman sat. 'He was later released after a gentleman up north, a Jasper Calamy, pleaded on his behalf due to his services in the war. Next time he won't be so lucky!

'Wilding is in debt.' The alderman's voice carried a note of finality. 'And he will pay for his transgressions. But we need to send a message, a message that the Company will not tolerate such actions.'

The plan unfolded before Robert's eyes, each detail a thread in a complex tapestry of deceit and strategy. The gravity of his role weighed heavily upon him, the realisation that he was to become the instrument of retribution sinking in.

‘You will break into my house.’ The alderman’s words were delivered with a sinister edge, a twist in the plot that sent a shiver down Robert’s spine.

Robert looked at Smythe and the alderman curiously. ‘What am I to do?’

Smythe knew what was coming and smiled cheekily.

‘You, my friend, will break into my house.’ The alderman sniggered. ‘Do you agree?’

A quizzical look on his face, he allowed the alderman to continue.

‘I will ensure the servants are in bed for the night so you will not be disturbed. You will break into the house using the boot room on the west side. You will make your way up the stairs to the master bedroom at the front of the house. There you will tiptoe to the chest of drawers and open the top drawer where you will find a valuables box. You will take the box and leave the same way you came in. The sapphire in the box is worth far more than the thirteen and a half shillings required for a thief to hang.’

Robert gulped. ‘Hang?’

‘Fear not, Robert Rushworth, Smythe will plant the idea about the position as a thief-taker to Wilding. He will be called to my house and there, I will offer him a warrant for your arrest. Wilding will also be offered a reward for returning the sapphire and the culprit who stole it.’

‘But I stole it, what if something goes wrong?’

The alderman’s assurances were tempered by a warning of the trials that awaited. ‘Have faith, Robert. The path ahead will not be easy, but your reward will match the risks you undertake.’

A heavy silence settled over the room as the weight of the plan settled upon them. Robert’s gaze shifted from the alderman to Smythe, his friend’s cheeky smile a beacon of camaraderie in the midst of uncertainty.

‘I am sure you are aware of how news travels on the streets of Leeds through the criminal underground, so once you have the necklace, you will flee. While you are gone and Wilding is in pursuit, Smythe will have time to organise matters.

'Now, Robert, whatever happens you must have faith and continue with the plan and under no circumstances is this to be linked with me and my wife or my associates. This would not good be good for… well… for business or for my position as alderman.'

Smythe looked at Robert. 'Like I said, one more job! You are to take the sapphire to a Captain Girlington in Hull to keep safe.'

The alderman continued, 'You will allow yourself to be arrested by Mr Wilding and brought back to the local court in Leeds. Here due to lack of findings, my colleague, the magistrate will order you to be taken to the Court of Assizes in York. There you will be interned in York Castle Prison to await trial.'

'Await trial?'

'Yes but don't fear, all will be well; however, I warn you this ordeal will not be pleasant.'

'Ordeal?' Robert gaped at Smythe then back at the alderman. 'An' what happens if your plan doesn't work? I could end up swinging from a rope!' stated Robert fearfully.

The alderman continued, 'Fear not, Robert, all will be well, and you will be handsomely rewarded for your time and efforts. Now, we really need to allow this plan to take its course.'

Robert took a deep breath.

'Now, let Mr Wilding follow you north. The next part of our plan will be difficult for you, Robert. Under no circumstances are you to tell your family. Now, are you up for this?'

Robert thought for a moment. He looked at Smythe. 'Well, I promised you one last job, didn't I?'

In that moment, a pact was forged in the shadows, a pact that would set in motion a chain of events that could shatter lives or rewrite destinies. With a deep breath, Robert Rushworth embraced his role in the alderman's intricate game, ready to navigate the treacherous path that lay ahead, guided by the promise of reward and the whispers of an uncertain future.

☆

'Such an elaborate plan! Only my father could have dreamed it up.'

Robert grabbed Ursula by the hand and pulled her into the bath, her towel fell exposing her nakedness. She giggled.

The water splashed over the edge of the bath, soaking the floor. 'Robert! Now look what you've done.'

Ursula smiled and gently wiped the water from Robert's face then leaned forward and kissed him. He reciprocated closing his eyes. He could feel the excitement in his loins. She sat up, straddled him then reached behind and guided his hardness inside. She tilted her head back, closed her eyes and quietly moaned.

The next morning's sun filtered through the curtains, gently rousing Robert from his slumber. He blinked, adjusting his eyes to the soft light that filled the room. His heart skipped a beat as he realized Ursula was nestled against his chest, her breathing steady and calm. Her eyelids fluttered open, revealing those captivating eyes that seemed to hold the secrets of the sea itself.

A coy smile played on Ursula's lips as she met Robert's gaze. Her fingers traced a tender path across his chest, leaving a trail of warmth in their wake. Slowly, her lips descended, placing delicate kisses on his skin, each one igniting a fire within him. Higher and higher they climbed until their lips finally met, sparking a passionate kiss that sent waves of desire coursing through Robert's veins.

Their longing was undeniable and Robert could feel his heart racing, echoing the rhythm of their urgent kiss. As their lips reluctantly parted, Ursula sat up, her silhouette a breathtaking sight against the morning light. Her graceful form was illuminated, every contour and curve casting a spell upon Robert's senses. He couldn't help but admire the way her hair cascaded down her back, a cascade of ebony silk that framed her beauty like a masterpiece.

With a languid grace, Ursula draped a towel around her waist, the fabric emphasising her slender waist and enticing curves. Robert's gaze lingered, drawn to her every movement as she sauntered toward a privacy screen.

Robert looked at her back; it was slim and feminine, and he liked the way her hair cascaded down it.

Her voice floated from behind the partition, laden with curiosity and uncertainty. 'Ursula, me father and Tommy must leave on the 'morrow to get back to Haworth. The reward I get from the alderman should be enough to pay the lease fines.'

Ursula spoke from behind the screen. 'Yes, I gathered, and I assume you will want to go with them?'

'Why don't you come with us? The moors are splendid this time of the year. I guarantee you've never seen anything like it.'

'I've been at sea a long time; I must speak to my father. Let me think on it.'

Ursula arranged new clothes for Robert; the clothes of a trader. He looked very dapper in his ochre leather tunic, dark brown breeches and knee-high boots.

There was a knock at the door.

Ursula called out, 'COME IN.'

Beaman appeared, walked over, and handed her a note. She read it then looked up. 'The alderman wants to meet with you tomorrow. '

In the evening, Robert stood and put his cloak and his black felt hat on.

Ursula smiled proudly. 'You look like a gentleman.'

Robert grinned, took off his hat and bowed to Ursula. He left through the door.

Ursula found her father on the aft deck. She climbed up the wooden steps to him. 'Robert has asked me to go with him. Daddy, I've been at sea for so long, I feel this is right.'

Captain Smythe held her hand. 'You should go, do you the world of good, but only with a guard.'

'Daddy, I'll be fine!'

'Ursula, it's a long way between here and Halifax. You must 'ave a guard and I will hear no more about it! Beaman will organise horses for you and Robert. Two of the crew will go with you.'

The captain ordered the cabin boy to get Beaman. A few moments later, Beaman knocked on the cabin door.

'COME IN!'

'Beaman, Ursula and her friend will be going on a trip. You and one of your best men will go with them.'

Beaman nodded, turned and closed the door behind him.

After they arrived in Leeds, Robert went straight to Red Hall.

The alderman sat in front of the fire in the sitting room while his wife sat beside him crocheting.

There was a knock at the door and the servant girl appeared. 'Sir, you 'ave a visitor.'

The alderman looked up. 'Ah yes, I've been waiting, please show him into the parlour, tell him I will be there shortly.'

She bowed and left.

'Please excuse me, my love, I have business to attend to.' He slowly stood and walked out the door.

The servant girl was standing outside the parlour and opened it for him.

'Ahhh, Robert, I hope your stay in the Castle Prison wasn't too unpleasant.

Robert stood. 'Alderman, it was a time I would rather not revisit.'

The alderman chuckled. 'Yes, I've heard. I believe you have something belonging to me.'

Robert reached into his coat and brought out the sapphire, dangling it at eye level.

The alderman smiled then took it from him, holding it in his hands allowing it to glisten in the candlelight. 'My wife will be most pleased.' He placed it gently on the table.

'Robert, Captain Smythe's relationship with the Company is long and trusted and he has proven time and time again to be a man of justice and principle despite his... other past times.'

'Your grace, I totally agree and if it weren't fer 'im... well...?'

'I, on behalf of the Company thank you for your efforts in this matter and it be God's will Mr Wilding no longer be a curse on the East India Company.

'Please accept this as a token of our thanks, it should be more than enough.' He handed Robert a fold of pound notes. 'Robert, I assume you will return home now. Go in peace, health and prosperity and God bless you and yours. My servant will see you out.'

Robert bowed. 'Your grace.' He turned and left through the parlour door, following the servant girl and out through the back door.

'Night.' She bowed and closed the door after him.

After Robert's encounter with the alderman and the exchange of the sapphire, his heart was light as he walked the familiar streets of Leeds. The weight of his recent trials seemed to melt away, replaced by a sense of anticipation. Little did he know that another surprise awaited him, one that would bring him unparalleled joy.

He reached the Upper Headrow then turned down Lands Lane and noticed Mary who was chatting with a gentleman of the night. Seeing Robert approach, he departed.

He put two and two together and assumed she also worked for Captain Smythe.

'Oh, tis a gentleman, would ya like some company, darlin'?' She smiled cheekily and winked at Robert.

Robert put a shilling in her hand, doffed his hat and went on his way. *It's a strange world,* he thought to himself. *One minute a copyholder's son, the next a gentleman with a fold of pound notes in my pouch.*

Robert felt he was being followed so he turned down High Street and quickly ducked into a doorway. A few minutes later, Beaman and another crewman came rushing past him.

After they passed, he stepped out of the doorway and whistled. 'OYE, LOOKIN' FOR SOMEBODY?'

Both Beaman and Edwin were out of breath, their hands on their knees. They both looked up and smiled. 'FER FUCK'S SAKE, Robert! Captain Girlington sent us ta keep an eye out.'

Robert strolled past them smiling. 'Come on let's get back.'

Arriving back at the Nags Head, they meandered in.

Ursula sat at a table, she looked up, she was waiting for them and looked down at her tankard. She was in deep thought.

Robert took a chair at her table.

She glanced at him but remained silent. *Should I tell him or not?*

Robert wanted to talk, but he knew something was wrong. He sat there quietly drinking his tankard of ale waiting for her to speak.

Beaman looked over and stood. 'Fer Christ's sake, will you two say something? GRRRRRR.' He shook his head and walked away, taking his tankard with him.

Both Robert and Ursula continued looking down at their tankards, neither of them ready to converse.

Robert glanced at her then looked around to see if anybody was listening in. 'Ursula…'

Robert glanced at her fearfully, dreading the bad news. He remembered the last time they parted.

Ursula took another chug of ale, then another and plonked the tankard back down on the table.

Robert was frustrated and stared at her. ‘And?’

‘Robert, I have something to tell you…’ Ursula’s words hung in the air, pregnant with uncertainty. Robert’s heart raced, bracing himself for the news that could potentially shatter the fragile peace he had found.

Ursula’s confession was delivered with a mixture of hesitance and resolve, ‘Robert… I am with child.’

Robert glanced up at her, confused.

Ursula rolled her eyes. ‘Robert, did you not hear me? I am with child… YOUR CHILD!’ She looked up to gauge his reaction.

It dawned on him, Robert raised his head and looked into her eyes. ‘MY… CHILD?’

‘SHUUUSH!’ She put her hand over his mouth and smiled. She leaned in to whisper, ‘Of course, your child!’

Robert was ecstatic but didn’t know how to show it. He didn’t know what to say or do. His eyes grew wide and white.

Ursula stared at him frowning, waiting for a reaction. ‘Are you disappointed?’

Robert couldn’t speak; he put his shaking finger up to his lips to shoosh her. He stuttered trying to say something but couldn’t.

He staggered over to the door and went outside, drunk with happiness.

Beaman watched him go then glanced back at Ursula who looked sad. He could see her eyes tearing up.

Outside, Robert raised his hands in jubilation. An ecstatic expression grew on his face, he screamed, ‘AHAHA, I’M GOING TO BE A DA! YES, YES, YEEEEEES!’ He dropped to his knees.

Inside, Ursula and Beaman exchanged glances, both moved by the scene unfolding before them. Ursula’s uncertainty had been met with a response she had not anticipated, and Robert’s uncontained happiness was a testament to the depth of his feelings.

Beaman looked over her shoulder. 'It seems Robert is most pleased with the news, Captain.'

Ursula turned quickly and wrapped her arms around him. 'Oh, Beaman, am I doing the right thing?'

Beaman remembered the times as a young girl when she would go to him after falling on deck; he would wipe her eyes and hold her close until her sobs ceased.

He tried to step back, lifting his arms uncomfortably unaccustomed to such affection from Captain Girlington. 'Ursula… ya 'ave ta follow ya heart, no matter what.'

Ursula walked out into the middle of the courtyard.

As Robert and Ursula embraced and shared a kiss that spoke of their shared journey and the future that lay ahead, Beaman watched from the sidelines, a knowing smile on his weathered face. In that moment, he recognised the power of love to transform lives, to bridge gaps, and to pave the way for new beginnings.

With Ursula in his arms, Robert felt a sense of completeness that transcended his past and his present circumstances. The road ahead would undoubtedly be marked by challenges and uncertainties, but the promise of new life had ignited a fire within him, one that burned brightly against the backdrop of the night.

And as the stars twinkled overhead, casting their radiant light upon the courtyard of the Nags Head, the celebration continued. For in that moment, Robert Wilding, a man who had risen from the depths of despair, found himself at the cusp of a future that held both promise and purpose.

☆

The morning sun seeped through the small window, rousing Robert from a well-earned slumber. His body felt both sated and weary from the passionate night he had shared with Ursula. As he squinted against the light, his searching gaze met an empty space where Ursula had been. A pang of longing tugged at his heart, and he pushed aside the bedsheets, his mind racing with questions.

Dressing quickly, Robert descended the creaking stairs of the inn, his thoughts consumed by the mystery of Ursula's absence. At the foot of the stairs, he was met by the sight of his father and Tommy, both waiting with solemn expressions. The cook placed a modest breakfast before them, and they began to pick at the simple fare. Weevils were plucked from biscuits and salted beef was chewed upon with a mixture of hunger and concern.

William was the first to speak as he chewed. 'Robert, we need ta get back home.'

Tommy agreed. 'Isabel and my daughters have been alone far too long.'

The cook brought Robert a bowl and returned to the galley without a word.

Captain Girlington climbed to the aft deck.

The three of them turned toward her.

Robert smiled with affection.

Tommy stood. 'Captain Girlington, we must make haste, we 'ave been away far too long and I fear for my wife and children.'

'Tommy, I am coming with you, the horses await.' William stood.

'William before you go, Robert and I have something to tell you. She whispered, 'You are going to be a grandfather.'

William turned to Robert. 'Come, the both of you, I am soooo pleased.' He put his hands out to embrace them both. Captain Girlington… Ursula.

William smiled proudly. 'This is grand news; you have made an old man very happy. Now we must go, we have been away from the moors fer too long and I miss the cold wind in me face.'

William and Tommy turned and started making their way out the back to their horses.

As William and Tommy mounted their horses and made their way toward the exit, Beaman's questioning gaze sought their departing figures. 'You're leaving, my friends?'

Robert and Ursula followed and stood beside Beaman.

Tommy saddled his horse.

William turned and put out his hand toward Beaman. 'Thank you, my friend, I am forever in your debt fer lookin' after me son.'

Tommy strode towards Beaman and put out his hand. 'Thank you. Goodbye Robert, Ursula, visit us in Haworth soon.'

Beaman smiled a big smile. 'Safe journey!'

William and Tommy mounted their horses then trotted through the archway.

Ursula stood beside Beaman, watching them depart. 'Beaman, organise the horses and yes, you're coming with us.'

'Comin' wi ya?' Beaman asked.

'Yes, Beaman, coming with us,' she demanded.

'But Captain, what about *The Pearl*? I need to get back.'

'Crew are on leave fer a week well, all except the watch.'

Beaman hesitated. 'And Captain Smythe? Does he know?'

Girlington glared at him. She took a step forward and looked up. 'First mate… I am the only captain you need to worry about.'

Robert felt the intensity of the look. He didn't want to see it again so he left them to it and went back inside.

She took another step toward Beaman, put one hand on her hip and the other on the handle of her pistol. She looked up into his nostrils; he towered above her and looked straight ahead.

'Is that clear, first mate? Besides, it was Daddy's idea.'

'Aye, Captain!' answered Beaman submissively.

Girlington smiled. 'I'm glad we understand each other, now arrange the horses and provisions for two days.'

'Aye, Captain.' Beaman hurried off.

Ursula went back inside the Nags Head. 'Robert, we're leaving before I change my mind!'

CHAPTER 32

Trails of Redemption

They left for Bradford on the hour and travelled west along Leeds Road. The journey from Bradford to Haworth was marked by a mix of determination and unease. Robert and Ursula cantered ahead, their horses' hooves pounding against the earth, while Beaman followed, keeping a watchful eye on the surroundings. Conversation between Robert and Ursula flowed effortlessly, their words intertwining with laughter and whispered promises for the future.

As they were riding along, he turned to her and asked, 'Why does yer father run the Nags Head, it's obvious he has money enough fer the finer things in life.'

Ursula's eyes darkened with a hint of sadness, and she cast her gaze downward. 'When you've lived the life my father did for as long, there are always going to be those who want to profit from his whereabouts. If his identity was known he would be hanged, drawn and quartered.'

'Very clever, who would think the great pirate, Captain Smythe would succumb to the life of a tavern keeper?'

☆

Time passed, and the landscape shifted beneath their horses' hooves. Two days later, as Tommy and William arrived at the cottage, a sense of urgency enveloped them. Tommy's anxiety manifested in the way he dismounted and handed over the reins to William. He hurried to the cottage's door, calling out for his family. 'Isabel, Morwen... Mirth?' *Where could they be?*

There was silence, the cottage was dark, cold and empty.

A few moments later William entered, strode over to the hearth and hovered his hand over the ashes. 'Stone cold, they 'avn't been 'ere fer a while.'

Tommy's frantic search led him outside, where he discovered the knocked-over dry-stone wall and the missing sheep. His heart sank as he realised the truth, and he bellowed, 'CALICO!'

They mounted their horses and galloped up Sun Street to Weavers Hill, then trotted down Spinners Way.

Calico heard the hooves of the horses and was outside his cottage. 'I've been waiting fer ya, you've been gone a while.'

The boy came out and grabbed the reins of the horses and they dismounted, following Calico inside.

Frustrated and annoyed, Tommy had no time for pleasantries. 'Where are they?'

William stared at his old friend.

'Please… sit.' Calico sat down in his embroidered chair. 'They are well and safe, do not fear.'

He recounted the events that had transpired in their absence. Isabel's refusal to vacate the property had been met with an order from Jasper Calamy himself. The lifehold lease was no more, and they were forced to leave. Calico's voice was laden with regret as he spoke of his inability to prevent the tragedy.

Tommy's anger and desperation erupted. 'WHERE ARE THEY?'

But Calico's soothing words urged caution. 'Calm yerself, Tommy.'

'Where are they now?' William asked with some concern.

'They are in the Haworth Almshouse. I have one of the women visit them every week and take them as much food as we can spare.'

Tommy ran out of the cottage, mounted his horse and galloped down to the end of the lane. He turned left on Sun Street, right on Bridgehouse Lane and headed north on Belle Isle Road toward the Crossroad. He jumped the low-lying shrubbery outside the stone house, dismounted and ran up to the door.

It was a two-story stone structure with three gables and a slate tile roof. There were seven deep recessed windows seven front doors and seven chimneys. He thumped on a central large oak door. 'ISABEL! ISABEL!'

He thumped on the door again. 'ISABEL!'

The door slowly opened and an old haggard woman stood there.

'TOMMY!' Isabel came running out of one of the seven doors down the end of the building.

He heard Isabel and turned to catch her as she ran into his arms.

'Tommy, I'm sa sorry, there was nothing I could do, they forced us ta go.' She sobbed.

'Shhhh, my luv, tis not yer fault, shhhh we'll sort it out, now come inside.'

'I was sa worried, you've been gone fer so long, I thought somethin' 'ad 'appened to ya.'

Tommy put his arm around her protectively and they went back inside.

Tommy gazed around and was taken back by the misery and desperation of the inhabitants in the room. There were another four people in the cramped, tiny space, all old, sick or disabled.

One old woman glanced at them, then turned back around to prod the small flame in the hearth. She coughed deeply, snorted then spat into the fire.

An old man sat on a stool at a small table, his leg amputated at the knee, he slowly massaged his stump.

Another old man sat on a straight back chair, his head leaning back against the wall. He was snoring and dribble was escaping from the corner of his mouth. He stopped breathing for a moment and bolted upright to catch his breath, shocked by the stranger in his midst.

'Tommy we've got to get the children out of 'ere; these people, they're all sick or dyin',' she whispered.

'Isabel where are the girls?' Tommy asked impatiently.

'They're down the other end interned with ten other children in a trainin' centre. They told 'em they would 'ave ta stay until they were sixteen!'

'Show me, grab yer things.' Tommy went outside and Isabel followed quickly behind.

Isabel rushed past him to the end door and opened it; the stone walled room was completely full of pauper children spinning and weaving. A man who was the overseer strode back and forth with a whipping stick.

Morwen and Mirth glanced up as the door opened and ran to their father. 'DAAA!'

The overseer lifted his stick. 'Here you two get back 'ere before ya get another whippin.'

Tommy bent down to embrace them, he closed his eyes. 'Morwen Mirth, tis alright, grab yer things were goin.'

The overseer marched over to Tommy. 'Here, ya can't be comin' in 'ere like this disturbin' things. Who da ya think you are?'

Tommy stood up and glared at him, then watched his children grab their cloaks. 'Hurry, daughters, go with yer mother.'

'I told ya, ya can't be comin' in 'ere disturbin' 'em! I'm gonna report you ta the authorities!'

Tommy squinted and bared his teeth. 'If I find you've put a finger on my daughters, I promise you I'll be back!' He turned and ushered his daughters through the door.

The overseer followed them. 'Here, you come back now, do ya hear? The constable will 'ear about this. BRING THOSE GIRLS BACK!'

Just as Tommy was lifting Morwen onto his horse, William arrived. He reined in his horse and jumped down.

Mirth ran to him and put her arms around his waist. 'UNCLE WILLIAM!' She closed her eyes and squeezed tightly.

William assisted Mirth up onto the saddle and pulled the horse forward.

Isabel walked beside them.

'And what of Will?' Tommy asked.

'We haven't seen him in weeks,' said Isabel, 'Still at the manor. Weren't allowed to see us at the alms 'ouse, no visitors they said.'

'We can't go back ta the cottage.'

Worriedly, Isabel glanced at Tommy. 'What are we ta do then, join the beggars on the road?'

William thought for a moment then stopped his horse. 'I've got an idea! Mirth, shove over, lass.' He climbed up on his horse and started trotting down the road.

Tommy called out after him. 'WILLIAM, WHERE YA GOIN'?'

William turned back and smiled. 'COME WI' ME, COME ON!'

Tommy moved Morwen forward, then pulled Isabel up onto the horse's rump. 'Come on, quick!'

Isabel giggled. 'Tommy, what's got into ya?'

Tommy dug his heels into the horse and trotted off after William. 'I think I know where he's goin'.'

Isabel frowned. 'Where 'ave ya all gone bonkers?'

Tommy followed William along Haworth Road. They followed the course of Bridgehouse Beck.

Down Sun Street, Isabel could see their cottage up on the hill, but rather than riding toward it, Tommy followed William down Marsh Lane. They turned into Moorhouse Lane toward the Hargreaves Cottage.

When Tommy cantered toward him, William was still sitting on his horse, Mirth with her arms around his waist, eyes closed and squeezing tightly.

The Hargreaves Cottage stood before them, a testament to the resilience of generations past. Its worn and weathered exterior whispered stories of the lives it had sheltered and now, it stood ready to embrace a new chapter in the lives of Tommy and his family.

Tommy and Isabel entered the cottage cautiously, their footsteps echoing in the dimly lit space. The room was musty and the air was heavy with the weight of neglect. The collapsed wall, the crumbling hearth, and the broken furniture were stark reminders of the challenges that lay ahead. Yet, amidst the decay, a glimmer of hope flickered in their eyes.

William, a little out of breath, said, 'Tis not much, but it's ours, along with the half acre behind it.'

'What da ya mean William, ours?'

'Belonged to yer grandfather on yer mother's side, John Hargreaves!'

Isabel was shocked. 'Ours?'

'Aye, John Hargreaves was a freeman, left it to ya Mother Agnes, so now it belongs to you, Tommy.'

Tommy was shocked. 'Why 'ave ya not told us this before, Uncle?'

'Because ya 'ad the lifehold and besides tis a very small parcel of land and the cottage, will take a lot of fixin' up. Where ya gonna get the coin fer that?'

Isabel was stunned. 'So we're landowners?'

William thought fer a moment, 'Aye, suppose you are, but don't get too excited – tis only half an acre! John Hargreaves sold most of it off after the war.'

Tommy jumped down from his horse, helped Isabel and Morwen down, then made his way toward the cottage.

The main section of the cottage wall was completely collapsed, the thatch mouldy and some missing. The chimney was missing a few stones and the hearth was full of cobwebs. Broken and rotting furniture was scattered everywhere.

William meandered up and put his hand on the mantle. 'I was only a young lad, but I remember when yer grandfather came 'ere to ask fer ya grandmother's hand.'

Morwen and Mirth called out, 'Oh, tell us, Uncle William, please tell us.'

'Not now, me darlins, it's late and I am tired. We need to get settled.'

'Ohhh, PLEASE, UNCLE WILLIAAAM?'

William gazed at the girls and smiled. 'Another time, tis gettin' late and we should start a fire and make a roof to get out of the wind. Girls go and find some kindlin'.'

'Don't you go too far now,' Isabel called out.

Isabel went over to Tommy and whispered, 'We need some things from the cottage.'

Tommy took out his steel and his knife, clicked them together repeatedly to create a spark on the dried grass and twigs the girls brought back.

Tommy went over toward his horse. 'I'm gonna go get some blankets and some grub. We might not 'ave a roof but we'll be warm this night.'

'Wait Tommy, I'll go, you stay 'ere with Isabel and the girls.'

'Ya sure, William?'

'Aye, course I'm sure! Besides there's something I 'ave ta take care of.'

Tommy and Isabel stared at him but said nothing.

'Now, is there anything else ya need from the cottage?'

'Some food for the girls would be good if there's some not been eaten by the rats,' said Isabel.

'Right, you are then, back in the shake of a gee gee's whisker.' He smiled and mounted his horse, and took off into the darkness.

☆

The wind whispered through the moors, carrying with it an air of uncertainty. The moonlight painted eerie shadows on the rugged landscape, casting a sense of foreboding over the tranquil scene.

Mrs Killsin sat in the red padded chair near the fire. She stood up and stepped to the door and called out, 'Milton, we need some more wood fer the fire.'

Milton was in the barn behind the cottage tending to the new lambs he brought in for the night. 'Okay, I'll be there in a minute, hold yer horses.'

Milton felt the tip of a pistol in the small of his back, he tried to turn. His breathing quickened.

'Don't move, put your hands behind you.'

Milton did as he was told. 'I have money in the house, you can have it all.'

The intruder turned him around and glared at him. He pulled the fabric from his face.

Milton gasped. 'YOU! You'll not get away with it!'

'Shut up you!' The intruder punched him in the stomach.

'Hmmffff.' Milton grabbed his stomach and bent over, coughing, hacking and trying to get his breath back.

'Now how does it feel ta get some a' yer own medicine back, ya fucker?'

He bound his wrists, gagged him then the intruder picked up a candle ushering him out the barn and back into the moors behind the cottage.

'Please, you can't do this. I'll report you; you'll spend the rest of your days in Castle Prison! You'll hang!'

'Keep walkin', ya fat little fucker!'

'Please, please, let me go. I won't tell anybody. I'll give them the land back.'

Pigshells pushed him forward. 'Keep walkin'.' They walked north through the forest on the edge of town.

☆

Mrs Killsin called out, 'MILTON, THE FIRE, IT'S GOING OUT!'

Mrs Killsin's heart raced as she stepped cautiously into the barn, her voice calling out for her husband echoing in the empty space. The candle's feeble glow barely pierced the veil of obscurity, casting long, twisted shadows that seemed to dance in sinister celebration. Something was amiss, and an unsettling feeling settled deep within her gut. 'Milton… Milton, where are you?'

She shuffled over to the bench where the candle sat and picked it up. She held it high moving it left and right trying to see through the darkness. 'Milton? Where are you, dear?' Her voice quivered, carrying a mixture of concern and growing unease.

Surely, he would tell me if he was going out, she thought to herself. Mrs Killsin shrugged her shoulders, picked up some dried peat and went back inside the cottage.

Outside, the wind howled, its mournful wail a haunting accompaniment to her anxiety. She pushed the door open a bit further, peering into the darkness beyond, her heart racing like a trapped bird against its cage. 'Milton, please, answer me!'

Her calls echoed into the night, fading into the distance without a trace of response. A chilling realisation crept over her – something was terribly wrong. Mrs. Killsin's breath quickened as panic set in, a cold sweat forming on her brow.

☆

William's return was met with a mixture of gratitude and anticipation. He dismounted his horse, a bag slung over his shoulder, and approached the cottage. The warmth of the firelight illuminated his face, casting a serene glow around him.

The bag contained blankets and provisions, a simple yet profound gesture of care and support. Together, they fashioned a makeshift shelter against the night's chill, using the blankets to create a sense of enclosure within the worn walls. As they huddled together, sharing stories and laughter, the cottage began to transform, infused with the spirit of family and resilience.

The girls were sitting on two stools Tommy pieced back together with twine. He made a small frame out of some bound branches and utilised some old thatch to make a slanted roof.

'What else did ya get?' Tommy asked.

'Got this salted lamb and cheese from the earth cellar and a bit of stale bread the rats 'ave been chewin' on, but tis better than nothin'.'

William peered into his pouch. 'I've still got the coin Smythe gave me in Selby, so we can go into the village tomorra and buy some food.'

Tommy looked up at the crumbling chimney. 'This cottage will need some fixin' so we can get some supplies and anything else we need from Hall Green.'

'Plenty of Water Reed and Longstraw about to re-thatch the roof, ' said Isabel. 'The girls an' I will collect some tomorra.'

While William was gone, Tommy told Isabel about the journey to Leeds and then York, the trial and Ursula.

Isabel was astonished. 'With child? A woman, the captain of a ship, pray Jesus, what next?'

Isabel made a makeshift bed out of branches and leaves to keep the girls off the ground then angled it close to the fire. She halved the blanket and laid them down.

The girls were fast asleep by the time she folded the other half of the blanket over them.

By the time she got back and sat down on one of the stools, Tommy and William were in deep conversation.

Isabel put her blanket around her shoulders. 'Tommy… please tell me about Leeds.'

Tommy stared into the fire. 'Never seen anythin' like it... so many people, so much noise, so much goin' on, nice place ta visit but wouldn't want ta stay there.'

Isabel was infatuated with the thought. 'Ohh, it sounds so excitin'. I wish I could go there one day.' She appeared melancholy knowing the opportunity would never eventuate.

William glanced at her, said nothing, stood, took his blanket and laid down in front of the fire.

Tommy knew there was something troubling him.

A few minutes later, Isabel took her blanket placed it beside Tommy and snuggled into him wrapping her arm around his waist.

As the fire crackled and the winds outside continued their gentle whisper, a sense of renewal settled within the walls of the Hargreaves Cottage. This was not just a new beginning; it was a testament to the enduring strength of the human spirit, a testament to love, family and the unbreakable bonds that tie them together.

CHAPTER 33

Unveiling the Truth

William didn't sleep much. He was up before the sun and tended to the fire before the others woke.

Tommy heard his uncle rummaging around and breaking branches. He sat up, putting his blanket over Isabel lovingly.

She stirred; he peered down at her. He reached over and slowly moved the dark hair from the side of her face with his fingertips.

Tommy stood, wandered over to his two daughters pulling the blanket up and tucking them in affectionately.

He stood and ambled over to William.

He was sitting on a stool in front of the fire lighting a twig, for no real reason, just lighting a twig and blowing on it to keep the flame alive.

Tommy sat down on the stool opposite him and lost himself in the small fire.

William treasured the presence of his nephew and the feeling he didn't have to speak. He sat there re-lighting the twig time and time again.

Tommy sat there watching him quietly.

The first rays of sun pierced the horizon, Isabel started to stir. 'Tommy, TOMMY!'

He raced toward her. 'I'm 'ere, luv, quieten yerself, all is well.'

Isabel was startled. 'I had a dream, a bad dream.'

Morwen awoke panicked and stressed from hearing her mother call out. 'Maaaaa?'

William turned to them. 'Tis orlright, you and yer mother are safe. Wake now, fer tis a new day!'

Morwen wiped her eyes. 'Uncle William, what's so special about a new day?'

'Any day you're alive is a good day, beautiful girl.' He reached down and tickled her and she cackled, which woke her sister.

'William, we need ta go, fix this roof before the night. We should all go, I'm not leaving Isabel and the girls here after what they've been through.'

Isabel raised the girls. 'Come on me darlin's we're goin' to the village.'

Mirth, always with the biggest appetite, said, 'Ma, I'm hungry!'

'I know, my luv, don't worry, we'll get some bread soon.'

Isabel peered at Tommy. 'Husband, we should stop by the cottage and get the cart and on the way back, grab mattresses, the cauldron and anythin' else we need.'

They left the fire smouldering.

The girls got on one horse and Isabel on t'other, William and Tommy led them along Moorhouse Lane then turned up Marsh Lane towards the cottage.

There were three horses tied up outside. 'TIS ROBERT AND URSULA THEY'RE HOME,' yelled Tommy.

Robert was waiting outside as they approached and Ursula came outside and stood beside him smiling as she watched his family coming up the hill.

Tommy called out, 'Oye, yer right? ROBERT, WHEN DID YA GET 'OME?'

Robert shook his hand and hugged Isabel and the children.

'Late last night, Tommy, we didn't know where ya were so we started a fire. Knew you'd come 'ere sooner or later.'

Ursula stepped forward. 'There's warm pottage in the hearth if Beaman hasn't gutsed it all.'

A deep voice came from inside the cottage. 'I 'EARD THAT!'

'BEAMAN? Beaman's 'ere?' William raced inside.

Ursula was right, Beaman was sitting near the fire with a large bowl, shovelling its contents into his gaping mouth.

He sighted William, raised the bowl to his lips and skulled its contents. The huge man stood, looking at him, smiling. His one golden tooth shined in the candlelight.

William walked up to him. 'Come 'ere, ya big lug!' He grabbed him in a bear hug slapping him on the back. 'I can never thank you enough fer what you did fer me, son.'

Beaman was unaccustomed to such affection from a man; he held his hands up uncomfortably then tapped William on the back. He took a step backwards his hand on his heart in a gesture of humility.

Tommy walked in. 'Beaman, it's so good to see you!' He held out his hand.

Ursula smiled at Isabel and her daughters. 'Come, we have news to tell.'

'You must be Ursula. I've 'eard so much about ya, and these are my girls Morwen and Mirth.'

Ursula embraced her and the girls. 'It's so good to meet you all.'

'Come in please, tis not much but it's 'ome or at least it used ta be,' claimed Isabel.

Isabel and the girls went inside; they felt glad to be home, a candle was lit, and the fire was on. She strode over and stirred the pottage. The girls raced up into the loft.

William took the legs of the trestle table from the wall and put the top on.

Tommy put stools and chairs around and they all sat.

Isabel pulled out a chair. 'Ursula, please sit. What a wonderful surprise ta finally meet you and I believe congratulations are in order!'

The two girls filled jacks of ale and put them on the table.

'And Robert, what plans 'ave ya?' William was curious.

Robert knew he needed to broach the subject. 'Firstly, Da, I wanted ta let ya know; I didn't steal the necklace.'

'You didn't steal it? Come on, son, I'm not stupid. I know the ways of the world and what goes on in Leeds! You should be ashamed of yerself.'

'Da, I was workin' fer Alderman Metcalfe. It was all a set up to get Jacob Wilding in front of a judge. I'm not going to reveal the rest because I've been sworn to secrecy.'

William was still not convinced and like all fathers, started to question his son's upbringing.

'Father, rest assured, I am my mother and father's son and proud to be. You 'ave nothing to be ashamed of.' Robert dismissed thoughts of his other misdeeds.

William could see it in his eyes. *He's telling the truth.*

'And what of the lease?' Robert asked.

'We've been turned off 'ere,' claimed Isabel sadly.

'It's orl right Isabel, we'll make do.' Tommy reassured her, 'We'll 'ave ta do up the old cottage and move in there fer a time. It's only half an acre but at least it's ours until we can get another tenancy.'

Robert glanced at Ursula. 'Shame, I've got the money fer the cloth and the reward, plus a bit extra, surely it'd be enough ta pay the lease and buy seed.'

William dropped his head. 'Tis too late, Robert, the month's up and Calamy won't…'

William was despondent. 'There's no use cryin' over spilt milk, lets hook up the cart and get to the market, get food and what we need ta fix the roof. We'll come back and get everything else later.'

They all climbed aboard the cart.

The air crackled with anticipation as the cart drew closer to the commotion up ahead. The clatter of footsteps, urgent voices, and the frenzied energy of the crowd stirred a mixture of curiosity and trepidation within the group riding on the cart. The sun hung low in the sky, casting long shadows that stretched across the cobblestone streets.

'Looks like somethin' big's happenin' up there,' Tommy mused, his grip on the cart's reins tightening. Isabel leaned forward, her brows furrowed in concern, as they all strained to catch a glimpse of the unfolding scene.

As the cart neared the heart of the commotion, a hush fell over the crowd, and all eyes turned toward them. Faces lined with worry and curiosity turned toward the newcomers, whispers rippling through the gathering like a gust of wind.

The crowd started running across the field toward the ducking pond.

'Uncle, stay here with Isabel and the children while I go and see what's goin' on.'

William grabbed the reins and moved over to the driver's seat.

Isabel was anxious about the commotion, the memories of the ducking pond still fresh in her memory. 'Tommy, you be careful!'

'Uncle William, where's Da goin'? Morwen was anxious.

'Don't worry, girl, ya da will be back soon.'

Tommy followed the crowd, hanging back as they tripped over the rutted paths, making their way around the ducking pond. He slipped and recovered then forced his way to the front of the crowd. Getting to the water's edge, he pushed back to stop from falling in.

The bailiff and Constable Pigshells were pulling down on the chain on the beam of the ducking stool.

The crowd started to yell, 'Let 'er up! Let 'er up!'

The bailiff and constable pulled down heavily, but they were having difficulty, so another two men ran over and assisted. They put more weight on the chain which lifted the beam and the chair out of the water slowly.

As the chair appeared, the crowd went deathly quiet and all around the pond froze.

Tommy peered across; it wasn't a woman at all. He recognised the person in the chair; it was Milton Killsin. He was naked and had been gagged, blindfolded and his hands and feet bound to the chair.

The men in the crowd gasped. The women turned away, disturbed by what they saw.

His body was pale white and there was significant trauma; his lips were enlarged, mouth open and his tongue white and swollen. His body was already decomposing and there was significant wrinkling. There was discolouration of skin and his stomach was bloating. Sloughing of the skin and rigor mortis had set in.

The bailiff and constable pulled down heavily and swung the beam around so it landed on the bank with a thud. The bailiff marched over; he cut the ropes on his wrists and legs and the body fell face forward, his large white buttocks prominent like two mounds of wet clay.

Mrs Killsin screamed and came running over. The bailiff held her back, she collapsed on the grass weeping, her hands trembling. 'NOOOO!'

The women helped her up and guided her away from the scene. 'Come, missis, let's get ya home.'

Tommy made his way around to the other side of the pond; he watched as Constable Pigshells and the others put the body on a blanket and lifted the corpse onto a cart.

Tommy strolled back then jumped back on the cart beside William. 'Milton Killsin, he's dead. Somebody left him in the pond to rot.'

They continued up Sun Street toward the village, past the manor and Weavers Hill.

It was only a matter of time. I knew somebody would get to him eventually, William thought to himself.

William and Tommy were glad to be home. The expanse of open Pennine countryside and moorlands on one side, the sun at its highest point casting shadows from trees on the other. The church tower of St Michaels a continual reminder of the distance and steepness of the climb to the square.

The news of Milton Killsin's death moved like wildfire through the village and everybody whispered about it.

One of the shop keepers who knew William called out, 'Did ya 'ere they just pulled Milton Killsin out a' the pond?'

William glanced at him. 'Did they now?' He continued looking at the course bread for sale. 'Let's get some bread and corn, tis gonna be a long day.'

Tommy took a sly glance at William, remembering he left them for a while the night before. *Nahhh, couldn't be. He wouldn't, surely,* he pondered.

After purchasing bread, grain and nails, they loaded them onto the cart and started on their way back to the cottage.

They passed the cart carrying Milton Killsin's body to the church. Pigshells had a malicious look on his face; he winked at William as he passed.

William's expression turned from one of curiosity to one of shock.

William, Robert and Tommy headed to the Hargreaves cottage to fix the roof.

They cut some trees to replace the ones rafters rotted and broken.

'Ker-chunk!' 'Ker-chunk!' 'Ker-chunk!'

Tommy was sitting on the roof; he wiped the sweat from his brow and shielded the sun from his eyes.

Griswold was riding up the road.

Tommy whistled to warn the family and jumped from the roof landing in a mound of thatch.

Isabel guided the girls to the back of the cottage. 'Shooosh my loves. Gew on, go play but don't go too far.'

Robert, William and Tommy stood in front of the cottage protectively, axes and hammers in hand.

Griswold called out, 'WILLIAM, TOMMY, HIS GRACE WANTS TO SEE YOU. IT'S URGENT, COME QUICK.'

William stepped up into the driver's seat, Robert and Tommy jumped on the back and they followed Griswold to the manor. Once there, they followed Griswold through the back door, through the kitchen and out into the great hall.

Master Calamy rose from his seat beside the crackling fire, his formal demeanour emanating an air of authority. A flicker of recognition crossed his features as he assessed the trio before him – William, Tommy, and the newcomer Robert. The Rushworths' reputation had evidently reached even the highest echelons of Haworth society.

'Welcome, gentlemen,' Calamy greeted. 'Robert Rushworth, I presume? Your name has made its way to my ears.'

'Aye! Robert Rushworth at your service.' Robert bowed.

'Your reputation proceeds you, sir.' His grace nodded. Calamy's business-like tone cut through the air. 'William, the reason for our meeting today is a grave one. Griswold has informed me of the unfortunate incident that occurred recently.'

William's eyebrows furrowed as he responded, his voice tinged with both sympathy and scepticism. 'Aye, it's a dreadful matter indeed. Poor Milton Killsin, may he rest in peace.'

Tommy exchanged an anxious glance with William, his curiosity piqued but his apprehension evident. He addressed Calamy with a voice tinged with concern. 'Master Calamy, have they found any leads on the culprit responsible for Milton's tragic end?'

Calamy's lips curved into a faint smile, his eyes glinting with a mixture of intrigue and calculation. 'The constable is conducting a thorough investigation. According to the night watchman, there were no witnesses to the incident, only the constable and himself.'

The Rushworths exchanged a knowing look, the truth of their suspicions lingering unspoken between them. Calamy's attention shifted, his gaze narrowing on William.

'William, I have asked you here to make you a proposal.'

Oh yeah, a proposal, this'll be good. William looked curious.

'As you know many of the tenants on my lands have renegued on their rack rents and have now left the area.'

William frowned. *Yeah, they left because they were forced off!*

'My man Griswold tells me currently, there is nobody to maintain the Killsin property.'

Tough luck! William shrugged his shoulders.

Calamy's tone remained composed, undeterred by William's assertion. 'Griswold informs me that the Killsin property, spanning some thirty acres, remains unattended. As your lifehold has now lapsed, I offer you a new lease, extending over seven years. This lease encompasses both your former land at Hall Green and the Killsin property.'

Tommy's astonishment was palpable, his voice echoing the disbelief that coursed through him. 'But what of Mrs Killsin, sir? What will become of her?'

'Mrs Killsin has family in Halifax and will return there very shortly to be with them. You may move into the yeoman's house which is much larger.'

Tommy was just about to say something when William butt in. 'Your grace, could we 'ave a moment?'

'Of course.' He held out his hand. 'Griswold, show them to the parlour.'

They followed Griswold across the stone floor, and he opened the door for them to enter. There was a stone fireplace and the fire was lit. They sat at the large table in the middle of the room.

As soon as Griswold closed the door, Tommy and Robert gazed at William.

He smiled cheekily. 'Before we go takin' on another lease, we need to realise we're in a good bargainin' position…'

A few minutes later, the door opened and they strode confidently back across to where his grace was waiting.

Calamy was curious. 'Have you reached a decision?'

William stepped forward. 'As the eldest, I will speak on behalf of the Rushworth family.'

'Very well, what say you, will you take the lease or not?' Calamy asked.

'Well… the way we see it, yer grace, as most of the tenants on yer lands 'ave been turned off, I believe it puts us in a very strong position. That is, if you want ta earn a good profit from the rearin' a sheep and the growin' a' grains.

'Now… me family 'as been on this land fer generations and always done the right thing to run it and improve it. We even 'ave the coin to pay the lease fines.

'Ohhh, splendid! I'll have Griswold draw up the lease.'

'Yer grace, as we are good tenants and as ya say, good tenants is 'ard ta come by, we would like some additional… conditions.'

Griswold stepped forward. 'This is undignified, you cannot hold his grace to ransom like this. You should be thankful he has made the offer.'

Jasper Calamy knew good tenants were becoming increasingly difficult to find and if they left, could quite easily lease land in Keighley, Oxenhope or Halifax.

Griswold was going to continue his rant when Calamy interrupted, 'GRISWOLD! Let them speak.'

'Thank you, your grace, we would like our lifehold back and you to pay the land tax and the tithe. Rather than paying the increased lease and fines, we go back to payin' the same rates as before.'

Griswold had a scowl on his face and he was fighting hard to hide his frustration.

Calamy thought for a moment. 'Agreed!'

William continued, 'I'm sorry, yer grace… we would also like improvements to the cottages and extra buildings fer livestock, also better drainage so the crops don't rot with the wet.'

Jasper Calamy thought about it fer a moment and was about to say something when Tommy nudged William.

'Oh, and one more thing.' William knew he was pushing his luck.

Griswold was almost at screaming point.

'What is it NOW?' Calamy was getting frustrated.

William glanced at Tommy. 'Mmm, beggin' yer pardon, your grace. We would like young Will to be allowed 'ome ta sleep and help on the property when he's not at the mill.'

Calamy rolled his eyes. 'YES! AGREED! AGREED! AGREED! Now please go… BEFORE ANYTHING ELSE COMES TO MIND! Griswold, show them out!'

The three men bowed, turned and followed Griswold across the great hall and out into the kitchen. He opened the back door for them. They strode confidently through, trying hard not to laugh.

William was the last out, the last thing he heard was Calamy calling out, 'GRISWOLD!'

They strolled down the driveway saying nothing, just comfortable with their thoughts. After they passed the manor front garden, Tommy and Robert started running and laughing. William followed but stopped short to catch his breath.

'Uncle, ya did it!' Excitedly, Tommy rushed up and put one arm each around William and Robert. 'Ya know what they say, when one door closes, another opens. Isabel won't believe it when I tell 'er.'

William stopped. 'I got an idea…'

☆

Back at the cottage, Tommy watched Mrs Killsin put her belongings in the small carriage and drive it down the path toward Sun Street. She turned left and headed toward the village.

The next morning, Tommy woke early. 'Come on, Isabel, up ya get. Gew on, girls, come on, Robert.'

William was hitching the horses and was waiting outside with the cart.

Robert assisted Isabel and the two girls into the back and Ursula into the seat beside William. Tommy jumped up and put his arm around his wife.

'Tommy, 'urry up put the blindfolds on. You too, Ursula. Tommy, make sure they're good and tight,' William demanded.

'Oh, William, 'ave ya gone starkers? What's it all about?' Isabel asked, not wanting to take part in their shenanigans.

Tommy put the blindfold on his wife. 'Tis a surprise. We want ta show ya the new cottage!'

'New, tis not new. Tis run down an' old!' Isabel was anxious about the surprise.

Tommy held her hand to calm her. 'We've fixed the roof, luv, want it ta be a surprise.'

'It'll be a surprise if it don't leak!' Isabel declared.

'Right 'old on tight, girls.' William flicked the reins and the horses trotted down the hill and rather than continuing a long Sun Street towards the Hargreaves cottage, turned up the rutted path towards the Killsin cottage.

He pulled up right in front of the two-story stone structure. 'Right, when I tell ya, take yer blindfolds off. One… two… THREE!'

Isabel and the girls took off their blindfolds. Isabel was the first to speak. 'Wha' on Earth are we doin' 'ere? We'll get in all sorts of trouble if we're found on private property.'

William allowed Tommy to speak. 'Tis ours, luv.'

Isabel looked bemused. 'What da ya mean ours?'

Tommy jumped down and held out his hand for Isabel. 'Come!'

Ursula and the girls smiled, seeing how happy Tommy was, and wanted to give them a moment.

Robert gazed at his father. 'Da, tis a fine thing ya did.'

Tommy strolled up to the front door and opened it then looked back at Mirth and Morwen. 'COME ON, GIRLS, YOU COME TOO.'

'Tommy ya can't be doing that. Mrs Killsin might be back soon. Come on now, what's goin' on?' Isabel felt anxious.

'We went ta see Jasper Calamy yesterday. He's offered us a new lifehold on not only our place but also this one. He's gonna pay the land tax and the tithe. We go back to payin' the same rates fer the lease and fines as before.'

Isabel looked at him in disbelief. 'Ohhhh, Tommy, I don't believe you.'

'Ask William and Robert.'

William strolled in. 'Tis true, Isabel. It's ours!'

'Oh my goodness, look at the place, its huge, far too big fer us.'

'Wife, you'll 'ave ta get used to it, we got thirty acres!'

'Thirty acres? Oh, Tommy. 'Ow we gonna tend so much land? We 'ad enough ta do with ten acres.'

'Don't you worry, me and William, well, we've got plans.'

'Plans?'

Tommy ushered her toward the stairs. 'Come now, don't you worry, go and look at yer new 'ouse.'

'Tommy, there's windows!' She shuffled over to the stairs leading to the bedrooms.

The girls stepped through the doorway.

Mirth was excited. 'Daaaa, Uncle William said this is ours!'

Isabel climbed the wooden stairs and Tommy bent down to embrace his two daughters. 'Aye, girls, tis ours, now go upstairs and find yer room.'

'Come on, Morwen, last one up the stairs is a plodge!'

William went over to the cupboard door under the stairs and opened it, then peered in the buttery with the adjoining pantry.

Ursula gazed out of the back window and marvelled at the rolling hills and blooming heather. Robert crept up behind her and placed his hands on her shoulders lovingly.

'Robert, will ya stay 'ome now, son, and help us run the property? With thirty acres, it'll take all of us, son.'

Ursula turned and stared at Robert then at William.

Robert was saddened but knew it was best to tell him. 'No, I'm sorry, Da, we 'ave ta return ta Leeds. We 'ave business ta tend to. We'll be leavin' early in the mornin'.'

William dropped his eyes sadly. 'I suppose when ya been to the big city, the moors just don't do it fer ya anymore.'

'Like ya once said about yer da, the heather seeded from the blood on his hands. Well, tis the same with me. The moors are in my heart and in my soul and never shall they go.'

William smiled. 'I'll come visit you and John sometime, maybe when the bairns born.'

'Aye, both John and Rosie would like that and so would I.' Ursula smiled, leant over and kissed William on the cheek.

When Isabel and the girls finished inspecting their new bedrooms, they came bounding down the stairs.

Isabel hugged Tommy. 'Ya should see the view from our bedroom, ya can see fer miles. Ohhh, Tommy, I'm sa happy. Tis too good ta be true.'

'Come on, luv, don't get all soppy on me now. We got much ta do, the chimney must 'ave three inches a muck on the inside; don't want the place goin' up in smoke before we've even moved in.'

They all went outside and Tommy closed the door behind him then stepped back to take one last look.

William smiled. ‘Come on, Tommy, it’ll still be ‘ere tomorra.’

Tommy laughed, ran over and jumped up on the cart with the others.

CHAPTER 34

Hearts and Roses

High above the village, in the quiet loft, Mr Dodds presided over an evening of solemn study. The Bible's verses echoed in the rustic space, accompanied by the rhythmic tap-tap of Mr Dodds' whipping stick on the table. Bobby and his companions read aloud, their voices blending with the aura of reverence that filled the room.

Mr Dodds sat at the table, in the loft, listening to Bobby and the others read the Bible.

'Right, you lot, there's work ta be done tomorra. Ta bed with ya!'

The boys went over to their beds and started to undress.

'No, not you, Rushworth. You go 'ome, but ya bloody well better be back 'ere tomorra before the sun rises.'

Time seemed to hang suspended for a moment, as if Will were caught in a peculiar dream. The other boys exchanged curious glances, but the fierce warning in Mr Dodds' eyes silenced any potential inquiries.

Will stood there for a moment thinking it was some type of joke. The other boys laughed.

Mr Dodds pointed at the door. 'Well… GO… before I change me mind!'

The other boys glared at Will then back at Mr Dodds questioningly.

'AND YOU THREE, NOT A BLOODY WORD, or so help me, the lot of ya will get a whippin'!'

Will put his tunic back on and raced down the stairs, past the barn towards the kitchen.

Margaret was standing outside the kitchen door with the other kitchen maids. She saw Will running and he raced past her and down the driveway.

She ran after him and shouted out, 'WILL, WHERE YA GOIN'?'

Out of breath, Will stopped, made his way slowly over to the bed of roses and picked a half-opened crimson flower. He turned and strolled back. Picking the thorns from it, he held the flower up to her.

Margaret smiled coyly and took the flower. 'Will! Yer gonna be getting yerself in all sorts a' trouble.'

Will saw the other kitchen maids peeking around the corner so he waved, and they giggled. He knew they were still watching so he leant over and gave Margaret a kiss on the cheek. He said nothing because no words needed to be said.

Will continued running down the driveway. The other kitchen maids giggled, oohed and ahhhed.

Margaret stood there, holding her cheek. In the fading light, she gazed down at the rose which she clutched tightly to her chest.

When Will got to Hall Green, he was so pleased to see the shutters open and the glow from the fire and the candles? He was out of breath so he slowed going up the hill. He could hear laughing and joviality and he smiled.

'Maa, Daaa!' He lifted the latch and went in.

His father stood to greet him. 'Will?'

Isabel ran to her son. 'Will, I've missed you so much!' She embraced him lovingly.

Will was surprised to see so many people in the small cottage. Ales were being poured and there were three dark, glass bottles on the table. There were pewter plates full of meat, pastries and fruit, the like he'd never seen before except on Calamy's table.

He stared at the end of the table and there was a full roasted chicken missing a leg. A very inebriated uncle was chewing in to it. 'What's goin' on?'

His father put his hand on Will's shoulder. 'Son, we 'ave some good news.'

William gazed around the room. 'Robert!' He strode up to Robert and held out his hand. 'Tis so good ta see ya, cousin!'

Robert shook his hand and introduced Ursula while William and the others watched on smiling.

Will paused for a moment, staring into Ursula's eyes. 'Robert, she's sa pretty!'

'Cheeky buggar, keep yers ta yerself!' Robert got Will in a headlock and started messing up his hair.

Ursula grabbed his arm. 'Oh, Robert, you're going to hurt him.'

'WHAT? This big lug? NEVER. Hard as nails, Will!'

Blushing, Will pushed Robert back and everybody laughed including Ursula. 'Now, Ma, what's this news you 'ave?'

Isabel glanced at Tommy and smiled. Tommy placed his hand on Will's shoulder. 'Sit down, son.'

They all sat down except for William who stood, swaying near the hearth, trying to keep his balance, and biting into what was left of the chicken leg. *Now a grandfather, wish me brother were 'ere ta celebrate with me! Suppose he is in a way!*

Tommy sat at the head of the table and Isabel sat beside him then Robert and Ursula.

Will stared blankly, wondering what was going on.

Ursula poured Will a goblet of wine out of the thick glass bottle and passed it to him.

He took it and peered inside. 'Looks like blood!'

Ursula smiled. 'It's an acquired taste, take a sip and keep it on the tongue before you swallow it.'

He took a sip and shuddered.

Robert smiled and watched him chug it all down then held out the tankard for more.

'Where did you get it?'

Ursula was going to answer then paused, 'My family runs import and export out of Hull.' She gazed at Robert and smiled. 'The wine… was… a gift.'

Will was warmed by the wine and it went to his head.

Tommy smiled. 'Will, we 'ave a new lifehold for the property. This property and the Killsin property.'

'You what? Two properties?' Will was astonished. Will took another swig of wine.

Tommy continued, 'We'll be movin' into the Killsin house.'

Will started to get a glazed look in his eyes. 'Killsin house. Aye, keep Mrs Killsin company? Haha.'

Tommy smiled. 'Aye, cause we 'ave thirty acres now, you will keep up yer apprenticeship at the manor but live at 'ome so ya can 'elp.'

Will lifted his head, a little tipsy. 'Aye, work at 'ome, sounds good ta me.'

'Hahahaha!' They all laughed hysterically.

Will gazed at the others, wondering what they were laughing about then his eyes drooped and his head dropped to the table. He rested on his forearms.

Robert looked at Will. 'It'll be a long day fer 'im tomorra… and my father by the looks of it.'

William was still standing by the hearth, trying to keep his balance and still chewing on his chicken bone. He gazed around blankly as if there was nobody else in the room. *A grandfather two times over, bless me soul.*

Robert gazed at his father, smirking at Ursula then back at Tommy and Isabel. 'We 'ave to leave early in the morning, as the sun breaks but before we go, we also 'ave news. Ursula has promised herself to me.' Robert put his hand on top of Ursula's.

Tommy stood. 'WE MUST CELEBRATE!'

Isabel glanced at Ursula and grinned. 'I think we've done enough celebrating fer one night!' She leaned across and put one hand on each of theirs then whispered, 'God bless you 'n' may you have many healthy bairns.'

Will lifted his head off the table, stood and yelled, 'WE MUST CELEBRATE!'

The room erupted with laughter.

He sat down again and put his head back down on the table, his arms dangling at his sides. 'What's in it?'

☆

William woke but couldn't open his eyes fully, his head felt heavy, and his mouth was as dry as ash. He sat up and pulled the blanket around his shoulders shivering because the fire was out.

He staggered over to Will who was still asleep at the table; he shook him. 'Will, the suns up. Ya must get ta the mill!'

Will lifted his head and staggered over to the door, opening it, he bolted up the hill toward Sun Street. William followed to watch him and grimaced.

Will slipped on the dewy grass and crashed into the dry bap wall. He stood and limped the rest of the way.

William closed his eyes to quieten the trumpets, then slowly reacted to the noise of horses behind the cottage. He could hear galloping and quickly went down the side of the cottage and peered over the moors, but all was still.

He became melancholy knowing his son and Ursula were gone and he turned back around and started back down the side of the cottage. When he got to the door, he was about to step inside but he thought he heard the neigh of a horse. He shook his head to clear it and was about to step inside but heard it again. He paused, looked up curiously, then turned around and ran.

The sun was far too high for his liking, so he shielded his eyes and looked over the moors. He blinked repeatedly then shook his head and blinked again. *It was him!*

The horse rose and *neighed* once again. He wore a black knee-length coat, a soldier's waistcoat and breeches with beige stockings and a ruffled shirt. Brown curly hair rested on his shoulders below a beige felt Cavaliers' hat decorated with a billowing plume.

The horse rose again and the highwayman lifted his hat and waved. William rubbed his eyes and looked again, he blinked and focused... but he was gone. He took a step forward, blinked again and rubbed his eyes and focused again then it dawned on him. *Robert the sly bugger, it was him! One last job aye, it better bloody well be!*

Isabel, with her blanket wrapped around her shoulders, wandered out and stood beside him, 'Ya orlright, William?'

'Aye, bit a' the bottle ache, tis orl.'

'Come on inside, nothing a hair of the dog won't mend.'

William followed Isabel inside and sat down on the stool near the hearth of the fire. He already missed his son, one minute there, the next gone.

He thought back to his days as a young man, watching he and John playing *'ball'* in the snow. *Robert always glanced back to make sure I was watching when he ran past John and touched the tree with the ball.*

Isabel handed him a leather jack. ''Ere, luv, drink this.'

William stared up at Isabel then sniffed the jack, pulling his nose up at the smell. 'Do I 'ave ta?'

Isabel rolled her eyes and put her hands on her hips. 'It'll make ya feel well, now just skull it!'

William gawked down into the jack.

Isabel shook her head in disgust. 'Right then, if yer gonna moan and complain the rest of the day, go somewhere else CAUSE I DON'T WANNA LISTEN TO IT.'

William skulled it, lifted his head and shuddered.

'What's all the yellin' fer?' Tommy climbed down the ladder from the loft, bleary-eyed and dishevelled.

'I'm sure the devil 'imself can 'ear ya.' He put his hands to his eyes, blinded by the light streaming through the cattle door which they left open. 'God wife, quieten yer words and get me somethin' ta quieten the drums behind me eyes!'

Tommy sat opposite William.

Tommy picked up the jack and skulled it. 'Right, what's ta eat? I'm starvin'.'

Griswold and Bobby marched to the barn, climbed the stacks of hay and peered over. 'Go on, Bobby, climb down there and bring up four tods of wool, oh and a bag a' corn fer 'is grace's pantry. I'll throw the rope down to ya.'

Bobby slipped over the top of the highest stack and peered down, feeling with his foot, trying to find the foothold.

Griswold became impatient. 'Come on, we don't 'ave all day!'

Bobby shook his head. 'Gi'me a minute.' He felt it, stood on it and took another step down, bracing himself against the wall of hay.

Down he went, slowly but surely, eventually reaching the bottom. He waited for his eyes to adjust then lit the candle in the lantern. He fumbled around feeling for the opening to the hidden wall and pushed it in.

He stepped inside and lifted the lantern. He called out, 'Mr Griswold, ya might wanna come an' 'ave a peep at this.'

'What da ya mean, ya silly lad?' Griswold climbed over the haystack and placed his foot on the stud protruding from the wall, made his way down carefully until he reached the bottom. He followed the light of the lantern.

Griswold was out of breath and irritable. 'Now, what seems to be the problem? Why on Earth 'ave ya forced me ta come all the way down 'ere!'

Bobby stood there motionless, looking around.

Griswold squinted, opened his eyes wider, took the lantern from Bobby and took a step forward. He turned and rushed to the other side of the barn. 'No… No… NOOO!'

The barn was empty, corn, wool even the dropped corn on the floor, from split bags. Gone!

One of Calico's men peeped from behind the wall of the mill, grinned mischievously then disappeared through the moor back to Weaver's Lane.

☆

In the shadowy corners of Haworth, a weary constable basked in the warmth of his hearth, a sly grin betraying his relief that his days as a constable were now a thing of the past. The crackling fire cast eerie shadows across the room and the flames dwindled. With a sense of cold finality, he reached for a brown leather ledger bearing the name of Milton Killsin, a name that would soon be lost to the world. Methodically, he tore page after page from the ledger, each rip echoing the secrets buried beneath ink and paper.

The yeoman's farmhouse with its tidy thatch roof and exposed timber and plaster walls painted with lime wash and tinted with ochre was marvellous. A rectangular structure with two stories, a couple of rooms and a large central chimney which towered way above the roof. It had iron, latticed windows and a rough timber plank front door. There was a small front garden and a hedge which separated road from property. The house contained four windows and a stair leading up into the bedrooms. The animals were moved to the barn outside.

Tommy looked at the cherry, pear, damson and apple trees lined down the side of the house and the cordoned off vegetable patch surrounded by a faggot fence.

He meandered through the field dragging his hands along the stalks of corn. Prices in York and London were rising due to demand, and life was good! It was a bumper crop, and almost ready for harvest. This good crop would see them through the winter.

He stopped for a minute and stared up at the blue sky allowing the sun to warm his face.

His white Vandyke collar glistened in the sun and his tall, felt capotain hat gave him a staunch gentlemanly appearance. He wore a new black buttoned tunic and breeches, and his woollen stockings were tight and tied below the knee with a brand-new navy-blue garter. His clean, black, shiny boots were cut several inches above the ankle and polished.

The moors of Yorkshire, green pastures and wayward hills, the colours of ochre, brown and pink coloured by a distant painter. Vivid green squares divided the land with brilliant white sheep with thick white wool dotting the hills and dales their bleating echoed through the valley. Long shoots of heather whispered their ancient secrets while swaying in the warm wind.

As the sun reached its highest point, the silvery beck glistened among the trees which lined the bank. The moors sang its songs, a chorus of chirping from the wrens and warblers trying to attract a mate.

Tommy stopped again. He raised his nose to smell the light, musky aroma of the heather drifting off the moors. He listened to the call of the Curlew announcing the start of Summer.

He was disturbed by Isabel calling in the distance, she came running at him, giggling, and jumped at him. He caught her; his hat falling from his head. He fell backwards on the ground, with her sitting on top of him. She leaned down and kissed him gently on the lips.

To be continued…

Step into a vividly reimagined past, where the echoes of history beckon with tales of courage, deceit, and the pursuit of fortune.

Unveiling a world where the past comes alive, 'The Lost Voices' invites you to traverse time and embrace the allure of a bygone era. The allure of adventure and intrigue awaits as you journey alongside brothers, John and Robert Rushworth, who leave the barren moors behind to chase elusive dreams in the heart of Leeds.

A Glimpse into the Shadows: Beneath the surface of the past lies a labyrinth of stories waiting to be unearthed. With the promise of adventure and the thrill of historical authenticity, this riveting tale offers an intimate window into the lives of brothers grappling with their aspirations and the shadows that haunt them.

A Struggle for Redemption: As the Rushworth brothers navigate the treacherous path of misguided choices, they confront fear head-on. Join Robert Rushworth on a riveting odyssey that takes you on an immersive journey to 17th century Leeds, York, and Hull—a world teeming with beggars, cutpurses, felons, and debtors. Amidst this tapestry of lives, the enigmatic *Shambles* serves as a crucible, a place where the threads of fate intertwine.

Judgment Awaits: In a time when theft bore the weight of a hangman's noose, a decision hangs in the balance – should Robert pay for his treachery and one last job? Brace yourself to be not just a reader, but the judge, jury, and executioner as the narrative unfurls in suspenseful twists and turns.

Intrigue and Deception: Prepare to unravel a web of murder, theft, and the shadowy allure of a tavern keeper named Smythe. As secrets reveal themselves in unexpected ways, be warned: not all is as it seems. The path to truth is shrouded in mystery, and the journey to the heart of the matter will keep you riveted until the very last page.

Dive into the Unknown: Embark on a voyage through time, where footpads, highwaymen, and pirates like the enigmatic Captain Girlington roam the pages. A captain's choice between the sea and the love that beckons provides a haunting backdrop, a testament to the complexity of lives lived in the shadows.

A Ruthless Pursuit: Amidst the tapestry of characters stands Jacob Wilding – a formidable presence, driven by ruthless determination. Will he capture Robert Rushworth and reclaim the alderman's reward, or will he meet an unforeseen fate of his own? The stage is set for a heart-pounding showdown, where the fate of these lives rests on a knife's edge.

Prepare to be transported into a world where history is alive, where choices are bound by the weight of consequences, and where the past whispers its secrets through the ages. *The Lost Voices* will envelop you in its intricate narrative, leaving you spellbound as the layers of 17th century life unravel in a symphony of suspense and revelation.

www.historiumpress.com